Nicole Arend is author of the VAMPS series. After travelling the world making documentaries, she wrote the book to accompany the C4 documentary series *Lost*. She enjoyed writing so much, she took a YA writing course at City Lit and became a fan of vampire fiction. She lives in London with her husband, her almost grown-up sons, her teenage daughter and two stunning Siberian cats.

NICOLE AREND

VAMPS

FRESH BLOOD

**SIMON &
SCHUSTER**

London · New York · Sydney · Toronto · New Delhi

First published in Great Britain by Simon & Schuster UK Ltd, 2022

Written by Nicole Arend

1 3 5 7 9 10 8 6 4 2

Simon & Schuster UK Ltd
1st Floor
222 Gray's Inn Road
London WC1X 8HB

Simon & Schuster Australia,
Sydney

Simon & Schuster India,
New Delhi

www.simonandschuster.co.uk
www.simonandschuster.com.au
www.simonandschuster.co.in

A CIP catalogue record for this book is available from the British Library

Paperback ISBN: 978-1-3985-1177-4
eBook ISBN: 978-1-3985-1178-1
Audio ISBN: 978-1-3985-1709-7

Typeset in Bembo by Palimpsest Book Production Ltd, Falkirk, Stirlingshire
Printed and bound in Great Britain by CPI Group (UK) Ltd, Croydon, CR0 4YY

MIX
Paper from
responsible sources
FSC® C171272

To Rob

1

New Blood

In a valley high up in the Swiss Alps nestles the tiny village of Arnes. Majestic snow-covered mountains tower over a cluster of wooden buildings and block the low winter sun, rendering it too cold and dark to be a popular ski resort.

At 5.30 p.m. on the first day of November, it was already pitch black. The soft glow of the street lanterns and the festive lights that garlanded the narrow high street were the only sources of light. The ancient village shop was closed; the white-washed church cold and empty. The faded green shutters that adorned each chalet were shut tight. Despite their jolly Christmas wreaths, every front door was barred shut.

Not a soul was to be seen. A thick layer of snow blanketed the entire village, and the silence was heavy. Even the soft spray of the waterfall, normally flowing down the east side of the mountain, was still — temporarily frozen in time.

The throaty roar of a powerful engine broke the stillness and, seconds later, a bright red Lamborghini Urus raced over icy cobbles and skidded to a stop in the town square. The passenger door opened, and a willowy girl stepped out. Ice-blonde hair fell in an immaculate, glossy sheet down her back. She was dressed expensively in skin-tight white jeans, a thick faux-fur gilet and matching knee-high boots.

Glancing up the high street with piercing ice-blue eyes, she exclaimed, 'Is this really it?'

A tall, handsome man, who didn't look old enough to be her father, stepped out of the other side.

'What did you expect, Celeste?' he growled. 'I warned you.'

'I was thinking of something quaint but sophisticated – like Gstaad.'

'Far too busy,' replied her father. 'Given our *special* requirements, this place is perfect.'

Some distance away, Dillon Halloran was uncomfortably aware that they were almost at their destination. A light sweat broke out across his forehead. He and his father, Gabriel, had travelled up the narrow valley in a sled pulled by eight huskies. Six kilometres out, one of the dogs had broken her harness, but despite Dillon's efforts, it hadn't sabotaged their journey; it only delayed them by half an hour.

Now, at the far edge of the village, long before the street

lanterns began, the dogs began to slow, then halt completely, forcing Gabriel to brake the sled hard. The pack stood motionless, eyes fixed on the distant village, and then, collectively, they let out a long low howl. Dillon leaned into his father, pointing at the agitated huskies.

'That's weird, Da. It's like they know there's something not right up there.'

Gabriel knew animals, and he knew to trust their instincts. There was a sense of unease in the air, and Dillon saw him fight back the desire to turn the dogs around and escape as fast as he could back down the mountain.

As the steam from the animals' nostrils rose in clouds around them, Dillon turned to Gabriel and pleaded, 'I don't want to go. Please don't make me.'

Gabriel sighed, 'Dillon, we have been through this. I promised your mother that as soon as you turned eighteen . . .'

'What makes you so desperate to keep a promise to a woman who didn't even care enough to stick around for us, Da?'

'I told you – it's complicated. She left to protect you, and I must uphold my promise to her.'

Dillon scowled. 'Protect me? Protect me from what exactly?'

'This is why you need to go. You need to learn about yourself and the world your mother comes from.'

Dillon shook his head angrily. 'She wasn't interested in my world – why should I care about hers?'

'You can't change who you are. Look, there is no time to talk now. You are already late.'

'C'mon, Da, none of this makes any sense. Can we not just turn back and go home?'

Gabriel said nothing but hugged Dillon tight.

'I've kept you safe all your life, son. But I can't do that anymore. And I think deep down you already know that.' Gabriel glanced at his watch again. 'You've got to go. You need to learn about yourself. But remember Dillon –' Gabriel pointed to his chest, thumping his heart as he spoke – 'This – this is what makes us who we are.'

As he pulled Dillon close, he slid an antique chain over his head. The strange fiery stone at the centre of the triangle-shaped pendant glimmered as it caught the moonlight.

'Wear this with pride, son. It means a lot to me. It was your ma's, but she wanted me to give it to you. Keep it on always and no matter what happens up there, never . . .' He broke off and cleared his throat. 'Never ever lose heart.'

There was no time to examine the chain now. Struggling to hold back his emotion, Dillon tucked it under the neck of his jumper and felt it heavy on his chest, just above his heart. After one final hug, he wrenched himself away from his father. Strapping on the snowshoes Gabriel had made for him back in Ireland, his eyes blurred. He blinked furiously and began to plunge across the snow, not trusting himself to look back. After a pause, he heard his father whistle to the dogs and then their excited yelps as the sled turned and headed back the way they had come.

He was so lost in his thoughts that he didn't hear the two snowmobiles until they were almost upon him. He swore loudly and threw himself to the side as one of the riders shouted something at him, swerved violently and hurtled past.

At the sound of snowmobiles approaching fast from the south, Celeste and her father both turned with lightning speed. Within minutes, the first one appeared, shot through the alpine trees and landed in a flashy circle, spraying snow and ice in a plume behind it. The drop-dead gorgeous boy straddling it cut the engine and, with the grace of a natural athlete, leapt off in a single high bound. His brown eyes were bright with the exhilaration of the ride, and he shook snow out of his dark hair. He clocked Celeste and struggled to tear his eyes away as, remembering his manners, he extended his hand towards her father and introduced himself.

'Hi, I'm Ace. Nice to meet you, sir.'

Celeste's father assessed him coldly before, ignoring Ace's hand, he replied, 'I'm Eric Torstensson, and this is my daughter, Celeste.'

Ace's eyes drank in her flawless face. 'Great to meet you,' he drawled in a relaxed American accent.

Celeste, clearly used to everyone falling at her feet, smiled graciously. 'Nice entrance.'

Ace ran a hand through his artfully long fringe. 'Yeah, well, this place is pretty remote. My folks had to stay back in Florida to sort out a couple of last-minute issues, so I thought I might as well have some fun.'

The two local men on the second skidoo had hurriedly unloaded a trunk and a leather holdall from a sled attached behind. Without stopping to say goodbye, they revved the engines and sped away, bouncing high over snowy bumps in their haste.

'Can't think why they didn't want to hang around.' Ace smirked.

Celeste chuckled, revealing perfect, slightly pointed white teeth and stepped closer to the Lamborghini as two blacked-out Mercedes G wagons and an Aston Martin DBX purred up. Romanian flags fluttered on the bonnets of the Mercedes and a chauffeur hastened round to open the back door of the first car. Bodyguards jumped out of the second car as a fine-boned, raven-haired boy dressed in a dark wool coat unfurled his long legs from the back seat.

'Bram Danesti,' he announced in slightly accented English, casting a somewhat haughty gaze over them and, unlike Ace, managing not to betray a flicker of interest in Celeste's beauty.

'Ah, Bram, you must be Alexandru's son. Is your father here?' Celeste's father asked, 'I need to talk to him urgently.' He strode over to talk to the striking but intimidating man who had emerged from the other side of the Mercedes.

Bram turned to Celeste. 'You'll probably know then that my father was chosen to lead his year for three years running. I'm expecting to follow in his footsteps.'

Celeste didn't blink an eyelid. 'Nice to meet you too.'

Bram's eyes narrowed slightly.

'I think you'll find that I'm a strong contender,' she continued with icy poise.

Bram smirked. 'Let's wait and see.'

Ace stepped forward, hand outstretched. 'Hi, Ace Ellison.'

Dragging his eyes away from Celeste, Bram also ignored his hand. 'Ah, you're the orange juice heir.'

Ace's perfectly chiselled face betrayed no hint of annoyance at the mocking tone. 'That's right, my father built his entire business empire on orange juice. He tells me that, even in our world, too much privilege kills ambition. One of the reasons I made my own way here,' he said, eyes sweeping over the two Mercedes and the bodyguards.

Bram's jaw tightened. He was about to reply, but Celeste spoke first.

'Now *he* looks interesting . . . ' she mused.

An exceptionally tall and muscled boy strolled towards them. Wearing just a casual T-shirt with jeans and appearing impervious to the cold, his huge biceps rippled as he slung a bag over his shoulder. His dreadlocks were finely twisted and drawn in a luxuriant ponytail down his back. A single ancient gold coin pendant gleamed against his neck. For a second, Celeste, Ace and Bram stared.

Unperturbed, he introduced himself. 'Hey, I'm Jeremiah.' His voice was deep and musical with a gentle Caribbean lilt.

Celeste recovered her manners first and, flicking her hair over one shoulder, smiled up at him, 'Hi, I'm Celeste.'

Jeremiah smiled an easy smile back at her. 'Celeste, nice name.'

'Thank you,' she indicated to her father, who was talking intently to Bram's dad. 'It was my father's mother's name. Have you travelled far?'

'I'm based just outside Montego Bay, so just a hop across the Atlantic, I guess.'

The loud throb of a sleek black helicopter appearing over the mountains filled the valley with noise. As it swept down and started its descent, Celeste winced and covered her sensitive ears with a pair of fur-lined earmuffs. Powerful landing lamps flooded the old outdoor ice rink with light and, as it neared touch down, the spinning rotor blades created a temporary blizzard. From the maelstrom of swirling snow and bright light, a boy and girl leaped out and, bending low to avoid the blades, sprinted with cheetah-like grace across the snowy ice towards the group.

Close up, the boy looked hard as nails. He had close-cropped fair hair and an impressive array of tattoos. He shouted over the engines, 'I am Aron and this is my twin sister, Ásta. We have travelled here from Iceland and we're excited to meet you.'

Ásta looked anything but pleased and shook her blunt blonde bob in irritation at her brother. Above razor-sharp cheekbones, her shrewd green eyes measured Celeste's stunning icy beauty.

Dillon was still battling through the snow towards the village. As he had flung himself out of the way of the skidoos, one of the straps on his left snowshoe had snapped. He had tied it back as best he could, but his progress had been painfully slow. The sight of the sleek black helicopter sweeping overhead added to his irritation and sweat dripped down his face as he dragged his left foot out of the snow yet again.

At last, he reached the main road into the village, and he was able to remove the snowshoes. Just as he started walking again, a Ferrari FF whipped round the last mountain bend and howled past him up the main street.

'God's sake,' he muttered. 'Who the feck are these people?'

The Ferrari screeched to a halt in front of the other cars and a wickedly gorgeous boy slid out of the impossibly low seat. He had the small, wiry frame of a racing driver and looked just as glamorous with his slanting, mischievous eyes, diamond earring and dark, wavy hair. He headed straight over to the group, leather jacket slung over a shoulder, and almost asphyxiated them with cologne. With a wolfish smile for Celeste and Ásta, he introduced himself as Angelo da Silva, son of world-famous polo player Seve da Silva.

Sparks flew as he and Ásta locked eyes. 'Delighted to meet you, Angelo,' she smirked, looking up at him through her heavily mascaraed lashes.

A lithe and exquisitely beautiful Nigerian girl who had arrived at the same time as the helicopter stood slightly to the side of the group of excited teenagers. Her instantly recognisable parents, who were famous scientists, were engaged in conversation with the other parents. She hung her head and stared at her feet, making patterns in the snow with the toe of her boot.

Ace was about to call her over but was distracted by the

sight of Dillon dressed in a shabby woollen jumper and walking up the high street with a rucksack and his snowshoes strapped to his back.

'Jeez, that's the dumbass we almost ran into back down the valley,' he exclaimed. 'What's he doing here?'

As he approached the group, Dillon's heart began to beat faster. He had never seen such a group of glamorous and intimidating people in his life. What was his father thinking?

Swallowing the urge to turn and run back the way he had come and not knowing who was in charge, he addressed both the teenagers and the small group of parents. 'Sorry I'm late, had a bit of trouble back there.' Every set of eyes turned to stare at him. 'I'm Dillon Halloran,' he added nervously. The boy he'd glimpsed roaring past him in the flashy Ferrari inched closer, narrowing his eyes, looking for all the world as if he was ready to pounce and eat him alive.

'What is he doing here?' he hissed.

'I was told this is the meeting place,' Dillon said, standing his ground but feeling his heart pound.

'Leave it, Angelo!' hissed the tough-looking girl next to him and attempted unsuccessfully to pull him away.

One of the tall, handsome boys standing in the main group broke the silence. 'Snowshoes? I thought they died out in the eighteenth century!' he joked.

Dillon shifted his feet awkwardly but lifted his chin and looked him in the eye. 'My da made these for me with his own hands. And they got me here, didn't they?'

'Ah, sorry . . . Dillon did you say? I'm Ace. That's very clever of your father. I wish I'd had them instead of my snowmobile,' he deadpanned.

Ace's expression was so smooth, Dillon wasn't sure if he was taking the piss or not.

'Yeah, those snowmobiles look a handful to drive,' Dillon shrugged. As most of the others were still staring at him, and he was unsure of the protocol, Dillon edged closer to the beautiful girl who was standing to the side and looked less intimidating than the others. 'Hi, I'm Dillon.'

As she looked at him with her huge brown eyes, he was reminded of a deer about to bolt back to the safety of the woods.

'I know, you just said,' she replied.

'Jaysus, sorry,' he muttered, feeling like a complete idiot. Clearly, she wasn't as shy as she looked.

She seemed to take pity on him. 'I'm Sade. You made quite an entrance.'

'Nice to meet you, Sade. You wouldn't know why everyone's staring at me, would you – or what his problem is?' he asked, inclining his head towards Angelo who, fortunately, had been distracted and was now showing the Ferrari off to the others.

'You really don't know?' Sade asked.

'Seriously, no. It's not the clothes, is it?'

'Well, I don't wish to be rude –' she fiddled with a gold bracelet as she spoke – 'but you look – how shall I put it – *different*. If you notice, none of us, lighter or darker-skinned, ever change.'

'What do you mean? My skin?'

'Well, sorry, but you look a bit hot and sweaty – your cheeks are flushed.'

Self-consciously, he pushed back his dark, messy curls and looked round the group. It was true. Despite the cold, everyone looked startlingly perfect. Not a single person's nose was red or running, and their skin was so smooth and uniform it looked poreless as if carved from marble.

'And we all heard that,' she added, pointing at his heart.

'Ah, well now, you'll have to excuse me for breathing!' he exclaimed.

'Shush!' she whispered, looking around nervously.

'Do you know everyone?'

'Not really, but I think the tall blonde is called Celeste. You already met Ace – he seems to have already made his play to be the joker of the pack. Ásta and Aron are the Icelandic twins. She distracted Angelo, who owns the Ferrari, for you. The moody, dark one is Bram, and the huge, stunning one is Jeremiah.'

'Ah grand, looks like I'm going to fit right in . . . as the mascot,' he joked and was rewarded with a smile that lit up her whole face.

A soft whistling noise distracted them, and they both looked up. A peregrine falcon and a raven glided over their heads and landed gracefully in the centre of the town square. Immediately, they transformed into a supernaturally beautiful woman and a sharp-looking man with a gleaming black beard.

An awed hush settled over the entire group. Dillon, who was staring open-mouthed, guessed the woman must be the headmistress. A headmistress who had just transformed from a bird. He shook his head in disbelief, but as her penetrating emerald-green eyes swept over him, he experienced a very real mixture of adoration and terror.

Although she looked small next to the teenagers surrounding her, she radiated power and poise. A hooded, fine woollen cape only partly concealed the thick auburn curls tumbling to her waist and perfect porcelain skin. A deep red velvet dress, the same colour as her lips, clung to hourglass curves, enhanced by a narrow filigree gold chain clasped about her waist.

'Welcome to Arnes, and congratulations.' Her voice was low and musical. 'I am Madame Dupledge, headmistress of the oldest and most exclusive vampire finishing academy in the world: *Vampire Academiae ad Meritum, Peritia et Scientia*. Commonly known as VAMPS, it stands for excellence, skill and knowledge. You are joining an elite group who have benefited from their education here and gone on to achieve great things in the world. I hope you will utilise your stay here well and, in time, fulfil your own potential.'

Surreptitiously, Dillon looked round at the others as Madame Dupledge spoke. Ace, Bram and Celeste looked determined. Ásta rolled her eyes and Angelo smirked back at her.

'This —' she gestured to the man next to her — 'Is Mr Hunt.'

The bearded man, who was wearing a sleek black ski jacket, bowed but didn't smile.

'He is our Deputy Head and will be instructing you on the next stage of the journey. The location of VAMPS is a closely guarded secret. We try to minimise travel to and from the academy as much as possible. As such you will be with us for the duration of the darkest months until the end of our year on March 31st.'

Dillon looked down at his boots to hide a wave of homesickness and horror. How was he going to survive five months with a bunch of hostile vampires?

'Now, we have disturbed the villagers enough for tonight. Please say goodbye to your parents and let us prepare to leave as soon as possible. Some students have already arrived and are waiting to meet you.'

As everyone collected their luggage and said goodbye to their parents, Dillon watched Bram's father draw Madame Dupledge aside and engage her in an intense conversation. After she graciously dismissed him to talk to another parent, his face darkened with fury, and he spoke to Bram urgently. Both shot Dillon a hostile glare. Hurriedly, he looked away, but he was pretty sure he'd got the message. The dark, brooding Bram and his father were not happy about him joining VAMPS.

To distract himself, he watched the casual farewells between the others and their parents. There was no sign of the emotional wrench that had occurred between himself and his father. Sade's parents appeared to be issuing instructions rather than hugs before they left, and he saw her hang her beautifully shaped head like a delicate orchid.

As the supercars and luxury SUVs began to drive away, Mr Hunt shouted out instructions. 'Listen up, everyone. I need you to form two groups: Fliers and Non-Fliers.'

Dillon had no idea what either was. 'Flier? What in the hell does that mean?' he whispered to Sade, who had kindly returned to stand next to him.

'If you don't know, you're a Non-Flier – trust me. I'm a Non, too.'

Dillon watched as Ace and Aron high-fived and whooped as they joined the flier group. Bram, Celeste, Ásta and Jeremiah joined them, grinning.

'I expect perfect behaviour on this flight,' Mr Hunt warned, his sharp, bird-like eyes raking over each of them.

'The rest of you will travel with Madame Dupledge. Leave your luggage; the school porters will be here shortly.'

'Shame,' Angelo muttered, shooting a snide glance at Dillon. 'I could do with a snack.'

Ásta snorted and tried to cover her smile as Mr Hunt directed a disapproving frown at them.

'Everyone coming with me: prepare yourselves.'

Ace, Aron and Jeremiah whooped again.

'Wanna bet on who gets there first?' Ace asked.

Celeste and Ásta sighed.

'Ready?' Mr Hunt leant forward, poised like a bird about to take flight. 'We go on the count of three.'

The teenagers stopped jostling each other and were instantly stone-still and alert.

'One . . . Two . . . Three,' roared Mr Hunt and suddenly they were gone.

Dillon started. 'Hold on a minute – where did they just go?'

Sade looked at him curiously. 'You really don't know much about us, do you?' she noted, not unkindly.

'No,' he admitted. 'Next to nothing. My ma left when I was born, and it was just me and my da. He shielded me from all of this. It's all doing my head in, to be honest. I only found out a week ago I was coming here.'

'My family is one of the elite vampire families. I have had to live up to my siblings and my parents' expectations my whole life,' she sighed. 'You are lucky to be free.'

'I wouldn't call this lucky,' Dillon replied with feeling. 'This is straight up weird.'

'Come now. Join me,' Madame Dupledge interrupted, beckoning the remaining group towards her in the centre of the town square.

With some trepidation, Dillon approached her. Sade and Angelo followed. Close up, her allure was palpable as was a sweet, overpowering scent. Dillon's head swam, and he felt overwhelmed with a desire to please her.

'Now,' she said, 'hold onto my cape, and whatever happens, do not let go.'

Still wary of Angelo, Dillon stood on the other side of Sade and, as he reached out and grasped her cape, he felt a jolt of electricity shoot through his entire body. Every nerve tingled and pulsed as if he had plunged into icy water.

'Well done.' Madame Dupledge smiled her approval. Turning to them all, she added, 'Enjoy . . .'

With a slight tremor, like the flutter of a bat's wing, they dissolved into thin air. Except for the abandoned piles of luggage, the village square was silent once more. Just one green shutter opened a fraction, and a young boy peered out before his mother shouted, and it slammed shut again.

2

First Blood

The cold mountain air stung Dillon's face like a hard slap. His cheeks smarted, and his eyes streamed. He gasped, incredulous that he was airborne and swore out loud. Instantly, the wind tore his breath away. They were shooting over clusters of fir trees and expanses of snow at an incredible speed. Every time they changed direction or height, there was a corresponding vibration through the cloak into his hand. A rising sense of panic and nausea threatened to overwhelm him.

'Come on, Dillon, keep it together,' he growled to himself. 'Just don't let go.'

Madame Dupledge led them. He, Sade and Angelo were strung out behind her in tight arrow formation. Her cape flapped wildly, and he clung on, petrified. As if sensing his panic, she turned, red curls flying and whispered to him. Somehow, despite the roaring in his ears, he heard her.

'Take deep breaths – it will pass. Try to enjoy it.'

He gulped mouthfuls of freezing air and as his eyes adjusted to the velocity, he glanced over at the others. Sade smiled encouragingly, and he relaxed a little. Madame Dupledge's cape, with its hum of invisible energy, flowed into his hand, calming him, and, as they began to head higher, the scenery below changed, becoming starkly beautiful. An abandoned ski resort swept past and, turning north, his body shuddered as they swooped up the eerie glistening face of a glacier. Climbing higher and higher, they finally emerged at the top, and Madame Dupledge pointed at something in the distance. Dillon couldn't see anything, just a series of pale mountain peaks disappearing into the distance on the far side of a huge frozen lake. Sade and Angelo obviously had sharper eyesight – or at least knew what they were looking for – as they both nodded and smiled. Madame Dupldege took them into a fast dive back down towards the lake and as his stomach howled in protest, Dillon focused on not throwing up rather than the view. As they sped low over the frozen lake, he began to feel more comfortable closer to the ground and paid closer attention to the way Madame Dupledge positioned her body. His grip on her cape loosened as he discovered that he could alter his direction by slightly rotating his shoulders. The sensation that he was actually flying sent a surge of adrenaline through him that went straight to his head, and he missed Madame Dupledge's warning to hold on tight. As she swooped suddenly to the right, her cape ripped out of his hand.

19

For a millisecond, he clutched at thin air, and then with a sickening plunging sensation, he dropped several metres. He was spinning, his arms and legs flailing wildly. The frozen surface of the lake plummeted up towards him. Instantly, Madame Dupledge dived, and he glimpsed Sade and Angelo's shocked faces before she grasped the back of his jumper. They skimmed the ice for a few seconds and they lifted off again.

'I told you to hold on,' she hissed, looking furiously over her shoulder. 'You have a lot to learn.'

Shocked silent and hyperventilating, he nodded. *More* than a lot. He was still so caught up in the internal agony of making a complete fool of himself that he didn't pay much attention to the landscape until they began approaching the first mountain range. There was something about it that made him look again and, as they drew closer, he realised the peak wasn't real at all. An incredible, futuristic building had been built into the mountain. Shaped like an inverted fang, it soared towards the clouds. It was entirely clad in gun-grey-metal diamond-shaped panels that gleamed silver where the moonlight caught them. There didn't appear to be any windows or doors. Dillon felt his heart thud with fear – it looked both stunning and supremely sinister.

Madame Dupledge swept them up the face of the mountain. Briefly, Dillon saw the four of them – and his pale, fear-frozen face – reflected in the building's shiny surface. When Madame Dupledge circled over the top, he realised that there were two projections, one at the front and one at the back, linked by two convex sides that curved down in the middle. What looked like an enormous oval magnifying glass set on a low metal and glass dome formed the roof. Dim light from the centre of the building softly illuminated the sky like a giant torch.

'Woah, would you look at that!' he gasped in surprise. He had been expecting some mouldy, old, gothic castle.

Madame Dupledge nodded and, as she took them on one more circuit around the roof, she gestured at another two mountain peaks in the near distance. 'Those are the lodges for the older vampires – they are known as Peak Two and Peak Three.'

Dillon peered over, but they looked like normal mountains to him; clearly, whatever was there was also well disguised. The next second, Madame Dupledge swooped them straight down the back of the building and a quarter of a way down the mountain face. He almost yelled out as she twisted and flew directly at a wall of rock. At the last second, a discreet metal door slid open, and they shot deep into the side of the mountain. His heart lurched again. There was no way he was getting out of here unless he learnt to fly. They continued along a wide concrete tunnel, lit with dim fluorescent lights and dotted with sleek CCTV cameras. After the stunning exterior, it seemed surprisingly utilitarian. Finally, they approached another door.

'Get ready,' Madame Dupledge said, putting on the brakes and landing them gently on the concrete.

Like an astronaut returning to Earth, Dillon's legs wobbled

as he acclimatised to the feeling of solid ground beneath his feet again. Silently, the door opened, and a rectangle of light spilled out. A vampire dressed in a tight black roll-neck and slim-fitting trousers greeted them.

'Welcome back, Madame.' He bowed. 'How was your journey?'

'Thank you Rufus, it was somewhat eventful,' she replied, casting an icy glance at Dillon that made him blush. Rufus's eyes widened in surprise, and Dillon felt Angelo twitch next to him.

Hastily, Madame Dupledge swept them all inside. A heady, bittersweet scent tinged with the hint of something darker enveloped them as, with a rush of cold mountain air, the door slid shut behind them. Dillon shivered slightly and fought the urge to run. They had entered a minimalist, white hallway. The school's black crest – with VAMPS written vertically down the centre in red – had been laid into an exquisite, tiled floor. Dillon shivered as he translated the Latin motto underneath: *In Tenebris Refulgemus* – 'In Darkness We Shine.' His Catholic education hadn't been a complete waste of time, then.

'Our school building has twelve floors,' Madame Dupledge explained. 'We are currently on the fifth floor. The sleeping quarters and the staff living areas are on the lower basement floors. The ceremonial hall where we will meet later tonight is on the top floor, in the roof.'

They had arrived at two lifts made from glass and steel.

Madame Dupledge turned to Rufus. 'Can you please show

Angelo where he can rest? He has had a long journey and appears to be nearing the limits of his control.'

Dillon dared to shoot a glance at Angelo, who eyeballed him and restlessly drummed his fingers against his thighs.

'Of course, Madame.' Rufus bowed and hurried Angelo into the lift.

Madame Dupledge turned to Sade. 'I want to speak to Dillon alone, but I would be grateful if you could come back when we are finished and accompany him to your rooms. Elias –' Dillon started as another vampire dressed in black appeared in the corridor behind them – 'will show you where to wait.'

Sade gave a small, nervous half-bow. 'Of course, Madame.'

Madame Dupledge turned to Dillon, and he half stepped back in shock. Her face was suddenly a mask of barely controlled anger.

'Dillon, I would like you to follow me to my office.'

She turned her back on him and entered the other lift so fast that Dillon blinked. With a deep sense of dread in his stomach and anger at his da, he dragged himself in after her. What had his da been thinking – sending him here?

Instantly, the doors closed, and they shot upwards. Despite the dark thoughts racing through his mind, Dillon saw that they were inside a vertical glass cylinder that seemed to go all the way to the bottom of the building. Looking up, he saw the night sky and realised it extended all the way to the glass roof he had seen from the outside. Each floor opened out from it. They stopped at what Dillon guessed was the ninth floor.

He half-ran, half-walked to keep up with Madame Dupledge, who incredibly didn't seem to make any noise as she walked. Dillon's thick boots thudded along behind her. They were now in a beautiful atrium that circled in a crescent around the central funnel. Madam Dupledge's office led off it and was just as impressive. A diamond-shaped window that he hadn't been able to detect when he had flown up the side of the building earlier dominated the outer wall and revealed the lake below. He presumed it must be tinted from the outside. The office door and curved inner wall were made of glass and drew in soft moonlight from the atrium. The room was exquisitely proportioned and minimal. The beautiful, gleaming parquet floor was bare and a magnificent aerial painting of the academy, perched amongst the mountain peaks, adorned one of the clean, white walls. Four portraits of previous VAMPS heads hung like a backwards journey through the centuries on the other wall. Dillon shuddered as he examined the elaborately dressed sixteenth-century headmaster, who grimaced, revealing long, cruel fangs and looked as if he was about to pounce on the portrait painter. Electric blinds lowered instantly, and dim spotlights came on as she walked behind a beautiful pale oak desk. Candles in glass cylinders gave off the same intoxicating bittersweet scent that he'd smelt in the hall. The blue glow from two large, ultra-slim computer screens on the desk lit up the cold anger on her face. Somehow, despite the sudden pounding of his heart, he found himself drawn towards her. He came to a halt in front of the desk and stood awkwardly. To his shame, his knees shook slightly with fear.

'Dillon, don't ever do a stupid thing like that again,' she hissed, her eyes like daggers. 'You could have killed yourself. Surely you know how privileged you are to be here?'

Scared almost witless and furious with himself for being so intimidated by her, he managed to mumble, 'Well, in fairness, I *don't* really know why I'm here. My father said I had to come as it was a promise he'd made to the mother I can't even remember.' He couldn't help the trace of bitterness in his tone.

Some of the anger in Madame Dupledge's expression turned to surprise. 'You do know what you are, don't you, Dillon?'

'I'm a dham . . . dhampir.' Dillon stumbled over the word. 'But there's been a mistake, honestly; there's no real sign of it, you know – in me, I mean.'

She ignored him and continued. 'A dhamphir is very rare as human-vampire interactions are taboo in our world. Mixed relationships are extremely dangerous for humans.'

Dillon swallowed; a light sweat broke out across his forehead.

'Very few produce progeny. The child rarely survives. But *you* did. This is why you are here, Dillon. This is why you are special. This is why you can't take stupid risks.'

Dillon couldn't take it in. 'Seriously, I still do not understand the half of this . . .'

'Dillon, your mother comes from a long line of powerful

vampires. Female vampires cannot normally have children naturally with male humans. We do not yet know how you survived. Her genes are so strong. This is why you need to be here now you have come of age – so that we can guide you, so that you do not become a danger to yourself or others.'

'I'm not dangerous!' Dillon protested. He immediately regretted it when he saw her face darken but this was batshit crazy – they must have got the wrong man.

'Who is my mother then?' he asked. 'My da never spoke about her and I didn't want to upset him.'

She stared at him intently. 'I'm sorry – for very good reasons, I can't tell you that, but she was right, this is the best place for you. This academy is for elite vampires or vampires who have the potential to excel. We believe that you have that potential, Dillon – even as a half vampire.'

None of it made any sense.

'I still don't understand what the big deal is?' he said, feeling his temper rise again.

Her eyes narrowed slightly. 'I understand it's a lot to take in. Just trust in us. It's safer this way.'

He clenched his fists in frustration as Elias appeared at the door, indicating the conversation was over.

Madame Dupledge spoke urgently to him. 'Just trust me, Dillon, and you will do well here.'

He shrugged, unsure of what to say. 'I'll do my best,' he muttered, turning to leave.

Just as he reached the door, she spoke again. 'Your mother. She had the strength of character to restrain her desires and

to protect both you and your father. You may not understand
yet how hard that was, but you will soon.'

He paused and looked back. She was staring out of the
diamond-shaped window at the ice lake below, her beautiful
face strangely sombre. Damn right, he didn't understand. So
what if he had some powerful vampire mother? It didn't
matter if neither Madame Dupledge nor his father would
tell him who she was.

'This way,' Elias gestured.

Dillon followed him back to the lift and down to the
fifth floor. Sade was waiting there.

'Okay?' she whispered as she joined him in the lift.

'Weird,' he said. 'I'll tell you later.'

They stood in silence on the way down, and Sade fiddled
with her bracelet. On the third floor, they stopped. Elias led
them into another circular atrium area and pointed to the
corridors that branched away on either side.

'This is the Peak One or P1 as we call it. Coffin corridor.'

Elias gestured at several open doors. Dillon's eyes widened,
but he followed Sade to the third door. Peals of laughter
were coming from the room. Inside, a tall, fine-boned girl
with short, dark hair and a pierced nose gesticulated wildly
as she described the succession of disasters that had led to
her missing the meeting point in Arnes and her luck at
bumping into someone else who was heading directly to
the school. Ace, who appeared to be lounging on a smooth,
chrome, oblong pod, was loving every minute of it.

Seeing Dillon and Sade, he drawled, 'Hey, what kept you?'

The girl stopped mid-flow, and her sea-green eyes widened in surprise. 'Good God!' she exclaimed in a cut-glass English accent. 'Are you the dhampir?'

Her reaction was so direct that Dillon smiled. 'Seems so. Apparently, I'm creating a bit of a stir around here.'

'How exciting!' she said, coming closer to peer at him. 'I have never met one of your kind before, and you must be the first to attend VAMPS. I wonder –' she paused to look him up and down – 'what's so special about you?'

Dillon smiled again, jolted out of his usual reserve. 'Being honest, I wish I could tell you. But this is all new to me. New, as in – last week.'

'You have got to be kidding me!'

'Seriously.'

'Well,' she said. 'I'm delighted to meet you, Dillon. This should make things much more interesting. I'm Cora de Courtenay by the way.'

Somewhat bewitched by her dazzling eyes, Dillon suddenly remembered his manners. 'Oh, and, of course, this is Sade. We flew here together.'

Cora turned her searchlight gaze on Sade, grabbed her and twirled her around. 'Exquisite!' she declared. 'Are you one of the Dauda family?'

A little embarrassed, Sade's face nevertheless lit up with a beautiful smile. 'Yes.' She nodded.

'No wonder,' Cora whistled.

Cora had the knack of bringing people out of their shells, Dillon noted.

'Have you found your rooms yet?' Ace asked.

'No. What's that?' Dillon pointed at Ace's oblong pod. 'Aw, come on, surely you don't sleep in that thing?'

Ace and Cora burst out in laughter.

'Of course, we do, dumbass — it's a coffin!' Ace snorted. 'That's why it's called the "coffin corridor".'

'How am I supposed to know, my da's not feckin' Count Dracula!' Dillon snapped. 'I thought sleeping in coffins was just a myth — something from the Dark Ages.'

Cora seemed startled by the force of his anger. 'Sorry Dillon, we didn't mean anything. It's just refreshing to meet someone, how shall I put it, so innocent about our world. Please ask me anything you need to know.'

Mollified but still scowling at Ace, he muttered, 'Fair play Cora, thanks. I'll remember that. I guess we'd better go find our rooms.'

He was damned if he was going to ask anything else in front of Ace. The other open doors revealed that most of the rooms were already taken. Celeste was unpacking her bags in the large room closest to the lifts that had windows looking into the centre of the building.

Celeste looked at Dillon. 'You're supposed to be sharing with me.'

She didn't seem pleased by the idea, so he turned to Sade. 'Would you like to swap with me?'

'If you're sure? This room looks great.'

'Of course.'

'Thanks.'

Grabbing his rucksack, he went back along the corridor and discovered the only free space was in the room furthest from the lift. A much smaller room than the one he'd just left; Jeremiah's huge frame almost filled it.

'Looks like we drew the short straw.' Jeremiah shrugged.

'Ah here – let's not start with the "short" gags, if we're sharing.' Dillon grinned, surprised that he seemed so friendly.

Despite its size, the room could have featured in a cool Scandi design magazine. Two sliding doors on an iron pole concealed the storage space for clothes. Two retro desks with shelves were fixed at opposite ends of the room. It would have looked completely normal except for the two coffin pods. Jeremiah had thrown his bag on the left one, which was about two feet longer and wider than the other. Warily, Dillon lifted the lid of the coffin on the right. It was lined with plush, black velvet.

'You have got to be kidding me! There is no way I can sleep in that.'

'Bit weird, I'll admit,' Jeremiah said. 'Back home, I don't sleep in one of these. This place is ultra-strict about tradition though. You should give it a go – it's a lot more comfortable than it looks. We're allowed to decorate them too.'

'I'll take your word for it!' Dillon closed the lid again. 'But I'm not sleeping with the lid shut. I breathe air after all.'

Jeremiah sat on his coffin and looked at him curiously. 'It's none of my business, but how did you end up coming here anyway?'

'I never knew my mother, so I think it's about learning all the things she never taught me. I turn eighteen, I find out she's a vampire, and suddenly this is the best place for me . . . so they reckon, anyway.'

'Probably is then. We'll all find out more at the Induction Ceremony.'

'Induction Ceremony?'

'We swear allegiance to the rules and – rumour has it – get to taste Madame Dupledge's blood.'

Dillon stared at him. 'Her actual blood?! No way, you're messing with me, right?'

'Don't worry about it.' Jeremiah grinned. His extraordinary hazel eyes turned black as his pupils became eerily huge and he added, 'It's supposed to be amazing.'

Dillon recoiled slightly. He was reminded of his cat at home when it was about to pounce. Jeremiah noticed and his face became more normal again.

'Sorry, can't help it. Guess you're going to have to get used to us.'

'And maybe vice versa, too? You're just all so . . .' he groped for the right word, ' . . . carnal.'

'That's one word for it.' Jeremiah laughed, but then said more seriously, 'That's why we're so dangerous, Dillon, and Dhamp, you must never forget it. It's why we come here – to learn to control the more *instinctive* sides of our natures.'

'Jeremiah, I don't even think I have any instincts yet!'

Cora's dark head popped round the door. 'Hey, sorry to

interrupt. I thought you'd like to know that we're all heading up to the great hall.'

'Thanks . . .' Jeremiah turned up the dial on his incredible smile, and Dillon chuckled as he saw Cora's slightly dazed expression.

'What?' she demanded.

'Nothing.' He shrugged.

'You can't laugh and not tell me why.' Her face was mutinous.

'Well, I'd guess that Jeremiah was testing his "charm the pants off everyone" spell, but maybe it failed?'

Jeremiah laughed. For a second, Cora looked embarrassed, but then she smirked.

'You're right. He is pretty irresistible, but I can assure you my pants are firmly in place . . . for now,' she said pointedly, looking at Dillon.

He felt his cheeks flush slightly.

'Um, I am here, you know,' Jeremiah interrupted. 'I don't like to be discussed like I'm all looks and nothing else. There's a fine brain inside here.' He tapped his head.

'Sorry Jeremiah,' Cora apologised. 'But . . . we know you have a fine brain because you're here, so cut us a little slack and let us admire you. We'll get over it soon enough.'

'Well . . .' Jeremiah grinned. 'Maybe not too soon.'

Cora threw her hands up. 'I despair! You guy vamps are so contrary. We have got to get going or we'll be thrown out before we've even begun.'

She began shooting down the corridor.

'Hang on,' Jeremiah called. 'It said "dress for dinner" on the instructions.'

'Did it?' She swore impressively, and Jeremiah's eyebrows shot up. 'I'll see you outside my room in five minutes. Ace should have finished prettifying himself by then, too – if he ever stops telling me how he beat everyone flying here.'

Dillon watched her disappear. He shook his head.

'Hey, sorry to keep wrecking your head with questions, but what does "dress for dinner" mean exactly? There's not some weird Dracula cloak or something, is there?'

'No, just a dinner jacket and tie.'

Jeremiah was already raking through his cupboard. Dillon swore again as he rooted in his rucksack. He didn't own anything like that. He doubted his father could have afforded a dinner suit anyway. With the extraordinary speed of a vampire, Jeremiah was already dressed in a perfectly cut black jacket, immaculate white shirt and velvet bow tie.

Dillon's mouth fell open. 'There's no way anyone's getting used to you wearing that,' he muttered.

Jeremiah grinned at him. 'I know. Now, let's go find you something to wear.'

Dillon hurried to catch up with him – not only were Jeremiah's legs a foot longer than his, but he was also shifting into vampire speed.

'Sure, you go on. I'll catch you up,' Dillon gasped, watching Jeremiah instantly vanish down the corridor.

By the time he arrived – out of breath – at Cora's door, a group had congregated, and Jeremiah was shaking his head ruefully.

'Sorry Dillon, no one has a spare dinner suit.'

Bram, who looked as if he had been born in a tux, glanced at Dillon's thick Irish jumper and jeans with distaste. A compact boy with striking fox-red hair and a happy-go-lucky face came forward and introduced himself.

'Hi, we haven't met. I'm Frederick. I just got here from Germany.'

Like Bram, he spoke perfect English with just a hint of a German accent.

As Dillon stepped forwards, he saw Frederick's nostrils flare and his happy face momentarily crumple. 'Hi, I'm Dillon,' he said quickly.

'Dillon the Dhampir,' Bram drawled. 'It has a nice ring to it.'

Frederick's happy face momentarily crumpled, and he looked confused. 'A dhampir? Really? I didn't—'

'Know VAMPS accepted dhampirs?' Dillon finished the sentence for him wearily, wondering how long this was going to go on.

There was an embarrassing pause that was broken by Ace's loud whistle. Celeste and Sade were walking towards them. Each complemented the other's beauty perfectly. Celeste was dressed in a backless, light-blue floor-length dress that shimmered over her slender curves. Sade was wearing a dusky-pink dress that warmed her glowing skin and revealed her tiny waist. She looked embarrassed by the attention, but Celeste revelled in it.

Celeste glared at Ace. 'I would prefer it if you didn't whistle like that Ace, it's uncouth, outdated and demeaning, especially if you have been well-educated like the rest of us.'

Not looking chastened enough, Ace bowed. 'I apologise. Sorry if I offended you. May I make amends by escorting you to the hall?'

Celeste inclined her head. 'You may,' she agreed and took his arm.

Together, they made a stunning couple. Ásta and Angelo followed suit. Ásta had changed into a tight black bodycon dress with diamond cut-outs that revealed her pale, toned waist. Vertiginous black Louboutin heels with blood-red soles made her the same height as Angelo, whose arm was wrapped around her, fingers gently stroking her bare skin. Embarrassed by the obvious heat between them, Dillon looked away.

Frederick clasped Sade and, making her giggle, danced her away even though she was a head taller than him. Cora dashed out of her room and stopped dead. Her tousled urchin hair and ethereal forest-green dress offset her luminous eyes and slender frame perfectly. Doc Martens boots added to the effortlessly cool image.

'All for me?' she exclaimed, seeing Aron, Bram, Dillon and Jeremiah.

Bram immediately offered to escort her, and Dillon was surprised when she linked her arm through his. With their matching dark hair and aristocratic bone structures, they looked almost like brother and sister. Dillon felt a twinge of something deep in his stomach he had never felt before. He couldn't imagine how he could ever be as cultured and socially confident as them. As if sensing his insecurity, Cora glanced back and smiled apologetically.

Aron shrugged. 'I guess we're left with each other, huh vamps? Hey Dillon, I don't have a spare dinner jacket, but I have a suit if you'd like to try it. We're about the same height.'

Dillon looked down at his jumper and jeans. He hadn't wanted to admit it, but he did feel uncomfortably under-dressed compared to everyone else. Ignoring the sound of his father's voice that said *be confident as you are*, he nodded and smiled gratefully. 'That would be great. Thanks a million.'

He was surprised that after their initial reaction, most of the vampires seemed to be okay with him being a dhampir.

'Come,' Aron beckoned. 'My room is the other side of the atrium. I'm sharing with Frederick.'

Aron and Frederick's room was way bigger than his. He and Jeremiah really had drawn the short straw. One side of the room was immaculate; Aron was clearly a neat freak. There was no sign of clothes chucked on top of his coffin or spilling out of bags. The latest iPhone and a pair of hand weights were the only items on his desk. Frederick's side was the complete opposite; it looked like a tornado had whipped through the tumble of clothes, headphones and personal belongings. Uneasily, Dillon noticed a crate of what looked like bottles of blood. Aron slid his cupboard door open and handed Dillon a dark charcoal suit and a white shirt.

'Are you sure?' Dillon asked, glimpsing the label – even he had heard of Tom Ford, and he could see that the suit was beautifully cut.

'Of course, but try it first. It may not fit.'

Dillon turned his back and pulled his jumper and T-shirt off. As he slid his arms into the shirt, it felt crisp and the cotton luxurious. His school shirts had always been itchy and ill-fitting. The jacket was just a tad big across the top of his shoulders and arms; Aron was hench, after all. The trousers fit perfectly. He turned back to face Aron.

'What a transformation!' Aron exclaimed and dragged him over to see for himself in a mirror on the back of the cupboard door.

Dillon gaped at his reflection. He didn't recognise the guy with the dark, tousled curls staring back at him. The suit made him look taller and broader and somehow brought out the startling blue of his eyes.

Aron handed him a dark tie. 'Now you just need this.'

'Thanks again.' He started to put the tie on.

'No, no, no,' Aron tutted. 'Like this . . .' His strong hands were surprisingly dexterous as he knotted the tie in a perfect V-shape and slid it up to Dillon's throat. 'This is a Savoy knot. Much nicer, no?'

As his hand accidentally brushed against Dillon's warm neck, he suddenly whipped it away and stepped back. Dillon saw his nostrils flare.

'Everything looks great, thanks again, Aron,' Dillon said rapidly.

'No problem.' Aron got himself back under control and clapped him on the back so heartily that Dillon pitched forward. 'We better get back.'

Jeremiah was still waiting for them in the corridor.

'Woah.' Jeremiah grinned. 'You scrub up well.'

Dillon grinned back and stuck a finger up at him.

'Hey, looks like we've got company after all,' Aron murmured.

A petite girl with blue streaks in her glossy black hair and huge, slightly heavy-looking dark glasses strode towards them. Two VAMPS staff struggled to keep up with her luggage. Close up, the boys saw that she had luminous skin and a delicate heart-shaped face. Diamonds glittered at her ears, and she was dressed in an immaculately tailored, slim-fitting jumpsuit with high boots.

'Hi, I'm Bik,' she announced, without removing her glasses. Dillon wondered if she had an eye problem. 'Sorry, I missed meeting you earlier. My father had business in London that delayed our arrival.'

'We're supposed to be in the great hall now for the Induction Ceremony – do you want to come with us?' Jeremiah asked.

Dillon watched as Bik tipped her head back to look up at Jeremiah and saw the usual spellbound expression on her face, although she quickly recovered her cool.

'Thanks, that would be great – although I haven't changed for dinner.'

'Don't worry.' Aron stepped forward. 'You look great as you are. I'm Aron, by the way.'

'Thanks Aron. Okay, I might as well come with you guys.'

Before Dillon could introduce himself, she suddenly whipped her neck round and stared at him through the glasses. He just about managed to hold his ground.

'What is he doing here?' she hissed.

Hastily, Jeremiah stepped between them. 'This is Dillon – he's a dhampir. He's the first to be admitted here.'

Glancing sideways, Dillon saw that Bik had calmed down, and her intelligent face was now scrutinising him. He saw faint green lights and figures reflecting onto her cheekbones from the glasses and suddenly realised they were augmented reality glasses. Jesus, these vampires were seriously wealthy.

'Fascinating,' she concluded. 'I can hear your heart, so you clearly still breathe, and I can see the blood in your skin. So what bits are vampire?'

'I don't really know.' Dillon shrugged, looking down at his feet, embarrassed.

'We'd better get a move on, or we'll be late. I do not want to get on the wrong side of Madame Dupledge,' Jeremiah said.

The four vampires disappeared down the corridor – they all moved so effortlessly fast. Dillon hurried after them but just missed the lift that the others were in. Cursing, he realised he had no idea how to call it back. Searching aimlessly for a button to press, he looked up and saw a sensor and hoped the lift must automatically know when someone was waiting. Sure enough, a few seconds later it arrived. As it glided smoothly upwards and he left the underground area, he glimpsed what looked like classrooms, a spectacular pool and a refectory of some sort, although that was confusing – as far as he knew, vampires didn't eat.

At the twelfth level, the lift opened directly into a stunning hall that took up the entire floor. The moonlit sky shone through the glass roof directly above them and the glass walls gave spectacular 360-degree views over the mountains on one side and the frozen lake on the other. Dillon realised that they must be inside the roof he'd flown over earlier. Candles in tall glass cylinders were placed on small tables around the room and on top of a beautiful ebony grand piano. Once again, the intoxicating sweet-but-dark scent unsettled him. There didn't appear to be any chairs and there was no sign of any of the utensils for food. His stomach growled, reminding him that he hadn't eaten since early that morning. The rest of the group was mingling, looking up at the view of the night sky. He had the surreal sense he was attending a red-carpet event for the richest and most beautiful people in the world. Even Sade was relaxed and laughing at something Frederick and Jeremiah were saying. Cora glanced over and saw him. He saw the momentary surprise in her eyes. Detaching herself from the group, she came towards him. In the soft candlelight, she looked even more gorgeous.

'Shite, okay, here we go,' he muttered to himself as he headed towards her. 'Be cool, do not go red.'

'Talk about hiding your light under a bushel!' she exclaimed, looking him up and down.

'It's mostly down to the suit Aron lent me – Tommy Ford,' he muttered as if that explained everything.

'You okay?'

'Yes, sound, why?'

'Nothing. But you are a dhampir in a room of vampires.'

'I'm hungry, that's all.'

'Aren't we all,' she said, licking her lips and then, laughing at his alarmed expression, she linked arms and led him into the room.

Madame Dupledge swept in with the sharp-eyed Mr Hunt. Several teachers glided in behind them, carrying a black leather Corbusier chaise longue, a pile of pristine white towels and several hi-tech silver cases. They moved a larger table to the centre of the room. One of the teachers arranged the chaise longue next to it, another opened the silver cases and began arranging test tubes and syringes on the table.

'Welcome, students.' Madame Dupledge's melodious voice filled the space. 'The Induction Ceremony marks the beginning of your three years here at VAMPS. By taking part, you are swearing allegiance not only to the academy but also to me during your time here.'

As her eyes swept over each of them, Dillon felt the hairs on the back of his neck rise.

'You are committing to learning and upholding the traditions and specialist knowledge that have sustained our community for centuries and have protected us from detection. We are blessed with immense speed, strength, acute senses, supernatural abilities and, sometimes, special talents that are only discovered and nurtured by what you learn here under the guidance of our excellent staff. Every one of the Professors you see before you is an authority in their field. You are from some of the most well-known vampire families in our world.'

'Not all of us,' hissed Bram under his breath – just loud enough for Dillon to hear.

'You have been chosen for your current aptitude and for your potential to preserve our community, but also to nurture your unique skills to enhance the world as a whole. This year is particularly special. For the first time in our history, a dhampir has been given a place at VAMPS. This is a rare privilege for the student in question –' Dillon felt a flush of embarrassment take over him again – 'but it is also a special opportunity for us to learn from him. He will have different needs at first and I trust you will all be considerate and help accommodate him, just as you would in the human world.'

Dillon could feel the curious stares of the others.

'Before we begin, I must draw your attention to some important rules that must be adhered to at all times. Rule number one: You are never to leave the castle alone; there must be a minimum of two of you and you must always have permission. Rule number two: You are forbidden to take blood from a human being, dead or alive – and you must never ever harm or kill a human without permission. The punishment will be instant banishment from the school if you harm a human and, in the case of killing a human, you will be put on trial in front of the vampire council. If found guilty, you will be put to death – unless the vampire council deem otherwise.'

Dillon gulped. He thought of the small sixth form college he had been attending back in Ireland where the biggest punishment was an occasional lunchtime detention.

'Rule number three: For your own safety, you may not take blood from each other or harm each other in any other way during your time at this school. Rule number four: If you develop the skill of compulsion or mind control, you are forbidden to use it on teachers, our staff or your fellow students while you are here.

'Make sure there are no transgressions of these rules. They have been put in place for your own safety and for the safety of our community and beyond. One of the most crucial lessons you learn here is to control your desires. This year we have a dhampir in our midst so it could prove particularly challenging. If any of you experience difficulties with any aspect of this, I encourage you to speak to me personally or to one of the other staff.

'Now, let us begin the ceremony. As tradition dictates, on your first night here, you take sustenance from me. This is how you swear your allegiance to me, and it allows me to gain some insight into your character.'

Dillon's head shot up in panic. What Jeremiah had said was true. He felt sick. He couldn't do it. Especially not in front of everyone and with Madame Dupledge. No way.

Cora touched his arm. 'What's wrong?' she whispered.

'I've never done it before.' He hissed back.

Like Jeremiah, her eyes widened in shock. 'Like never?'

'Yes, like never. I've never tasted a single drop of another person's blood.'

After staring at him for a couple of seconds, her face dissolved into a grin. 'That explains why you smell so intoxicatingly human. You're going to love it – trust me.'

'But, before you take sustenance from me, as is also customary, we must collect a vial of blood from each of you. You may use the traditional vampire method to draw blood –' Dillon's heart jumped into his throat as she held a hunting knife up, its razor-sharp blade glinting in the candlelight – 'or Dr Meyer will be happy to assist you with the more contemporary blood taking equipment.'

She gestured at the tray of needles and syringes. 'Now line up please.'

The students split into two groups. Nearly everyone chose the knife queue, only Dillon and Sade chose the needle. Dillon watched in horrified fascination as Aron removed his dinner jacket and rolled up one of his white shirt sleeves. Flexing his rock-hard bicep, he gripped the knife and drew it without hesitation across his skin, taking care to avoid the intricate tattoos. Dark-red blood instantly dripped down his arm and into a large vial one of the teachers held out for him. Dillon was mesmerised by the blood, the knife and Aron's tattoos. It was like a bizarre horror movie ritual.

'Maybe don't look?' Sade advised.

'I'm fine,' he snapped and then instantly felt bad when

he saw the hurt look on her face. 'Sorry,' he whispered. 'It's all a bit much.'

'It's okay. It must be strange for you.'

Sade watched Dr Meyer carefully as she inserted a needle into her arm. As blood spurted into the syringe, Dr Meyer quickly attached a vial. It was full in seconds, and she removed the needle. Sade gently licked the puncture point. Dillon blinked. He remembered Jeremiah's words: *That's why we're so dangerous Dillon and you must never forget it.* It was way too easy to forget that exquisitely beautiful Sade was a blood-loving vampire. Ásta was next in the knife queue. Her green eyes held Angelo's as she slid the knife provocatively across her bare arm and watched her blood drip into the vial. Once full, she handed it to a teacher and licked the wound sensuously, without dropping her gaze. It looked like Angelo was having difficulty holding himself back. Aware that every eye was on her and loving every minute of it, Ásta sashayed back across the room to his side. Standing so close to her that no one from the front could see, Angelo slid his hand through the cut-outs at her waist and massaged her lower back.

'Arm, please,' Dr Meyer snapped. Her tone indicated she must have asked Dillon a couple of times already.

'Um, sorry.'

He removed his jacket and rolled up his sleeve. She looked up at him, paused for a second and rooted around her first aid box for a tourniquet. Clearly, she'd decided to treat him like a human rather than a vampire. She snapped

45

the tourniquet on his upper arm and inserted the needle in the vein on the inside of his elbow. As his blood flowed into the vial, he was surprised to see her nostrils flare. She controlled herself in seconds but refused to look at him as she removed the needle and turned to label the vial and place it next to the others.

'All done, you can join the others now,' she snapped again and then, as if remembering something, said, 'Hold out your arm again. I'll lick it for you.'

Dillon squirmed as she lowered her head and her tongue flicked across his arm, instantly healing the small puncture. She noticed his discomfort as she finished and smiled.

'My saliva has stronger than normal vampire healing abilities. It is the reason I became a doctor.'

Jeremiah had revealed his huge bicep and as he sliced the knife across it, there was an almost audible sigh from the watching vampires. Dillon grinned as he returned to stand next to Sade and Cora. Ace, Bik, Celeste, Bram and Cora were quick and efficient. Frederick was the last to let his blood, grinning happily as if slicing his arm open was just as fun as tucking into a German sausage. As the vials were labelled and placed carefully in a secure case, Madame Dupledge's voice sang out again.

'Well done everyone. And now it is time to begin the ceremony in earnest. Bram Danesti. You are first.'

As she arranged herself on the chaise longue in the centre of the hall, Dillon was reminded of a sacrificial table and swallowed – his throat suddenly dry. Without her cape, her voluptuous curves were on full display. The red velvet dress draped artfully over the chair and her auburn curls cascaded around her. Mr Hunt and the rest of the teachers stood in a protective row to her side. Bram attempted a swagger as he crossed the hall, but his face was dark with suppressed emotion as he approached her. Dillon had to admit he looked the part.

He bowed to Madame Dupledge and then formally asked her, 'Madame Dupledge, may I drink from you?'

Madame Dupledge swept her hair away from her left shoulder and exposed her creamy throat. 'Drink,' she commanded. As much as he wanted to look away, Dillon could not take his eyes off them. He had never expected to witness anything like this in his whole life.

Bram's lips pulled back revealing his fangs and he bent gracefully as if he had been doing it his whole life. Almost languorously, his mouth found her neck and he gently grazed her skin. Instantly, his eyes snapped shut and he began to drink powerfully but in perfect control. Dillon watched horrified and enthralled as Madame Duplege tipped her head back and closed her own eyes, completely acquiescing. After what seemed like ages, she seemed to come back to herself and at some unspoken command, Bram drew away courteously. She took a while to open her eyes.

Dillon got a brief glimpse of the puncture marks on her throat before they healed over. Bram's eyes gleamed darkly; his pupils were distended, and he looked dazed. A teacher handed him one of the hand towels for the tiny drop of blood that still stained his lips. Dillon couldn't suppress a shiver.

'Thank you, Bram,' Madame Dupledge said approvingly, 'that was a masterclass in how to take blood.' She then said something to him in a such a low murmur that even the vampires seemed not to be able to hear. Dillon leant forward, straining to pick up her words.

'What's all that about? What is she saying?' Dillon asked Cora in a whisper.

Cora frowned. 'I can't tell – something about confidence and bravery,' she said.

'Thank you, Madame Dupledge.' Bram's dark eyes glowed with triumph and the recent blood. Despite his studied refinement, he couldn't resist a discreet fist pump with Aron as he returned to the group.

'Sade, you are next.'

Sade seemed self-conscious in front of everyone and, rather than bending, she knelt at Madame Dupledge's side, with her back to the group. Delicately, she pushed up the soft velvet of Madame Dupledge's sleeve and lowered her head to the translucent skin of her inner elbow. Dillon was surprised; he thought all vampires drank from the neck. All he could see though was the back of her long, delicate neck and Madame Dupledge's face. Once again, as Sade began to drink, Madame Duplege's eyes closed, and she appeared to enter into a deep trance. When she finally reopened them, Sade lifted her own head.

'What control you have, Sade.' Madame Dupledge smiled

and, as she had with Bram, said something that Sade alone could hear.

Sade's face broke into the heartbreaking smile Dillon had seen earlier. 'Thank you, Madame Dupledge,' she replied, her voice slow but clear.

As she returned to Dillon's side, he asked her, 'What's the story with the inner arm? Why did you choose there?'

She shrugged. 'I prefer it, it doesn't gush as much as the neck.'

He gulped, actually unable to believe he was having this conversation. 'What did she say?'

'It's private. It's about me.'

'She can – what – tell what you're like, just by you drinking her blood?'

Sade shrugged again. 'Yeah, I guess.'

Mr Hunt shot them a warning glance and Dillon shut up. 'Angelo, come.'

Angelo was by Madame Dupledge's side in a blur and, as he turned, Dillon could see that his eyes were huge and dark again. He bent over her, the tips of his fangs already exposed.

He said something to her, and Dillon's mouth hung open as she sighed and slid her dress up, revealing a beautifully shaped pale leg. Bending it, she placed her delicate high-heeled laced boot on the leather chaise longue.

'Control, Angelo,' she warned, and he paused just a second before sinking his fangs into the soft flesh of her thigh – seeking out the fast-flowing blood of the femoral artery.

Dillon glanced round the room and noticed Ásta lick her own lips as she watched Angelo drink lustily. Madame Dupledge broke the trance and opened her eyes sooner than she had for the others and Dillon could see him struggling to slow down.

'Stop!' Madame Dupledge commanded out loud.

Mr Hunt sprang forward, ready to rip Angelo off. As every tendon in his neck strained, Angelo tore himself away.

'Sorry Madame,' he growled, his voice still husky and eyes bloodshot.

'Angelo, you have great passion, but you will have to learn self-control to be able to harness your abilities.' She advised him out loud, a little ruffled by the encounter.

'Yes, Madame,' Angelo nodded and, refusing a towel, licked his bloodstained lips with enjoyment. With a wild, restless expression, he returned to Ásta's side.

'Now, Cora you are next.'

Cora, not so confident now, in fact looking deathly pale and completely unlike herself, walked towards the chair. Dillon could see that something was wrong. She bent over Madame Dupledge. Looking into the headmistress' eyes, she hesitated and then, as if she had made her mind up about something, her lips parted, exposing glistening pearly fangs. Hovering for just a second, she sank them into Madame Dupledge's throat. Her eyelashes fanned over her cheeks, and she began drinking with almost the same wild abandon as Angelo. Madame Dupledge's eyes flicked open for just a fraction of a second in surprise. To his embarrassment, Dillon felt a powerful desire sweep through him. It was the most erotic thing he had ever seen. Glancing round the room again, he was relieved to see that the others were equally transfixed. Bram's coal-black eyes burned with lust, Ásta and Angelo stirred restlessly and even Jeremiah and Bik looked shaken out of their cool.

As Madame Dupledge transmitted her silent order to stop, Cora's elegant hands clenched and unclenched, and she struggled to control herself.

'You can do this, Cora,' Madame Dupledge murmured, and Cora slowed and gently pulled herself away, blinking and dazed. Her cheeks had a faint creamy colour, and her green eyes were slightly unfocused and huge in her face. 'Well done, you did well in controlling yourself, Cora,' Madame Duplege said, before lowering her voice. Dillon just about caught the words 'zest for life'.

'Thank you, Madame Dupledge.' Cora looked relieved and incredibly beautiful as she crossed the hall.

Bram's eyes followed her every step and he shot Dillon a malevolent stare as she stood next to him. Dillon didn't think he could take much more. His thoughts swirled in a confusion of fear and loathing and yet fascination and desire. The raging hormones zipping round the room were palpable. The atmosphere was charged with suppressed emotion, heightened by the heady scent and the slight, sickly sweet smell of blood. As Cora stood near him, he felt his entire body tense. Every millimetre of his being was acutely aware of her, and he forced himself to stare straight ahead.

'Dillon, you are next.'

Dillon sensed his feet stumble forward, but his head felt like it was somewhere else. His heart pounded and he was uncomfortably aware that everyone else could hear his fear. He could see that the teachers were watching with interest, which made it worse. Slowly he approached the chair.

'Um, Madame Dupledge,' he spoke as softly as possible, hoping that no one would hear. 'Just a heads up – I've never done this before.'

'Don't worry, Dillon. No one has,' she murmured back.

'No, not that. I mean, I have never had blood before. I should have mentioned it when we were back in the office.'

'Oh.' She looked momentarily taken aback and then thoughtful. 'Of course. Perhaps I will not let you drink as long as the others, but don't worry. I am here to guide you. The vampire side of your nature should take over. You saw the others do this. Place your mouth close to my throat.'

Dillon's heart was now pounding so hard his vision was blurring, but as Madame Dupledge looked into his eyes, he felt most of the fear drift away. Slowly, in a dream-like state, he bent towards her neck. Once again, her powerful, sweet smell overwhelmed him. As his trembling lips touched her smooth, cool skin, he almost jumped back as he felt a painful burning in his gums and a stabbing pain as sharp fangs forced through the tender skin, their pointed edges grazing his bottom lip.

What the fuck? He forced himself to remember his da's words: '*don't lose heart, Dillon.*'

'Now, let your instincts take over,' Madame Dupledge whispered.

Shivering all over, his teeth sank clumsily into her neck and his eyes instinctively fluttered shut. As her blood began to flow into his mouth, he momentarily gagged. It was metallic and surprisingly cool, but then something deep inside took over and he swallowed. With a small groan, he began to drink deeply. It was the most intoxicating thing he had ever tasted in his life. He could feel it spreading through his bloodstream, making his body tingle with energy. He groaned again, deeper this time, lost in the sensations that flooded through him. He drank faster and more deeply, and he sensed some sort of internal struggle in Madame Dupledge. She wanted him to stop, but as he drank, it seemed to be drawing her deeper and deeper into his core being. They were both lost on a wave of surging power. It was too much for him. His head began to spin and, as he somehow wrenched his mouth away, everything went black and he felt himself falling.

3

Blood Awakening

Dillon came round in the ultra-hi-tech Sanatorium. Pads and wires were strapped to his chest and clear liquid was being transfused through a plastic tube into the vein on the back of his hand. As his vision cleared, he gasped – it was like he had suddenly flicked the high-definition switch in his brain. Colours were way more intense and the detail was incredible. For a minute he stared, transfixed, at the liquid travelling down the IV tube. He could see minute eddies and splashes as if it was a full-sized river. The moment of peace was shattered as recollections of the ceremony and dark visions of knives, blood and the sensations of drinking Madame Dupledge's blood flooded his mind. Tentatively, he ran his tongue over his gums and was surprised that they felt normal. The only sign of the fangs were two slightly tender bumps high up above his canines. His hearing seemed more acute too; he picked up the sound of soft footsteps and a second later, Dr Meyer came in.

'You passed out,' she explained. 'Madame Dupledge's blood is powerful for one who has never tasted it before.'

She clicked her tongue in annoyance as if they should have expected such a poor performance from a dhampir. He tried to sit up, but she stopped him.

'Rest. You are taking some fluids in. I believe your human system was dehydrated and had low blood sugar. The rehydration will help your body assimilate the vampire blood. It may take some time for you to adapt to running two systems at the same time.'

'How does it work?' Dillon asked.

'I believe a good analogy might be a hybrid electric and petrol car. You can function on either vampire blood, human sustenance or both. The only element your human side can't do without is air, although you will be able to utilise oxygen much more efficiently now, your heart will begin to slow down, and you will be able to hold your breath for long periods of time.'

'Okay.' He nodded.

'Yes, it will be interesting to see where one side is more dominant than the other or if the two systems work equally together. In certain areas, you may be stronger than a pure vampire. Obviously, your human side has been dominant for the last eighteen years as you have not had any blood to stimulate the vampire side.'

As the doctor spoke, he noticed Jeremiah and Cora

standing behind her outside the open door. He sank back on to the bed, cringing in embarrassment as he recalled losing control in front of them. He was certain he would never live it down. From what he had seen so far, vampires didn't take any prisoners. But, as Cora's scent filled his newly sensitised nostrils, electricity flooded through him again. The machine that the wires connected to beeped a warning. The doctor hurriedly checked it before noticing Cora and Jeremiah at the door.

'Ah,' she said, raising an eyebrow.

Inwardly, he groaned. Could this evening get any more humiliating?

'I'm feeling much better. I think I can go now.' He tried to persuade Dr Meyer.

'We'll keep an eye on him,' Cora called out.

'I'd rather he stayed here for a while. He needs rest. You may stay with him. I have to finish up at the ceremony but inform me immediately if there are any changes,' she instructed, looking sternly at them.

'Of course,' Jeremiah agreed and, as usual, his steady manner persuaded anyone in authority that he was reliable.

As Dr Meyer left and Cora moved closer, Dillon closed his eyes, willing himself to remain calm. He wondered if this was how vampires always felt after taking blood or if Madame Dupledge's was particularly potent.

'Are you okay?' Cora asked.

Reopening his eyes, he looked into hers for the first time since the ceremony and was shocked to see the electricity reflected back at him. For a second, they stared at each other. The machine went wild.

'Ahem.' Jeremiah cleared his throat. 'Shall I turn that off for you?'

'Thanks, that would be great, you know, thanks,' Dillon spluttered.

'I think I might catch up with you guys later. I just wanted to check you're okay.'

'What about Dr Meyer?'

'I'll tell her Cora has everything under control,' Jeremiah said, shooting Cora an amused glance. 'Maybe catch you at the pool later?' he added as he disappeared out the door.

'The pool?' Dillon enquired.

'Yeah, after the ceremony, everyone gets to let off steam in the pool. It's on the eleventh floor.'

'Ah yes, I saw it on the way up to the ceremony. Do you want to go?' he asked Cora, anxious that he was ruining her fun.

'All in good time,' she replied. 'Dawn is still a long way off.'

Of course, he hadn't really thought through the implications of the nocturnal vampire lifestyle. The blood was making him feel restless and awake.

'Do you mind me asking – how do you manage?' Dillon asked.

'What do you mean?'

'With the whole day-night thing in the human world?'

'None of us, except maybe Ace and Jeremiah, have had

much contact with the human world yet – that's why we're here. But, to answer your question, we're okay in the day if we stay behind tinted glass or out of direct sunlight. We don't need much sleep to regenerate. Also, often we can sleep in the day standing or sitting without seeming as if we are.'

'Sort of makes sense, I suppose.'

'How are you feeling?' she asked.

'Okay, I think. There's so much going on – I lost track of "normal" way back.'

'Let's remove this, then.'

She started to peel the tape holding the transfusion tube to his hand. As she touched him, little sparks of electricity darted up his arm.

'What are you doing?' he asked, alarmed.

'You worry too much, Dillon,' she replied. 'It's time for some fun. We're all feeling the effects of Madame Dupledge's blood. Everyone is . . . how shall I put it . . . ? Bonding. I have to say, it is the most amazing thing I have ever tasted. You're lucky, you know, to have started with the best.'

He closed his eyes as the vision of Cora drinking from Madame Dupledge leapt unbidden into his mind and once again, electricity suffused his body. Cora grinned, revealing slightly extended fangs, and leant over him, lowering her lovely face towards his. He literally stopped breathing. In his new HD-vision she was even more beautiful – he could see tiny gold stripes radiating out from her pupils. Then, fast as lightning, she pulled away again.

His head reeled.

'The doctor. She's coming back.' She hissed. 'Try to get yourself out of here.'

There was a slight disturbance in the air as she whipped round to turn the machine back on just as Dr Meyer hurried back in with some of the equipment from the ceremony.

She tutted her tongue again when she saw Dillon.

'Why is he flushed?' she asked, staring daggers at Cora.

'Beats me,' she said, shrugging her shoulders.

Dr Meyer still looked suspicious. 'How are you feeling?' she asked him.

'Um, much better,' he mumbled. 'I think I'm good to go.'

She stared into his eyes, and he had the uncomfortable feeling she was somehow probing deep inside his body.

'Your body seems to be dealing with the blood, but I think you should stay a while longer. You've had enough excitement for one night. I'll remove the drip and the wires now though,' she said, beginning to peel the pads off his chest.

'So, what was the story with the rest of the ceremony? How did things go?' he asked Cora to ease the tension.

'Frederick was hilariously clumsy and funny, although I'm not sure Madame Dupledge appreciated his humour. Jeremiah looked like the god he is, Bik was cool as a cucumber but Madame Dupledge had to make her remove those glasses. Ásta lost it and Mr Hunt had to pull her off – Madame Dupledge wasn't pleased, to say the least. Ace was cocky. Celeste was super gorgeous, all of us were drooling, but she didn't like Madame Dupledge's private comment afterwards and refused to tell any of us what she said.'

'Oh right.' Dillon absorbed that for a second and then asked, 'What did she say to you?'

'Something like I have a zest for life, and I break down social barriers, bring out the best in people that sort of thing. I'm definitely into breaking down the dhampir–vampire divide . . .'

Dr Meyer couldn't pretend not to have heard Cora's last comment. 'I think you should let Dillon rest now,' she said pointedly, tutting.

Cora sighed dramatically. 'Okay, I'll catch you at the pool later, Dillon.'

'Yeah, sure,' he smiled as she backed out the door, making signals behind the doctor's back that he should get out as soon as he could. As she disappeared, he sank back onto the trolley bed. Cora was incredible and he couldn't believe she seemed to like him but, when she was near, he felt way out of control, like everything was happening in fast forward.

He wondered where his da was. That morning they had been just father and son. Now he'd taken vampire blood, he was different. Maybe he'd even try to hurt him. A wave of longing swept over him. Dr Meyer came over and shone a torch into his eyes.

'Everything seems to be fusing nicely,' she said approvingly.

'May I come in?' Sade's gentle voice interrupted the spiral of his thoughts.

'Hey, Sade. Of course.'

'How are you feeling?'

'Good, thanks. All went a bit off the rails back there.'

'It's normal to be overwhelmed,' she replied. 'We're all feeling it. You should see the others. I had to get away for a bit . . . And I wanted to see how you were,' she added, looking at him shyly.

As he looked into her huge, earnest eyes, he felt calm radiate through his body for the first time since saying goodbye to his father.

'Jaysus – that's you! How are you doing that?' he blurted out in surprise.

'What?' she asked, looking puzzled.

'That calming thing.'

'I don't know what you're talking about.'

'Maybe Madame Dupledge's blood has brought something out in you?'

'What do you mean?'

'Maybe it's what we call a "charm" in Ireland – you calm people.'

Sade looked unconvinced.

'It works on me,' he said, shrugging.

'Really?' she said, looking pleased.

He felt his heart contract. Shite, it had been all over the place since he'd arrived. No wonder vampires had dispensed with something so volatile.

Dr Meyer drifted over. 'Ah, you're looking much better now, Dillon,' she said, glancing approvingly at Sade. She checked his temperature. 'Just a bit above average now, which is normal for a dhampir. I think you should be fine to go. If anything changes come back straight away. I will be here until dawn and then the day nurse will take over.'

'Thank you, Dr Meyer,' he said as he shrugged Aron's shirt back on. For a moment, he caught Sade staring at his chest. He had worked outside on the land in Ireland all his life and had the lean, muscled torso to prove it. Quickly, she looked away and he fiddled with the buttons.

'What do you want to do?' she asked.

'Cora and Jeremiah mentioned the pool. Do you fancy checking it out?' he asked, folding Aron's jacket over his arm. 'We don't have to stay long,' he added.

'Okay,' she agreed, 'I think it's on the eleventh floor.'

His legs felt unbelievably strong and light. He had no trouble keeping up with her as they flew down the corridor and, not bothering to take the lift, bounded up the curved staircases that snaked, helter-skelter like, between each floor. He felt a surge of exhilaration, amazed that just one drink of blood had given him such speed and power. Sade turned back and smiled at him, her own eyes bright. As they reached the final curved staircase, he heard a buzz of conversation and a thumping bass track. Bounding up the steps, the laughter and excited shouts grew louder until they emerged into a circular room.

'Woah, this is a long way from home,' breathed Dillon.

An incredible pool curved round one side of the glass tubular lift shaft. Huge diamond-shaped windows, invisible from the outside, lined one wall. The pool was lit with underwater lights and appeared to float amongst the mountain tops. Steam rose from the surface, adding a magical feeling to it all. The others were grouped around the pool half chatting, half dancing to the music. The high–octane atmosphere had dialled up a notch. Ásta and Angelo were locked in a passionate embrace against the furthest windows. Dillon looked away, embarrassed as Ásta's leg snaked round Angelo's thigh, drawing him to her. Angelo's hands slid below her exposed waist and disappeared beneath her dress, pulling her even closer. Ace had exchanged his dinner suit for swim shorts. A perfect dive took him the length of the pool and, without needing to breathe, he returned with the beautiful gliding stroke of a vampire who had been swimming in Florida pools his whole life.

Loving the fact that everyone was watching, he leapt out at the end and shook the water out of his hair. In the up–lights that had turned his pale skin golden, he looked like a dripping Oscar statue. Celeste sauntered across the room towards him, her dress cut so low it revealed the whole of her perfect, smooth back. Sweeping her waterfall of blonde hair over one shoulder, she whispered something in his ear. He grinned and slowly ran a finger down her back. Dillon's stomach lurched as he noticed Bram, still looking darkly handsome in his dinner jacket but now with his bow tie loose and his shirt open, flirting with Cora. She had hitched her long dress up and was standing barefoot, talking intently to him.

Frederick almost crashed into Sade and Dillon as he burst

in behind them with the crate of bottles Dillon had noticed earlier.

'Sorry, want one of these?' he asked, waving a bottle at them.

'What is it?'

'Bottled blood – we've started making it at my father's drinks factory. All hush hush, of course.'

Sade looked unconvinced. 'What's in it?'

'A high-grade vodka and one hundred per cent pure preserved blood.' Frederick licked his lips.

Dillon gagged and couldn't hide his relief when Sade answered for him.

'We'll pass this time – thanks though.'

'Your loss!' Frederick shrugged his shoulders. 'Woah! Look at Jeremiah and Aron!'

Beetling vampire-fast round the pool, he joined Jeremiah, Bik and Aron who were standing talking. Jeremiah and Aron had both removed their jackets and opened their shirts, revealing their jaw dropping chests. Only Aron accepted a beer and Frederick leant in and kissed him lasciviously on the lips. Dillon blinked, momentarily surprised.

Sade noticed his confusion. 'The vampire world is very open when it comes to sexuality,' she explained. 'We have preferences but few boundaries. I don't like labels but I think in the human world, you might call us pansexual?'

Dillon nodded, even though where he came from sexual orientation was still stuck in the dark ages.

'Some of us are more extreme in our desires than others,'

she added as Ásta wrapped both legs around Angelo and he carried her, mouth crushed against hers, to a circular steam room with a dark-tinted floor-to-ceiling window.

Dillon had the familiar feeling of being out of his depth as the glass began to steam up and Ásta's dress flew out the door, followed by Angelo's jacket. Bik laughed at something Jeremiah said and followed Celeste into a small changing room on the other side of the pool. They reappeared in miniscule bikinis, their arms wrapped around each other. For once, Bik was without her glasses. Dillon stared for a second and then forced himself to look away – nervous he'd be called out by them. Ace had no such reticence, looking at Celeste's flawless body appreciatively. His eyes darkened as she and Bik slid into the steaming water like a pair of beautiful but deadly water nymphs. He dived in, and Celeste screeched as he swam underneath her and emerged with her on his shoulders.

'Water-polo time!' he yelled.

Jeremiah grinned and, stripping down to his Calvins, tumble turned into the water and lifted Bik onto his shoulders.

'You better be good, Jeremiah,' Ace jibed.

Celeste leant forward and sensuously kissed Bik on the lips. 'For luck. You'll need it, Bik.' She smirked as she pulled away.

Frederick and Aron whooped and followed suit. Someone found a ball and, within seconds, it was shooting back and forth over the pool, moving so fast Dillon could barely see it. Bram and Cora were still deep in conversation, completely entranced with each other. Dillon was shocked by the wave of jealous fury that swept over him. He wasn't normally aggressive but he wanted to smash his fist into Bram's arrogant face.

'Do you want to head on?' he asked Sade, not wanting Cora to see him. 'Go, I mean.'

'Okay, sure,' she said, scrutinising him. 'It's not really my scene anyway.'

As they started to leave, there was a loud snapping noise and huge cracks spread across the steam room door as Angelo and Ásta crashed into it. The water polo stopped for a second as the others looked round to see what it was. Ace laughed; Bram noticed Dillon and smirked at him. Dillon almost tripped over Sade in his haste to escape.

'Are you sure you're okay?' she asked.

'I've a favour to ask of you. Would you be able to show me how to sleep in a coffin?'

Sade smiled. 'Really? That's what you're worrying about?'

'I've never even seen one close up before today, let alone slept in it.' It wasn't a lie.

'I know,' she chortled. 'I was with you when you asked Ace what the coffins were for, remember.'

'It's not that funny.'

'Okay, sorry. I'll show you.'

Away from the madness of the pool, he felt better. Once again, he exulted in his new physical strength as they returned to the coffin corridor.

'You smell different now, you know,' Sade said.

'What?'

'Not bad or anything,' she added hastily. 'Just, you don't smell quite so intoxicating now you have had a bit of vampire blood.'

'I'm heartbroken,' he joked. 'But I guess not smelling so tasty to you lot is a good thing, right?'

'I guess, although your scent is still . . .' she groped for the right word, 'provocative.'

'Ah that explains it.' He grinned at her. 'No one is normally that interested in me.'

She looked at him earnestly. 'Even though we live forever, we tend to live fast. When we want something, we take it. That said, some of us are more sensitive than others.'

'I get that. You don't seem like the others.'

'My brothers and sisters are all brilliant extroverts, but I'm not. I'm used to being the quiet one.'

'Quiet doesn't mean you're not equally brilliant. Just a bit more modest.'

'That's kind, Dillon, but you don't know my family.'

He led the way to the little room at the end of the corridor. The two coffins gleamed malevolently.

Sade pointed at his shorter coffin. 'I assume that's yours?'

'How did you guess that?'

'Very funny. Take the stuff off the top and open the lid.'

He did as she asked.

'There are controls on the inside panel. Once you turn it on, the interior of the coffin will stay at the perfect temperature and humidity for your body all night. You can lock it from the inside too – although dhampirs are not so sensitive to sunlight so it's not such an issue for you if someone opens it in the day.'

'Never thought of that,' he said. 'It would be the only time you're vulnerable.'

'Yes. Vampires pay a lot for secure coffins and, when we travel, for daytime security. Actually, dhampirs sometimes help the most important vampire families.'

'Oh, the help. That explains Bram's attitude towards me.'

'I think that's Bram's attitude towards anyone, except maybe Cora. Her family is virtually as old as his. They're like the royalty of the vampire world.'

He almost gasped at the jolt of jealousy that shot through him again at the mention of Bram and Cora.

'Can I keep the lid open?'

'You shouldn't – but maybe just a crack for your first time. You don't have to lock it.'

'What do you wear in it?'

'Most vampires sleep naked,' she said, glancing at him from under her lashes.

'Oh, right. Cool,' he shrugged, affecting nonchalance.

Jeremiah's lilting voice boomed up the corridor. 'I won fair and square, Bik, that was the deal.'

Dillon lifted an eyebrow as the next second, Jeremiah shot into the room.

Jeremiah grinned. 'She's furious with me for winning a bet.'

'I wouldn't want to be on the wrong side of her.'

'No, despite her petite stature, she is a force to be reckoned with.'

Sade headed to the door. 'I'll leave you two alone.'

'Thanks, Sade. I owe you one.'

'You're welcome.'

Jeremiah shook his head as she disappeared.

'Watch that one,' he muttered.

'What do you mean?'

'Look, I'm not prejudiced in any way but I heard her family are very strict. They would never let her associate with anyone they hadn't approved, let alone a dhampir.'

'We're not "associating". We're just friends,' Dillon protested.

Jeremiah raised his hands. 'Don't shoot the messenger. I'm just telling you.'

He began removing his somewhat crumpled dinner suit. 'Despite Madame Dupledge's premium blood, I am now running on empty. It's coffin time.'

Dillon turned to remove Aron's suit trousers and laid them and the jacket carefully on the desk. Jeremiah was already in his coffin. Dillon switched off the light and discovered that his night vision had also improved. He had no difficulty finding his coffin in the dark. Tentatively, he climbed in and sat down. The lining was surprisingly comfortable. He inched himself down until he was lying flat, looking up at the ceiling. Following Sade's instructions, he pressed the temperature-control button.

'What was the story with that bet, by the way?' he asked casually, hoping Jeremiah didn't fall asleep as quickly as he moved.

Jeremiah chuckled. 'That Cora and Bram would get together despite her fascination for you. I've never seen anything like Cora drinking from Madame Dupledge – she's a dark horse for sure.'

Dillon clenched his fists. Why the hell hadn't he tried to get out of the Sanatorium earlier? For a second, he tortured himself with images of Bram and Cora together.

'Morning, Dillon. Sleep well,' Jeremiah's voice drifted over.

'Cheers. You too.'

He heard the lid of Jeremiah's coffin shut with a soft thud and he lay there for a while, debating whether to close his own lid or not. The weight of the chain against his collarbones, reminded him of his da's parting gift and he examined it more closely. Even with his new vision it was difficult to see details in the dim light, but he could just make out the gleaming, gold triangular pendant with a fiery, dark orange stone nestled in the centre. Peering even more closely, he could just make out a star-like pattern etched into the gold and radiating out from the stone. Rather than feeling comforted by it, Dillon shivered. Feeling too vulnerable without his clothes, he got up again and pulled his boxers and a second thick jumper out of his rucksack – he'd left the first in Aron's room. Finally comforted by the scent of home and the soft, well-washed feel of the wool against his skin, he curled up as best as he could in the coffin. Surprisingly, as he began to relax, he felt a deep, sinking feeling as if he was floating in water and the coffin felt increasingly spacious. As he drifted off to sleep, he didn't even notice the lid automatically closing.

4

Blood Never Lies

Dillon woke with a start; his heart was pounding and, for a second, he had no idea where he was. It was pitch black. He fought to stay calm. Forcing himself to take two slow breaths, he fumbled along the side of the coffin for the lid button. The lid opened instantly, and he sighed with relief. The room was still dark, but he had the feeling it was daytime. He glanced at his watch; it was three in the afternoon.

The throbbing pain in his bladder reminded him of why he'd woken up. He swore silently. He clearly hadn't switched to full-vampire mode yet. *They* obviously didn't have this problem. Jeremiah's coffin was silent and closed. Groping around, he changed into tracksuit bottoms and slid quietly into the hall.

It was empty and silent, winter daylight from the centre of the building gently illuminated the atrium area and lift shaft. He headed towards it, trying to think where they would put toilets. Would they even have human visitors? Probably not, he reasoned. It would be too dangerous. Besides, only helicopters or mountain climbers would be able to reach this place.

The school looked different in daylight, starker somehow. Vampires didn't do 'cosy' by the looks of it. He stopped on the fifth floor but there weren't any signs in the entrance hall. Stepping back into the lift, he took it up to the eleventh floor. The pool area was silent and cold in the grey afternoon light. The extreme isolation of the building was even more obvious. It didn't look so glamorous now either, although there was still some evidence of the party the night before. Angelo's jacket remained on the floor where he'd flung it, and a huge spiderweb of cracks spread across the sauna room door. With a pang, he saw Cora's Doc Marten boots, left carelessly by the windows.

Desperate now, he checked the changing rooms and cursed again. There must be somewhere he could go. The huge pot plants by the windows caught his attention and he slid behind one, praying there weren't any surveillance cameras.

Picking up Cora's boots, he headed back down to the sleeping quarters. He caught sight of a couple of black-clad vampires noiselessly scurrying about, preparing for the rest of the vampires to wake up.

Quietly, he placed the boots outside Cora's room and almost bumped into a barefooted Angelo in a crumpled white shirt, creeping out of Ásta's room next door. She had managed to claim one of only two single rooms on the

73

corridor. His eyes were bloodshot and his olive skin, deathly pale.

Warily, Dillon stepped back.

To his surprise, Angelo spoke, 'Help me out, amigo, give me a taster. Dhampir blood is the best.'

'Whaat?' Dillon stammered, taking another step back. 'Leave it out.'

'Just a little pick me up. I didn't get any sleep. She's one hell of a vampire.' He gestured at the door.

Dillon squirmed. 'Um, I don't think I can help. Isn't it against the rules?'

'No one would know. A spoonful would do. I'll show you how to do it. We don't have to use fangs.'

Dillon shuddered. This was insane. Holding his hands up, he backed away. 'Why don't you ask Frederick – I think he has some bottled stuff.'

Angelo looked hopeful. 'Really? Do you know which room he's in?'

Dillon pointed down the hall. 'The third one on the other side of the lift.'

'Okay, great.' He shot down the corridor like a bullet.

Dillon sighed with relief and whipped back to his room before Angelo changed his mind. He hoped Frederick wouldn't mind being woken up but figured that Aron was tough enough to deal with Angelo if things got out of hand.

He was aware that he could do with a wash, especially since he now knew just how sensitive a vampire's sense of smell was. Cora had smelt incredible last night. Grabbing a towel, he checked the corridor again. There was no sign of Angelo, so he slid back out. Halfway along, he noticed an opaque glass door. Sure enough, when he opened it there was a trendy white tiled communal shower area and a sleek metal trough-like basin with a long mirror above it. There were no doors or locks. Uneasily, he re-checked the corridor, but everything was as silent as before and he guessed he had another half hour before everyone started waking up.

Carefully placing his towel where he could grab it in case Angelo appeared, he stripped off and turned a shower on. He almost yelled out as the water hit his body. It was powerful and too hot – a complete contrast to the cold dripping excuse for a shower he was used to at home. The hi-tech controls made no sense so he gradually inched himself under the scalding water and was enveloped by thick, swirling steam.

He nearly jumped out of his skin when he realised someone had joined him. Covering himself with his hands, he peered through the steam. A completely naked Celeste was washing her hair, her perfect body seemingly impervious to the heat. Somehow, even though he knew it was wrong, he couldn't look away. He'd never seen anything like it in real life before.

Suddenly, she noticed him. 'What the hell are you looking at? Pervert.'

Flushing as red as the rest of his body, he looked away. 'Um, sorry, you surprised me.'

'Yeah, right.' She raised an eyebrow and looked pointedly

at his hands, still covering himself up. 'Just a bit of advice. We don't stare at each other in the shower, and we don't have a problem with nudity.' Glancing again at his lower stomach region and enjoying watching him squirm, she added, 'I presume you dhampirs have nothing to be embarrassed about.'

'Um, no . . . nothing more than usual,' he mumbled, cursing to himself that he couldn't be cool and nonchalant, but he hadn't had much practice at strutting around in front of stunning, naked female vampires.

Celeste smirked as he turned away and grabbed his towel. 'Nice pendant by the way. You must have some good vampire connections somewhere.'

'Um, thanks,' he said, touching it self-consciously, not understanding what she meant.

Celeste smirked again, and he hurried out of the shower, almost crashing into Ace, whose lower-body tattoo and rock-hard ten-pack were now on full display.

'Hi,' he mumbled as he edged past him.

Ace looked surprised. 'What's the rush? Is the water okay?'

'Ah no, actually, it's getting a bit too hot for me.'

'Oh, okay.' Ace looked bemused. 'Catch you later,' he said and disappeared into the steam.

There was no shriek of protest from Celeste – obviously, he was well drilled in vampire-shower etiquette or she didn't mind sharing the shower with him. Judging by the giggles and gasps that emerged a moment later – it was the latter.

The dim lights in the corridor had come on, and Jeremiah was awake when he got back and collapsed against the door.

'Everything okay?' Jeremiah asked.

'Well, since we last spoke, Angelo wanted to drink my blood and Celeste just humiliated me in the shower, but apart from that, yeah, dull and boring.'

Jeremiah grinned. 'Sounds like you've had a busy time. It's going to take you a while to adapt to us, but you'll be fine.'

'Hope so. There's a lot of adapting necessary. Do you know what happens today?' he asked, pulling his jeans and jumper on.

'We have to meet at the great hall again and we choose the VE.'

'VE?' Dillon raised an eyebrow.

'Vampire Elect. The best vampire in each year.'

'How do we do that?' Not another humiliating ritual, he hoped.

Jeremiah shot him a sideways glance. 'By tasting each other's blood.'

Dillon blanched, of course. How else would vampires do it?

'Like we did with Madame Dupledge?'

For a horrifying minute he imagined drinking from Bram or worse, Ásta or Angelo or, worse still, but for different reasons, Cora. No way could he do that.

'No, from the samples we gave last night – so that we don't know whose blood is whose.'

It was better but not by much.

'Okay, so let me get this right. I have to drink twelve samples of blood, including my own and then vote on my favourite?'

Jeremiah nodded. 'That's about it.'

Dillon swore. Just when he'd thought things couldn't get any worse.

'Don't worry though, our blood is nowhere near as potent as Madame Dupledge's, and it won't be as intense as drinking from the source.'

Dillon winced and wondered yet again why he had to do all of this. He would never fit in. He might be half vampire but this world was just too out there. A sudden, intense wave of homesickness almost floored him.

Jeremiah was checking messages on a state-of-the-art iPhone and Dillon realised he had no way of contacting the outside world. The cottage in Ireland was so remote; there was no phone signal or internet access so there was no point. Quite a few of the kids at school who lived as far out as he did went without phones. He guessed that it would be the opposite here, Bik had those AR glasses for Christ's sake.

'How much does one of those cost?' he asked Jeremiah, pointing at the phone.

'About twelve hundred dollars. Why?' he replied.

Dillon's mouth hung open. 'Shite. Really?'

'I have an old handset as a spare if you want to use it. You just need a sim card. Bik might have one – you should see the kit in her room. Her dad runs some massive tech company in Shanghai. She's sharing with Cora now, by the way. She was freaking out about sharing with Angelo last night so Ace offered to swap. Rather him than me – Angelo's wild.'

'You're not joking!'

'Let's go and see her now. She should be awake,' Jeremiah said, springing up.

'Um, okay, sure.'

Dillon followed him out and watched as Jeremiah tapped on the door. Dillon fidgeted awkwardly behind him, unsure about seeing Cora after last night. He noticed that her boots had disappeared.

Bik came to the door without her AR glasses on and, for the first time, Dillon saw she had vivacious, dark-brown eyes that sparkled when she looked at Jeremiah. Jeremiah smoothed his dreads and smiled down at her.

'Hey Bik, sorry to disturb you. Dillon needs a sim card.' He waved the old phone.

Bik took the phone. 'I'm not sure I have anything for something this outdated. I'll have a look.' She opened the door. 'Come in.'

Dillon glanced over at Cora's coffin, it was open and empty, but her dress had been tossed over a chair and her boots chucked in the corner by the desk. Pictures of stunning vampires bearing a strong family resemblance to her covered the inside lid of her coffin.

Bik saw him looking. 'Cora's in the bathroom,' she explained.

He could smell her lingering scent and felt desire flood through him. Christ. What was wrong with him? It was like she had bewitched him.

Bik was rooting through a suitcase full of chargers, leads

and hard drives. As Jeremiah had said, she had some serious kit. A sleek laptop hummed on the desk next to a Chanel handbag and her glasses were charging next to the coffin.

'Ah, this might do it.' In seconds, she fitted a sim into the phone and switched it on. The screen lit up. 'Do you want me to set it up for you? I can save all Jeremiah's stuff and then take it back to factory settings.'

He shrugged and looked at Jeremiah. 'Sure that's okay? You won't need it?'

'Sure, but I think I've taken everything off it already.'

Bik plugged the phone into her laptop together with a flash drive and her fingers flew over the keys.

'All done.' She handed the phone and the flash drive to Jeremiah.

'Thanks, Bik. I owe you one.'

'No problem,' she said.

Dillon smiled to himself, noticing her eyes sparkle again as she looked up at Jeremiah, who was flexing his biceps as he smoothed his hair back yet again.

'Catch you later.' Jeremiah waved as they headed out the door and encountered a dripping Cora wrapped in a towel.

'Hey Cora,' Jeremiah smiled at her.

'Hey Jeremiah.'

Dillon's heart lurched; her wet eyelashes were stuck together like starfish and she looked more delicate somehow without the black kohl around her eyes. Her legs went on for miles under the short towel.

'Um, hi. I put your boots by the door,' he mumbled.

'Ah, it was you – thank you, Dillon.'

He suddenly realised he was still staring at her. 'Um, well, I'm in contact with the world now,' he said, waving the phone, looking everywhere but at her. 'Bik has sorted us out.'

She was smiling like he was funny. 'Oh great. Well, see you later.'

'Yeah, or you could call me,' he replied, 'on this.'

'I'll *see* you later, Dillon' said Cora.

Jeremiah grinned as he caught up with him. 'That went well.'

Dillon groaned. 'Mind yourself, Jeremiah or I'll . . .' he glanced at Jeremiah's huge biceps, ' . . . probably do nothing.'

Jeremiah chuckled. 'You want my advice?'

'Advice about what in particular?' asked Dillon. He admired the phone as they waited for the lift and then pocketed it. 'Networks? Call charges?'

'Come on, man. You're crazy about her.'

'So, it's that obvious, is it?'

'Look, play it cool. She'll come back to you. You're too much of a temptation.'

'Me, a temptation?'

'She's a rebel and what's the best way to defy traditional family expectations?'

'Hang out with a dhampir?' Dillon guessed.

'Exactly. Bram may be dark and dashing but ultimately he's exactly the type of vampire her parents would like her to hang out with.'

'I'm not sure. Isn't he like vampire royalty? Lot more to offer than me. Anyway, what about your bet with Bik?'

'That was last night. We were all feeling – how shall I put it . . . amorous. Madame Dupledge's blood was . . . special.' Jeremiah grinned. 'I'm still feeling the rather delicious after-effects today.'

Dillon stopped. 'Does drinking blood always do that?'

'Yes, but not as much, and the effect doesn't last as long. She is a very powerful vampire and she's lived a long time. Her blood is the most amazing I've ever tasted.'

'Cora said the same.'

'It's true – look what it did to you.'

'Don't remind me!'

The candles in the ceremonial hall flickered and cast restless shadows on the floor as Dillon and Jeremiah shot in five minutes late. Dillon was surprised to see it was full of vampires, most of whom turned to stare at him, some curious, some hostile.

He looked away awkwardly, realising they must be the Peak Two and Three vampires waiting to watch the Blood Tasting, and he felt his stomach clench with nerves. What if he did something stupid, like pass out again – in front of the whole academy?

His year was hovering near a stunning girl who was chatting to Madame Dupledge.

Mr Hunt glanced at his watch. 'Ah Mr Halloran and Mr Lewin, nice of you to join us.'

'Sorry, Sir,' Jeremiah apologised.

Madame Dupledge turned, and Dillon saw a strange, almost tender expression flit across her face. Instantly, she controlled it and smiled.

'Dillon, welcome. I trust you are feeling better.'

'Yes, Madame. Thank you, Madame.' His voice squeaked, and he saw Bram smirk at Ace.

Cora and Bik slid in at the back of the hall and Bram's expression became unreadable. Whatever had happened the night before, he wasn't giving any clues away.

Madame Dupledge introduced the girl standing next to her. 'Mahina Ikaika here is our Peak Three Vampire Elect. As the third year is the final year at the school, it is an especially great honour to be selected. She has faced many difficult tests over her first two years here and has become a strong and powerful young vampire as a result.'

Celeste, standing next to Sade, shot Bram a triumphant glance and smiled at Mahina. Looking at Mahina, Dillon was unsurprised. She had a strong, brave beauty with long, rippling black hair and wide cheekbones. In another world she could have just stepped off a surfboard in the North Pacific.

'She is going to show you around and answer any questions you might have about the school,' Madame Dupledge continued. 'But first, a word about the behaviour last night.'

A nerve in Angelo's jaw twitched. Ásta, in skin-tight black jeans and a body-hugging cashmere jumper, stared forward stonily.

'I'm aware that meeting each other for the first time can be overwhelming and emotions were running high, but breaking school property is not acceptable. The pool is out of bounds until the glass in the sauna is fixed.'

Ace suppressed a groan.

'I hope the culprits will come forward so that the cost can be added to their bill, otherwise, it will be shared amongst all of you.'

Dillon's heart sank. He had no idea how his father was affording all this. Madame Dupledge had mentioned a scholarship but there was no way they could pay for anything extra. That sauna would probably cost a fortune to fix.

Ásta put her hand up. 'My father will see that it is paid for,' she announced.

It wasn't exactly an admission or an apology, but Dillon sagged with relief.

'Thank you, Ásta.' Madame Dupledge inclined her head. 'You will come and see me in my office later to discuss the details.'

Ástsa scowled. 'Yes, Madame.'

The nerve in Angelo's jaw was still going but he remained silent; Ásta shot him a furious glare.

'I would also like to remind you that the only blood you will consume is provided by the school.' She held up one of Frederick's empty bottles. 'This is not acceptable.'

Frederick fidgeted and fiddled with the zip on his jacket.

'If I find anyone drinking illegal blood such as this, they

will be instantly suspended.' Her green glare swept over them. 'Now, Mahina, perhaps you can introduce yourself.'

'Thank you, Madame Dupledge.' Mahina stepped forward. 'Hi everyone. I guess you already know how lucky you are. VAMPS is awesome and it will make you into the best vampire you can be. I am not from one of the pure-blood vampire families . . .'

There was a slight stirring amongst the vampires in the hall, and Dillon saw Bram glance at Cora with a raised eyebrow. Surprised again at the surge of violence that welled up inside him, he clenched his fists and tried to focus on what Mahina was saying.

'When I first arrived here, I had no idea how strong or powerful I could become. Since then, I've discovered that I'm up there with the best at misting and hypnosis. I'm going to work in international diplomacy and intelligence under Countess Bibiana Fassano. That could be any one of you.'

Sade, Celeste and Bik were virtually swooning. Countess Fassano was obviously someone big in the vampire world.

'I'll show you around the building – feel free to ask me anything you want.'

As she strode to the lifts, Celeste and Bik virtually flew across the floor to be in the same lift as her. Bram pulled in Cora and Ace, and Jeremiah and Aron jumped in at the last second.

Dillon found himself in the other lift with Sade, Angelo, Ásta and Frederick. He pressed himself against the glass, as far away from Angelo as possible. Even so, as the doors closed and they headed towards the basement, Angelo inched closer, nostrils flaring.

'Why didn't you own up?' Ásta hissed at him.

Shaking his head and dragging his eyes away from Dillon's neck, Angelo shrugged. 'My father would kill me if he heard that I'm in trouble already. Things have not always gone well at my other schools.'

That was no surprise, thought Dillon. Angelo's family must be pretty important in the vampire world for him to have got a place. Not that *he* could talk. He had no obvious talent either – apparently just an impressive, powerful vampire mother.

'Don't worry, I can give you the money.'

'The money is nothing!' Ásta exclaimed. 'It's the principle. I thought you were strong, Angelo.'

'I am,' he protested.

'Prove it.'

'What. How?'

'The blood they provide here will be sanitised, tasteless rubbish. Find me some real stuff.'

Angelo fidgeted and his fingers drummed against the glass wall of the lift.

Sade intervened. 'I'm not sure that's a good idea, Ásta.'

'Stay out of it, Sade,' Ásta snapped.

'Hey,' Dillon said as he stepped forward.

Frederick stood between them. 'Hey!' he exclaimed in German. 'Cool it, vamps. Look Angelo, I can help – I have contacts.' He turned to Ásta, 'It will cost.'

She put her hands on her hips. 'Like I said, money isn't an issue. But Angelo needs to prove he's vampire enough for me.'

Angelo grew about two inches taller. 'I don't need to prove anything to you.'

As they stared furiously at each other, their anger erupted into lust. Angelo pushed Ásta up against the glass and crushed his mouth against hers. Dillon looked out the window; the other lift looked like the picture of respectability.

'Careful.' Frederick grinned. 'We don't want any more broken glass!'

Fortunately, the lift doors opened at the basement and broke them apart. Dillon shot out like lightning, Sade just behind him. Almost the entire floor was taken up with an incredible state-of-the-art gym space, complete with MMA-style ring, huge climbing walls and what looked like a couple of wind tunnels.

Mahina pointed them out. 'That's where you practise your flying skills – they help to increase your speed. The climbing walls speak for themselves; some of us are fantastic climbers.'

Aron, looking completely at home in the gym, demonstrated by scaling one the vertical walls like a spider. Dillon clapped in awe but then felt like a complete idiot when he realised no one else looked remotely impressed. Maybe they could all do it? Sure enough, Ásta followed and scaled it even faster.

Mahina continued, 'We practise combat plus strength and endurance in here. We're way stronger and faster than humans but we learn to be strong and wily to defend ourselves against some dangers. There are ways to kill us, including stakes made of Aspen wood through the heart and fire. Nightshade and silver can weaken us. Sometimes we have to track and even destroy rogue vampires. The hardest is when it's someone you know.' Suddenly, her face looked stricken.

There was silence as the group took this in.

'Did it happen to you?' Cora asked, her tone combative and her face hard.

Dillon glanced up at her in surprise. There was a pause while Mahina and Cora stared at each other.

'Sort of.'

Dillon swallowed. He could easily imagine Angelo going rogue but couldn't fathom having to track him down and 'destroy' him.

For the first time, he realised that he was now one of the hunted. People or other vampires might want to kill him. This school wasn't about getting an A in Geography – it was about survival.

Ace, Jeremiah, Ásta and Aron were pacing round the gym like they wanted to start immediately. Ásta karate-kicked a stray punch bag across the room as if it was made of polystyrene.

Jesus, thought Dillon, he was starting to understand why Angelo had been so desperate for a blood hit earlier on.

'How long did it take you to get good at flying?' he asked Mahina.

She studied him. 'You must be the dhampir everyone's talking about.'

'Um, yeah, I guess.' He squirmed under her scrutiny. Her beauty was intimidating.

'Not long.' She smiled. 'But misting worked out better for me. It takes a lot of mental strength.'

She was still staring at him, and he had the same strange sensation he had with Dr Meyer that she was probing his mind.

'I believe you will be good at it too,' she said finally. 'It's odd for a dhampir. From what I have studied, your skills are less enhanced than a full vampire.'

'That I can believe,' Dillon replied with feeling.

'Yeah, well, I wouldn't be so sure.' She stared at him a second longer and then raised her voice. 'Follow me everyone, I'll show you the Blood Room. All three Peaks drink there twice a month although some Peak Threes only need a top up once a month.'

They didn't bother with the lift this time, taking the circular stairs that linked each floor. The Blood Room was on the tenth floor. It was empty and looked surprisingly normal. There were long tables and cool Scandi chairs. The only evidence that blood was served here were two empty racks on wheels.

Mahina pointed to a reinforced door with a porthole window and a security keypad, 'All the blood is kept in the storage room behind the door. Professor Dukan looks after it and he works out the optimum blood type for you.'

Dillon could see hundreds of blood bags hanging eerily from steel racks.

'There is also a bar –' Angelo and Frederick perked up – 'where you can buy artificial blood shots or foams if you get thirsty.'

Their faces fell, and Dillon grinned to himself. The blood bar was clearly not the type of bar they had been hoping for.

Mahina smiled. 'We had better get back to Madame Dupledge. Does anyone have any questions?'

'Has anyone ever been expelled?' Cora asked.

Mahina looked a little startled by the question. 'A few people but it's rare. There has to be a major transgression.'

'Anyone in your year?' Cora pressed on, ignoring her.

Dillon saw Mahina study Cora's nose ring and her black-ringed eyes for a second.

'What's your name again?'

'Cora.'

Recognition flitted across her face, followed by that stricken look again. 'You know there was.'

She turned abruptly away and was immediately monopolised by Bik and Celeste as they made their way back down the stairs. Bram had gone ahead so Dillon caught up with Cora.

'My brother was expelled,' she hissed under her breath.

'Jaysus. What happened with him? Where is he now?'

'I'm not sure. He escaped and they went after him. Mahina and he were *together*, and she was one of vampires who hunted him down, but he evaded them, and no one knows what happened to him.'

'What do you mean?'

Cora clammed up. Madame Dupledge met them on the sixth floor. His mind was reeling, full of questions about Cora's brother.

'Thank you, Mahina.' Madame Dupledge's resonant voice interrupted his thoughts. 'I hope you were all suitably impressed by Mahina's incredible achievements.'

Bik, Sade and Celeste nodded, and the others looked a bit sheepish. At least he'd asked about flying, Dillon thought.

As Mahina left to join the rest of the Peak Two and Three vampires, Madame Dupledge's eyes swept over them again. 'And now we will choose our Peak One Vampire Elect. A screen has been set up in the hall so that the other years and the teaching staff are able to witness the Blood Tasting.'

She led them to a large lab style room. Twelve test tubes containing two centimetres of blood each were lined up on each workbench together with state-of-the-art laptop–tablet hybrids and an electric pen.

Everyone fell silent. Bram's eyes blazed with confidence. Ace and Celeste looked meaningfully at each other – like they had a pact of some sort. Cora looked as if she couldn't care less. The others were all somewhere in between.

Sade turned and gave him a little smile. God, she was so sweet, the only one who seemed to get how weird this all was for him. He hadn't really spoken to her much this evening.

He eyed up the vials. Weirdly, he didn't feel as revolted as he had expected. With a mounting feeling of disgust, he realised he was looking forward to the hit from another shot of blood.

As the others headed for the workbenches, Madame Dupledge drew him aside. 'Dillon, are you sure you are feeling restored? Are you able to cope with this?'

'Yes. Honest, I'm fine,' he said, avoiding looking at her in case it brought back the incredible sensations of drinking her blood.

Feeling light-headed and conscious that the other years were watching, he slumped onto the only remaining workbench right at the front, next to Sade.

'Listen carefully everyone. You will take one sip of each vial of blood, and you will give it a ranking on the laptop provided. Each vial is numbered and only myself and Mr Hunt know whose blood is in each vial. As there is no way you can identify the blood, do not attempt to. Instead, close your eyes and let your instincts take over. You will know when you taste the blood of the candidate you want to be Vampire Elect this year. You may choose yourself. Although it is rare to be unsure, you may take one more sip from any of the vials if you need to. As always, the Blood Tasting is broadcasted live to the hall where the teachers and Peaks Two and Three will watch it on the big screen.'

Great. His tension ratcheted up another notch. Not only could the whole class see him but the entire academy. He willed himself not to pass out again. The room was completely silent. Bram tapped his foot impatiently.

'You may begin. You do not have to taste the vials in order. Bik, please remove your glasses. They will only act as a distraction for this particular task.'

There was a faint whirring noise as the fixed cameras, high up in the corners of the room, zoomed in. Fingers trembling slightly, Dillon reached for vial number seven. The blood was a vivid crimson colour. It seemed like the two sides of his nature were having a tussle. One side wanted to gag, the other wanted to rip the cap off and gulp it down. He forced himself to unwind the cap slowly and put the test tube to his lips. The metallic, sweet smell of blood filled his nostrils and he jerked back as, once again, fangs shot out of the tender bumps at the top of his gums. He almost dropped the test tube out of surprise. He had thought fangs only came out if 'flesh' was involved.

Closing his eyes and trying not to think of everyone watching, he held his breath and took a sip. Clumsily, his fangs clunked against the glass rim and the blood shot into the back of throat. The shock made him choke and everyone looked up. Dreading a scene like the night before, he swallowed hard and, like a shot of good whiskey, he felt the blood flow down his throat with a pleasant burn. As the warmth spread throughout his limbs, his entire body tingled, like every cell was waking up again.

He liked it. He liked it a lot. It seemed like he'd hit the jackpot straight away. But the next vial was even better. As the blood hit his system, the power rush was incredible. His pulse raced, every muscle tensed involuntarily, and his eyes pinged like they were popping out of his head. A surge of confidence followed and for a minute or two he felt he could do anything he wanted. He craved another slug but, taken aback by his body's strong reaction, he didn't dare risk it.

He continued tasting, but none of the other samples elicited the same powerful response as the second one. On close inspection, he noticed that each vial varied ever so slightly in colour, consistency and smell but it was the flavour that really set them apart and it was hard to analyse why he liked one vial more than another. They were simply 'pleasurable' to a lesser or greater degree. He decided not to try working out why and instead just gave an instinctive score to each sample he swallowed.

Only one vial slightly confused him – it had a rich aroma, with a wonderfully light silky texture that lingered pleasantly on his tongue but, after a few seconds, left him with an ever-so-subtle bitter aftertaste. He couldn't quite work out whether it was good or bad, so he ended up giving it a mid-range score.

Having tasted all twelve vials, one sample stood out as a clear 10 out of 10 – it was the one that had given him the extraordinary power surge.

Just to make sure he'd got it right, he tasted it again. This time, the powerful reaction was even stronger, and he felt absolutely convinced that this was the right one. Deep inside, he felt it was probably Jeremiah's.

Satisfied with his selection, he completed the spreadsheet and was the first to hand his in. Glancing round the room, he noticed that some of the others were still deliberating. Bram in particular appeared to be struggling.

Madame Dupledge spoke again. 'Remember everyone, let your instincts take over. Ignore your mind and everything you have been told before you entered this room – it will only confuse you and ultimately could lead you to make mistakes.'

Bram pinched the bridge of his nose and frowned. Finally, he forced his eyes shut and completed the last of his choices. Bik was the last to finish. She too had found it hard to turn her logical brain off.

'Thank you everyone,' Madame Dupledge said. 'Mr Hunt has been logging your responses and we will take a small amount of time to process them. The announcement will be made in the great hall. Do not discuss your choices with each other. As I have said already, they are deeply instinctive and should not be open for discussion or –' she paused to look at every single one of them – 'any form of criticism.'

Dillon looked around for Jeremiah as they filed out of the lab room. He was chatting to Bik so Dillon hung back to wait for them.

Bik was complaining. 'It's ridiculous in this day and age to rely on instinct and not scientific reasoning. My glasses would have helped me assess the properties of each sample from a logical perspective. Emotions can cloud effective decision-making.'

'You're right Bik,' Jeremiah soothed, 'but this is a system that has worked for centuries and our innate powers as vampires can't be disregarded either. I have to say, personally, I wouldn't have had a clue which sample to choose if I hadn't let my instinct take over.'

Reluctantly, Bik agreed. 'But I still say they should check the scientific properties of the blood and cross match them with our instinctive choices. What if the blood showed a marker for insanity that we didn't pick up?'

'Come on, we're vampires – we've all got a mad streak. Anyway, they probably do that already. This place is pretty hi-tech.'

'Well, there is that possibility,' Bik conceded. 'They have had the samples since last night. I will discuss it with Madame Dupledge.'

'Good idea.' He glanced over at Dillon. 'How did it go for you, Dillon?'

'Good, I think. I'm still getting used to the whole fang thing.'

Jeremiah chuckled. 'At least you're getting better at it – you didn't pass out this time.'

An air of nervous anticipation filled the hall as they returned. The rest of the vampires and staff mingled in front of the screen that had relayed the live pictures of the Blood Tasting. Once again, several of them stared at him cold-eyed and a few high-fived Bram, who looked confident, like he had it in the bag.

The most ambitious students in the year, Bram and Celeste, grouped together with Ace. Bram beckoned Cora over and despite the fact she looked bored, he felt physically ill when he saw Bram gently stroking her arm as he talked intently to them.

Suddenly Cora glanced across the room and caught him staring at her. Looking back at him with a resigned expression on her face, she shrugged her shoulders and looked away again. What the hell did that mean?

Sade joined him, Bik and Jeremiah. 'How did your Blood Tasting go?' she asked.

'Well, I wouldn't want to do it every day,' he joked.

'No. It is strange tasting so many different samples. I feel a little light-headed myself.'

'Is it like that every time you take blood?'

'No, the blood we drink for nutrition is human blood that's been treated and sanitised. We all have optimum blood types and they each have their individual taste but there isn't the sense of character you get with vampire blood.'

Dillon remembered Ásta's ultimatum to Angelo in the lift earlier and shuddered.

Madame Dupledge swept into the hall followed by Mr Hunt. There was an instant hush. The sense of anticipation ratcheted up a few notches. Dillon saw Bram's posture stiffen as they all focused on her, waiting for the result. Even though Dillon didn't really care who was picked, he found that he too was hardly daring to breathe.

'Thank you for your patience,' Madame Dupledge

addressed them. 'We have the result, and it has been verified by myself, Mr Hunt and Professor Dukan, Head of Blood Technology.'

Dillon hoped that Madame Dupledge's voice masked the pounding of his heart.

'For the first time in the history of this school, one candidate has received all twelve nominations.' There was a gasp and the vampires shifted restlessly. 'Before I announce the result, I would like you to remember one of the most important tenets that VAMPS has been based upon. *Blood. Never. Lies.* With that in mind, I am pleased to announce that the person with all twelve nominations is —' she paused — 'Dillon Halloran.'

5

Tainted Blood

The whole hall went silent. Dillon felt like he was watching the events from far away – like his body was there but his mind was floating somewhere up on the ceiling.

Then there were gasps of horror and surprise.

'Christ,' was all he could think to say. Had he heard right? There must be some mistake.

Bram's already pale face went deathly white. Ace thumped the wall and Celeste's normally flawless forehead was marred by an angry frown.

'That can't be right, he's not even a full vampire,' she hissed.

Madame Dupledge ignored her. 'To reiterate, the process and the results have been triple-checked by myself, Mr Hunt and Professor Dukan. There is absolutely no doubt that every single one of you, including Dillon himself, voted him as Vampire Elect.'

Bram found his voice and although it was tight with anger, he spoke clearly and fluently. 'This is an outrage. He shouldn't have been included. It's no surprise his blood would taste alluring to us – he is half human.'

There was a small murmur of agreement from some of the watching vampires.

Madame Dupledge turned to Bram. 'Mr Danesti, if the human element in Dillon's blood was so identifiable, or "alluring" as you put it, why did you pick it?'

Bram floundered for a second. 'I didn't say the human element was identifiable, I said his sample would stand out and it's obvious why we all picked it and why the result is so different to other years.'

'Be honest, Mr Danesti. What did your instincts tell you about the blood?'

Bram looked away. 'I can't remember exactly.'

Madame Dupledge turned to Cora. 'Cora, what did your instincts tell you?'

Cora looked fierce. 'It was the sample I had no doubt about. It was incredibly powerful, and it had something else I couldn't put my finger on.'

'Thank you, Cora. Bik?'

Bik's glasses hid her expression. 'Pretty much the same as Cora. I felt like this blood, Dillon's, I suppose, was the standout choice. Although, I am surprised.'

'Celeste?'

Celeste shrugged. 'It was different but maybe not in a good way.'

Madame Dupledge ignored her. 'Jeremiah?'

'There must be more to Dillon that meets the eye,' Jeremiah quipped. 'His blood was strong, very strong.'

Angelo raised his hand. 'I'm no Dillon fan, but his blood tasted incredible – almost as good yours.'

Madame Dupledge raised an eyebrow. 'Thank you, Angelo.'

She turned to Bram. 'Not one of you has mentioned a sense of human "allure" in Dillon's blood, including yourself. There is no doubt you too would have made an excellent Vampire Elect, Mr Danesti. I would like you to demonstrate those qualities by accepting today's result.'

Bram bit his lip and, clenching his fists, gave a small bow. 'I accept the result, but I am not convinced that my father will.'

Madame Dupledge smiled. 'Your father is not your concern Bram. At VAMPS you are encouraged to make your own choices. However, I will speak to him, as indeed, I shall speak to all of your parents.'

Dillon was still frozen with horror. Not in a hundred, million years did he want to be leader of a bunch of crazy, arrogant, super-strong, super-intelligent vampires.

At last, he managed to speak. 'Look, I don't want to be causing any trouble – I realise I'm still learning about how things work here. I'm happy for there to be another vote.'

For the first time, Madame Dupledge's eyes blazed. 'Dillon, you have been chosen as leader in a tried and tested cere-mony that has worked for centuries. As I said: blood never lies. You do not *step down*. You accept the mantle, and you live up to it. Your second-in-command will help to guide you when it is a matter of knowledge about our school or the vampire world. None of you have attended this academy before so it is a learning experience for everyone.'

Now, as well as the paralysing fear, he felt a stab of shame in his stomach. He'd already failed the first test.

Glaring at him for a second longer, Madame Dupledge moved on. 'The person with the second-highest number of votes and our Peak One Deputy Vampire Elect is Bram Danesti.'

Bram became eerily still – as if he was morphing into stone. Not a flicker of a muscle or a single blink of an eyelid betrayed his feelings, which was somehow more intimidating than the anger he had displayed before.

'This is outrageous,' Celeste protested. 'This school is obviously centuries behind in terms of equality.'

'Celeste.' Madame Dupledge turned to her. 'As you should know, the ceremony doesn't differentiate by anything other than who is the best vampire for the role. In my view, that is true equality. Mahina is Vampire Elect of Peak Three and surely you don't need me to remind you that I have been Head here for over a hundred years. There have been countless female Vampire Elects over the years, as any cursory research into the history of this academy would have informed you.'

Ouch, thought Dillon, *that's put her in her place*.

Celeste's face went very still and mask-like. There was no

outward sign of it but, somehow, he could tell that inside she was seething with anger.

Bram was also eerily still and, like Celeste, Dillon had the impression he was thinking at ninety miles an hour. Coming second to a dhampir was probably worse for him than not being chosen at all.

'Bram and Dillon, I will go over the responsibilities of your positions with you in my office. The rest of you may spend the remainder of the evening enjoying some downtime before the full timetable begins tomorrow straight after dusk.'

'Yes!' Angelo and Frederick fist-pumped, seemingly completely unaware of the tense undercurrents of emotion.

As the others drifted away, Dillon wished he could go with them. He didn't want any of this. He didn't want to be at this academy, he didn't want to be half vampire and he certainly didn't want to be Vampire Elect. It was like he had no say over anything anymore – even the thing he had for Cora felt wildly out of control.

He noticed that Bram had already taken his phone out and was messaging someone – probably his father. With any luck he would demand to have Dillon removed and sent home. Feeling like he had the weight of the world on his shoulders, he followed Bram and Madame Dupledge back to her office. A few vampires from the other peaks who hadn't dispersed yet stared at him as he walked past, some hostile, some curious.

As usual, her sweet, intoxicating scent made his head swim, and he was furious that he couldn't even control his own body. He forced himself not to think about her smooth, creamy throat. Bram stood next to him, looking cool and collected.

Madame Dupledge analysed them for several long seconds. Irritated with himself, Dillon averted his eyes as another vivid flood of memories threatened to overwhelm him.

'Well done both of you,' she said finally. 'As you know, I gain some insight into your characters at the Induction Ceremony, and I believe that you are both special candidates.'

Strange word, 'special', thought Dillon. He noticed that she hadn't said 'best'.

'Bram, I realise that you are disappointed that you weren't chosen as Vampire Elect but I believe you can embrace the role of deputy and be a great help to Dillon. Both of you, for different reasons, will face many challenges and you must be prepared to make difficult decisions that might put you at odds with your peers on occasion. I want you to put any differences aside, to live up to those challenges and deal with them to the best of your ability. I am here to guide you.'

Bram seemed impassive but Dillon's negative thoughts threatened to spin out of control. It had been hard enough to fit in before and now it would be impossible. Bram – the vampire who had been groomed for the role since he took his first taste of blood – wouldn't help him. The whole thing was crazy.

With her strange insight, Madame Dupledge turned to him. 'Dillon, I would like to speak to you alone. Bram, think hard about what I have said and remember what I said to you after the Induction Ceremony.'

'Yes, Madame,' Bram said, completely blank-faced. He half bowed and left the room.

Madame Dupledge analysed Dillon for several uncomfortable seconds. Finally, she spoke. 'Dillon, I know it must have been a great shock to have been chosen as Vampire Elect but let me reassure you that the Blood Tasting has never been wrong in all the time I have been at the school. That said, you are going to have to learn fast and you are going to have to be extremely resilient. We would like to run some more tests on your blood. We will need a couple more vials if you would oblige.'

Dillon coughed. He was convinced that despite her words, she didn't trust the result. Why else would they want to test his blood again? Screwing up his courage, he forced himself to ask the question that was bothering him.

'Are you sure I wasn't chosen just because I'm a dhampir? Like you said, a dhampir has never been accepted at the school before.'

Privately, he agreed with Bram; there must have been a mistake, something about the half human element that confused everyone. He had never displayed a single leadership quality in his life.

She stared into his eyes, and he wanted to blink or look away, but he found himself mesmerized by her hypnotic emerald-green gaze.

'Dillon, it may seem surprising that you, a half vampire,

have been chosen, but there has been no mistake. Take my word for it. As I mentioned before – your mother has a powerful and impressive bloodline.'

He found himself agreeing with her. He could rise to the challenge. He may not have been prepared for the role, but he was tough. He'd grown up in the wilds of Ireland; Bram and the others appeared to have lived a life of luxury.

Madam Dupedge nodded. 'Better. Believe in yourself, Dillon.'

Jaysus. She really could see inside him.

'I will accompany you to the Sanatorium.'

As she turned and walked around the desk, the positive vibes she must have been transmitting faded and he blinked hard to prevent his thoughts from tumbling back into negativity.

He followed her as she glided out of her office to the atrium area and floated down the stairs to the seventh floor. Dillon recognised the hallway and the Sanatorium door. Dr Meyer was inside dealing with Frederick, who, in the short space of time since he'd last seen him, had gashed his head open and was perched on the bed looking sorry for himself.

Dillon's eyes widened as the normally austere Dr Meyer began tenderly licking the wound. Frederick didn't bat an eyelid. Instantly, it healed.

'There, that's better Frederick,' she said, stepping back and admiring it before noticing Madame Dupledge and Dillon at the door. 'Ah, I won't be a minute, Madame. Frederick had an accident in the gym. Head wounds take a while to heal on their own.'

Dillon remembered that Cora had said Frederick was clumsy. Being accident-prone seemed out of character for a vampire.

'Sorry.' Frederick smiled ruefully. 'It seems I am not as kickass as Aron and Jeremiah in that department.'

'I'm sure you have other talents, Mr Keller,' Madame Dupledge said crisply.

'*Ja*, for sure,' Frederick agreed, beaming.

'Now, if you will excuse us, Dillon and I need to speak to Dr Meyer.'

'Ah, no problem.' Frederick bounced off the bed and left the room, raising his eyebrows as he passed Dillon.

Dillon gave a tiny shrug back. Madame Dupledge clearly didn't want his classmates to know about these blood samples.

As soon as Frederick had disappeared, she spoke to Dr Meyer. 'Could you provide us with another two samples of Dillon's blood and bring them to me personally?'

'Of course, Madame,' Dr Meyer agreed and began opening and shutting drawers as she set up the blood-testing kit.

'Thank you.' Madame Dupledge nodded and spoke to Dillon again. 'I will see you tomorrow for your first Desire and Control lesson.'

'Um, yes, thank you,' Dillon stuttered, flushing yet again. 'Looking forward to it.'

As she swept out of the door, he slumped on to the bed with a sigh of relief.

'Okay?' Dr Meyer asked.

'Yes, I think so, thanks. Things happen fast around here,

that's all. It's like my body is still going wild after all the Blood Tasting.'

'You will get used to it.'

'That's what everyone keeps telling me.' Although how did they know that if he was the first dhampir here? He wondered.

As she inserted the needle into his arm once again, Dr Meyer's expression softened a little. 'It must be hard for you, but Madame Dupledge obviously believes in you. She doesn't suffer fools. Try not to worry too much.' She removed the needle and turning to her desk, carefully labelled the vial. 'There, it will heal by itself, but you may lick the puncture point if you wish. You should have some healing ability in your saliva now.'

He looked down at his arm and licked it tentatively. The end of his tongue tingled as it came in contact with the small drop of blood.

'Thanks, then,' he mumbled. 'Can I go now?'

'Yes, thank you, Dillon. I'll see you in lessons at some point if you take the Vampire Medicine option.'

'Okay, yes, maybe I will. Bye then.'

He backed out of the door and stood in the corridor debating what the hell to do next. He needed Sade's calm advice. Surely, she wouldn't mind him being Vampire Elect?

She wasn't in her room. His spirits crashed down again. Paranoia was really setting in – he imagined his classmates scheming against him. After pacing up and down the corridor, he decided he had no choice but to face them. He couldn't hide away forever.

First, he tried the swimming pool, but it was still cold and quiet – the sauna room was now taped off. That left the gym or the blood bar Mahina had mentioned.

It was dark and shadowy in the basement atrium area, and he stood for ages outside the black door with 'Blood Bar' written on it – building up the courage to walk in. Finally, he grabbed the handle and pushed it open.

He found himself in a short, dark corridor lit with icy-blue neon lights. It was way darker than it had been outside, and he blinked a couple of times as his vampire night-vision kicked in. A strange sickly-sweet, slightly synthetic smell invaded his nostrils. He could hear laughter, muffled conversation and the sound of balls clunking together coming from somewhere inside. Walking towards the noise, he rounded the corner and stared. It was like no educational common room he'd ever seen.

The others and a few Peak Two vampires were lolling in low, comfortable chairs and on bar stools at a long black rectangular bar. More ice-blue neon lights, this time in the shape of icicles, appeared to hang down the front and sides of the bar. Mirrors and smaller icicle lights lit up the wall behind the bar. Frederick and Aron were playing pool on a table to the side of the bar – in typical vampire fashion, both appeared to pot every ball in one go. Ásta was ostentatiously sitting on Angelo's lap in the middle of a plush, red velvet sofa.

He could hear faint hissing and gurgling noises and steam drifted upwards adding to the smoky underground atmosphere. It came from a huge machine on the bar which appeared to be a sophisticated 'coffee' machine for artificial blood. He realised that the blood bar was literally a 'Starbucks' for vampires except that – he grinned to himself – it should be called 'Starbloods'. A menu on the back wall offered: Foaming Blood, Silky Blood, Blood Shots, Blood Bubbles and Iced Blood. He forced down a wave of revulsion as he realised that they came in different flavours like O Positive or AB Negative.

None of the others had seen or heard him yet. He hoped that meant his heartbeat was not as loud as it had been.

Celeste, perched on a bar stool next to Ace, was clutching a tall glass with a frothy, pink liquid in it. 'It's rigged,' she said. 'He's not even a real vampire. Madame Dupledge just wants someone she can manipulate. Someone who knows nothing about this school and what has been going on for the last few years under her leadership. My father says that she believes our bloodlines have become weak and we need to introduce some *rough* blood. It's a crazy idea – Mahina being a common vampire is bad enough. He's not going to sit by and let her allow this.'

Unfortunately, Bram, who was also at the bar, glimpsed him in the mirrors and he smiled round at the others. 'I couldn't agree more Celeste. Cora, why don't you repeat what you were just saying about there being a mistake too so that Dillon can hear it for himself.'

With their lightning reflexes, the others all turned at the same time and stared at him. Some of the stares were downright hostile, others excited, like they were looking forward to a confrontation. Ásta, he noticed, having ignored him up to now, was suddenly eying him with interest. Impatiently, she slapped one of Angelo's wandering hands away. Sade, sitting in a comfy chair next to the pool table, looked down at her feet.

As Bram's words filtered into Dillon's brain and he realised what he'd said about Cora, he almost choked. His eyes sought hers.

She held his gaze but if vampires could blush, she would have been scarlet. Then, recovering some of her usual insouciance, she turned to Bram. 'You know I didn't mean it like that Bram – I said it wasn't fair on you Dillon, you know, to have to lead us unruly lot – even though your blood was great.'

'Well, that's one way to interpret it.' Bram smirked.

She glared at him and hissed, 'Stop acting like a dick, Bram.'

Furiously, they glared at each other until Bram shrugged and spoke again, 'Look Dillon, I may have my faults – although admittedly, it's hard to think of any off the top of my head – but one thing I am not, is two-faced. It's no secret that I wanted to be Vampire Elect, and I think everyone would agree that I'm the best vampire for the job—'

'Ahem.' Celeste raised her eyebrows.

'Every Danesti has been Vampire Elect in Peak One going

back for generations. There has obviously been a mistake and my father will insist that there is an investigation. Madame Dupledge is not listening to reason. Just because a system has been used for centuries doesn't mean mistakes can't be made. Let's face it Dillon, you don't want to be Vampire Elect – you're probably pissing your pants as I speak.'

Dillon found himself agreeing with everything Bram was saying – his beautiful voice was hypnotic and he was so self-assured – it all made perfect sense. Bram's eyes were beginning to gleam, sensing triumph. Then Dillon caught Sade's eye. She gave an almost imperceptible, sharp shake of her head.

He thought back to his feelings when he had tasted his own blood – he had experienced a raw, surging power. He might not be the most cultured or dynamic leader, but he must have something. As the thoughts raced through his head, Bram watched him impatiently and the gleam in his eyes darkened as Dillon lifted his chin.

'You know what, Bram? I agree with you – you'd be a great Vampire Elect. But here's the simple fact: your blood wasn't picked. I was the one who was chosen.' He turned to look around at the others who were avidly watching him with that strange vampire stillness. 'You all believed in my blood.'

Bram's eyes blazed and the muscle in his jaw twitched. 'Don't be an idiot, Dhampir. I'm telling you now – stand down or face the consequences.'

Dillon felt as if tiny sparks were attacking his brain and a high-pitched buzzing noise rang in his ears. The sensation was painful and disorientating. He shook his head to get rid of it. Jeremiah who had been sitting back, lost in the shadows, quietly got up and stood next to him, arms folded across his chest.

'I wouldn't try that if I were you, Bram. Vampires who want to be VE don't use mind games.'

Dillon had no idea what he was on about, but Bram's eyes, still focused on him, narrowed.

'Sit down, Jeremiah. This is not your battle,' he hissed.

The painful darts of electricity in his head eased off a little but he was starting to feel dizzy.

'I said, drop it, Bram,' Jeremiah insisted.

Reluctantly, Bram dragged his eyes away from Dillon's and locked onto Jeremiah's instead. There seemed to be a silent battle of wills going on between them. Occasionally, one or the other winced slightly and noticing that he couldn't feel anything anymore, Dillon realised Bram had been wielding some sort of mind power that he'd now switched to Jeremiah.

Jeremiah was still solid and mostly impassive, but Bram's fingers began shaking and his face was slowly turning grey. Whatever they were doing was taking a tremendous amount of effort. Both were starting to shudder now, and Bram's eyes were popping slightly.

Suddenly, Cora sprang up and stood between them. 'Stop it! Both of you! This is crazy.'

'Get out of the way, Cora,' Bram hissed again and tried to push her to the side. 'This doesn't concern you.'

There was a resounding thwack as she raised her hand and slapped him hard around the face. Instantly the room went quiet – the only noise was the gentle hissing of the blood machine. Bram and Jeremiah slumped slightly.

Cora covered her mouth with her hand. 'Oh, my God. Bram, I'm so sorry, I shouldn't have done that, but I had to break the mindfuck between you two.'

Without a word, Bram spun away from her and stalked out of the room. Cora looked dazed for a second, then she gave Dillon an apologetic smile and rushed out after him.

The deathly silence was broken by Ásta slow-clapping, her face unusually animated.

'Round one – Dillon,' she drawled and, unfurling herself from Angelo's lap, she sashayed up to Dillon, took his face in her hands and kissed him passionately on the lips.

6

Blood Hurts

Ásta had clearly had tons of practice; Dillon's knees buckled.
Then he remembered that everyone was watching.

'Woah. Ásta!' he said and, with some difficulty, broke away
and stumbled backwards. Ace smirked.

Ásta smiled knowingly. 'You should stand up for yourself more
often, Dillon. You become very attractive when you're angry.'

'I never thought it was that attractive a trait,' he mumbled.
She made him feel like a little boy.

Angelo stood up and Dillon cast a quick glance at him.
Luckily, rather than looking like he wanted to suck Dillon's
blood dry, he seemed stimulated by the incident.

'Dillon, I need to go over the timetable for next week
with you remember?' Sade stood up too and looked at him,
raising her eyebrows.

'Ah, yes.' He had no idea what she was talking about, but
it seemed a good time to exit.

He looked around for Jeremiah, but there was no sign of him. He must have slipped out when he was in the clinch with Ásta. He followed Sade down the dark corridor and, as the door closed behind them, he cringed as he heard a burst of laughter.

'You okay?' Sade asked. 'It looked like you needed rescuing.'

'Fair play, thanks for spotting that. I owe you one.'

'Two now – the coffin lesson? Remember?'

'You're right. Seriously, I am grateful.' Just outside her door, he shot her a sideways glance. 'Are you okay with all the stuff about me being VE?'

She hesitated, her hand on the door handle. 'I won't lie. I was surprised that the blood was yours.'

'Why?'

She opened the door and he followed her into the room. Celeste's desk was covered in photos of her looking glamorous with her father at several glitzy vampire events. Her bikini from the night before was drying on the end of her coffin and expensive clothes and shoes spilled out of the cupboard. Sade's desk was covered in books and a top-of-the-range MacBook Pro. Her coffin was open and, like Cora, she had stuck pictures of her stunning siblings and a sleek pet cat on the inside lid. Dillon blinked at the picture of her parents receiving the Nobel Physics Prize on the wall.

'It's hard to put into words,' she said slowly, sitting at her desk, 'but I had a powerful reaction to it.'

'Same! I did too – I had no idea.'

'And, well, Angelo was right, it was . . . amazing. I can still taste it.'

'Oh, right. Um, thanks,' he said, not sure how to respond to that.

He sat near her on the coffin pod. 'Look, I'm not meant to discuss this, but Madame Dupledge wanted more of my blood.'

'What for?'

'She didn't say. But maybe there's been a mistake like Bram says? Why else would she want it?'

'She wouldn't have announced it if they thought that. They'd have made an excuse for the delay and reanalysed the results or repeated the Tasting. It's more likely that they want to know more about your blood. I didn't tell you this before, but after you passed out at the Induction Ceremony, Madame Dupledge looked pretty shaken herself. I thought it was because you had fainted but now, I'm not so sure. Did she speak to you about it?'

'No.'

'That's strange, don't you think?'

It was true. Madame Dupledge hadn't said anything to him about the Induction Ceremony. He thought back to it. He had been overwhelmed by the experience but, just before he passed out, he remembered sensing her loss of control too.

'The only thing she's mentioned twice now is that my mother is from some strong line of vampires.'

'Really?' Sade sat up taller. 'Look, maybe we should do

some testing of our own? Find out more about where you come from.'

'How could we do that?'

'I'm good at bio-chemistry. All I would need is access to the labs but that shouldn't be too hard – I'm choosing the blood analysis option. There must be a blood database of all the vampires who've come here. We just have to find a match for yours.'

'You can test my blood?'

'Yes – keep up, Dillon.'

'If vampires can tell stuff by taste, why do you need to? Shouldn't you just try some more of my blood?'

'We all identified your blood as special but that doesn't tell us where it's come from or anything about it. We could find out if you have any extra proteins or antigens or if there's something different about your DNA. Vampire DNA is different to human DNA; we have genetically adapted to an all-blood diet.'

Dillon grimaced.

'We are designed to attract and catch prey. That means greater strength, better senses and our brains have developed some clever tricks – hence Bram's little display on you.'

'That wasn't a little display – my head was wrecked.'

Sade ignored him. 'Our metabolic and circulatory systems have become incredibly efficient, and our hearts beat so slowly we're not even aware of them – listen.'

She beckoned to him to come closer and guided his head to her breastbone. She was wearing a thin, long-sleeved

V-neck top that stopped about an inch above her joggers, revealing a small strip of stomach. Her skin was cool and incredibly smooth. He could just about hear the occasional soft beat of her heart — like the beat of a butterfly wing.

'Wow, that's amazing,' he murmured as a wonderful sense of serenity crept through him. Having felt like his own heart had been attached to a bungee wire most of the night, he could literally feel it slowing down now in response. She smelt amazing, not as bewitching as Cora or as intoxicating as Madame Dupledge but simply delicious, like a fresh apple tart or wheaten bread just out of the oven.

The door flew open and light from the corridor spilled over them.

'Dillon, there must be something about you I'm missing. I certainly didn't witness it in the shower.' Celeste smirked.

Dillon and Sade sprang apart.

'It's not like that,' he blurted out. 'I was listening to her heart.'

Celeste raised her perfectly arched eyebrows. 'Sure you were, but don't mind me. I'm going over to Ace's room to compare timetables. Maybe I'll "listen to his heart" while I'm there. You two carry on.'

She scooped up her laptop and swept out again.

Sade was head down, absorbed in retying her Nike laces. 'What happened in the shower?' Her voice was slightly muffled.

'Nothing. She seems to enjoy winding me up.' He scowled.

Sade was still for a moment. 'Yeah, I guess I can see that. She's actually okay behind the ice-bitch facade.'

She looked up at him and Dillon blinked, momentarily surprised. 'I'll have to take your word for that.'

She turned back to her desk and opened her laptop. 'Do you want to look at the timetable? As soon as I start Blood Analysis and swing access to the labs, we can start doing some testing of our own.'

'Why?'

'Why, what?'

'Why are you helping me?'

Sade paused, hands poised over the keyboard. 'I'm not sure, I guess I've never met anyone like you before. I've always lived amongst vampires and a lot of the time,' she paused, 'I don't feel like I fit in. Also, like I said, I want to find out why your blood tastes so good.'

'You're different too – most of them seem selfish, out for themselves. Da always said you had to watch yourself around people focused too much on themselves. Although,' he corrected himself, 'Jeremiah's not like that.'

'Yeah, he's a good 'un,' Sade agreed and peered back at the screen. 'So, we start with Combat, Hunt and Protect with Mr Hunt in the morning – apt name.' She grinned. 'Then Desire and Control with Madame Dupledge tomorrow afternoon. The other main subjects seem to be Flying Skills, Living Amongst Humans, Blood Analysis, Enhancing Mind Power, International Relations and Vampire Diplomacy. It looks like we study those for the whole of our time at Peak

One, although Enhancing Mind Power and the International Diplomacy lessons appear to start later, after January. Combat, Hunt and Protect and Desire and Control are clearly the areas they want us to master – they take up nearly all our time. There are some voluntary modules too. The main ones appear to be Vampire Science and Medicine, Enhanced IT Skills and Vampire History. Oh and by the way, VEs tend to excel at everything.'

Dillon grimaced. 'Are you trying to make me feel better or worse?'

'Just saying.'

'Yeah well. This VE is hanging on by the skin of his teeth – or fangs should I say. I better head off, check Jeremiah is okay.'

'Okay, make sure you lock your coffin tonight – now we all know your blood tastes as good as it smells.'

She smiled one of her heartbreaker smiles.

Dillon grinned back. 'Very funny.'

Jeremiah was lying in his coffin with the lid open when he got back.

'Are you okay?' Dillon asked.

'Yeah, I'm just chilling.'

'What was that going on back there? Magic?'

'We're able to harness electro-magnetic energy inside the brain and direct it in the form of high amplitude pulses into someone else's. Some vampires are better than others. Bram is strong.'

'You looked stronger.'

He shrugged. 'I'm not so good at harnessing it, but I have learnt to become good at blocking it.'

'How long does it take to recover?'

'Depends on how long you do it for and it takes less effort as you get better at it. I'm pretty much restored now although I could murder a shot.'

'Do you want me to get you one?' It was the least he could do.

'If you think you can stay out of trouble. O Positive with extra froth, thanks.'

Dillon gulped. 'Ah yeah, sure. Back in a minute.'

He breathed a sigh of relief that the blood bar was empty. The blood machine was simple to work out and he watched, fascinated and revolted, as the steaming shot of blood frothed into the takeaway cup. When he picked the cup up, the same sweet, slightly synthetic blood-smell hit his nostrils, and he was surprised by an overwhelming urge to taste it. He felt his fangs tingle.

Shocked, he shoved the cup away and put a lid on it. He refused to start craving any type of blood now or ever. All the way back, he fought the impulse to open the lid and as he handed it over to Jeremiah, he slumped with relief onto his own coffin.

'What's up?' Jeremiah asked, sipping at the pink froth.

'So help me, I really, really wanted a sip.'

Jeremiah chuckled. 'Welcome to our world, my friend. Now you know why the Desire and Control lesson is on day one!'

Dillon swore. 'I've never had cravings like this before.'

'The craving does lessen as you age. Madame Dupledge probably survives on a couple of sips a month.'

'Thank Christ for that – although, if I start eating "normal" food again, I guess the craving stops?'

Jeremiah raised his palms. 'Who knows. The bloodlust is strong – once you've awakened it, I'm not sure you can just "lock" it away again.'

'Shite. I hope that's not true.'

'I've got to hit my coffin.'

'Yeah, me too.' He fished the phone Jeremiah had given him earlier in the evening out of his pocket. 'How do I pay for my calls on this?'

'I think Bik put a pre-paid sim in, so you can just top it up with your credit card.'

'Ah, okay, thanks.' He decided not to mention that he didn't have a credit card. At home, he'd always worked for his da, and there was never any spare money. His da didn't agree with spending what you didn't have. He changed the subject; he was different enough to them all already. 'Look, thanks for earlier, too. For standing up for me.'

'No problem. I normally stay out of that kind of rivalry crap, but I don't like it when someone abuses an unfair advantage.'

'Yeah, well, I appreciate it.'

'How are you feeling about being VE?'

'I still think there's been a mistake.'

'Nah – now I've thought about it, there was something

different about your blood. Like I said before, there must be more to you than meets the eye.'

'Or maybe it's all just a big mix up – I swear I thought it was yours!' Dillon said, grinning at him.

'Get out of here!' Jeremiah waved at him and lay back down in his coffin, out of sight.

Dillon stepped outside and dialled the home phone in Ireland. It rang and rang. Strange – his da got up long before dawn, so he should be awake. Sighing, he rang off and crept back into the room. Jeremiah's coffin lid was firmly shut. Sighing again, he stripped off and lay in his coffin. The small knot of worry about his father prevented him from falling asleep. Where was he?

In the silent, inky darkness of the coffin, his mind began to drift and a vision of his father talking intently to a woman popped into his head. It was dark and they were outside somewhere. He could see stars in the sky. He strained to see the woman's face, but she remained hidden in the shadows and, as fast as the vision appeared, it disappeared.

He spent the rest of the night worrying. The vision had felt too realistic to be a dream. Had all the talk of his elusive vampire mother triggered some memory? Somehow the vision hadn't felt dated, and it would explain why his da wasn't picking up the phone at home. He felt a stab of irrational jealousy – if it was his mother, his da hadn't waited long to meet up with her again. Finally, just before sunset, he fell into an uneasy sleep.

★

A loud tapping noise woke him.

'Hey Dillon, wake up.' Jeremiah's voice was muffled. 'Combat, Hunt and Protect starts in thirty minutes.'

'Shite!' Dillon clutched his head and swore loudly.

He arrived at the gym feeling like death.

'Ah our new VE.' Mr Hunt's piercing black eyes spotted him immediately. 'Setting us all an example. Welcome to Combat, Hunt and Protect or CHP. If you're late again, you'll be the prey on our next hunt.'

The others sniggered. Dillon gritted his teeth and nodded curtly. Mr Hunt stared at him for a few seconds longer and then carried on. Dillon was surprised to realise how small he was – his powerful persona made him seem bigger. It explained the tiny vampire syndrome.

'We are predators,' Mr Hunt said, looking around the whole class, his gaze lingering on Dillon once more, to emphasise his words. 'There is no point denying it. We are designed to catch prey – in our case humans – and to evade capture ourselves. Now, obviously, we no longer hunt humans like our ancestors. Blood banks and private human blood donors have enabled us to survive without hunting. But we cannot simply ignore our instincts. Anyone want to tell me why?'

Ace raised his hand. 'We'd go nuts?'

The class tittered.

Mr Hunt acknowledged Ace with a small smile. 'That's a succinct way of putting it, but yes, we can't suppress centuries of instinct without suffering some mental and physical consequences. It's like putting a cat in a cage and surrounding it with birds. Any other reasons?'

'There might still be occasions when we need to hunt?' Celeste suggested.

Clearly not immune to Celeste's beauty, Mr Hunt flashed her a big smile. *Sexist git*, thought Dillon.

'Absolutely. If we were stuck somewhere on the planet without access to blood, we would be forced to hunt. We would turn to large meat-eating prey first – deer, big cats and so on – but if it was a matter of survival, as a last resort, we would be forced to hunt humans. When else might we have to hunt?'

Bram, looking dark-eyed and moody, spoke up. 'When vampires go rogue or when a bunch of humans go rogue, and we need to maintain the status quo.'

'Correct.' Mr Hunt nodded his approval. 'One of the aims of this school is to prepare you to advance a civilised vampire community and to direct our enhanced skills in the right direction. Some less well-educated vampires do not accept our vision for the future and wish to drag us back to the dark ages. It is our job to bring them into line. Our Vampire Secret Service is an international organisation that some of you may have the aptitude to join when you leave here. Usually, one or two of our graduates make it each year. We operate within our own jurisdiction but occasionally we co-operate with the elite human secret services. Very few humans know about us, only those right at the top of the secret services and their governments. For good reason. Our existence is top secret and that is why we are expected to control our own kind – so that we remain invisible to most of the human world.'

Dillon noticed that Aron was literally hanging off every word. No guessing what he wanted to do when he graduated.

'Sometimes they call on our *special* expertise for issues that arise and threaten world security.'

Dillon was gobsmacked. His understanding of how the world worked had just been turned upside down. Vampires were embedded in the highest echelons of power. He had assumed that they just existed in their own weird world on the edges of society.

A few of the vampires were beginning to shift restlessly.

Mr Hunt's sharp eyes noticed. 'Right. Enough talking. Any more questions?'

Dillon had hundreds, but he stayed quiet.

'So, as vampires we need to hone our skills. We need to know how to fight—'

'Yes!' Ásta pumped her fist.

'—against humans, weapons, enemy vampires and occasionally, other supernaturals. We need to know how to track, how to survive, how to stay hidden and, despite our existing advantages, we must become physically tougher. Over the next weeks, we will prepare for a challenge that will take you to your limits. It is contested every year and this year it will be the Ice Challenge.'

Ace and Aron whooped, and Mr Hunt acknowledged them with another small smile. 'Ace, Aron, I like your enthusiasm — let's hope you will still be celebrating afterwards.

The Ice Challenge is one of our most difficult physical and mental tests. It is designed to make you work together and to take you to your individual limits and beyond. You will have a task to complete that will involve spending a significant amount of time under the ice to avoid detection by hostile "rogue" vampires. Top VSS operatives act as the rogue vampires and will attack you at the first opportunity. Only the teams that pull together will stand a chance of defeating them. There are two opposing teams, one led by the Vampire Elect and the other by the Deputy Vampire Elect.' His eyes flickered over Dillon. 'Assuming they have mastered the required skills.'

Dillon blanched.

'Those of you who excel will receive "colours" and are likely to be put forward for the VSS – the Vampire Secret Service programme.'

As the others burst into excited conversation, Dillon raised his hand. 'Sorry, but would you mind saying exactly what you mean by "rogue" vampire?'

Bram and Celeste rolled their eyes.

Mr Hunt eyed him impatiently. 'Vampires who don't follow our rules and who prefer to kill humans for sustenance,' he said.

Dillon blanched again as he remembered Mahina had mentioned having to hunt rogue vampires down.

Mr Hunt turned back to the class. 'Right, let's get a move on. We'll start with a warm-up and then we'll practise in the sensory deprivation room. This will help you prepare for what it could be like under the ice.'

He glided to an area covered in mats with a Mixed-Martial-Arts-style ring to the side and eight hanging punchbags. The warehouse style ceiling was over fifteen metres high and four of the punchbags hung from it.

A terrifying, muscle-bound vampire appeared from a tiny office at the side of the gym Dillon hadn't noticed before. He had a tough, battle-scarred face and longish blond hair pulled into a bun on top of his head. The fact that he looked older and had scars made Dillon think he must have been human or, he looked again, maybe even a Viking. He was wearing a tiny training vest and short shorts, both of which revealed too much of his rough-hewn but impressive physique.

'Uh oh, Jeremiah's got competition!' Celeste jested and earnt a scowl from Bik. Jeremiah just ignored her.

'This is Borzak, your fight teacher. Former World MMA champion. He used to be known as "Dr Iron Fist" before he transitioned from human to vampire twenty years ago. He's the current World Vampire Combat Champion. We are extremely privileged to have him as a teacher here.'

Dillon stared at him. Why would he have transitioned to a vampire? Then he had a horrible realisation: he must have died or almost died in a fight at some point.

'Hi.' Borzak waved one of his enormous fists at them. 'I am here to turn you into some of the toughest – and most combat savvy – vampires on the planet.'

Bik raised her hand. 'Is this really compulsory for all of us?' she asked. 'It does not seem the best use of my talents.'

Borzak stared at her and, reaching out a long arm, plucked

her glasses off. Bik blinked as her pupils contracted in the dim gym-lights and immediately began to protest.

'You cannot rely on stuff like this in a life-and-death situation,' he growled. 'You must rely only on yourself.'

Bik stretched to her full height. 'This is the twenty-first century. It's extremely unlikely that I will allow myself to get into that position – you clearly don't understand that my glasses give me constant feedback on my environment and whoever is around me. From their stats, I could tell you that Sade, Dillon and Frederick are scared, Ásta, Jeremiah and Aron are eerily calm – they've trained for this situation already. Angelo is wildly over-excited; Bram is burning with repressed anger. Strangely, so is Celeste to a lesser extent. Cora's stats are the most difficult to read, but she seems one of those competitive types who tries to pretend they're not. Nevertheless, I deduce that Bram is the most volatile and to be avoided.'

Borzak grinned, revealing a mouth of missing teeth. 'In combat you can never predict how a person will react. The strongest person becomes a pussy . . .' Mr Hunt winced. 'The weakest . . . becomes a tiger. Let's begin.'

Borzak began pairing them up. He put Aron with Bik, Frederick with Bram, Cora with Celeste, Ásta with Ace and Jeremiah with Angelo. Dillon suppressed a sigh of relief that he had been forgotten. It would give him a chance to assess them first. The pairings seemed strangely ill-matched.

'Dillon and I will begin.'

Dillon stared up at his mountainous six-foot seven-inch frame in horror.

'You've got to be kidding me,' he protested, backing away.

'I never joke,' Borzak assured him, pointing at the ring. 'After you.'

Dillon glanced at Mr Hunt, who nodded, eyes gleaming. Presumably he wouldn't let Borzak kill him, Dillon reasoned, feeling his legs turn to jelly as he stepped into the ring. As Borzak adopted a crouch position, Dillon turned slightly to the side in the boxing stance he'd learnt at school in Ireland and raised his fists to protect his face.

He didn't even see the first strike. Low and lethal, Borzak's leg shot out, instantly dropping him to the floor.

'Get up.'

Warily, he dragged himself back up, every nerve in his body on high alert.

Once again, he didn't even see Borzak move. Like lightning, Borzak twisted his arm behind him and at the same time flipped him onto his back, knocking the air out of his body.

'Get up.'

Dillon took his time. Borzak knocked him down again before he had even stood up properly. He heard Bram's snigger and Ásta's snort of disgust.

'Tune into your instincts, Dillon,' Jeremiah called out and was shushed by Mr Hunt.

He didn't have time. A trickle of blood ran from his nose, and he could feel his right eye swelling up.

'Come on Dhampir,' Borzak goaded. 'You are a mummy's boy, no?'

He had never had a mother. Something in Dillon flipped and, with a roar, he launched himself at Borzak, using the weight of his whole body to jam a right hook at his chin. Borzak's head snapped back and he staggered a little.

'That's more like it, Dhampir,' he growled.

A red mist descended over Dillon's eyes as he laid into Borzak again. His rage at every new change in his life burst like a dam and, as he rained punches, he didn't think of what he was doing, he just let his body take over.

'Dillon! Easy mate, easy, chill, come on.'

He heard Jeremiah's voice but continued punching and ducking until he felt two powerful arms wrap around him and drag him away.

'Leave me alone. Do not touch me,' he grunted, trying to wrestle his way out of Jeremiah's iron grip.

'Cool it down a bit, yeah?'

As he returned to reality, he saw that the others were all watching, some shocked, some amused. Sade, eyes wide, came over to him.

'Are you okay?'

He could feel sweat dripping off his forehead and was surprised to see cuts crisscrossing Borzak's eyebrows and a swelling eye that was slowly beginning to heal. Borzak grinned and grabbed Dillon's fists.

'How did you learn to do this?' he asked.

'Uh, do what?'

'Punch hard like that?

Dillon shrugged. 'Ireland.'

'Right everyone, show's over,' Mr Hunt called. 'Let's get on with the rest of the session.'

Borzak adjusted the pairings slightly. He put Dillon with Sade and Jeremiah with himself. In what seemed like a crazy move, he sent Bik into the ring with Aron.

'What happened there?' Sade asked softly as they circled each other.

'I'm not sure.'

'You were like a mad thing.'

He shrugged. 'Have you never heard of the fightin' Irish. Everyone learns how to box where I come from.'

'It seemed so unlike you.'

'It is. Everything that's happening here is unlike me. Flying. Fighting. Blood.'

'It's okay. I understand. I keep forgetting how hard it is for you.'

'Sade, seems like you're the *only* person who realises that.'

'Come on you two,' Mr Hunt called, 'this is a sparring session, not a coffee morning!'

He returned to strolling around the other pairs and Dillon scowled at his back. 'Gobshite.'

Sade snorted. 'What did you say? Gobshite?'

'It means a big mouth. Mr Hunt and Bram fit the bill, all right.'

'I like it.' Grinning, she threw a half-hearted punch at Dillon's head, and he feigned throwing his head back as if she had hit him.

'Gobshite!' she smirked, aiming a roundhouse kick at him as he mock dived backwards.

'Well done, Sade!' Borzak called over, and they both ducked to hide their stifled laughter.

Surreptitiously, everyone began watching the ring as Aron and Bik circled each other, eyes narrowed. Just as Aron sprang, Bik flew up into the air and landed on his back. He staggered but managed to hold his balance, twisting to throw her off. Once again, light as a feather, she floated away and darted in with a spinning kick to the back of Aron's knee that dropped him to the floor.

Borzak, who was sparring with Jeremiah, roared across the room. 'I knew it Bik. You're a tiger without those piece-of-shit glasses.'

Mr Hunt who had stopped to watch Celeste and Cora, winced again. 'Thank you, Borzak.'

Aron seemed reluctant to attack hard.

Borzak roared again, 'Come on, Aron, she can stand up for herself. See Bik, Aron is lethal, but against you, he's a teddy bear. You never know someone until you fight them.'

'I don't want to hurt her,' Aron protested and groaned as Bik smashed a roundhouse kick into his stomach and spun out of his reach again.

'Aron!' Ásta warned, not breaking her concentration for a second as she and Ace maintained a deadly dance round each other.

Only when Borzak roared that he would fail the class did Aron lash out with a fast, deadly and efficient sequence of moves. There was a horrible cracking noise like a pistol shot as Bik's collarbone snapped. Blood streamed from her nose.

As Borzak looked over to check she was all right, Jeremiah took great delight in connecting his right fist into Borzak's chin and sent him flying across the room.

'Bik, I'm so sorry.' Aron fell to his knees beside her.

Bik winced. 'No problem, Aron, it'll heal. I got overconfident.'

Jeremiah gently stroked the hair off Bik's forehead. 'I'll accompany her to Dr Meyer to make sure she heals properly,' he told Borzak, who winced as he rubbed his jaw.

'Okay fine, good punch, Jeremiah. But remember to keep a cool head when someone you have an interest in is fighting. She is good. She can deal with vampires as strong as Aron without your help.'

'You don't need to tell me that,' said Jeremiah with a small smile.

'Um, excuse me, I know that too,' Bik interrupted. 'I'm just not that interested, but I'll concede you're right about one thing, Borzak – I need more practice. Jeremiah, I don't need you to accompany me to the Sanatorium.'

'Are you sure?'

'Yes.'

Two seconds after she had left, Jeremiah waved Bik's glasses. 'I'd better take these to Bik,' he said, whipping out of the gym before Mr Hunt stopped him.

The rest of the class grinned when he returned five minutes later.

'I guess Bik didn't need you, Jeremiah?' Celeste taunted.

Jeremiah ignored her and Dillon turned to him. 'Is Bik okay?'

'She and Dr Meyer kicked me out, so I guess so. She won't let Aron get away with that next time, that's for sure.'

Mr Hunt decided they need a change of scene.

'Right, stop everyone, let's have a go at sensory deprivation to prepare you for the Ice Challenge.'

He led them to a door adjacent to the horizontal wind tunnel. 'Behind this door is a large room. It is filled with dry ice and it is pitch black. The only senses you can rely on will be hearing and smell. Even with a vampire's heightened senses you will become disorientated. The winner in each pair will immobilise their partner for a count of ten. Borzak and I will be watching on an infra-red camera. There are no rules. Cora, you go with Dillon. Ace, you go with Sade. Bram, you go with Aron. Angelo, you go against Frederick, Celeste, you go against Ásta.'

Dillon peeked over at Cora. He did not want to go up against her for so many reasons.

'Bram and Aron, you go first.' Borzak ordered, handing them both headphones and dark goggles. 'When you enter the room, walk in the direction I tell you. When you hear my command, you take the headphones off, and you begin. Got it?'

Aron and Bram nodded. Bram tried to look bored but the gleam in his coal-black eyes and the tension across his shoulders gave him away. Aron, with his hard-as-nails body, revealed by a slim-fitting black T-shirt and black combat trousers, clenched his fists in anticipation.

'Okay, goggles and headphones on.'

Borzak guided them inside the room and shut the door. He and Mr Hunt peered at a screen by the door. The rest of the class huddled round.

The picture was black and white and not very clear. Dillon could just make out their shadowy figures creeping round the sides of the room, feeling along the walls with their hands.

Borzak spoke into an earpiece. 'Headphones and goggles off now.'

The shadowy figures responded, and a closer camera picked up the eerie, white glare of Bram's eyes. Both vampires had shifted forward into a defensive stance and were standing still. Only their heads rotated, as they tried to find each other. Suddenly, Aron clutched his head and sank to his knees just as Bram sprang across the room and landed in a deadly pincer move on top of him.

Ásta took a sharp intake of breath and shook her head.

'He picked up Aron's electromagnetic brain signals,' Jeremiah muttered under his breath, 'then directed his own in that direction. Not only does it hurt Aron, it also enables him to pinpoint where he is. Unless he's stronger than I think, he won't be able to maintain it once Aron counter attacks.'

Sure enough, as Bram attempted to grapple Aron to the floor, Aron twisted out from underneath him and, in a lightning flip, had Bram on his back. They rolled into a dense dry-ice patch and by the time the infra-red cameras picked them up again, it looked like Bram was on top. Aron's hand shot out like a cobra striking and slammed into Bram's throat. Bram shot backwards and landed sprawling on the other side of the room.

'Yes! Destroy him, Aron,' hissed Ásta.

A second later Bram was up, prowling around the walls of the room. Aron crouched forward. Dillon could see him straining to pick up any clues. Bram had stopped; he whipped his head round and focused in Aron's direction. A second later, Aron executed three perfect backflips and dropped low to the floor. Snake-like, once again, he crawled on his stomach. Bram's head whipped left and right working out where he had gone; Aron grabbed his ankles from behind and toppled him to the floor once more. This time Aron wrapped his legs and arms around him in a death hold and Bram, thrashing around, was unable to throw him off.

Borzak started the count. 'Three . . . Four . . . Five . . . Six . . .'

Bram went completely still. Almost instantly, Aron began shaking his head in pain as the electromagnetic pulses fired into his brain, but he managed to hold on.

'Eight . . . Nine . . . Ten!' Borzak roared and pressed a button. A horn sounded and a red light flashed, indicating the fight was over. Slipping his earpiece off, he strode to the door and opened it.

Bram, face like a thundercloud, stormed out of the gym. Aron followed, wincing as his eyes adjusted to the light and massaging his forehead.

Arms folded, Ásta eyed him coldly. 'Not bad, brother. But you need to work on the mind blocks.'

Frederick hugged him. 'Are you okay?'

'Of course, he is okay,' Ásta hissed. 'He is tough – unlike you,' she added, looking pointedly at Frederick's slightly untuned physique.

'Ásta!' Aron glared at her and grinned down at Frederick. 'Chill, Fred. He's strong with the mind games but I am better at combat.'

Borzak clapped Aron on the back. 'Good work. Right, Cora and Dillon next.'

Dillon's stomach clenched into a tiny ball. As he approached the door, he caught Cora's eye. She grinned at him.

'May the best vampire win!'

'Ah, you've some notions of yourself,' Dillon replied, hoping he sounded more confident than he felt.

Borzak gave them goggles and headphones. 'Cora, Dillon, remember – take the goggles off and throw the headphones to the corner of the room once I tell you to start.'

Dillon and Cora nodded. He could feel the electricity crackling between them and already his senses were becoming overwhelmed by her.

Borzak tutted. 'Did you hear me?'

'Sorry, headphones in the corner when you say so, yeah?'

'Get ready.'

As soon as he put them on, he was plunged into complete darkness and silence. He felt Borzak's huge hand on his back guiding him through the door. The acrid, pungent smell of dry ice filled his nose and he coughed as it hit the back of his throat. He sensed that Cora was still standing next to him, but he could no longer smell her bewitching scent.

Borzak's voice came through the headphones. 'Okay, Dillon, walk straight forward until I tell you to stop.'

It was the strangest feeling, to be walking forward into nothing. Involuntarily, he stretched his arms out, feeling his way through the acrid air, taking one hesitant step after another, hearing nothing but his own breath and his heartbeat.

He was aware that his pulse was speeding up and he fought down a rising tide of claustrophobia. 'It's just a room,' he growled to himself. He had known true darkness back at home, in the nights of the bleak Irish winter when even the light from the stars was hidden. Then he'd delighted in the strange sensation of his vision being the same whether his eyes were open or closed. But this was a different situation, where rather than relishing the darkness, he had to find a way to 'see' through it.

'Okay, Dillon, you can take the headphones and goggles off now.' Borzak's voice broke through the rising panic.

He couldn't see much more with them off, just swirling smoke and a dim, dark-greyish light. For a second, he remained dead still, straining his senses to pick up the slightest hint of where Cora was. Absolutely nothing. Just the occasional whooshing noise as more dry ice was pumped into the room.

She was probably standing still too, he reasoned. Slowly he turned in a circle, peering into the gloom. Nothing. Where the hell was she?

The tension was unbearable. Any second, he expected her to leap out of the darkness. He closed his eyes again.

Where the hell is he? I should be able to hear his heartbeat.

His eyes shot open. 'Cora?' he spoke out loud.

There was half a second's pause.

Got him!

He felt her surge of emotion, followed by a rush through the air a second later, and dropped to the floor just in time. What the hell?

Cora flew over him and he heard a soft thud as she hit the floor.

Shit! He's faster than I thought.

He froze as it finally clicked that he was hearing Cora's thoughts, not her voice. There must be more to the dry ice than they'd admitted – some weird vampire sense of humour.

He could feel exactly where she was. What would he do now? He didn't want to hurt her. The only way to finish this was to take her down as gently as possible.

Slowly, he crawled in the direction of her thoughts.

I can hear his heart. He's near.

Shite.

Spin, Cora you idiot. You're faster than him.

He sensed her thoughts whirl as she spun away from him.

He had to slow his heart rate down. He needed a couple of seconds before she heard him. He rolled onto his back and breathed out in one long, slow, silent breath and then a slow breath in. He repeated it five times. Confident now that he'd bought himself a bit of time, he trained in on Cora again.

Stand still, listen out for his heart and attack. Come on, Cora, you can do this. Cute or not, he can't beat you.

Dillon grinned in the darkness – Cora found him 'cute'.

Slowly transferring into a crouch position, he closed his eyes again, focused on Cora's thoughts and sprang across the room. The impact threw her backwards to the floor and he landed on top of her.

Fuck. How did he do that?

Abruptly, he lost contact with her thoughts. All he was aware of was her scent, her satin skin and the wonderous feel of her body underneath him. She froze. He could feel his heart thudding against her chest.

Instinctively, his mouth lowered towards hers.

Suddenly, she twisted and rolled on top of him. What the hell? She was incredibly strong. Pinning his arms to his sides with her hands, she wrapped her long legs around him.

He writhed about, trying to loosen her hold and managed to roll her over again. The darkness added to the intense physical sensations between them as she rolled on top of him again.

Finally, he managed to release a leg. Just as he was about to knee her in the back, he paused. Hissing with effort, she slammed her forearm into his throat, winding him and then holding him down. He tried to get his heels underneath to buck her off, but she pushed down harder. He strained against her but, with her whole body pressed against him, he struggled to focus his thoughts.

The red light flashed.

Instantly, Cora rolled off him, and they both lay on their backs for a second. He was panting hard.

'Sorry,' she whispered, before springing up as the door opened and dim light filtered through the gloom.

7

Blood Contract

The scalding hot water pounded onto his head and Dillon began washing the sweat and dry-ice smell out of his hair. He decided he wasn't going to the Desire and Control lesson. He'd only end up humiliated again.

'Dillon? You in there?' Jeremiah's lilting voice cut through his furious thoughts.

He didn't want to speak to anyone but there was no point pretending he wasn't there when it was obvious that he was. ' . . . Yeah.'

'Desires starts soon.'

'Yeah, I know. I'm gonna give it a miss . . .'

'Come on, Dhamp.'

Jeremiah's face appeared through the steam as Dillon turned the shower off and wrapped a towel around his waist.

'It wasn't that bad.'

'It was.'

'Look –' Jeremiah glanced over his shoulder to check they were alone – 'anyone would lose it with Cora on top of them!'

'It's not funny. You heard what Borzak said in front of *everyone*.' He imitated Borzak's accent. '*Never allow lust to cloud your mind*.' He paused for a minute. 'Thank Christ Bram wasn't there. I'm not sure what he would have enjoyed more; lording it over me or landing one on me.'

'He still might,' Jeremiah observed with a wry smile. 'There's not a hope in hell he won't hear about it. No one's going to forget the . . . *unusual* rolling around technique you two were employing.'

Dillon dropped his head into his hands and groaned. 'Are you supposed to be helping?'

Jeremiah grinned again. 'Look, just be there, okay? You don't want Madame Dupledge making your life harder than it already is.'

He had a point.

'Suppose so. Last thing I need today is more grief.'

Jeremiah slapped him on the back. 'Good decision. Hey, one more thing. In that room, how did you know where Cora was? You were like a heat seeking missile.'

'Oh that, yeah, I'm not sure. I just . . . I guess I feel a strong connection to her.'

He wasn't going to tell anyone that he had briefly heard her thoughts. If it happened again, he'd talk to Madame Dupledge. He trusted Jeremiah but the last thing he needed was more attention.

Jeremiah frowned. 'Okay. Must be a mighty strong connection to spring across a room right on target.'

'That or beginner's luck.' Dillon adjusted his towel, adding, 'Head on without me – I'll catch you up when I'm ready.'

The second he walked into Madame Dupledge's classroom, he clocked that Bram was sitting next to Cora. Bram shot him a hostile glare. He'd heard what had happened all right. Cora was talking to Celeste and didn't notice him come in. Jeremiah was next to Bik and the only other empty chair was next to Sade. She didn't look at him as he sat down.

'Hey,' he said.

'Hey,' she replied.

Madame Dupledge swept in. She had changed her more traditional vampire dress for tight black leather trousers, high-heeled boots and a fitted jacket over a silky blouse. Her lustrous red hair was piled on top of her head and emeralds that matched her eyes glittered at her ears.

'Good evening. I hear that your CHP class went well earlier and that some of you discovered strengths that you didn't know you had.'

Dillon's felt his cheeks begin to burn.

'Aron, I hear that you in particular excelled, and Dillon, I hear that you were a surprise too.'

A faint snicker went round the classroom and Dillon's face inflamed. Out of the corner of his eye he saw Cora grin.

'So, how do we define desire? A strong feeling of wanting

to have something or wishing for something to happen. As vampires, we are susceptible to strong desires. Our strongest and most primitive is for blood, particularly blood taken directly from a human. The hunger for blood is almost as constant as breathing is for humans. Simply because without it, we cannot survive; it is hardwired into our brain and it is absolutely the most difficult desire to control.'

She looked around the class.

'Never, ever underestimate it. At the Induction Ceremony, some of you proved that you have already learnt great restraint. Some of you less so.'

Her gaze fell on Angelo and Ásta.

'Because losing control could involve injury or even death to a human and risk our exposure, it is imperative that you gain complete mastery of it. It will be our primary focus this year and will culminate in a weekend trip to a nearby ski resort where you will be expected to manage close contact with humans. If I, or any of the other staff, do not feel that you are ready, you will not be allowed to go. The risk is too great.'

She continued, 'Most of you have had very little exposure to humans. Dillon –' she turned to look at him – 'has obviously had a completely different experience. He has lived amongst humans for his entire life but his desire for blood has only just been awakened. His need could become strong – maybe even stronger than yours at first and I would like you to help him as much as possible. As Vampire Elect, his control must be exemplary.'

Dillon thought of his craving for the fake-blood froth the night before. Just how bad was this going to get?

He raised his hand. 'Can I counter desire for blood with normal human food?'

'As far as we know, only if you completely abstain from swallowing blood. If you do that though, your vampire traits of greater strength, senses, intuition, speed, special skills and so on will also diminish and eventually return to hibernation.' She gave him a small smile. 'Most dhampirs do not wish to give those up and, as you have had the great honour to be chosen as Vampire Elect, you are obligated to maintain the vampire side of your nature for as long as you hold that role.'

Dillon sighed inside. No one had told him that being chosen as VE meant he was tied into a blood-drinking contract for a year.

'Okay, thanks,' he muttered.

Madame Dupledge turned back to the class. 'So can anyone describe what it feels like to have an intense desire for something.'

Angelo looked up and spoke with feeling. 'You can't think about anything else; your mind and body are totally obsessed with it.'

'Absolutely right, Angelo. So, in relation to bloodlust, how might we reduce such strong feelings?'

'By making sure we never get too hungry?' Ace offered.

'Correct. That is why you have a compulsory midnight blood-drinking session and have twenty-four-hour access to the artificial blood bar. That is also why you must always be prepared. On long journeys, you take spare blood bags in case you are delayed or can't access blood where you are going. Angelo, I think you will agree that you made that mistake on your journey here.'

'Yes.' Angelo grimaced. 'Our private jet was delayed for forty-eight hours and when I first smelled Dillon in the town square, I wanted to suck the living daylights out of him. Sorry Dillon, but I was bone dry and your blood smelt incredible – tastes even better,' he added in an undertone.

The class snickered and Madame Dupledge smiled. 'Yes, thank you, Angelo. You have already enlightened us on your enjoyment of Dillon's blood.'

'Is that part of the reason he is here? To test us?'

'No Angelo, Dillon is not here to tempt you – although clearly, his presence has had that effect. How have you controlled yourself around him until now?'

'I drank your blood, which was even more mind-blowing, and then I drank the twelve samples and then four double shots in the blood bar and the blood bee—'

Frederick coughed and cleared his throat loudly. 'Sorry, Madame Dupledge,' he apologised.

Madame Dupledge frowned at him and returned to Angelo. 'This is where all of you have to be careful, you do not want to replace one desire with overindulgence of another. You must learn control; to take only what you need. You need to understand your desire for excess, Angelo. Why are you feeling unfulfilled?'

'Um, I wouldn't say I was unfulfilled,' Angelo replied, shooting a smouldering glance at Ásta. 'I just happen to have used up a lot of energy in the last couple of days.'

Dillon saw Ásta smirk.

'I have a fast metabolism. I've always needed more.'

'Let me put it another way. You think you need more blood than most vampires, but do you indulge in many things to excess – alcohol, sexual desire or adrenaline sports for example?'

Angelo shrugged. 'I guess.'

'So, my point is that you have to learn control otherwise you will be forever trying to fill a black hole of desire.'

'Dillon, would you mind standing here, at the front?'

He was about to refuse but as her mesmerising green eyes rested on him he found himself, as usual, agreeing.

'Um, sure.' He hoped that this was not the prelude to more humiliation.

'Angelo, I want you to stand really close to Dillon without touching him.'

Angelo prowled up to him, stopping only an inch away.

'Now close your eyes Angelo and inhale Dillon's scent.'

Dillon wasn't reassured by the glazed look in Angelo's eyes before his eyelids fluttered closed. He squirmed as Angelo sniffed him like he was a rare truffle or an expensive bottle of wine. The others watched expectantly.

'How do you feel now, Angelo?'

Angelo groaned. 'Worse. He still smells mouth-watering.'

'I would like you to taste him.'

'What?' Dillon jerked back and stared at her in shock.

'Not blood, skin.' Madame Dupledge said.

'Ah, okay. I understand.' Angelo nodded.

'Hang on!' Dillon took another step back.

'Trust me, Dillon,' she commanded.

Flinching, he managed to stand still. As Angelo lunged towards his neck, Dillon recoiled but Angelo's strong hands clasped his head firmly, as if it was his beloved Ferrari's steering wheel. Tentatively, he lowered his mouth and flicked his tongue over Dillon's skin.

Involuntarily, Dillon shivered. Angelo's fangs shot out, making him jump. The whole class watched, spellbound. Angelo sighed deeply and sniffed once more, filling his nostrils with Dillon's scent. Running his tongue one last time from Dillon's jawbone to his collarbone, fangs gently grazing the skin, he suddenly let go and stepped back.

Dillon realised he had been holding his breath and, slumping forward, hands resting on his thighs, he took several breaths.

The vampires looked at him in surprise.

'Well done, Angelo.' Madame Dupledge approved. 'How do you feel?'

Furiously, Dillon looked up at her. What the hell? How did Angelo feel? She should be asking how *he* felt. Angelo could have flipped and chomped into his neck at any point.

'Better,' Angelo admitted. 'I can't deny Dillon is a temptation, but just standing close to him and getting used to him helped.'

'Exactly, sometimes controlled exposure can help us to learn control.'

Madame Dupledge turned to him. 'How do you feel, Dillon? Do you trust Angelo?'

'No.' He didn't want to admit that despite his fear, or maybe because of it, he had found the experience disturbingly erotic.

The class laughed.

'Starting from our next lesson, I would like you two to pair up.'

Dillon repressed a sigh as he returned to his seat next to Sade. Great. So now he had the extra challenge of avoiding Angelo's bloodlust.

'What happens if it doesn't work?' Sade asked. 'What if Angelo becomes more obsessed?'

Dillon could have hugged her.

'Then it becomes more interesting. Angelo has managed so far though and it should only get easier as Dillon's system becomes more vampiric.'

'It still seems a bit risky,' Sade insisted.

'It would be riskier if we didn't confront it and learn from it in a controlled environment. In this class, we learn to trust each other and, if Angelo and Dillon are honest, we can all help with any issues that arise. That will be invaluable for the ski trip.

'Now, imagine you must go on a night out with your colleagues. Normally you would refuse but you can't on this occasion. In the nightclub that night is one of the most delicious humans you have ever smelled. Your fangs begin to tingle, your pupils begin to dilate, your desire for that blood starts to cloud your judgement. What do you do?'

'Run,' cracked Ace.

'Avoidance is an excellent technique. But what if you can't run away?'

'You distract yourself?'

'Another excellent technique. You could talk to someone else, dance, message someone. This time, however, it's gone beyond that. You're starting to lose rational thought. All you can think about is drinking that person's blood. They're dancing so close to you, they smell amazing, your fangs start to surface, you lower your mouth to their neck, your lips caress their skin. How do you stop yourself at that very last point? The point of no return?'

Dillon sat up. The whole class were on the edge of their seats again.

'You can't.' Ásta broke the silence.

'Correct, Ásta. Only a mature vampire with extraordinary willpower would be able to stop them themselves at that point. It is a skill that we develop as we age, but as a young vampire you can never allow yourselves to become too close or to drop your guard. It is simply too dangerous.'

Dillon felt cold all over. It was what he had worried about that first night in the Sanatorium. He thought of his father. Could he be a danger to him now? Having an uncontrollable urge to drink his blood made him want to throw up.

'Some vampires must get close to humans or dhampirs wouldn't exist.' Celeste remarked, staring at him pointedly.

'Nowadays, human-and-vampire relationships are taboo because of the danger. Occasionally, of course, they still occur, and if the vampire has tremendous control, they may endure. However, they are extremely rare. Hence why we have never had a dhampir at this school before.'

There was a momentary silence.

Dillon realised he had never asked how his father and mother had got together and he hadn't known enough, until now, to think to ask how they had made it work. He knew she had supposedly left to protect him, not his father. Did that mean she had been able to control herself around her father but not him?

Madame Dupledge suddenly turned to him, as if she had picked up on his inner turmoil, but continued to address the class.

'To prepare you for the ski trip we will be breaking down the psychology of bloodlust and we will be looking at methods to control it. One is to keep reminding yourself of the consequences of losing control. Picture the object of your desire as cold and lifeless. All turn to your partners and visualise what they would look like – spare no details.'

No one seemed keen to look at their partner. Dillon stole a glance at Sade. Slowly, her eyes travelled up his face and, silently, they looked at each other.

Madame Dupledge's voice continued, slow and hypnotic, 'Think of them lying limp, their skin – grey and lifeless, their eyes – staring and empty, their neck – ravaged and torn, blood congealing at the edges of the wound. Think how you would feel about yourself, how you would tell the people who love them . . .'

Dillon took in Sade's beautiful face, her gleaming skin and finally her huge, glowing brown eyes. He'd been struck by her eyes before, but he'd never really stared into them. It was like sinking into a cool, dark pool. He felt a sense of her subtle strength and serenity shining out and, every time he tried, his mind shied away from any image of them empty and lifeless. He tried to imagine himself ripping out her throat and sucking her blood. He simply couldn't.

A loud scraping noise followed by a rush of air and the sound of the door slamming broke the tension. Sade's long, curly lashes came down like shutters and she closed her eyes. He shivered and blinked, surprised to see pink moisture seeping out under her eyelids.

'Hey,' he whispered. 'You okay?'

She reopened her eyes but kept them on the desk. 'Yeah.'

Looking around the class, Dillon realised that it was Cora who had run out. Bram was visibly disturbed and several of the others looked unsettled. Teen vampires had feelings. It was not what he had expected.

Madame Dupledge watched them intently. Her voice, when she spoke, was soft. 'You have learnt an important lesson today. Visualisation is a powerful tool. Use it wisely. It might stop you from doing something you would regret for the rest of your lives.

'We will finish with an exercise to help you to understand and to strengthen your willpower. The blood bar is shut for the rest of the night and, to make it harder, each of you will have a shot of untreated human blood delivered to your rooms. It will measure exactly forty-five millilitres. If it measures less than that in the morning, you will fail your first homework assignment. Your first formal blood feed is midnight tomorrow. All of you should be able to hold out until then.'

There were a few gasps of dismay and Angelo sighed dramatically.

Madame Dupledge ignored them and continued, 'I will give you one piece of advice: if you start to waver, try to think about our higher purpose. For us, that is the desire to become progressive, civilised creatures that have an important role to play in the world. Stay strong and believe in yourselves.'

As he followed Sade out, Madame Dupledge called him over, 'Dillon, could I have a word, please?'

She waited until the rest of the class left.

'You seem disturbed about something, Dillon?'

'I'm a bit freaked out about my da. Why did no one explain that once I had blood, I might not be able to control myself around him?' He sounded angrier than he had intended to.

'You won't attack your father, Dillon.'

'How do you know? My mother obviously didn't trust herself.'

Something like sadness flashed across Madame Dupledge's

expression. 'I'm sure the reasons your mother left were more complicated than that, Dillon, and it is extremely unlikely you will be a danger to your father. He brought you up. You have his genes. That will stand for a great deal.'

'But I can never be one hundred per cent sure that I won't?'

'No,' she admitted. 'But cases of dhampirs attacking the human parent are almost unheard of.'

'Maybe I shouldn't have any more blood.'

'You have no choice, Dillon. You cannot change what you are. You are Vampire Elect now.'

'Maybe I shouldn't be! I don't want all this! I don't want to stay away from my father. I can't even get hold of him since I came to this place.'

'I understand that this is difficult for you, Dillon, but you have to accept that this is the way it has to be.'

'So what happens if I just refuse to drink blood? Where's your Vampire Elect then?' he snapped, his anger fuelled by fear.

'Dillon, please trust me. You must follow this path. Your father wants this for you too.'

That startled him. 'He does? Have you spoken to him?'

'Yes, I have.'

He was lost for words. 'Does he know all the implications?'

'He does. That's why he sent you here.'

'He said it was a promise he made to my mother.'

'That is true. But you must realise, Dillon, that your father wanted you to come here just as much as your mother did.'

★

Cora was waiting for him in the corridor when he left the classroom.

He walked towards her. 'Are you okay? Why did you run out?'

She paused and when she spoke, her voice was halting. 'While I was visualising, Bram's face turned into my brother's. It was so realistic.' As she finished talking, her eyes shone with moisture.

He looked over his shoulder. 'Look, can we go somewhere? Somewhere more private.'

She brushed her eyes impatiently and gave him a small smile. 'As long as you're not planning to ambush me again?'

He flushed. 'Look I'm sorry about—'

She waved his apology aside. 'Don't worry about it. Look, I do know a place. It's up by the pool but you have to promise to keep it a secret.' She grabbed his hand. 'Follow me.'

Trying to ignore the distracting sensation of her hand in his and the extremely pleasurable electric shivers up his arm as they headed for the stairs, he shook his head. 'How do you know about this "secret" place?'

'Because I'm amazing!'

'And modest?'

She mock swiped at him. 'Watch it or I might suck the living daylights out of you!'

'Hey, get in line – Angelo's still at the head of that queue.' They both chuckled.

'Lighten up, Dillon. Angelo can't do anything to you –

not now you're his "control" experiment. I have to admit, watching him lap at your neck was very disturbing.'

They had reached the pool floor and he paused. 'Disturbing in what way?'

She smirked at him. 'You must have felt it. There's a magnetism between you two.'

'Sort of,' he mumbled, looking away in embarrassment.

Cora grinned and dragged him towards the newly fixed sauna room.

He hung back. 'Not the sauna?' He didn't think he could manage being with Cora in there. Not after Ásta and Angelo's display.

'No, better than that.'

Tucked behind the sauna room was a narrow metal door, hidden by a screen. Cora reached for the handle.

'Won't it set an alarm off?'

She shrugged. 'Doesn't seem to.'

Opening the door, she began climbing a narrow metal staircase that travelled past the hall floor and into the roof. At the top was a clear hatch. Cora went first and, pushing back the hatch, disappeared into the starry night sky. He followed, shivering at the blast of cold air as he emerged. The gleaming roof stretched out in front of them.

He breathed in great lungfuls of fresh air. It was bliss being outside after the confines of the school. For a moment, he revelled in the complete silence. Cora turned to face him; her pale face illuminated by the soft building lights shining through the roof.

'It's stunning, isn't it?'

'Incredible,' he agreed and then, unable to stop himself, said, 'Does Bram know about it?'

Her face closed off and he wished he'd stayed quiet. 'No. My brother told me.'

'How did he find it?'

'He probably worked it out from the design of the building – he's clever that way.'

He touched her arm. 'You must miss him. What's his name?'

She looked over the mountains. 'Zach. I miss him every single day. He was a rebel but he was also brilliant. He shouldn't have been chucked out. He discovered something and they found a way to get rid of him.'

'Madame Dupledge?'

'No, not Madame Dupledge. Despite appearances, she's not the most powerful vampire here. There's a ruling elite in the vampire world. Many of them are on the Board of Vampire Governors. Bram's dad, Celeste's Dad and Sade's parents are on it. She's more progressive. They're more traditional and they have a lot of sway. I don't know what he found out, but Bram's dad had something to do with it.'

She turned back to him. 'That's why I have to be with Bram, Dillon. Do you understand?'

Distracted by her luminous eyes, he struggled to make sense of his thoughts. 'Does Bram know?'

'Yeah, he knows – about my brother – not that I'm trying to find out about him.'

'But . . .' Dillon was still struggling to understand. 'Bram's not stupid. If you're using him to get to his father, he'll know.'

'No, he's not stupid,' Cora agreed. 'But he's egotistic enough to believe that I like him. Anyway, I'm not using him to get back at his father. I'm just trying to find out more. I'll tell him at some point.'

'What does his father think about you two?'

'His father doesn't know about us. He told him to stay away from me but . . .' She quirked her lip. 'I guess it's lucky that he seems drawn to me.'

'Cora, if Bram's father finds out, they could find a way to expel you too.'

She shrugged. 'It would look too suspicious. I couldn't care less anyway. I just need to clear my brother's name and find out if he's alive. It's not like him to not contact me.'

'What did he discover that's so bad?'

'I don't know. That's why I need your help.'

'Me? How can I help?'

'You're VE. You'll have privileges,' she reminded him. 'You might have access to vampires and places that I won't have.'

'Probably not for much longer if Bram's father is as influential as you say he is.'

'Not even he can mess with the blood vote.'

'Maybe not that,' Dillon mused, 'but he's still got the dhampir trump card.'

'I hope not.'

All rational thought drained away as she closed the distance between them and, resting her cheek on his chest, put her arms around him.

'I just really need to find my brother.'

Tentatively, he tilted her chin up towards him. For a long moment they stared at each other and, just as he had imagined in his dreams, he lowered his mouth towards hers. She pressed against him and her mouth parted, sending his heart into overdrive. But, just before their lips touched, she turned her face away and placed her hands on his chest.

'I'm sorry, Dillon. I really like you, but I can't do this to you.'

He stumbled back, head reeling, fangs half extended. 'Come on, Cora. You feel it too, I know you do – remember the Sanatorium.'

She sighed. 'Look, you smelt amazing, and Madame Dupledge's blood went to my head, I guess. I can't risk upsetting Bram – besides, he's good for me.'

'Good for you? What the hell does that mean? What am I, just the dumb dhampir you twist around your little finger?'

'No! It's not like that. I said it already . . . I like you.'

'Fuck off, Cora. I'm sorry about your brother but go and find someone else to play your little games with.'

He saw the hurt in her eyes.

'Dillon, I'm not playing games. I've been completely straight with you.'

He couldn't stop himself lashing out again. 'But you're not being straight with yourself. I'll catch you later, Cora.'

He stalked back to the open hatch.

'Dillon. Wait. Please!'

Jeremiah was in when he got back to their room.

'What now?' he said, with one glance at Dillon's face.

'Cora. Everything.'

'Did you two fall out?'

'I'm not really in the mood to talk about it. That okay?'

Jeremiah raised his hands. 'No problem, Dhamp. I'm here if you need me.'

He felt himself cooling down. 'Thanks.'

Jeremiah turned back to the book he was reading. Dillon grabbed his phone and slipped back outside to call his father. Once again, the phone just rang and rang. Where was he? It was six o'clock in the morning. How come Madame Dupledge had spoken to him? He needed to find out if she was speaking the truth.

Elias and another assistant were delivering the blood home-work in glass measuring beakers to each room. He handed Dillon the last two on the tray.

'Good luck,' he murmured.

'Thanks.' Dillon caught a whiff of the blood and his fangs immediately shot out. It was far worse than the fake-blood froth.

Elias scurried away. 'Stay strong.'

Dillon kicked the door with his foot, careful not to spill the blood.

Jeremiah started out of his chair and then grinned as he

clocked Dillon's fangs. 'We'd better lock you in your coffin tonight.'

'It's not funny!' Dillon said with a lisp, unused to talking with his teeth hanging over his bottom lip. 'Where shall we put it?'

'Well, I'd cover it up for starters and, like I said, either lock yourself or the blood in the coffin.'

The smell of the blood was driving him crazy. Saliva was running in weird rivulets down his tongue. 'I think I'll put it in the coffin. Can you do it for me?'

He thrust the beakers at Jeremiah, whose nostrils flared comically as he covered them with a T-shirt and carefully placed them in the coffin.

'Both?' Dillon questioned.

'Yeah, or you'll smell my beaker all night.'

The tantalising smell lessened somewhat but Dillon couldn't stop thinking about it. 'Was it like this for you?'

'Our parents give us small amounts of blood early on but it's harder once we become teenagers. Cravings become more intense and it's difficult to work out if you're into someone or their blood sometimes.'

'I thought it was just human blood that you craved?'

Jeremiah shrugged. 'Yes, but we still sometimes crave each other's blood too. You know what Madame Dupledge's felt like. Drinking your partner's blood . . .' He grinned. 'How shall I put it . . . heightens the experience.'

'Oh . . . right.' Dillon stared at him. 'Isn't it against the rules?'

Jeremiah's grin widened. 'It is – here. Outside, you can do what you want.'

'So what's the secret? How do you know if you like someone or just their blood?'

'You don't. It's all part of the allure.'

'Jaysus,' he groaned. 'Is there nothing that's easy about all this? Tell me, do you crave Bik's blood?'

'None of your business! Talking of Bik, I need to ask her something.'

He jumped up and then paused at the door. 'Will you be okay with the . . .' He pointed at the blood in the coffin and tapped his fangs.

Dillon waved him out. 'I'll be grand. You go. I'll catch you later.'

The minute he was gone, Dillon began to obsess about the blood in the coffin. He wished Jeremiah had padlocked it somehow. Sighing, he turned the light off and, making one jumper into a pillow, curled into a ball. Two seconds later, he sat up and put another one over his head.

He really wanted that blood. With a huge effort, he willed himself to think about something else. His mind jumped straight to the argument with Cora. He felt bad about losing his temper. Maybe she had been straight with him. However much she liked him – her priority was her brother.

He must have fallen into an uneasy sleep. He woke with a start, instantly alert, eyes straining in the dark. 'Jeremiah?'

'Dillon, it's me, Sade.'

'Sade? What are you doing? Where's Jeremiah?'

She shrugged. 'Probably with Bik. You need to get up. There's a group of parents here.'

Dillon groaned. He struggled to take in what Sade was saying – the scent of the blood in the coffin was over-whelming.

'I suspect it's about your election as VE. They expected it to be Bram and Celeste and they are used to getting what they want.'

Dillon shook his head, desperately trying to shift his focus away from the blood. Whatever problem Sade was talking about would be easier to face if he could just have a tiny, little sip.

'Celeste told me. Her father's here. So are my parents apparently – not that they've asked to see me.'

'So? What can we do about it?' The desire for the blood was making him short-tempered.

'We need to find out what's going on. Knowledge is power – that's my father's motto.'

'But maybe he wants rid of me too. You might be going against his wishes. You've already said that he's a traditionalist. Why would you do that?'

She took a deep breath. 'My parents invent sophisticated satellite technology. They wanted to make sure even the most remote parts of the world are able to communicate but, since they have been feted by powerful vampires and humans alike, let's say they have lost touch with their original principles.'

He rubbed at his eyes. 'But what has that got to do with me?'

'They want me to get together with Bram.'

Dillon sat up. 'What?! Look, no offence, but Bram's pretty obsessed with Cora.'

'Yeah.' She lifted her chin. 'And I'm not the slightest bit interested in him, but our two families would represent a powerful alliance.'

Dillon raised an eyebrow. 'Does that medieval shite really still go on?'

'In powerful vampire circles, yes.'

He could see her eyes gleaming in the dark. 'And will you do it? Or at least try to?'

She paused. 'No I won't.'

He sat back, surprised at the relief he felt. 'This whole world is crazy. Ruling families. Vampire Elects. Arranged marriages. Dhampir prejudice.'

'I know, but we can't just sit back.'

He was silent for a second. 'Okay, let's go –' he pinched the bridge of his nose – 'the smell of that blood is driving me crazy.'

Sade chuckled. 'I put a bowl of lemon oil in our room. It helps to neutralise blood odour.'

He got up. 'Cheers for not sharing that earlier.'

They both crept out. Winter sunlight illuminated the end of the corridor.

'What time is it?' Dillon whispered.

'Afternoon.'

'Why are they meeting in the day?'

'They obviously see it as urgent.'

Silently, he followed her to the stairs. It was the first time he'd seen sunlight. The sky had been steel-grey or dark up to now, and school hours were all between sunset and sunrise. Stunning prisms of rainbow light bounced off the glass roof and sprinkled the interior with colour.

The building was completely wasted on vampires, Dillon reflected as they crept up the circular staircases between each floor, bending low to stay hidden beneath the chest-height balustrade walls that enclosed them – far enough away to mask his scent. The noise of angry voices increased as they drew closer, and Sade slowed on the eighth-floor staircase. Step by step they approached the level of the ninth floor.

A powerful male vampire's voice rose above the others. 'I am removing Bram from this academy if you persist with this ridiculous experiment, Lily. Yes, the dhampir's blood might taste different, but Bram said he had never taken blood before – that means his blood would undoubtably have a different allure.'

There was a rumbling of agreement from the other vampires.

Madame Dupledge's musical voice rang out with just the slightest hint of exasperation. 'Why don't you just try his blood, Alexandru, perhaps then you will understand why he was chosen? As you know, I have an insight into each student at the Induction Ceremony. I feel his potential.'

Sade's eyes widened, and Dillon shook his head at her as if to say it was news to him.

'What about Bram's?' Alexandru exploded.

'I have no doubt Bram will be an accomplished vampire too.'

'Lily, we know you have special powers of intuition but be realistic. This dhampir. Who is his father? Do we even know him?'Alexandru demanded.

'What does it matter? On his mother's side—'

'You keep saying that, Lily,' Alexandru interrupted. 'Of course it matters who his father is. And who exactly is his mother? We know that female vampires rarely bear progeny with male humans.'

'That is precisely my argument. He is special. As far as we know, he is the only dhampir with a vampire mother and a human father.'

Alexandru chuckled. 'Come now, Lily. That novelty doesn't make him more special than a dhampir born to a human mother and a vampire father.'

'His mother's heritage and a half human foetus surviving in a vampire body is special. Need I repeat? As far as we know, he is the only one.'

'That may be so, but why would his place be here? It beggars belief that a boy of questionable upbringing and with complete lack of knowledge should lead the year when Bram's bloodline is impeccable.'

There was another rumble of agreement from Alexandru's supporters.

'You should never have included him in the blood vote, Lily. He doesn't belong here. There is no need to keep an eye on him – he needs to leave.'

'I told you,' Dillon mouthed at Sade.

'Just taste the blood,' Madame Dupledge insisted. 'We saved some from the Induction Ceremony, before he drank from me.'

Another voice, quiet but authoritative, spoke. 'We should taste it, Alexandru.'

'My father,' Sade hissed under her breath.

'It's beside the point. Whatever his blood tastes like, he is unsuitable for the role,' Alexandru argued.

'That may be so, but at least we will have a better under-standing of it and if there has been a mistake or not.' Sade's father pointed out.

'Very well, let's get it over with then. I'm supposed to be in Romania in two hours.'

Sade and Dillon peered over the balustrade as the parents disappeared inside Madame Dupledge's office.

She hadn't closed the blinds so they could see her handing out a small vial to each parent, keeping one for herself. There was silence as they each sniffed it and then, closing their eyes, took a sip and swilled it around their mouths before tipping back their heads and swallowing. Dillon grimaced. It was like a bizarre wine-tasting for connoisseurs – Blood de Dillon.

Madame Dupledge took only one sip and her eyes remained closed for several minutes. Finally, she spoke. 'Well, I think we have our answer.'

Sade's father spoke. 'It is incredible, like nothing I have tasted before. Are you sure he is a dhampir?'

'Of course, he hadn't tasted blood until the Induction Ceremony.'

Bram's father remained silent.

Madame Dupledge turned to him. 'Alexandru?'

'I'll admit it's powerful, Lily, but I still don't think a dhampir belongs at VAMPS.'

'You want to overturn centuries of tradition? You know better than anyone that blood never lies, Alexandru.'

'You overturned centuries of tradition when you granted him a place. This is a finishing academy for elite vampires – the best of the best. Unless you want the year deprived of some of the most talented vampires of their generation, I suggest you come to your senses. The blood vote is invalidated this year. As to whether he stays at VAMPS – that conversation is to be continued.'

'As you know, Alexandru, any decision has to be agreed by a majority vote. I will arrange a full board of governors' meeting as soon as we can all assemble. Until then, he will remain Vampire Elect.'

There was a splintering of glass as Alexandru flung his vial to the floor. Dillon and Sade ducked as he turned on his heel and walked out. The lift whirred into action, and they glimpsed his thunderous expression as he passed on his way down to the fifth floor entrance hall.

'Alexandru is upset, Lily. We'll discuss the implications of the dhampir's blood in the full board meeting. Until then, keep the dhampir out of trouble,' Sade's father advised.

A voice cold with anger spoke out. 'I want to make it known now that I agree with Alexandru, Lily.'

'Celeste's father,' Sade hissed.

'I shall remove Celeste too, if necessary. What about *her* potential? Have you even considered her future?'

'Celeste is an extremely clever young vampire, Eric. No one is denying that, but you cannot deny the strength of Dillon's blood either. Let us wait for Professor Dukan to take more samples and allow the full board to make a decision.'

After Eric, looking as furious as Alexandru, left with Sade's parents, Madame Dupledge and the group of teachers continued talking. Dillon and Sade strained to hear. Mr Hunt's voice was unmistakable.

'Lily, you are skating on thin ice here. I'm not sure he's worth it.'

'I've faced far greater challenges than Alexandru Danesti in my tenure here, Alastair. You must focus on teaching Dillon as much as you can for the next few weeks.'

Mr Hunt's voice moved towards them. 'You think you can drag it out for weeks?'

'We need to get out of here,' Sade hissed, turning and streaking silently back down the stairs. Dillon followed. Back on their floor, Sade stopped outside her door. 'We need to start finding out about your blood as soon as we can. You'll need to give me some blood ASAP. Are you okay with that?'

'I wish I could talk to my da about all of this.' Dillon sighed. 'He always knows what's right. We've always been close but now I can't talk to him. Why's he not answering my calls?'

Sade reached out and touched his arm. 'He must have his reasons. Maybe he thinks it's best for you to immerse yourself in this world now. It must be hard for him too.'

'Yeah, maybe you're right. Thanks Sade.'

'You're welcome. Now go!'

Dillon had forgotten about the bloodlust homework. As he crept back into his room, the pungent smell coming from the coffin burnt his nostrils. Jeremiah still hadn't returned. Saliva began spilling out of the corners of his mouth. A glance at his watch told him he had an hour until darkness and two hours before lessons started. The desire to rip the coffin lid open was overwhelming. Clammy sweat broke out across his forehead.

Stumbling back out, he leant against the door, feeling weak and sick. He forced himself back up the corridor, intending to head for the Sanatorium. Maybe the day nurse might be able to give him something. As he neared the lifts, he caught the faint sound of music coming from Aron and Frederick's room. The music immediately went silent as he tapped on the door, and he heard faint scuffling noises. Frederick's face appeared two seconds later.

'Oh, it's you. Thank God for that. We thought it was Hunt or Dupledge.'

'What are you up to? I can't sleep.'

Fred's face broke into a knowing grin. 'Having trouble with your bloodlust?' he asked.

Dillon nodded.

'You've come to the right place then, my Dhamp!' he said, throwing the door open.

His side of the room was even more chaotic than before; clothes and empty blood bottles littered the floor, and discarded blood-flavoured vapes rested precariously around the edges of his coffin.

Ásta and Angelo lolled on Fred's desk wearing very little clothing, and Aron had passed out half-in and half-out of his extremely neat coffin. Both Ásta and Angelo's eyes were feline-like, their pupils scarily huge.

'Ah, it's my delicious Dhampir.' Angelo beckoned him in. 'Turn the music back on, Fred.'

Fred obliged, filling the room with a deep, insistent drum-and-bass beat.

Ásta jumped up. 'Dance with me, Dillon,' she purred.

'Um, actually, I was just heading up to the Sanatorium.'

'Not so quick, Dhampir,' Ásta growled, pulling him to her and beginning to grind against him to the music.

The music was hypnotic, and Dillon found himself moving with her as she gyrated her toned body up and down his.

Fred whistled. 'Go Dillon!'

After all the repressed emotion with Cora, he was embarrassed to feel the heat rising between them. Angelo watched from the desk and then suddenly jumped up. Holding Ásta firmly around the waist, he began to dance against her back. Ásta sighed with pleasure and rotated her hips, pressing into him. As Dillon, caught in a bizarre erotic threesome tried to draw away, Angelo pulled him closer. Suddenly, the scent of Dillon's heated blood grew too much. His eyes changed and as his fangs shot out, Dillon struggled to release himself. Ásta, caught in between them, twisted round and put her arms round Angelo's neck.

'Cool down, Angelo. You don't need it.'

Angelo's hold around Dillon's neck loosened a little.

Ásta's strong arms held him. 'Come on, Angelo. This is your chance. You don't want to get kicked out of here.'

Angelo struggled for a second or two and then slowly came back to himself. 'Oh god,' he moaned. 'I'm sorry, Dillon. It's just very hard for me with you.'

For the first time, Dillon had an inkling of what he was on about. 'I understand. It's driving me crazy.'

Ásta turned to him. 'How bad is it?'

'Like I'm struggling to think about anything else.'

Ásta's eyes gleamed. 'We can help, Dillon.'

'Shush, Ásta. We can't,' Frederick hissed. 'He's VE.'

'Maybe not for much longer,' Dillon muttered.

'What do you mean?'

'I just saw an entourage of parents. Bram's dad along with Celeste's and Sade's parents were just with Madame Dupledge. They've given her an ultimatum: them or me.'

'Then it's not a problem.' Ásta smirked. 'She won't risk losing any of them. Their parents pump money into this place.'

Frederick looked him in the eye. 'Can you be trusted, Dillon?'

'Yes, but I have no idea what you're talking about.'

'We can help you to feel better.'

Dillon's heart sank.

'We've drunk all the bottled blood, but I smuggled in something better – the real deal. I haven't got much but I've got a contact on the outside who can help me restock. He works at a health clinic in the Alps not far from here. It's going to cost though.'

'Woah . . .' Dillon backed away. 'Look, thanks for the offer, Frederick, but I haven't got any money – at all.'

'Don't worry about it, Dillon, I'll sub you for today,' Ásta insisted.

Dillon backed into the door. 'Thanks Ásta, but no. My da always said never take something you can't pay back.'

Frederick, Angelo and Ásta drew closer, 'Come on Dillon, don't be boring. It will make you feel amazing again.'

If he takes even a sip, I'll have influence over him for the rest of the year.

Dillon jumped. 'What?' he asked, staring at her.

Ásta looked at him as if he was crazy. Shite. He must be hearing thoughts again.

Ásta moved closer still. 'Come on, Dillon. Fred, pass me the blood.'

Frederick went to his cupboard and removed a blood bag from a chill box. The contents were bright red, and a large O printed in black stood out on the label. Ásta opened the small nozzle on the top and wafted it under Dillon's nose. Instantly, the insides of his nostrils burned, and a river of

176

saliva erupted into his mouth. He swallowed hard, trying not to inhale more of the blood scent.

This is going to be easy.

Dillon leaned closer. So what if Ásta had leverage over him. He was leaving anyway. God, it smelt amazing. He closed his eyes. Ásta squeezed the bag so that the blood oozed up the tube to the nozzle and placed it against his lips. Just as Dillon opened his mouth, he heard Madame Dupledge's voice: *Think of the higher purpose.*

With tremendous effort, he turned his head. 'Take it away. Seriously.'

His head buzzed as he felt her anger.

'Come on, Dillon. Don't be a pussy,' she growled.

'Leave him alone, Ásta. He doesn't want it.' Aron had woken and swung his legs over the side of the coffin.

'Stay out of it, Aron. We're helping him. Dillon has a bad case of bloodlust.'

'Yeah, but he said he doesn't want it.'

Dillon didn't dare look at Aron.

Ásta and Aron stared at each other. No one moved.

'Fine.' Ásta stepped back and, staring deep into Dillon's eyes, she sucked deeply from the bag. Almost instantaneously, her pupils reacted, growing even wider, so that her slanting cat eyes looked almost all black.

Dillon's stomach clenched and he fumbled for the door handle, 'Fred – don't get me wrong, I really appreciate the offer. But I just can't—'

Frederick grabbed his arm, squeezing more tightly that Dillon anticipated. 'Remember Dillon, a gift that is refused can have repercussions. You know nothing about this, *ja*?'

Dillon nodded. 'Yeah, yeah, of course.' He mimed zipping his lips. 'You can trust me on this. Honest. I know you were trying to help.'

He half-fell out of the room and clutched his stomach. Stumbling back to the lifts, he made his way back up to the roof. Dusk was falling and, sobbing with relief, he lay down on the cool glass and stared up at the moody sky, wondering if his father was awake, looking up at the same stars. His improved night vision brought even more detail to the stars – filigrees of galaxies, swirling and twisting. As he stared at the sky, he felt the tension in his neck and shoulders easing. He exhaled deeply, emptying his lungs and allowing the fresh mountain air to rush back in.

'I'm sorry. I didn't mean to intrude.'

He jumped at the sound of Cora's voice. He hadn't seen her huddled by an air vent.

Unable to move, he turned his head. 'Nah, I'm the one who's sorry.'

She inched over and lay down next to him. He felt her hand reach for his. The moment was so perfect, he ignored the little sparks shooting up his arm and let the thick, heavenly silence envelope them.

8

Golden Blood

Dillon woke to an inky-black sky. Cora was watching him. He didn't want to break the perfect moment. They lay together in silence, both aware that the wrong word would kill the moment.

'You don't have to help me, Dillon. I shouldn't have told you.'

'I want to help you find your brother but, honestly, Cora, I don't think I'll have VE privileges for much longer. Bram's family want rid of me.'

'You get why I have to be with Bram, don't you? How important this is to me?'

His heart twisted. 'Yes, I get it. It's family. I understand. Blood's thicker than water. I'm starting to understand just what that means now.'

Cora shifted next to him. 'Bram is competitive; he's going

to take every opportunity to put you down. You can see that right?'

Dillon's heart twisted again. After the sensory deprivation debacle, Bram knew that he liked Cora – and was bound to use it against him.

'I can handle it.' He reassured her, unsure if he could.

'I don't muck people around,' she suddenly blurted out. 'Bram's dad is a dick, but Bram is okay. He just doesn't dare show anyone that side.'

Each word was like a knife in the heart. 'I'm sure he has his hidden talents.'

'I just don't want you thinking I don't have principles. If I hated Bram, I would find another way.'

Dillon wished she would find another way. He didn't know what she needed from him. He just wanted to lie here and stare at the sky with her, not hear more about Bram's supposed nice side. He checked his watch. 'We should go.'

'You go first. We better not be seen together.'

He felt the anger rise again. 'Can we not be seen as friends? Is he that much of a control freak?'

Her own eyes flashed with anger. 'You said you could handle this. We can't be friends if you can't.'

He wasn't sure if he *could* handle it, but the thought of no contact with her at all was worse. He took a deep breath.

'Okay.'

As soon as Cora left, Dillon felt a stabbing pain attack his insides and groaned. The sensation was agony, like his guts were being turned inside out. Hunched over, cradling his stomach, he somehow made it to the sixth floor for the first Living Amongst Humans lesson. Jeremiah was with Bik, but he took one look at Dillon and was by his side, helping him stand, in an instant.

'You need blood.'

'I'm fine,' Dillon muttered.

'You don't look it.'

'I only have to wait until midnight. I'll be grand.'

Jeremiah looked sceptical but shrugged. 'If you say so. It's your funeral.'

Dillon was still crouched over the desk when Sade arrived, followed by the teacher and, as she sat down, she shot him a concerned look.

'Good evening, everyone. I hope your assignment from Madame Dupledge went well.' The new teacher spoke with a slight Indian accent. She was petite with long, trailing black hair, flared jeans, sandals and mischievous brown eyes enhanced with a strong flick of black eyeliner.

'I am Professor Sandhu, and I will be teaching you tips on how to live amongst humans. I was human and a musician until I was turned during the 1960s. What a decade that was!' She smiled round the class. 'I am also a professor of music and teach individual music lessons. Please talk to me at the end of the class if you would like to learn more about music here.'

She rested her gaze on Dillon. 'We are lucky to have an expert in all things human in our midst this year. What have you noticed most about our differences, Dillon, and what would be your biggest piece of advice to help us blend in?'

Dillon thought for a minute. 'Apart from not looking like you want to pounce on anyone with blood and hiding your fangs, I guess the biggest things would be your eyes – they don't look human when you think about blood and –' he paused – 'you're all too perfect-looking.'

Professor Sandhu chortled and the class grinned. She had a naturally infectious laugh. 'You're right.'

'We can't help being good-looking,' Ace pointed out, lifting his chiselled jaw and smoothing his floppy fringe back.

'No, but many vampires wear tinted glasses in the human world. They help disguise our eyes and deflect our beauty.'

'I refuse to wear glasses,' Celeste said.

'Celeste, vampires fall at your feet – what do you think humans are going to do?' Sade reminded her.

Celeste looked at her as if she was mad. 'So?'

'So, you don't want to draw attention to yourself?'

'Okay, okay everyone,' Professor Sandhu interrupted. 'Dillon's right. We stand out more than you realise. For obvious reasons, we have biological advantages that draw humans to us. It's better that we do everything we can to prevent that – no matter how good your control, it causes complications.'

She handed out mirrors. 'Take a minute to look at yourselves.'

Dillon was shocked to see how pale he looked. His normally vivid blue eyes were cloudy, and a sheen of sweat clung to his forehead.

'I look like shite!' he exclaimed.

'He's only just realised?' Bram drawled.

'Can you see how you might look to a human?' Professor Sandhu asked.

'Not really,' said Celeste admiring herself in the mirror.

'Yeah, sort of.' Jeremiah grinned, and the rest of the class chuckled.

'Jeremiah, you need a balaclava!' joked Bik.

'You don't have to do anything radical – just be aware of it,' Professor Sandhu advised, 'and play it down whenever you think you need to – particularly if you are with a group of vampires. I would advise having a pair of dark glasses with you at all times. You will have to become masters at observing human behaviour. They eat a lot, they take regular trips to the bathroom, they fidget and sit down far more than us and they move painfully slowly.'

'How dull.' Ásta sounded bored.

'We're not asking you to be best friends, just to remain unidentified. As you know, you have the ski trip coming up and you will have to mingle with them unnoticed. As they find us compulsively alluring, you must learn how to deflect their interest. Madame Dupledge is in charge of preventing you from losing control. I will teach you to stay under the radar.'

She groped about in a fringed suede bag and, opening a vial of blood, wafted it around the room. Instantly, the entire classes' fangs shot out, and she grinned.

'The biggest giveaway that we are vampires are our fangs.

Lift your top lip, please – let's have a look at them. Fangs are sort of like a vampire's fingerprint, each of us has individual quirks.' She peered at Angelo. 'What have you had done to yours, Angelo? I've never seen that before.'

'I had them engraved,' he said.

'Fascinating,' she said. 'Come and show the class.'

Angelo lifted his top lip. His fangs were intricately patterned with black ink. They looked incredible.

'I learnt how to do it, if you're interested.'

Professor Sandhu smiled. 'Thanks Angelo, they suit you but I'm not sure it would work for me.'

'Aron, what happened to yours?'

Aron pulled back his lips back and Dillon saw that his left fang was shorter than the right.

'It was damaged in a fight with Ásta when we were young,' he explained.

'It's very rare for a vampire tooth to be damaged for life,' Professor Sandhu exclaimed.

'Yeah, you don't know Ásta,' Aron said, with a rueful, lopsided smile.

She peered around the rest of the class. 'Jeremiah, those are beautiful!'

Jeremiah grinned, revealing tiny golden filigree crests plated onto his fangs. 'My father had them done for me when I turned eighteen. I'm proud of him and honoured to display our family crest. They're made from the gold from our family mines.'

'Of course, Jeremiah. I guess the human equivalent is a signet ring.'

'Anyone else?'

Celeste put up her hand and revealed a tiny, flashing diamond on her left fang. Dillon wasn't surprised; it matched her ice-cold beauty.

'Beautiful!' Professor Sandhu exclaimed. 'Fang art has really come on since my day.'

'I can set you up with someone who can do it for you,' Frederick offered.

'Thank you, Frederick, but as I said to Angelo, it wouldn't suit an old vampire like me.'

Dillon glanced at her incredulously, she didn't look a day over twenty-five. He made a mental note to ask Jeremiah or Sade how the vampire ageing thing worked.

'Works of art they may be, it is important that you keep your fangs retracted in human environments. Your ability to stop them popping out will improve as you age but I do have a trick up my sleeve if you are really struggling.' Rifling in her bag once again, she produced a small, crescent-shaped, clear gum shield. 'Another piece of armour. A specially enforced plastic guard that will stop your fangs descending.' She snapped it over her teeth. 'It just looks like an invisible human brace.'

'*¡Qué Alivio!* Thank goodness,' Angelo sighed dramatically.

'I'll arrange for each of you to be fitted for one before the ski trip,' she promised him.

Dillon was starting to lose it, and Sade raised her hand. 'Professor Sandhu, I think Dillon needs to be excused,' she said.

Professor Sandhu walked over to Dillon's desk and felt his forehead. 'He's as cold as ice.'

'No, I'm grand,' Dillon slurred, checking his watch. His vision was doing strange things but eventually he made out: 11.40 p.m.

'I can wait twenty minutes, seriously. No bother.' He smiled at her, and then slowly slid off his chair to the ground.

The last thing he heard was Professor Sandhu saying, 'Jeremiah, can you take him to Dr Mey . . .'

Dr Meyer took one look at him and tutted.

'You shouldn't have waited so long, Dillon. You need regular small amounts of blood at the start.'

Dillon didn't have the wherewithal to argue that he didn't know the first thing about drinking blood.

'I'll speak to Madame Dupledge. Go up to the blood room now. It's only a bit before midnight. I'll let Professor Dukan know you are coming up early.'

The gleaming-white blood room had been transformed. Dark-red blood bags hung from steel racks that were grouped into blood type. Professor Dukan, whose spare frame and long legs were encased in an ancient tweed suit, clutched a scanner in one hand and a touch pad in the other.

'It's not midnight,' he called over.

'Dillon isn't feeling well. He needs something now. Dr Meyer cleared it,' Jeremiah explained.

'Ah, Dillon Halloran.' Professor Dukan looked at him with interest. 'Amazing blood, we're still identifying it. We're running more tests to decide the blood type that will suit you best but for the moment I obtained some Golden Blood for you. It has no antigens and so shouldn't react with your blood. It's almost impossible to get hold of – there's only two donors willing to give it to us – so don't waste it. One unit should be more than enough for the moment. I'll just go and remove it from the secure fridge – we have to keep it locked away.'

After swiping a card over the door lock and peering into a facial-recognition camera, he disappeared into the hi-tech storage facility behind.

Something strange happened to Dillon's peripheral vision. It was like he was peering through a tunnel and his throat felt like parched desert. Although he was ice cold, sweat began running off his forehead.

'Jesus,' Jeremiah swore. 'How long is he going to take?'

Professor Dukan finally emerged looking even more eccentric in a surgical head covering that looked like a blue shower cap and rubber gloves. After scanning the barcode and logging it into his touch pad, he reverently passed the bag with the precious blood to Dillon.

'Whatever you do, don't drop it.'

Dillon's stomach clenched in agony at the mere sight of it, and it was all he could do to stop himself grabbing it. Students from the other peaks, eager to witness any newbies losing control at the first blood drink, had started to trickle in from their lodges. Seeing Dillon's glazed eyes and Professor Dukan's concern, several of them began to crowd round him expectantly. Jeremiah stretched his long arms out.

'Give him some space please.'

Professor Dukan opened the nozzle at the top of the bag and slightly averted his nose. 'Go ahead,' he encouraged. 'But take it easy, do not gulp it down.'

As Dillon lifted the bag, he caught the smell of the blood for the first time and his senses went crazy, it was simply the most delectable thing he had smelt in his entire life. His fangs shot out instantly. The older vampire students leaned in as they saw the expression on his face. Several caught scent of it themselves and there was an almost comical wave of nostrils flaring and eyes darkening.

'What the hell's he drinking?' someone whispered.

Aware that Professor Dukan was watching him closely, Dillon forced himself to take a small sip. As the blood slid to the back of his throat, his eyes shut in ecstasy. The taste was pure liquid gold, different to the power of his own blood or the intoxicating quality of Madame Dupledge's. Vampire blood was like strong whiskey with after-effects – human blood was more like caviar – simply delicious. He began to sip faster, allowing the blood to slip down his throat like nectar. Almost instantaneously, he felt it hit his system and as a warm flush sped through his arteries, it soothed the stomach cramps and eased his muscle aches.

The throng of vampires around him increased and there was a commotion as Angelo, Ásta and Frederick pushed through. Dillon's eyes shot open just as Frederick's jaw dropped,

'He's drinking Golden Blood,' he hissed to Angelo and Ásta. 'That's about ten thousand euros a sip.'

Unable to control himself any longer, Dillon drained the bag in two last gulps and sighed with pleasure. The transformation was incredible. From feeling like death, he now felt like he'd never been more vibrantly alive. Colours were vivid again and everything around him seemed to glow with an unseen energy. He was reminded of Dr Meyer's hybrid car analogy – he'd gone from a rusty old banger to a Formula 1 car in a matter of seconds.

'I want some of that,' a Peak Three vampire joked.

'I had no idea he was so good-looking – for a dhampir,' another Peak Two vampire mouthed to her friend.

Professor Dukan's bright eyes scrutinised him. 'Seems like that did the job?'

'Fuck yes,' Dillon growled, his voice unusually low and husky. Immediately he clapped a hand over his mouth. 'I'm sorry, sir.'

Frederick and Angelo grinned.

Professor Dukan tried to look stern and failed, such was his excitement. 'I'll put that down to the effect of Golden Blood, Dillon – just this once.' Turning to the rest of the vampires, he shouted, 'Show's over. Can everyone see me for your blood type so I can scan your blood bag.'

Everyone milled around Professor Dukan, and Dillon caught several angry mutters: 'It's not fair. Why do we have the bog-standard crap and he gets the best. He's a dhampir, for Christ's sake.'

Sade rushed up. Her eyes widened when she saw Dillon. 'What happened?' she asked.

'Professor Dukan gave him Golden Blood,' Jeremiah replied.

Sade's eyebrows almost hit her hairline. 'Wow. The real thing?'

'Yup. Try standing next to him when he's drinking it.' Jeremiah grimaced.

Dillon looked at him in surprise. He'd shown no obvious signs of discomfort but then again, he hadn't been in a state to notice.

Jeremiah patted him on the back. 'Sorry mate. It's just that Golden Blood is the stuff of vampire fantasies. I never thought they'd hand it out here. You must have some shit-hot rare blood type.'

'It would make sense,' Sade mused. 'We've all found it difficult to be around him at times.'

'What? Are you serious?' Dillon blurted out, looking at her in disbelief. 'Even you two?'

'Even us.' Jeremiah grinned. 'Why do you think I keep escaping to Bik's room.'

Bik had arrived unnoticed and was standing behind Jeremiah. 'Thanks Jeremiah,' she said crisply.

Jeremiah swung round, and in one smooth movement lifted her up and kissed her. 'And because of your intelligent company, of course.'

'Put me down, Jeremiah. You keep lifting me up. I'm not a doll!' she protested.

Dillon felt the prickle of Bram's hostile glare before he saw it. He and Cora were queuing for their blood bags on the other side of the room. Dillon noted that he was in the bog-standard O queue and smiled sweetly at him. Bram scowled back and looked away.

The mood was exuberant by the time the first flying class started. Dillon was beginning to understand that rollercoaster highs and lows were part of teenage vampire life. They all suffered from massive 'hanger' issues for sure. He wondered how much practice it took to become as controlled as Madame Dupledge or Mahina, the Peak Three VE. He'd noticed her calmly savouring her blood as he'd left the blood room.

Even Mr Hunt seemed less sarcastic than usual, he must have enjoyed a midnight tipple too. 'I hear that something special happened in the blood room tonight. I can't remember the last time we gave anyone Golden Blood. I hope you realise how lucky you are, Dillon? You've probably got around a hundred thousand euros of the most exquisite blood in the world in your system right now.'

'Yes, sir. I have been made aware of that.'

'Well, make sure you don't take it for granted.'

'It feels out of this world, Mr Hunt.' Dillon beamed, still feeling the bliss of the Golden Blood. 'I'd never take it for granted.'

Mr Hunt glanced at him suspiciously, unsure if he was being sarcastic or not.

'Right, let's get on with flying. Those of you who are already flying but need to work towards your flying certificate, stay with me in the horizontal tunnel. Everyone else, head over to the vertical wind tunnel. Our flying instructor Chiro will be guiding you through your flight techniques.'

Sade, Dillon, Angelo, Jeremiah, Frederick and Bik headed over to the glass space age vertical cylinder. Huge fans at the top were just visible through the special ceiling. The base looked like a hi-tech trampoline.

Chiro was small and bat-like with a slight stoop and reddish eyes. He greeted them in a skin-tight black suit that enhanced the flying rodent impression.

'Welcome,' he lisped with a strong Brazilian accent. 'My task today is to connect you to your innate ability to fly and, hopefully, if there's time, show you some tricks.'

He grinned, revealing a set of razor-sharp teeth. Imperceptibly, the group shifted back and Chiro's grin widened.

'Once you've mastered the basic body position and you develop control of your movements, you will practise in the horizontal tunnel to make sure you are flying as aerodynamically as possible. Then we move outside.'

He fiddled with the computer set-up to the side of the tunnel and a screen began recording windspeed, air pressure and forces. The huge fans at the top whirred into action and, once they had picked up speed, he dived through the entrance at the side. Instantly, his awkwardness on the ground disappeared as he performed graceful arcs and spun upside down in the air. As he hovered on his stomach, literally floating on air, he spun in graceful circles, changing direction with small movements of his hands or feet.

'If you bend your legs, you go down,' he rasped. 'Straighten your arms and legs at the same time, and you'll go up. It's the same when you're flying for real. This gives you the chance to feel what the air pressure feels like at high velocity. We can fly roughly between seventy-five to one hundred and fifty miles an hour. The faster you go the less control you have but you can make quicker moves.'

The monitor revealed that the windspeed had reached one hundred and fifty miles per hour.

'You must have equal pressure on the wind with your arms and legs. Keep your core tight, push your hips forward, chin up and relax.'

He floated gracefully to the top of the funnel and then pirouetted upside down to peer at them through the glass. His leering face was even more gruesome upside down.

'Who wants to go first?'

Angelo, face alight with excitement, stepped forward. Chiro flipped the right way up and used a remote-control device to lower the windspeed.

'Lean in Angelo, until you feel the air pressure. Dhampir, you follow him.'

Dillon started. 'Sorry? Me?'

'Yes, you're the dhampir, no?'

'My name is Dillon.'

'Yes, Dillon the Dhampir,' shouted Bram, who had been watching from across the room. 'Easy to remember.'

With a bony hand, Chiro guided Dillon in. 'Now, Dillon, lean into the air . . .'

Dillon followed Angelo and copied the way he leant into the air stream and appeared to float into the wind, perfectly balanced. As soon as the wind hit him, he plunged down headfirst, arms and legs flailing. Chiro grabbed him around the middle and rebalanced him.

'Come on, you should be good at this. Lift your chin, arch your back a bit.'

He glimpsed Jeremiah and Sade's grinning faces as he wobbled and fought for balance.

Chiro grew impatient. 'Feel the wind. Keep your body still. Press your elbows and knees into the wind equally.'

Dillon tried. His arms and his legs shot up as he seesawed up and down in the air. Angelo floated up and down the tube around him in perfect control, and Chiro gave him a thumbs up. Finally, in frustration, Chiro let go of Dillon. He instantly shot up to the top of the tube and down again, crashing into the side as he fell. Chiro pushed him back to the entrance.

'Enough for today.'

'Complete natural,' Jeremiah said, giving him a thumbs up.

'I'm not sure flying is your forte.' Sade smirked.

'Ha! So funny.'

Chiro called through the entrance and looked admiringly at Jeremiah. 'You with the muscles – you go next,' he called, upping the windspeed.

Jeremiah scowled at him. 'I'm a lot more than my physical appearance,' he growled, before leaning in and letting the force of the wind support him. With just a few wobbly adjustments he was off, zooming up and down, while Chiro followed him, grinning like a demented bat.

Sade was equally graceful, Chiro just made small adjustments to her feet and hands. Only Frederick was as aeronautically challenged as Dillon but he didn't seem to care, grinning happily as he crashed and tumbled time and time again.

Finally, Chiro stopped the fans and ducked out, looking strangely awkward back on the ground.

'Watch the others in the horizontal tunnel now. It will help you to see how they adjust their body configuration in order to fly forward faster or slower.'

They made their way over to the horizonal tunnel. This time huge fans, rather than sucking the air up, pushed it along the tunnel. Ace and Ásta were inside, and Dillon could see instantly that they were brilliant. Although the force of the wind whipped the hair off their foreheads, they hovered in perfect control, arms by their sides as Mr Hunt looked at the monitors and yelled out instructions.

'Lift your left knee a little, Ásta, and you'll be more aero-dynamic – it should add another 10mph to your top speed. Turning the speed down now.'

As the windspeed lessened, Ace and Ásta slowly pulled themselves upright, landing gently on the floor.

'Excellent, you two. You should stand a good chance of winning the outdoor Flight Trial in a couple of weeks.'

As Ásta and Ace high-fived, Mr Hunt noticed the newcomers. 'Dillon, let's get you in next.'

'To be honest, I need more practice, sir.'

'Don't be ridiculous. You're VE. All VEs are superb flyers.'

Dillon's heart sank. Why did he get the feeling Mr Hunt wanted to humiliate him?

Mr Hunt looked over the group. 'Cora, you're a strong flyer. You go in with him.'

'Chiro said Dillon's not ready,' Sade argued.

'He's just had Golden Blood. Anyone can fly on that. It's like high-performance jet fuel,' Mr Hunt snapped. 'Both of you in the tunnel.'

'But he crashed,' Sade tried again.

Mr Hunt ignored her and turned to Chiro. 'Chiro, tell him what to do.'

Chiro shrugged and leaned into the tunnel microphone. 'Dillon, concentrate. Close your eyes, feel the blood in your system, connect with your innate ability to fly.'

Dillon shut out the crowd of curious faces. Mr Hunt was right; he could still feel the blood surging through his body. As he and Cora took their positions, he heard the fans whir into life and wind began buffeting him.

'Don't overthink it Dillon, just start to feel a sense of weightlessness,' Chiro growled.

The wind was picking up speed, Dillon had to lean forward to avoid being pushed back. His feet began to slide along the floor and Cora reached for his hand to stop him being pushed further back. The electricity that shot up his arm whenever she touched him ignited something dormant inside him. He pitched forward and felt his feet leave the floor.

Like stage two of a rocket launch, the surge of excitement he felt at the thought he'd left the ground set off another explosion of energy and he found himself shooting towards the fans, dragging Cora with him.

He just caught Chiro's surprised face before Mr Hunt tapped the controls and whacked the windspeed up. Dillon saw it jump to 100 mph but they were still shooting towards the fans. Finally, somewhere around 120 mph, they stopped moving and hung suspended in the air. Cora managed to grin at him without losing her balance. Their clothes whipped close to their bodies and his eyes streamed as the wind slammed into them. The smallest movement pitched him to the side. If a leg or an arm lowered a fraction, the wind immediately dragged at it, threatening to spin him out of control. As he learnt to make his body more aerodynamic, they began moving forwards again, until the windspeed held them stationary again at 150 mph.

'Reducing windspeed,' Chiro shouted. 'Get ready to lower your feet.'

As soon as their feet touched the ground and the fans slowed to a stop, half the class burst into applause.

'Woah,' gasped Cora, dropping his hand and smoothing her wind-blown hair. 'That was good for a first flight.'

'Really? Glad you liked it!' Dillon grinned, absurdly delighted that he'd managed to impress her for once.

Bram came up and wrapped a possessive arm around her – making his 'stay away' message abundantly clear.

'Did you see that?' she asked him.

Once again, Dillon had to clench his fists to stop himself ripping Bram's arm off. As if he understood exactly what Dillon was thinking, Bram smirked and turned to him.

'Seems like it's easy with Golden Blood – you heard what Mr Hunt said. Let's see how well you do when we're outside, Dhampir. It's completely different.'

'Not bad, Dillon.' Mr Hunt's cold, black eyes appraised him and Bram. 'As Bram said – let's see what you can do outside in the Flight Trial.'

'Okay. Thank you, Sir.'

Jeremiah pumped his hand, and Sade, excited for him, gave him a spontaneous hug. As her voluptuous body pressed against his and her soft hair tickled his cheek, another sudden surge of energy confused him, and he stepped back. Instantly, her happy smile wavered, and he saw the hurt in her eyes.

'Um, I've got some reading to do.' She faltered. 'I'll see you later.'

As she walked off, his heart constricted.

'Sade . . . Wait . . .' he said as she began to walk away.

He tried to follow her, but Frederick dragged him away.

'What's the secret, Dillon? You've got to show me.'

'Hang on a minute, Fred,' he said, turning back towards her. But by the time he'd shaken him off, she was gone.

9

Blood Rivals

Over the next week, while the effects of the Golden Blood lasted, Dillon went to the flying tunnel to practise outside of class. Chiro, despite his creepy appearance, was surprisingly keen to offer advice and tips. After perfecting his ability to control his flight line, they worked on increasing his speed. Chiro took great delight in buzzing around him and rapping any bodypart that slipped a millimetre out of position. The problem was his take off. Without Cora, he struggled to access the sudden explosion of energy that he needed to power up his muscles.

Ace, Bram and Ásta arrived as he was leaving a particularly gruelling session with Chiro, utterly frustrated that he still hadn't cracked it.

'It's going to take more than a few wind tunnels to catch us, Dhampir,' Bram taunted.

'Just give it a rest, Bram,' Dillon snarled, pleased to see him flinch slightly in surprise. 'I'm not in the mood.'

'Yeah, give it a rest, Bram. All this fake machismo, it's so boring,' Ásta drawled.

Bram's eyes darkened and he glared at her. 'I'll leave you to your dhampir then, there's no accounting for taste,' he said, stalking back out of the gym.

Ásta shrugged and rolled her eyes. 'Do you want to practise with me and Ace, Dillon?' she asked.

'I've just finished, but thanks, Ásta.' He was under no illusions. He knew she was fiercely competitive and just wanted to keep an eye on him.

As he headed back to his room to change, Frederick intercepted him once again.

'Dillon, come with me,' he hissed, his eyes sparkling with excitement. 'I've got something to show you.'

'No blood, Frederick.' Dillon warned.

'No, no, better than that.'

Frederick dragged him back to his room.

'Look,' he said proudly, pointing at his laptop screen.

He was taking illegal bets, offering early prices on the upcoming Ice Challenge. The screen listed the odds. Dillon was at 5-1. Bram was 3-1, behind Ace. Aron and Ásta were both at 2-1. Frederick had put himself at 50-1.

'You never know,' he said, grinning when Dillon raised his eyebrow. 'Want to place a bet? The odds might change, a couple of vampires from Peaks One and Two are backing you.'

'I would, but I'm sorry. Like I said, I don't have any money.'

'I'm sure you can sort it, Dillon. Sade's got bundles – she'll lend you some. I'll keep the odds good for you.'

He was so exuberant that Dillon found himself agreeing.

'I'll try,' he said, starting to back out of the room.

'Are you sure you don't need any blood?' Fred asked hopefully.

'Nah, I'm good, thanks. Professor Dukan said I should stick to Golden for now.'

As he left Frederick's room, despite it being the middle of the night, he pulled out his phone and tried the home number again. To his surprise, his father answered on the first ring.

'Da?' he gasped.

'Dillon, how's about ye?'

At the sound of his father's warm Irish voice, a large lump formed in his throat. He wanted to blurt out everything that had happened since they'd parted – the blood, the flying, his role as Vampire Elect, but he couldn't seem to say a word.

'Dillon? Are you there?'

The more his da spoke, the more Dillon felt his longing for home rise – winter nights by the fireside with his da telling long, rambling stories, the early walks through their land with the mists still rising around their ankles, swimming in the sharp, cold water of the Atlantic . . .

'Dillon? Can you hear me?'

His father's voice cut through his reverie. Dillon breathed deep.

'Where have you been, Da? I got a phone and I've been trying to ring you every day.'

'Sorry, Dill. I got held up on the way back. Had to meet someone.'

Dillon remembered the strange dream.

'Did you meet my mother? I dreamt I saw you with a woman?'

He tried to ignore the sense of abandonment he felt – his da had been part of every day of his life prior to VAMPS.

There was a pause.

'I can't lie to you, Dillon. Yes, I did, but look, the phone isn't secure, I'll explain more when I see you—'

'Madame Dupledge said *you* want me here,' Dillon interrupted. 'It wasn't just a promise to my mother.'

There was another small silence and his father spoke slowly, like he was choosing his words carefully.

'They think there might be something special about you, Dill. For your mother's sake, I can't hold you back and it's safer for the moment.'

'Did she say anything about me being a danger to you now? I'm not allowed to stop drinking . . .' He paused, embarrassed to talk about it in front of his dad. ' . . . Blood. I mean. Drinking blood.'

There was another silence.

'I know about the blood, Dillon. All about it. I know what it meant to your mother. And I know it will mean the same to you, given time.'

'Why didn't you prepare me, Da?'

His father chuckled. 'Funnily enough, I've never been to vampire school.'

'Yes, and neither had I when I got here,' Dillon countered, knowing his father's way of turning a serious conversation into something lighter and less real. 'Why didn't you tell me more about it all? About Ma? About my weird blood?'

He heard his father sigh. 'I didn't know anything about your blood, Dill. Just try to trust that I love you and your ma loves you.'

'I've always trusted you, Da,' Dillon said. 'Always. But, in here, on my own, not being able to contact you. It's been hard.'

'I promise you'll understand – soon.' Dillon could hear something muffled on the other end of the phone, then his father came back on. 'Look, Dill. I've got to go – something's up.'

'Seriously? You've got to go? Da, I need to . . .'

'I love you, Dill. Don't lose heart.'

The line went dead. Heart thumping, Dillon stared at the phone. He immediately hit 'redial' but this time – as with all his previous attempts, the screen instantly returned 'call failed'. Incredulously, he stared at the phone, unsettled by how strangely his father was behaving.

'Hey.'

He started. He had been so absorbed; he hadn't heard Sade approaching.

'Are you okay?' she asked, fiddling with the zip on her bag. He hadn't seen much of her since the first flying lesson.

'I've just had this really strange conversation with my father.'

'All my conversations with my parents are strange.' Sade shrugged.

'Yeah, but normally we're so close, you know? He was saying that the phone wasn't secure or something. I used to be able to tell him everything. Now it feels like he doesn't want to know.'

'Maybe he's missing you?'

'Nah, it's more than that.'

'Like I said, we need that sample of your blood so we can find out if it matches anything. Then you'll have your answer.'

'How?'

She stopped fiddling with her zip and looked up at him again, with a small smile. 'By breaking into Professor Dukan's office.'

'You're joking, right?'

She smiled sweetly at him and began walking off.

'I'll wake you at midday.'

'Sade—' There was just one more thing he had to bring up. 'About the other night . . .'

'What?'

'At the end of the flying lesson . . .'

She raised her hand to interrupt him. 'Forget it, Dillon. It's fine,' she said, unable to look him in the eye. 'Desire and Control starts in five minutes.'

★

Madame Dupledge stood behind her desk in a beautifully tailored pencil-skirt and fitted jacket and high, spiky heels. She looked up from her laptop as Dillon shot in.

'Goodness, Dillon. What's the rush?' she asked as he sat down next to Angelo.

Frederick coughed and muttered 'Golden Blood' under his breath, and the rest of the class grinned.

'If you have something to say Frederick, please say it. I hope you all understand why Dillon has been given Golden Blood?' Madame Dupledge asked.

'Because he's VE?' Fred said deadpan, smirking at Dillon.

'I am not going to dignify that with a reply, Frederick – but let me tell you all that Professor Dukan is giving Dillon Golden Blood as a precaution while he runs some tests on his blood. His vampire side is still developing and so is his blood. It has nothing to do with special treatment or favouritism. Now let's move on. I have the results of your blood homework here and well done everyone, all except one of you managed to abstain.'

Surreptitiously, the class looked round at each other, wondering who had lost control. Dillon sensed Angelo stiffen but his heart thudded when Jeremiah spoke up.

'I'm sorry, Madame Dupledge. I won't lose control again.'

Dillon remembered that he'd spent the rest of the blood homework night on the roof with Cora. By the time he'd got back to his room, the blood had gone. Jeremiah must have come back and had a sip or two before Elias collected the samples. A second later, he realised what a good friend

Jeremiah was. He could easily have taken it from his beaker and blamed him. None of them would have believed a newly converted dhampir.

'Thank you, Jeremiah. As your behaviour has been exemplary since you have been here, you will not receive a note on your record for this. However, to make sure that you have gained control of your bloodlust, you will have to repeat the test in a month or two. In the meantime, I suggest you speak to Professor Dukan to make sure you are receiving the correct amount of sustenance.'

'Professor Dukan has worked it all out perfectly, Madame Dupledge. I have had no problems with control since the blood feeding.'

'That is good to hear, Jeremiah.' She looked around the rest of the class. 'How did everyone else find it? Did anyone find it hard?'

Fred and Ásta kept their eyes glued to their desks, and Bram suppressed a bored sigh.

'I found distraction was the best technique,' Celeste offered, shooting a coy look at Ace, who winked back.

'Yeah,' Angelo agreed and then shut up as Ásta scowled at him.

'Well, I must say I am pleased that you were able to resist at least one form of temptation, Angelo. How are you coping with the lure you feel for Dillon?'

To Dillon's surprise, Angelo leant close to him and took a deep sniff.

'Still tempting, but it is less potent since he started taking blood,' he declared, sitting back, totally relaxed.

Despite her high heels, Madame Dupledge glided silently over to their desk and leant down so that they were both enveloped by her sweet, powerful scent. 'Angelo, you understand that using props in the desires class is not only extremely dangerous for you, but for the whole class and could put the ski trip at risk? You will not be allowed to attend if we cannot trust you. In this class we must have complete faith in each other. I suggest you remove those nose plugs immediately.'

Dillon gasped and clutched the desk as a tidal wave of humiliation and inadequacy washed over him. It took him a second to realise that, somehow, he was feeling what Angelo was.

Angelo hid his feelings well and smirked defiantly at her as he pulled a tiny, almost invisible golden wire under the central part of his nostrils and carefully removed two cylindrical nose plugs. Maybe Madame Dupledge had sensed his feelings too as she ignored the smirk and spoke more gently.

'Props to help you live amongst humans have their place, but they are for your lessons with Professor Sandhu; my lessons are about learning mind control over our primitive desires. You have a passionate nature and strong desires, so you will have to work harder, but I am confident you can do it.'

Angelo's smirk faltered and Dillon felt his shock that someone like Madame Dupledge believed in him turn into a rush of determination and hope.

'Thank you,' he muttered. 'Jesus, Dillon,' he whispered, after she moved away to teach the rest of the lesson. 'I thought I'd had it there.'

'Like she said, she thinks you can do it – I do too.'

He had meant it as a platitude but, as he said it, he realised that he meant it.

Angelo's caramel eyes gleamed at him. 'I can't promise that I'll do it, Dillon, but I'm going to try.'

At the end of the class, Madame Dupledge asked Bram and Dillon to wait for her outside her office while she had another word with Angelo and as he emerged into the sixth-floor atrium, Bram made sure Dillon was in sight before giving Cora a lingering goodbye kiss. Once again, Dillon was struck by how perfect they looked together and a gut-wrenching stab of jealousy almost floored him. Cora seemed a little embarrassed for a vampire and tried to smile at him as she left but he turned away.

'You may have VE, Dhampir,' Bram mocked, as they made their way to the ninth floor. 'But I've got Cora.'

Dillon was unable to keep a neutral expression and Bram smirked at him.

'Let me know when you're ready to swap.'

Like it had in the gym, a red mist descended in front of his eyes and before he knew what he was doing, he punched Bram, sending him flying across the atrium, and sprang on top of him.

'Don't you dare speak about her like that,' he hissed.

'It's got nothing to do with you,' Bram hissed back, shoving the heel of his hand hard into Dillon's chest.

'Mr Halloran!'

Mr Hunt dragged him off.

'Save this sort of behaviour for combat lessons, Dillon. This is not the way a VE behaves.'

'Certainly not.'

Dillon winced at the steely sound of Madame Dupledge's voice. He hadn't heard her arrive.

'What were you thinking, Dillon?' she asked, eyes blazing.

'It was my fault. Something I said provoked him,' Bram spoke up and his fake apologetic tone in front of Madame Dupledge made Dillon want to punch him again.

'I apologise too,' he ground out between gritted teeth, avoiding Bram's eyes.

'You'd better come into my office,' she said, flipping the switch for the automatic blinds as she walked in.

Trapped inside her office, her sweet, intoxicating scent wrapped around him, confusing his thoughts.

'What is going on here?' she said, scrutinising them. 'I cannot have a warring Vampire Elect and Deputy Vampire Elect. Bram, you promised that you would put your disappointment aside and show me that you are ready to become a great leader.'

'I have Madame Dupledge, but with respect, it is unsettling for all of us – not knowing if Dillon will be VE for much longer.'

Dillon winced as he saw her eyes blaze.

'What a waste of your time and energy, Bram. Let me assure you again that, while I am head of this school, Dillon will be VE.'

Bram shifted his feet, looking slightly less sure of himself. 'But my father—'

'What is happening between your father and myself is not your concern. You need to be focusing on leading your year with Dillon and proving to me that the Blood Tasting was right.'

Bram was clearly not used to being put in his place and, for a second, he looked like he'd just swallowed a lemon. Dillon grinned to himself until she directed her attention to him.

'Dillon, I understand that taking blood is still new for you and it might have had a —' she paused — '*rousing* effect on you, but you must gain control of yourself. It is unseemly for a Vampire Elect to brawl in the corridor like that.'

He nodded. 'I'll try. I'm sorry.'

'I presume your disagreement was over Cora?'

Once again, her eyes flicked between the two of them. Neither vampire spoke.

'For what it's worth, I think Cora is more than able to fight her own battles and you should both respect that.'

Bram's face remained impassive, but Dillon shifted uncomfortably and stared at his trainers.

'Right. Let's move on. One of the most important vampires in the world will shortly be visiting us, and you will act as the representatives for your year. I will expect you, along with the other deputies and elects, to greet her and, wherever possible, display your leadership qualities to her.'

'Who is it?' Bram asked.

'Countess Fassano, previously known as Bibiana Fassano.'

Bram's eyes widened.

'We are extremely privileged that she has managed to find the time in her schedule. Dillon, she leads diplomatic relations between our world and the human world. The name of every leader in the modern world is on her speed dial and she has ultimate responsibility for our vampire secret service.'

Dillon saw Bram's fangs nearly shoot out at the thought of sucking up to her. Dillon's first thought was what the hell was an eighteen-year-old dhampir from the wilds of Ireland going to say to the vampire equivalent of Hillary Clinton.

'She is also one of my oldest friends.'

Wonderful – even more pressure. There was no way he could muck this up.

'She will be watching the Ice Challenge as well as teaching a lesson on mind control techniques and international diplomacy. It is an opportunity for her to get to know you better – she is always on the lookout for new recruits. We will work out the finer details over the next few weeks. Bram, I know your family already know her, but both of you should do as much research about her as you can – she doesn't suffer fools.'

As they turned to leave, she called him back. 'Dillon, could I have a quick word?'

Bram scowled at him and left silently, leaving Dillon to

face Madame Dupledge on his own. With nothing to distract him from her creamy throat, once again, he found it hard to block out the memories of his first blood drinking. Paranoid that she would know what he was thinking, he forced himself to recall the names of the world's longest rivers. *Nile, Amazon, Yangtze* . . .

There was a pause and then, as if realising what he was doing, she smiled. 'How are you doing, Dillon?'

'I'm better since I had blood, thanks.'

'Good. Professor Dukan is still running tests and until he has more information, he will keep you on Golden Blood.'

'Isn't Golden Blood very expensive?'

'It is, but we have a duty to keep you healthy while you are here. Professor Dukan thinks there is a possibility that your system is developing slightly differently to pure vampires and it could prove dangerous if you are given blood that reacts with yours. We just don't know yet.'

'Okay.' He nodded. 'Surely, I can't stay on it forever?'

'Like I said, let's wait and see how your system develops. Professor Dukan thinks that your blood may become so powerful that you might be able to exist on hardly any human blood at all.'

Dillon stared at her, hardly daring to hope. If that happened, it would mean he wouldn't be a danger to his da. Abruptly, Madame Dupledge changed subject.

'Try to understand Bram, Dillon. He has been told he would be VE since he was small. It was a great shock to him not to be chosen and he is under a lot of pressure from his father. He will be a help to you once he grows accustomed to it. Just try not to antagonise him further. It is obvious that you are drawn to Cora, and I can see why, but try not to rock the boat any further.'

Dillon felt his face flush – clearly, it was *that* obvious.

'I understand your frustration – just don't do anything stupid is all I'm saying.'

She turned to the slim computer screen at her side.

'Now, if you will excuse me, I need to prepare for the governors.'

'Of course,' he muttered.

'Try to enjoy Countess Fassano's visit, Dillon. She is intimidating but she is also extremely insightful and will be able to offer you some guidance,' she said as he was halfway out the door.

He turned and frowned, unable to see how such an important vampire would have time for him. 'Why me?'

Madame Dupledge looked up from the screen and paused for a second. 'It is her job. You could be an asset to her.'

Cora was waiting for him outside his room, twisting one of the piercings in her ear.

'I heard that things got heated between you and Bram. Are you okay?' she asked as he approached.

Dillon glowered; it was impossible to get away with anything in this place.

'He said something I didn't like, something disrespectful, so I threw a punch at him. Mr Hunt broke it up, no big deal.'

Her eyes widened. 'Jesus, Dillon. What did he say to rile you up so much?'

He hesitated, longing to drop Bram in it, but he didn't want to hurt her or reveal how strongly he felt about her.

'The usual dhampir – I should have been VE rubbish.'

She looked relieved. 'I thought it might have been about me. He'll get over the dhampir thing. It's just the way he's been brought up.'

'I can't wait,' he said sarcastically.

Cora grinned. 'I'd better find him. I just wanted to check you're okay.'

He shrugged. 'Yeah, I'm fine.'

She tilted her head to one side appraising him. 'You're changing, Dillon. I'll catch you later.'

'What the hell does that mean?' he asked out loud as she disappeared down the corridor.

Jeremiah opened the door. 'What?' he asked.

Dillon pushed past him and opened his coffin. 'One guess,' he said, stripping his clothes off.

Jeremiah raised his eyebrows at him. 'Cora? Bram?'

Despite himself, Dillon smirked at him as he climbed in. 'I popped Bram one on the nose.'

'I guess he deserved it,' Jeremiah said, grinning back.

'Yeah, and I probably won't get another chance; Madame Dupledge warned me not to antagonise him, even though *he's* the one who's got it in for *me*.'

Jeremiah whistled. 'You better stay away from Cora.'

'If only it was that easy,' he sighed and started as his coffin vibrated. He'd left his phone in a pocket at the side. Fumbling with it, he hoped it was from his da, but it was a DM from Sade: *I'll see you later . . .*

Sighing again, he closed his eyes. Right now, finding out about his mother wasn't at the top of his priority list.

10

Blood Thickens

He was grouchy and disorientated when Sade tapped on his coffin at midday.

'Do we have to do this now?' he said, sitting up and blushing as, even in the dim room, he saw Sade's eyes widen infinitesimally and remembered he was stark naked.

Looking surprisingly awkward, she averted her eyes and kept them locked on Jeremiah's coffin. 'Shush, you'll wake Jeremiah, and yes, we do have to do this now. Or at least as soon as you're dressed,' she whispered, backing out. 'I'll meet you outside.'

The sixth-floor atrium outside Professor Dukan's office was stark and empty.

'Is there CCTV up here?' Dillon whispered, looking round uneasily.

'Yup,' said Sade, jumping up and pointing out a minute camera in the opposite direction. 'But they don't pay close attention to it. Guess they think there's nothing a bunch of vampires can't deal with on the inside.'

She tried Professor Dukan's door. 'It's locked,' she said, and swore.

Dillon grinned at her. 'That's the first time I've heard language like that out of you!'

She ignored him. 'Do you know how to pick locks?'

'No. Of course not. This is the real world. Where I come from we never even lock our doors.'

'How very rural and charming, Dillon! Help me, then. I know a bit.'

She removed two pins from her hair and a mass of soft, tight curls cascaded to her shoulders. Dillon stared – long enough for Sade to notice.

'What's the problem?'

'Er, nothing. I've just never seen you with your hair down before. It looks . . . nice,' he ended tamely.

'Oh.' She blinked and turned awkwardly to the door. 'I'd better get on with this.'

She opened one of the pins into a long piece of wire and made a loop at end. She bent the other one into a right angle. Dillon watched as she inserted the right-angled pin into the lock and turned it one way and then the other. Satisfied, she used her other hand to slide the longer pin in and jiggled it around. Dillon heard a small click.

'First one is the hardest,' she grunted, 'the others should be easy.'

A bit more jiggling and clicks and she turned the bottom pin all the way.

'Turn the handle!' she said to Dillon as she held the pins in place in the lock.

The door swung open.

He turned to her, impressed. 'Fair play. How did you learn that?'

'I read about it once. I've never actually done it before.'

He narrowed his eyes. 'You read about it *once!*'

'Yeah, I'm good with that sort of stuff.' She shrugged.

Inside, Professor Dukan's office was as eccentric as he was. Two skeletons hung from stands in the corners of the room and a collection of vampire jaws, complete with fangs, crowded one of the shelves. A strange, metallic smell hovered faintly in the background. Loose stacks of papers covered with calculations and spidery, scrawled notes rested precariously on the desk next to an ultra-hi-tech computer. Books and more untidy stacks of scientific papers were packed onto shelves that lined an entire wall. A spare tweed jacket and a white lab coat hung from the back of the door. Even though the diamond-shaped window on the outside wall was tinted, he had shielded it with a Japanese-style screen.

Dillon peered more closely at the skeletons. One had a stone in its jaw, and he repressed a shiver as he saw the large holes in the sternum and femur bones of the other.

'They're medieval "vampire" skeletons,' Sade informed him. 'We disintegrate into ash if we die so they're probably human skeletons they believed to be vampires. The holes are from the stakes they used to pin the dead "vampire" to its grave. They believed it would prevent them from rising up in the night and feeding.'

Dillon swallowed, once again uncomfortable with the knowledge that he was now one of the reviled. 'What's the stone in the jaw for?' he asked.

'To stop the "vampire" from using its fangs.' Sade mused for a second, 'Of course, they could be dhampir skeletons. As far as I know, you don't turn to ash. We should ask Professor Dukan – he's probably analysed their DNA.'

'Oh, right.' Dillon absorbed that for a second.

'If you're interested in this stuff, you should take the Vampire History option,' she suggested as she darted across the room to a door at the back of the office. 'It's fascinating – especially what medieval people thought about us.'

'I probably should do,' he agreed. 'What's in there?'

'Professor Dukan's private lab area,' she said, opening the door. 'I help him with research in here.'

She revealed a windowless room, lined with cupboards and work tops. Trays of vials and machines linked to computers were arranged on the worktops. A faint humming sound came from a large stainless-steel fridge in the corner.

'What are those?' Dillon asked, pointing at the machines.

'Haematology analysers. They read the composition of blood: red and white cell counts and platelets, stuff like that. You'll find out more when we start blood composition in Blood Analysis lessons.'

She opened the fridge and peered inside. 'Damn, it's just full of reactants and chemicals, none of the blood samples.'

'There's a surprise,' Dillon said dryly.

Sade thought for a minute. 'Vampire blood doesn't degenerate like human blood so I can take a fresh sample and send it to my eldest sister in Zurich, if I can't find the answers myself.'

'What does she do?'

'She's a leading scientist in rare blood diseases. I told you, all my siblings are brilliant.'

'Of course.' Dillon might have guessed. 'How will we take a sample?'

She raked around in the cupboards and emerged with two sample vials.

'I can't find a scalpel. You'll have to use your fangs.'

Dillon grimaced. 'I'm not sure I can,' he admitted.

'Do you want me to do it?' she asked, glancing at him from behind her hair.

He shifted uncomfortably. 'Can you?'

'I should be okay. I have strong control. I won't swallow it.'

Dillon gulped. 'Okay. Are you sure?'

'Yeah, it's important right? The quicker we find out more about your blood and your mother the better.' She bent over his arm like she had for Madame Dupledge and glanced up at him. 'Do you mind not watching?' she asked.

'Oh, yeah, sure,' he mumbled, looking over his shoulder.

He felt her hair trail over his arm as she lowered her head

and gently turned his inner elbow towards her. As her soft lips pressed against his skin, he repressed a shiver. A second later, he gasped as her razor-sharp fangs sliced through the skin. For a second, she went still, and he thought he felt a faint sucking at the wound. Shocked, he turned to see her struggling to pull away.

'Sade!'

Rearing up so fast she almost hit him in the face, she grabbed a vial. 'Hold this,' she said, springing further away from him and completely hiding her face behind her hair as she searched in a drawer for the lids.

The blood flowed freely now, filling the vials in seconds. Still not looking at him, she took the full vials and placed the lids on the top, taking care to keep her nose averted. He looked at the small wound and licked it tentatively. Once again, he noticed the slight power surge on the tip of his tongue as it made contact with his blood. It tasted even better than it had done at the Blood Tasting when they voted for VE.

'Are you okay?' he asked.

'Yes. Sorry, Dillon. You know your blood is . . . enticing,' she blustered. 'And I can taste the Golden Blood in it so it was harder than I expected. I'm okay now.'

'Did you swallow any?'

She fiddled with the vials. 'Just a bit. But don't worry, it won't change anything. It's not like we're together.'

He wasn't sure what she meant. 'Did you taste anything different?'

'Yes, it was even stronger than before.'

'Shite. That's what Madame Dupledge said might happen.'

'Did she?' Sade pushed her hair back, eyes alight with interest. 'Maybe that's why you're here. If your blood turns out to be super powerful, the whole vampire world will be interested in you.'

'In what way?'

'You've seen the reaction to Golden Blood and that's just human.'

She had a point.

'We better get out of here,' she said, checking to see that she'd left everything as it was and, as they walked back into Professor Dukan's office, she tucked the vials inside her top. Dillon tried not to think about how she was hiding them, about the vials of his blood sitting right against her skin. He raised his eyebrows.

'Just in case we bump into someone on the way back,' she explained.

The building was still eerily quiet as they streaked back down the stairs. As they approached the coffin floors, Dillon wondered where Madame Dupledge's coffin was. They stopped outside Sade's door.

'Good luck – with my blood,' he said, noticing with surprise that her nostrils flared slightly at the mention of it.

Suddenly awkward again, she turned away and fumbled with the door. 'Yeah, see you later,' she said, slipping inside and shutting it in his face.

11

Blood Pressure

His early evening flying practice a week later wasn't going well. He was tired and covered in sweat. Chiro was pleased with his speed, but his take-off was still hit and miss.

'Come on Dillon,' Chiro growled. 'The Flight Trial is coming up fast. You've got to master this.'

'I know. My da would tell me to find a way, but I don't know how – it's just not happening today.'

Dillon raked his hand through his hair, sick with nerves. Leaving Chiro in the flight tunnel, he went straight to the roof. The pressure-cooker atmosphere of the school was increasingly driving him to the limits of his endurance. It was exhausting, and it never let up.

He messaged Cora as he made his way to the top of the building, *Meet me on the roof?*

He was practising his take-off again when she finally appeared.

'I didn't think you were coming,' he grunted.

'It took me a while to get away.' She shrugged. 'Don't get mad, but I think I know what the problem is,' she called out after the fifth botched attempt.

'What?' he snapped.

'You're too tense.'

He gave an ironic laugh. 'Doesn't take a genius to see that.'

'You should go with Ásta or Angelo. Burn off some frustration.'

'What?' He stared at her. 'Are you mad? They scare the hell out of me.'

Cora's lips twitched. 'I'm sure you can handle them.'

He drew closer and allowed himself the luxury of examining every detail of her face. The short, tousled hair had grown out a bit and softened her fine bone structure. The small gold nose ring that gleamed at the side of her nose every time the moonlight caught it. The thickly lashed aqua eyes, enhanced by coal-black eyeliner. It was like he was possessed.

'There's only one vampire I want,' he said softly.

Her smile faded as she held his gaze and they stared on and on at each other.

'You know I can't,' she whispered finally.

'How can I make myself good enough for you?'

Finally tearing her eyes from his, she looked across the vast ice lake. A tiny muscle tensed in her jaw.

'Don't say that, Dillon. Maybe *I'm* not good enough for

you,' she said in a low voice. 'Anyway, you know, it's not about that.'

He shook his head. 'If I do find out about your brother, will you give me a chance?'

She sighed. 'It's not a contest.'

'But would you?'

'Okay, okay,' she raised her hands in defeat.

He tipped his head back and whooped into the sky.

'I'm meeting Countess Fassano, head of the Vampire Secret Service and everything else, it seems.'

'Are you really?' she asked, her eyes suddenly alight with hope.

'We all are, but I'll find out for you, I promise,' he said, reaching for her hands.

As the instant crackle between them ripped through his body, he felt the energy flood his muscles. He let go and, focusing for a second, he willed his feet off the glass roof.

Cora whooped as he shot upwards.

'Do it again without me,' she shouted.

'The CCTV cameras,' he reminded her, landing again.

'Just lift up a couple of metres, they're probably focused outwards.'

He closed his eyes and focused his mind again. Deep inside himself, he felt the strength of the blood running in his veins and the stored energy in his muscles. He visualised the spark that shot through his body whenever he and Cora touched and he kept his mind on it until it flared, electrifying his muscles as it sped like lightning through his nervous system. Like a rocket, he felt himself lift off and his eyes shot open.

'That's it, Dillon!' Cora crowed. 'Do it again.'

He tried another two times, each time imagining the spark he felt with Cora.

'Jaysus, that's it,' he panted as he landed after the third take off. 'Feckin' flying!'

He paused, trying to control his exuberance.

'I will speak to Countess Fassano for you and find out about your brother and I'll make everything better for us – I mean, for you.'

She placed her finger on his lips and he held his breath.

'Don't make any promises.'

'If you don't mind me asking . . . Is Bram helping you?' he asked hoarsely, his lips tingling with heat where her finger had been.

'I've told him now and he's trying, but his father is difficult; he has to be careful not to arouse his suspicions.' Her voice shook. 'It's taking so long – I just want to know if he's alive.'

Deep in thought about Cora's brother, Dillon almost crashed into Professor Dukan on his way down from the roof.

'Ah, Dillon, you're just the person I wanted to see. Can you come up to my office?' Professor Dukan asked.

Even with vampire speed, Dillon hurried to keep up with Professor Dukan's long legs. He whipped though corridors and flew upstairs, twitching with nervous energy. Inside his office, he paced the room at a slower but still vampiric speed, making the papers on his desk flutter each time he passed by.

'I'm having trouble analysing your blood, Dillon,' he confessed. 'This has never happened before. I'm going to have to use another more sophisticated lab.'

'What are you looking for? Is there something wrong with my blood?'

'A whole new blood type, Dillon. It could be an incredibly exciting discovery.'

He showed Dillon the screen of the tablet device he held. The screen was full of indecipherable medical graphs and information.

'And incredibly dangerous for you, too, of course.'

'Hold on now – incredibly dangerous for *me*? How?' asked Dillon.

'A whole new blood type in a world where the Apex Predators live on blood? Come on, Dillon, show some intelligence, please. Vampires and humans alike may want to get their hands on it. Madame Dupledge has been called away, but we need to discuss the implications.' He paced more rapidly. 'You might need more protection while you are here.'

'What do you mean *more* protection?' asked Dillon.

'I don't think you understand. I explained how rare and precious Golden Blood is, yes? Your blood could be even rarer than that, like the rhodium of blood types.'

'Rhodium?'

'The rarest, most expensive precious metal in the world. It's used in catalytic converters, but that's beside the point.'

'I get that it's rare, but so what?'

'Dillon, you have seen the reaction of your peers – your blood is alluring to other vampires and it's not just because of your human side. We think it may have powerful properties. The problem is that its composition is still changing.'

'Because of the Golden Blood?'

'Maybe, perhaps more likely is because of the other bloods you have ingested and because your vampire side is waking up.' He stared at him. 'For the moment it will be best if you keep this to yourself, Dillon. Don't even tell your closest friends.'

Dillon looked away guiltily. 'Um, okay. Why?'

'At this stage, the fewer the people who know, the better. These things have a habit of getting out.'

'What did Professor Dukan want?' Sade asked him the minute he found her in her room. 'I saw him rush you into his office.'

'I'm not supposed to tell you,' he teased. 'Seriously, Professor Dukan said so.'

Seeing her face fall, he gave in.

'Like you thought, he thinks I may have this rare blood – he still can't identify it. He said I might need extra protection but that seems a bit dramatic.'

Sade shook her head.

'I don't think so, you're already causing shockwaves in the vampire world and if they find out you've got some precious blood, it's going to cause major ructions.'

'Have you found anything?' he asked her.

'Um, not much,' she admitted, looking away and ruffling the papers on her desk, 'Your white blood cells are scarily high, but that's probably because of all the different blood you had in the Tasting. It could also mean you're good at healing. I've sent some off to my sister for DNA analysis, but don't worry she can be trusted to keep it secret.'

He glanced at her for a second. She still wouldn't meet his eyes.

'What's going on Sade? Why are you acting so weird?'

She fiddled with a book on her desk. 'I'm disappointed I couldn't do more myself, I suppose.'

He crossed the room to her. 'Come on now – if Professor Dukan can't do anything with all the gear he has here . . .'

Sade turned huge, troubled eyes to him. 'I'm disappointed in myself.'

Dillon moved closer and reached out to comfort her. Instantly, she stepped back and hung her head but not before he saw her nostrils flare and her eyes darken.

'Sade!' he exclaimed. 'What's going on with you?'

'I'm sorry, Dillon. Ever since I took your blood sample, I'm finding it a little hard to be around you.'

Realisation dawned.

'You mean, since you tasted my blood?'

Shamefaced, she nodded.

'Oh right,' he said, unsure what to say. 'Can't we try gradual exposure like Madame Dupledge suggested for Angelo?'

'Maybe,' she said, a small flare of hope in her eyes.

He took a tentative step towards her and then another until they were almost touching. Sade shuddered.

'Should I touch you?' he asked.

She nodded, eyes still downcast, curly lashes fanning her high cheekbones. He pulled her to him and held her against him, letting her delicious scent fill his nostrils. He didn't experience the sense of calm he usually felt near her. She quivered all over and tried to pull away.

'Just a wee bit longer – you can do it Sade,' Dillon whispered.

As her hands inched up to his neck and traced his carotid artery, Dillon held his breath. Suddenly, she pulled his neck towards her and, surprised by her strength, Dillon yelped. For the briefest second, he felt her lips, butterfly-soft against his skin.

The door flew open, and Celeste strode in. 'I just need to charge my laptop, Sade,' she said, stopping dead.

Dillon and Sade sprang apart.

'Now Celeste, seriously, it isn't what you think,' he said.

Celeste ignored him and continued to stare at Sade. 'You look like you're suffering from a bad case of bloodlust, Sade. I do hope you haven't broken the rules?'

Sade's eyes had darkened, and she looked mortified.

'Of course not,' Dillon said furiously. 'It's my blood. The

scent of it. I know it's tricky for all of you.'

Celeste came up close and slowly lowered her head until her nose was just centimetres from his neck. 'Challenging, I'll admit,' she announced, ice-blue eyes gleaming, 'but not overwhelming.'

'Okay, Celeste,' Sade snapped. 'I like Dillon. You like Ace. It's no big deal.'

Dillon's eyes widened in surprise.

'I *like* Ace,' Celeste agreed. 'I'm not obsessed with his blood. I'll catch you later.'

'Shite,' Dillon swore as she disappeared out the door.

'Dillon, I'm sorry I said that, I . . . I know you like Cora.' Her voice wobbled. 'But I had to get her off my back. If they find out I've tasted your blood, they could throw me out.'

'They would never do that Sade; you're a model student. You'll get on top of it and don't forget, without you and Jeremiah life would be pretty unbearable for me in here.'

She managed a small smile.

'Thanks, Dillon.'

As he left her room, his head was a mess. Maybe he shouldn't have told her about his blood, but she had always helped him. The problem was that he didn't know how to help her.

12

Blood Trial

The night of the Flight Trial, Jeremiah found Dillon cowering in the shower room, stricken with the stomach cramps that signalled he needed blood and nerves about the upcoming flight.

'Come on, mate. It's midnight, time for pre-flight blood,' he said, helping him up.

The crowd of Peak Two and Three vampires waiting for their blood rations turned to stare at him as they arrived in the blood room. He wished they had a different blood drinking night.

'See, Dillon,' Professor Dukan murmured, coming up to him. 'They all want to see you drink Golden Blood. Imagine if yours is even more special?'

As he tapped in the door code to the blood storage room, Dillon noticed Sade loitering, watching closely.

'Sade, I know what you're up to,' he whispered in her ear.

She jumped back, nostrils flaring. 'Dillon! Don't creep up on me like that.'

'What's going on with you two?' Bram drawled.

Dillon whipped round – he hadn't heard him approach.

Sade shrugged. 'Nothing to interest you, Bram. Just something private between me and Dillon.'

Bram's eyes flicked between the two of them. 'I see. I'm sure your father will be delighted to know how you are . . . becoming close to Dillon, Sade.'

Sade's eyes narrowed. 'Keep out of it, Bram. Like I said, it's got nothing to do with you,' she snapped.

Dillon glanced at her in surprise – he'd never seen her rattled before.

Bram raised his hands and stepped back. 'Woah, Sade. No need to get het up, sorry if I touched a nerve.'

Dillon could feel her fuming as she watched him walk off.

'He's such a dick.'

'Sade! You can't talk about the Deputy Vampire Elect like that.' Dillon teased. 'I mean, what if people start thinking it's true?'

'Shut up!' she giggled.

As Professor Dukan re-emerged from the storage room, the crowd surged forward, desperate to get a whiff of the Golden Blood.

'You better come in here, Dillon,' he said. 'Stand back everyone.'

'Check out as much as you can, any computers, any login

233

codes – find out where your original samples are,' Sade hissed in his ear and stepped back quickly, but not before he saw her nostrils flare again.

'Hurry up, Dillon.' Professor Dukan waved an impatient hand.

Dillon hurried after him and the door closed, sealing them into the private space. Inside, the quiet calm of the blood storage room was eerily beautiful. Hundreds of blood bags, the vampires' life force, hung silently from stainless steel racks, belying the hidden power within them. Professor Dukan thrust a head covering and gloves at him.

'Put these on before I open it.'

This time, as soon as the professor opened the bag, Dillon struggled to control himself. He wanted it so badly. The minute he swallowed the Golden Blood and then felt it hit his circulation, his system was electrified. He felt like a firework about to take off.

'Woah – here we go,' he gasped. His head was spinning.

'Put your head between your knees for a minute,' Professor Dukan advised.

The Golden Blood danced through every particle of his body, and he struggled to think rationally. He thought of Sade waiting outside. What did she want him to do? Oh yes, he remembered now.

'Where are my original samples?' he asked. 'You must need them to record the differences.'

'They're not here. Madame Dupledge has some and the lab has some. The data is on a secure computer in here.

Don't worry, they're under high security. Are you feeling better?'

His head was still spinning slightly, but he felt he had some control back and his nerves were now fizzing with energy. 'Yes, much better now, thanks.'

'Take it easy for a bit. There could be a second wave . . .'

There was a hush as he left the storage room, and Frederick rushed up in front of Sade.

'What did he give you this time?'

'Just Golden Blood again.'

'*Scheiße*! I mean, shit – Dillon, what do you mean, "just"? What was it like this time?'

Dillon grinned. 'It was just incredible. I'll see you at flying.'

Leaving Frederick open-mouthed and feeling like he was walking on air, he walked round him to join Sade.

'Did you see where your blood might be kept?' she hissed out of the corner of her mouth. He pretended not to notice her stepping away from him a little.

'Absolutely,' he told her, swaying slightly.

'Are you going to tell me then?' she said, staring at him, crossing her arms.

'What? Oh, sorry. Yes, of course.' He tried to pull himself together. 'It's the Golden Blood,' he said, pointing at his head.

Sade tried to hide a smile. 'I'll have to take your word for it, Dillon. I've never tasted Golden Blood,' she said.

'You should do,' Dillon said earnestly. 'It's, it's . . .' he gave up and raised his hands to the ceiling.

'Dillon,' she said, grinning at him. 'Just concentrate and tell me what you know.'

'Not much, the original samples aren't in the building and the data is on a computer in there. Unless you find a way to get past the facial recognition system, you'll have to find a way to hack into it.'

'Damn it,' Sade snapped. 'We'll have to involve Bik. Do you mind?'

Dillon hesitated. 'Professor Dukan specifically told me not to tell anyone. He's been kind to me; I feel bad going behind his back.'

'I understand, but you're not telling Bik – I am. I trust her, she's extremely clever with computer science and she's not into the power politics like some of the others.'

Despite his reservations, he agreed.

As soon as he saw the gym, Dillon's nerves returned with a vengeance. Mr Hunt, dressed in his sleek black flying jacket, stood next to Chiro and called the class to attention.

'This is your first outdoor flight without Madame Dupledge or myself. As it is a major part of vampire survival, you must prove that you are proficient if you want to graduate from VAMPS. The very best amongst you will be considered for special flying operations in the VSS and elsewhere. This is a competition so fly to win, but remember, any transgressions of the rules could lead to a suspension from the academy.'

He looked around the group. 'Pay attention: You must stick to a thirty kilometre radius around the school. Non-VAMPS vampires are not allowed to enter it unless they have clearance from myself or Madame Dupledge. Likewise, do not let yourself be seen from the ground. Make sure you stay high and avoid humans. The nearest village is Arnes and it's out of the thirty kilometre radius so stay well away from it. Finally, do not fly alone – always stay with your partner.

'As this trial was planned according to the lunar calendar, the moon is waning and there is good cloud cover. Even so, I'm providing black flight suits to help you to remain camouflaged. You have just taken blood so you should have enough energy, but try not to do anything stupid.'

His eyes drifted from Frederick to Angelo and back towards Dillon. He chucked the flight suits at them.

'Hurry up and change, we will head for the entrance in ten minutes. Dillon, you fly with Cora. Jeremiah, you're with Sade. Ace, you will fly with Aron. Bram, you fly with Angelo. Bik and Ásta, you will fly together, and Frederick, you fly with Celeste.

Ace and Aron punched fists. 'Yes!'

'You've got to be joking,' Celeste said, staring daggers at Frederick.

'Flying may not be my strongest skill but at least I'm not a stuck-up bitch,' Frederick retorted as Aron placed a warning hand on his arm.

'How dare you,' Celeste said, blue eyes cold as ice.

'You started it,' he said, shrugging nonchalantly.

Hissing under her breath, Celeste turned on her heel and stalked off to moan to Ace. Frederick winked at Aron.

'Don't do anything stupid, Fred. You want to still be alive when you get back,' Aron warned.

'Stop fretting, Aron,' Fred protested. 'I can handle the ice queen. I may not be an ace at flying but if anyone can handle themselves outside of here, it's me.'

Dressed in their black suits, they made their way to the entrance hall where Mr Hunt handed out wristbands. 'These are tracking devices – they record your vital statistics so we'll know where you are if there's a problem. They will beep a warning as you approach the thirty kilometre boundary. I would like all of you to fly directly north to the boundary and then fly a complete semicircle, passing over VAMPS, before heading back here on the same route that you took out. It should take approximately an hour, depending on how fast you fly. We are not designed to make long flights at full speed so make sure you pace yourself. Chiro will be out there with you, but he will keep out of your way unless there is an emergency. Remember, you must stay in sight of your partner, but we will be analysing individual performances. Once VAMPS is in sight, you may leave your partner and fly back at your fastest speed. One final thing: hand your phones to me, their signals represent a security risk outside of the academy building.'

Dillon swallowed, his throat dry and his body taut with nervous tension as he handed over his phone over. Frederick suddenly looked shifty and triple-checked his was turned off and locked before he handed it in.

'I do not want Hunt getting hold of my contacts,' he hissed under his breath to Dillon.

'Prepare yourselves,' Mr Hunt warned, opening the door and revealing the tunnel that led to the opening in the mountain.

Dillon took his place next to Cora and she turned to him, eyes huge with nervous anticipation.

'Ready?'

He nodded, trying to ignore the out of body feeling he was experiencing and focused on the dark circle at the end of the tunnel.

Ace and Aron and Bram and Angelo pushed their way to the front along with Ásta, who dragged a reluctant Bik with her.

'Keep up, Bik,' Ásta hissed under her breath.

'I'm trying, Ásta,' Bik snapped.

Mr Hunt raised his hand. 'Okay, countdown starting. Five, four, three . . .'

The whole class pitched forward, poised for take-off.

' . . . two, one!'

Like bullets out of a gun, Ace and Aron shot down the tunnel, with Bram and Angelo hot on their heels, and disappeared. Ásta, with Bik straining to keep up, shot after them. The others, including a slightly wobbly Frederick, followed seconds later.

Dillon had failed to take off. His feet felt leaden like they were stuck in concrete.

'What are you doing?' Chiro screeched.

'I'm not sure, something is wrong,' Dillon muttered, desperately trying to summon up the spark that usually lifted his feet off the ground.

Cora flew back down the tunnel and landed next to him.

'What's going on?' she asked, disappointment clouding her eyes.

'He needs a jump start,' Chiro snarled.

In a beat, Cora leant forward and crushed her lips against his. His body jerked as if he had been electrocuted with a thousand volts.

'Cora, stop that immediately,' Mr Hunt snapped.

Just in time, she broke away, and he catapulted down the tunnel. Bursting into the cold night air, he sensed her on his heels and flipped onto his back.

'Hold my hand,' he yelled. 'We'll be faster together.'

Flipping over again, he checked his speed for a second until he felt Cora's hand clasp his. The second bolt of electricity shot them both forward and he almost lost control. Bram was right; flying in real air was completely different. It felt denser somehow and sudden air pockets pitched them down. Wind and air currents pummelled at them, threatening to spin them off track. Keeping as flat and straight as he could, he pressed into the wind, increasing their speed. The rugged mountains blurred beneath them.

Celeste's face was a picture as they sped past her and Fred, who was still moaning about his phone and struggling to maintain his body line. Sade and Jeremiah whooped as they caught up with them. They headed due north straight over the mountain range until Cora's wristband began beeping.

'This is the thirty kilometre radius – we turn clockwise here,' she shouted into the wind.

Dillon glanced at his wrist, trying not to make any big moves that would send him into a flat spin; his wristband was silent. Either it hadn't been set properly or it was broken.

'Ready?' he shouted back.

In unison, they dropped their shoulders and swooped right, heading back round towards the academy. They passed Bik and Ásta as if they were floating in mid-air, and Ásta hissed with rage.

They were approaching the academy building fast from the east, which meant they were halfway round the circuit. He could just make out the Peak Two and Three vampires and Mr Hunt watching from the roof. Bram and Angelo were up ahead, just behind Ace and Aron.

'Come on,' he shouted to Cora, straining every sinew, determined to catch Bram. They were flying on the edge now, he could literally feel the air wobbling beneath him, like he was balancing on an invisible skateboard. He tried to remember Chiro's words: *the faster you go, the less control you have but you can make quicker moves.*

Seconds before approaching VAMPS, they levelled with Bram and Angelo's heels.

'Now!' Dillon shouted to Cora.

Flying dangerously close to their limits, they dived lower, gaining yet more speed. The watching vampires threw themselves to the glass roof to avoid being hit, as Dillon and Cora flew underneath Bram and Angelo, just skimming the roof, and overtook them. Dillon just glimpsed Mr Hunt's irate face as he sprang back to his feet.

Bram swore loudly and, yelling to Angelo, they lengthened out to increase their speed, gradually gaining on Dillon and Cora. As they inched up, flying neck and neck now, Cora stared straight ahead, not wanting to catch Bram's eye, biting her lip with the effort of maintaining her flight line.

Still incandescent with rage that he'd been overtaken in front of the Peak Two and Three vampires, Bram lost his head halfway round the west side of the circuit and lurched forward, determined to regain the lead. The sudden increase in air speed caught Angelo unawares and pitched him into a flat spin, sending him tumbling towards the ground.

'Shite!' Dillon swore, as he and Cora lifted their heads, and he almost lost it himself.

Straining against the wind, they slowed down just enough to see Angelo, struggling to regain control. Without thinking, Dillon dived, leaving Cora with Bram. He plummeted down after Angelo, who couldn't seem to stop his fall and was spiralling fast towards a cluster of chalets, set on the side of a small forest clearing. Despite the rushing in his ears, he could hear the insistent beeping of Angelo's tracker. They must have fallen outside of the thirty kilometre boundary.

Forcing himself into an even steeper dive, he caught up with Angelo just above the level of the alpine trees and grabbed hold of the back of his flight suit. Angelo slumped with shock, and Dillon swore as he struggled to put the brakes on.

'Come on, Angelo – for feck's sake, lift your chin!' he yelled.

Angelo flattened out but Dillon didn't have the power to pull them out of the dive in time and they both slammed into a snow-covered roof.

It was lucky the snow was so deep, Dillon thought as he lay stunned on the roof, Angelo sprawled next to him. The shock of the fall had caused him to pass out, and Dillon willed him to be okay and open his eyes.

The sound of a door opening and human voices shocked him into action.

'Angelo!' he hissed. 'We've got to get out of here.'

Eyes shut. Angelo groaned. 'Leave me alone, Dillon. I'm fucked.'

'Keep it down and get up, for Christ's sake. There're humans down there.'

Staggering on the slippery roof, he hauled Angelo up. 'Can you fly?'

'*No se*,' Angelo mumbled, slipping into his native Spanish. 'Bram's fucking crazy. I've got no energy left.'

The voices were heading around the side of the chalet. With a single flying leap, Dillon grabbed Angelo and sprang off the roof, landing lightly on the ground. Pulling Angelo with him, he bounded towards the dense forest at the back of the chalet and shoved him behind a tree, out of sight.

'What the fuck, Dill—' Angelo hissed, eyes wild with adrenalin.

As a man came into view, Angelo's head instantly whipped round and he strained to get away from Dillon.

'Don't be stupid, Angelo—'

Dillon suddenly caught the scent and, instinctively, he turned towards it too. It was the first living human blood he'd smelt since he'd woken up his vampire half. He could hear it pumping around the man's body as loud and insistent as a drumbeat. Now he understood what Sade and the others had heard when they first saw him. He felt his blood surge and, for a second, a red mist clouded his vision.

Angelo's fangs popped out and, like dominos falling, so did his own.

'Shit, shit, shit,' he lisped. 'We've really got to get out of here.'

But Angelo's eyes had glazed, fixated on the human.

'Think of the higher purpose.' Dillon tried. 'Think of the consequences.'

But Angelo was beyond hearing him, and he struggled to hold him against the tree. The red mist across his own eyes was fading now as he focused on Angelo, trying to bring him back. He racked his brain; Madame Dupledge had advised distraction. Desperate now, he unzipped his flying suit at the neck and leant towards Angelo.

'Come on, Angelo. Have a whiff of this.'

Angelo's head whipped back. '*Dios mio*,' he growled. 'Holy shit, Dillon. What are you doing to me?'

His lips had pulled back, exposing the whole of his decorated fangs and, with sudden iron strength, he pulled Dillon's head towards him.

Dillon struggled against him. 'Not now, Angelo, we've got to get out of here.'

Angelo stared at him, his pupils wide, his eyes black with hunger, and Dillon found himself losing the will to resist, enthralled by his strong, feral allure. He froze as Angelo ducked his head and as he felt his fangs graze the delicate skin at his neck, he shuddered, once again shocked by the eroticism of it all.

'Yes,' Angelo growled softly.

Something whistled through the air above them, momentarily distracting Angelo, and Dillon shoved him away. The next second, a black shape darted through the sky like lightning and grabbed Angelo, immediately pulling him into the air.

Looking up, he saw Chiro's red eyes gleaming in the dark and Angelo hanging suspended underneath him. 'Focus, Dillon. Connect to the energy flowing in your blood,' he hissed. 'You need to take off now. It's not safe. There's another vampire around.'

Dillon shook his head to clear it; his blood was still surging. Closing his eyes, he searched for the illusive spark he needed to ignite the energy in his muscles. The relief was palpable when he found it and, as he focused hard on it, he felt a burst of exhilaration as his feet left the ground.

'At last,' Chiro growled. 'Let's get out of here. Stay close to me, both of you. Like I said, there's another vampire out here – we need to fly clever.'

Chiro disguised it well, but Dillon felt a thud of fear as he sensed his anxiety. Whoever was out there wasn't flying for fun. As they burst out above the tree line, Chiro's red eyes scanned the sky constantly. Dillon marvelled at his flying skill and strived to copy his every move as they hurtled through the night sky, sticking to the cloud cover where they could. Focused utterly on staying in the air as they skimmed through gorges and soared over mountain peaks, he couldn't tell if there was anything on their tail. He himself sensed nothing.

As VAMPS appeared in the distance, Chiro banked hard to the left and roared, 'Fly as fast as you can. Don't look around until you are in.'

Fuelled by their fear of what could be behind, Dillon and Angelo streaked like fighter jets over the huge expanse of ice and raced up the side of the academy, high into the sky before descending behind it and shooting into the entrance tunnel.

The other vampires were still waiting in the tunnel as he landed, legs trembling with exhaustion and bent forward, hands on his thighs. Angelo wobbled in just behind and collapsed, utterly spent, on the floor.

'What took you?' Bram mocked.

'What do you think? Angelo would have been in serious trouble if I hadn't helped him,' Dillon said furiously, raising his head and glaring up at him.

'Someone had to stay with Cora,' Bram drawled. 'Or did you forget about her?'

Mr Hunt flew up, landing with an angry thud right in front of Dillon. 'That was a stupid, dangerous move by you and Cora over the roof. I will be investigating what happened tonight with Angelo. Give me your tracker, Dillon.'

'It wasn't working,' Dillon told him.

'I'll be the judge of that. You, Angelo, Bram and Cora will see me in my office once I've analysed the tracking data and spoken to Chiro.'

'Chiro's still out there. He might need help; there was something after us.'

'Chiro will be fine. He'll be back soon, I'm sure,' he snapped and, turning on his heel, he stalked off.

13

Blood Inquisition

The mood was subdued as they removed their flight suits. If looks could kill, Celeste and Ásta's would have finished off Frederick and Bik. Cora and Bram were silent too; they had returned third and fourth but were likely to be disqualified for returning with the wrong partners.

Only Ace and Aron, who had returned first and second, were pumped up.

'What happened to you, Dillon?' Ace asked, chucking his flight suit in a pile on the gym floor. 'I guess outdoor flying sorted the vamps from the dhamps.'

'Cora and I were flying well but Angelo got into trouble. I helped,' Dillon said, shortly.

'He didn't look like a dhampir when he passed us,' Jeremiah spoke up. 'Made me and Sade look like we were going backwards.'

Ace grinned. 'Yeah, well, I'm not flying scared yet. Cora's

not gonna be around every time he needs a little help with . . . lift off.' He laughed.

Dillon glanced at Cora, wondering how Ace had found out about the botched take off. She shook her head slightly.

He was relieved when Chiro walked in, his eyes redder than ever but only looking slightly ruffled.

'Mr Hunt's ready for you,' he growled.

Dillon waited until the others had gone ahead. 'What happened?' he asked Chiro.

'Whatever it was took flight once I turned. I chased them back to the thirty kilometre border radius but I lost them after that.'

'What did they want?'

His red eyes darkened. 'They wouldn't normally dare enter the thirty kilometre zone. The academy is a protected space, and the zone cannot be entered without huge risk unless you are specifically invited here. I'd guess they wanted you.'

Dillon went cold. In the bubble of the academy, he hadn't really believed Professor Dukan that other vampires may want his blood. He felt the fear roll over him; how would he see his da if vampires were after him every time he left the academy?

Mr Hunt's black eyebrows were drawn together in a dark frown, and he looked up coldly as Dillon and Chiro followed Bram, Cora and Angelo into his office.

It was completely different to Madame Dupledge's. Whereas hers was light and uber-modern like the rest of the academy, his wouldn't have looked out of place on a Dracula movie set. The walls were dark and covered in heavy, framed pictures of castles and previous champion flyers. His slim laptop and the hi-tech GPS equipment looked out of place on the heavy gothic desk, next to a ram's skull and a brass lamp. Dillon shuddered when he spotted the malevolent stuffed raven, its beak as sharp as a dagger, hunched over a wooden perch. A brass bell hung below.

Mr Hunt launched straight in. 'We don't have any data from your flight tracker, Dillon, which seems suspicious. They were all working when I handed them out. I hope you didn't intend to sabotage the results after your disastrous start?'

'Seriously?' Dillon blurted out. 'No, of course not. I wouldn't have a clue how to disable it.'

'Why did Angelo suddenly lose control? Up to the point you and Cora passed him, the data on his tracker shows he and Bram were flying fast and smooth. We all witnessed your dangerous stunt over the roof of the academy.'

'Cora and I didn't do anything. Bram accelerated to overtake us. Angelo wasn't prepared and he lost control.'

'Why did you go after him when I told you to stay with your partner?'

Dillon felt his temper rising; this was more like an inquisition.

'Shouldn't you ask Bram why he didn't go after him?' he snapped. 'It was a split-second decision. Angelo was falling fast.'

'Would you say your rivalry with Mr Danesti got in the way of making a cool-headed decision?'

'What? It had nothing to do with that.' He thought for a second. 'At least my decision didn't, I can't speak for Bram. If I hadn't dived after Angelo, he would have been in serious danger.'

'It's true.' Angelo nodded.

'Why did you fly out of the thirty kilometre boundary knowing it was against the rules. Is that why you disabled the tracker?'

'What?' Dillon was flabbergasted. 'What is this about? Come on. We were flying on the edge of the boundary, and when Angelo lost control we must have spiralled out of it. It wasn't intentional. My tracker didn't alert me to anything.'

'What happened on the ground? Was there human contact?'

'We managed to disappear before they saw us, although there wasn't time to hide our tracks.'

'Why didn't you leave the scene straightaway?'

He glanced at Angelo. 'Angelo was still recovering.'

Mr Hunt's eyes grew even colder. 'How did he regain his strength?'

'Chiro arrived.'

No need to add that Chiro had literally plucked Angelo off him.

'What happened to Cora and Bram?' Dillon asked pointedly.

'They followed protocol and flew back here as fast as they could to raise the alarm.'

Dillon looked at him incredulously. 'Are you saying I shouldn't have helped Angelo?'

'We are trying to understand why you and Angelo flew out of bounds and made contact with humans – both of which were against the rules – and put yourselves and Chiro at risk.'

Bram looked like the cat who had got the cream. Dillon clenched his fists. He could feel his blood starting to heat up.

'There was nothing suspicious about it. We didn't make contact with anyone. It was exactly as I told you.'

'Why did you bare your neck to Angelo? As you know, giving blood to another vampire is against VAMPS rules.'

Shite. How did he know that? Out of the corner of his eye, he saw Angelo twitch.

'No blood was shared,' he said.

'Because Chiro arrived?' Mr Hunt interrupted.

'Well, yes, but I wouldn't have let Angelo anyway.'

'You are extremely privileged to have Golden Blood, Dillon. You shouldn't use it as currency with your peers.'

He struggled to stop his blood boiling over. 'Angelo's always had a thing about my blood. I would never use Golden Blood as "currency",' he said, furiously.

'That remains to be seen.'

If we can get him suspended, he'll lose VE and Alexandru will put pressure on Madame Dupledge.

Dillon started and stared at Mr Hunt for a second. Instantly, he understood what was going on. This was more than a telling off; he was determined to get rid of him. Mr Hunt's face darkened as he saw Dillon's reaction and the mind connection disappeared abruptly. Dillon needed a moment to gather his thoughts and work out how to get through this unscathed, now that he knew he couldn't trust Mr Hunt.

Cora broke the momentary silence. 'Dillon's done nothing wrong. He wanted to help Angelo, that's all. I saw him dive after him and we all know that Angelo has a penchant for Dillon's blood. I'm sure Dillon didn't offer it to him and, if he bared his neck, it must have been for a good reason.'

'He did it to distract me from the scent of the human. I admit my control is sometimes not as *fuerte*, sorry – I mean as *strong* as it should be.' In his agitation, Angelo slipped back into Spanish.

Mr Hunt ignored him. 'Both of you infringed three important rules. Flying out of bounds, risking contact with humans before you are fully trained and possibly exchanging blood. It is more than enough to suspend you and, in Madame Dupledge's absence, I have made that decision.'

'You can't do that!' Cora gasped. 'Dillon's VE. He'll lose the position.'

'Rules are rules, Miss de Courtenay, Vampire Elect behaviour must be exemplary at all times. Mr Danesti will take on the role for now.'

Now Dillon knew why Bram hadn't dived: his quick brain had calculated the implications.

'Trying to save a vampire from injury or discovery *is* exemplary behaviour.' Cora's voice rose. 'You said it yourself in the first Combat, Hunt and Protect lesson.'

'Control yourself, Cora,' Mr Hunt hissed.

'It's not worth it, Cora,' Bram said, trying to hold her back.

She shook him off, shaking with rage. 'I don't care.' She glared at Mr Hunt, 'Suspend me too on some bogus charge. You did it to my brother—'

Mr Hunt's eyes turned colder still and gleamed like black onyx.

'Cora, you haven't done anything wrong.' Dillon cut in, desperate to stop her from doing anything stupid.

Cora shut her eyes and, if she'd been human, she would have taken a deep breath. When she reopened them, they sparked with passion. Dillon couldn't help but think that he had never seen her look so beautiful.

'I haven't done anything wrong, nor has Dillon, and Angelo doesn't deserve to be punished, it was an accident that he ended up in a situation that tested his control. He is brave and loyal.'

The room went silent.

'I don't know what's going on here but, Cora, you have just proved yourself to be a young vampire with exceptional character.'

Everyone in the room spun around like lightning at the sound of Madame Dupledge's voice. She stood in the doorway, dressed in her floor-length black travelling cape, immaculate as always, with just a hint of weariness around her vivid, green eyes.

'Ah, thank goodness, Madame Dupledge. You have arrived just in time to help us sort out a major transgression of the rules.'

Mr Hunt was suddenly all charm and smarm as he bowed her in. It was shocking to Dillon to see how fake it was. To think he had trusted him.

Madame Dupledge smiled. 'It sounded like Cora was doing a good job of that, but do update me, Mr Hunt.'

Mr Hunt drew himself up. 'Dillon and Angelo broke several rules during the Flight Trial, which I believe are serious enough to justify suspending them for a week.'

Madame Dupledge's expression gave nothing away. 'I see, and what exactly were their transgressions?'

'They flew out of bounds, made contact with humans and there is evidence that Dillon gave Angelo his blood.'

'Serious indeed.' She turned to Cora. 'But you disagree with that assessment?'

'Like I said, Angelo got into trouble, Dillon tried to save him – they did what they had to. I wasn't there, but I know them.' Cora's voice shook slightly.

Madame Dupledge turned to Chiro. 'You flew with them, Chiro. Did you see this?'

Chiro cleared his throat. 'Bram increased his speed suddenly to overtake after Dillon and Cora pulled ahead of him. Angelo wasn't ready and it sent him into a flat spin. Dillon dived to help, but he only managed to catch him just before they crashed into a chalet roof just on the wrong side of the border. They jumped off and I lost them in the trees for a bit but when I saw them again, their fangs were extended. I saw Dillon attempt to restrain Angelo and I removed Angelo until he came back to his senses. They were both low on energy at that point. We had to move fast as I saw an unidentified vampire flying low over the woods and I realised we were in a dangerous situation. Once we took off again, the vampire stayed on our tail and both Dillon and Angelo demonstrated some impressive flying to keep up with me and hold whoever it was off. I left them when the academy was in sight to give chase to the unknown vampire. Dillon and Cora flew the first three quarters of the course together and her tracker shows that they flew faster than anyone else in the race. I have reason to believe they would have won had Angelo not lost control.'

Bram stifled a snort and Mr Hunt went very still.

'Thank you for that, Chiro,' Madame Dupledge said, making no mention of the unknown vampire. 'I would like to speak to Dillon and Angelo alone. Bram, if you could wait outside, I will speak to you when we have finished.'

As Chiro scuttled out followed by Cora and Bram, Madame Dupledge turned to Angelo and Dillon. 'I would like you to explain why your fangs were out.'

Angelo glanced at Dillon but made no effort to speak. Dillon cleared his throat, playing for time. 'We were both distracted by the scent of the humans. Angelo's fangs popped out and so did mine. I got control of myself, but Angelo was struggling so I attempted to distract him—'

'By letting him drink your blood,' Mr Hunt said. 'It's unlikely that you regained control so soon.'

'I didn't let him drink my blood.'

Madame Dupledge glanced at Mr Hunt and then back to Dillon and Angelo. 'Thank you for your honesty, Dillon, but I need to know that you and Angelo can control yourselves before we go on the ski trip. Can you assure me that this won't happen again?'

Angelo bowed his head so that his black curls hid his face.

Dillon swallowed. 'Yes.'

'Good. If you have any cause to believe that yourself or Angelo or any of your peers are not ready for the ski trip, it is your duty to inform me. Lives could be at stake. Now as regards your punishment.' She glanced at Mr Hunt. 'Chiro has explained that the flying out of boundary wasn't your fault, so I believe a suspension is unnecessary. However, Angelo will take part in extra control lessons with me. Dillon, your position as VE is under review as is your participation in the ski trip.'

Dillon bowed his head; it was better than the humiliation of a suspension, but it was still harsh in his opinion. Mr Hunt's face remained marble still, but the malevolence in his eyes matched that of the stuffed raven next to him. If Mr Hunt had disliked him before, he definitely hated him now.

As he and Angelo reached the door, he remembered that Madame Dupledge had said nothing about the vampire who had followed them.

'What about the vampire who was chasing us?' He asked turning round again.

Her expression turned sombre. 'There will be an investigation. I will speak to Chiro.'

She immediately walked away, leaving Dillon with yet more questions he'd not be given answers to.

14

Blood Bond

Twenty minutes later, Bram steamed into Dillon's room without knocking.

'You should be out on your fucking ear, but instead Dupledge has just given me a massive bollocking,' he hissed. 'I would have beaten you and you know it. Dupledge can't save your bacon for much longer.'

Dillon raised an eyebrow; Bram's language was usually more refined.

'Cora and I beat you, Bram. You lost your head.'

Back in control, Bram smiled and placed both hands on the coffin between them. 'Enjoy it while you can, Dillon. Like I said, Dupledge can't hold out forever. There's a barrage of opposition forming against her. She's losing her control over this school. Even Hunt's come over to our side.'

Dillon shrugged. 'Fine. I wish you good luck. You said I need to know something about Countess Fassano's visit?'

Bram eyed him coldly. 'If you're still VE by then, we need to welcome her along with Mahina and George when she arrives.'

'George?' Dillon interrupted.

Bram rolled his eyes. 'George Gyllenborg, the Peak Two VE. Madame Dupledge wants us to impress her with our intelligence and charm, so you'd better leave the talking to me.'

'I'm sure she'll end up thoroughly schooled in the subject of "BRAM" if you're doing all the talking,' said Dillon, deadpan. 'What else?'

'After the Ice Challenge, she'll present colours.'

'Colours?'

'God — you really know nothing.' Bram sneered. 'If it's full colours, the VAMPS crest is tattooed in blood on the body. It's a huge honour.'

'Blood?'

'Yes, blood from our Ancient founders is mixed with a lifelong preservative and needled into the skin.'

Dillon fought to hide a wave of revulsion; he wasn't against tattoos but using the blood of some old vampire?

'Does the Countess have one?' he asked to change the subject.

'Of course, they say she excelled in her challenges. Her mind skills are legendary.'

'Like what?' he asked.

'She can read minds with a clarity that no vampire can match, and she can inflict pain that will completely immobilise an opponent.'

Dillon winced. 'Like the thing you do?'

'Yeah, but far more powerful. I'll get stronger, though.'

'Is that what you want to do?'

Bram's smouldering eyes lit up. 'It's the best job in the vampire world, but my father doesn't agree with the direction she is taking us.'

For the first time, Dillon felt a minute twinge of pity for Bram always having to be the best and having to do exactly as his father said. But it didn't last long.

Bram leaned forward over the coffin and hissed, 'By the way, if you even try to get near Cora again, you'll be sorry.'

Dillon held his gaze. 'You heard Madame Dupledge. Cora can make her own decisions.'

Bram's eyes narrowed, and Dillon winced as a band of pain and a buzzing noise filled his brain.

'I mean it,' he hissed again. 'Stay away from her. She's got a glittering future with me – you'll just drag her down. She has an annoying habit of feeling sorry for underdogs like you, you know? She likes novelty and she's never known a dhampir before. You'll only lead her into trouble – like you almost did today.'

Just as Bram had intended, every word pierced his heart like darts thudding into a bullseye. He forced himself to smile, determined not to show Bram he'd hit home.

'Like I said, Cora's her own vampire.'

'She'll soon realise that underdogs . . . are the runts of the litter,' Bram hissed, turning on his heel.

As soon as Bram left, Dillon went straight to the roof,

making sure that no one saw him. He didn't want to see Cora. For once, the view of the chalky mountains against the inky black sky and the luminous green of the ice lake stretching away in the opposite direction failed to soothe him.

Bram's words still rang in his head: *you'll just drag her down.* It was true. Madame Dupledge had applauded Cora's courage earlier, but it could easily have gone the other way. He would not let her get kicked out because of him.

'Hey.'

His heart sank when he heard her voice.

'Hey,' he replied, turning to face her.

'I thought I'd find you here. What happened?' she asked as soon as she saw his expression. 'Shit, you haven't been suspended have you?'

'No, I just needed some fresh air,' he said, waving a hand at the mountains.

'Come on, Dillon. What did Madame Dupledge say after we left?'

'They're deciding if I can stay VE and take part in the ski trip.'

'Why?' she said, furiously. 'Just because Angelo can't control himself?'

'She was fair, Cora,' he said gently. 'This isn't your fight. You impressed her; you heard what she said. Don't ruin that for my sake. I'm just something a bit different for you.'

'What the hell, Dillon? What does that mean?'

He raked a hand through his hair. 'Cora, you are destined to fly high; I don't want to drag you down.'

Her eyes shone in the reflected light of the mountains and her bottom lip trembled with anger. 'That is total bullshit, Dillon.'

'Like you said, Bram is good for you, I'll just hold you back.'

As if controlled by an invisible force, she closed the distance between them and gently clasped the back of his head, pulling his lips down to hers. He tried to pull away.

'It's tru—'

'Just shut up, Dillon,' she whispered and, as her cool, full lips met his, he trembled and his resistance crumbled. As he cupped her delicate face with his hands, she wound hers into his hair and pressed closer to him. The feel of her against him sent heat surging round his body. It felt so right, better than his wildest dreams and, for a few glorious moments, he forgot Bram's words.

'Ouch.' Cora jerked her head back as the electricity sparked between their lips, shocking her.

He leant forward, desperate to reconnect, but the shock seemed to bring her to her senses.

Gazing at him, their faces still only inches apart, she whispered, 'I'm sorry, I didn't mean . . . just never put yourself down, okay?'

'Don't,' he said, sharply. 'Just don't.'

Tearing himself away from her, heart beating, pulse on fire, he walked to the edge of the roof, taking gasping breaths and breathing out long clouds of steam into the cold air.

'Dill . . .'

'I'd like to be alone,' he said, refusing to look at her.

There was a pause and then he heard the hatch shut.

'Fuck!' he roared, into the silence.

He jumped as his phone vibrated in his pocket and he saw he had a missed call from his da. Fingers shaking on the keys, he called him back, sagging with relief when he answered.

'Da? Did you want me?'

'Hello, Dill. I passed the fir tree we chose for Christmas today, the one down in the copse. It reminded me that it'll be our first one apart.'

For a moment, Dillon couldn't answer. At the beginning of December, he and his da always felled a fir tree on their land and carried it back to the cottage together. It had been so intense over the past weeks; he had completely lost track of time outside the academy. December was only a couple of weeks away.

His da broke the silence. 'I'm sorry, Dill. I know I shouldn't have disturbed you. It was just the tree . . . I know vampires don't celebrate Christmas . . .' His voice trailed off.

Dillon swallowed hard. 'You're not disturbing me, Da,' he croaked. 'It's been tough on my own. A lot of vampires are not happy that I'm here.'

'I know, Dill. Stay strong. You're better than them. Madame Dupledge is on your side.'

He wanted to tell him about Cora and about flying, about everything that had happened to him, but his throat closed with emotion.

There was another small silence.

'Will you put the tree up?' Dillon blurted out.

'Maybe not, there doesn't seem much point this year,' his da said, finally. 'Look, you'd better get on.'

'Da, thanks for calling. I . . . I miss you.' His voice cracked.

'Miss you too, Dill. Like I said, stay strong, believe in yourself.'

As the phone went dead, Dillon stared at it. He had a suspicion that a finger or two of whiskey had weakened his da's resolve not to call. Sade had been right about that.

15

Blood Skills

He avoided bumping into Cora as December approached and the nights grew longer. The schedule was ramping up. As well as starting Blood Analysis lessons with Professor Dukan, they were training in earnest for the Ice Challenge now. In their Combat, Hunt and Protect lessons, Borzak began teaching them more advanced MMA techniques for self-defence and close combat.

Mr Hunt, standing in front of the fight ring, was in a foul mood and directed most of his sarcastic taunts at Dillon. Whereas before Dillon had attributed Mr Hunt's antipathy towards him to disdain at having to teach an ignorant dhampir, now he knew it was personal.

'You already have strength, speed and lightning-fast reactions,' he told them. 'Your senses are highly attuned, and some of you may have extra sensory skills that enable you to predict an enemy's next move.' His eyes flicked towards

Dillon and moved on round the rest of the class. 'Tonight, we will learn techniques for the rare occasions that you find yourself trapped and are forced into close hand-to-hand combat.'

As one, the vampires stirred restlessly, and Ásta and Aron strained forward, eager to start. Borzak took over. He was still dressed in his shorts and vest outfit and the spotlights lighting the dim gym space highlighted his scarred and craggy face. Once again, Dillon found himself fascinated by Borzak's past and he wondered why the scars of his human life had remained after he was turned. He assumed that certain features were such an integral part of a human's persona, they survived the transition. Borzak wouldn't look right with perfect, porcelain-smooth vampire skin.

'The rule for all close combat is maximum damage, minimum time.' Borzak spoke slowly, making eye contact with each of them to emphasise the importance of his words. 'That means go in fast, go in hard and get out quick. The faster and harder you attack, the more advantage you gain. With knowledge of these techniques comes a deep respon-sibility. They should only be used for self-defence.' He paused. 'Never, ever forget that they are designed to kill. I know that better than anyone.'

The whole class was stone-still now, hanging off his every word. Sade looked slightly sick.

'Why?' Ásta asked.

'I once let a jealous rage get the better of me,' he replied, his craggy face suddenly tormented.

No one dared ask him anything else. Dillon was convinced it had something to do with him becoming a vampire.

'Why can't we just use our fangs?' Frederick asked, looking alarmed at the idea of intense physical contact.

'It's hard to get close enough in an attack situation, Fred,' Aron said.

'Exactly right.' Borzak nodded. 'And remember, we are talking about combat against rogue vampires here, not just humans. Fangs are much less effective against other vampires. Don't forget, humans are also likely to have weapons that can make it extremely hard for you to get close enough to use your fangs.'

'Don't worry, I'll help you,' Aron whispered, looping his hand behind his back and entwining his strong hand in Fred's.

'Suits me. I'll be in charge of combat logistics.' Fred grinned back.

'Don't be so fucking soft, both of you,' Ásta hissed at them. 'This is not a game.'

Even though Dillon had grown used to the undercurrent of danger around vampires, he was shocked by this latest raising of the stakes.

'Will we really be faced with something like this in the Ice Challenge?' he asked.

Bram's top lip curled as he sneered at him. 'Of course – if you want to be the best of the best.'

Borzak smirked, showing off his missing teeth. 'It is true. You need experience. Many people and vampires want to hurt us.'

Turning, he vaulted his heavy frame into the MMA ring.

'To be dangerous you need a big variety of techniques for any situation. You will become experts at holds, throws and paralysing blows that lead to severe injury or death. Your main weapons will be your head, fists, elbows and feet. If you are able to hold close contact, fangs are lethal. You already have speed on your side, but the moves must become instinctive. Aron, get up here.'

Aron flipped over the ropes, landing next to Borzak, who immediately grabbed his arm, twisted it behind his back and kicked his feet out from under him. As Aron dropped, his arm was almost wrenched out of its socket. He hissed with pain.

'First rule of close combat, always be aware of your surroundings and never stop assessing a situation for danger. Aron, you dived in without thinking.'

He let go of Aron's arm. Aron sprang to a crouch and butted his head into Borzak's stomach. Instantly, Borzak gripped him around the shoulders and kneed his groin three times in quick succession, ending with a sharp chop to the back of his neck. As he had been on the night of the Induction Ceremony, Dillon was both sickened and enthralled. The raw power and speed of the deadly moves was almost graceful. Aron was still sprawled on the floor. Frederick moved towards the ring, but Ásta grabbed him back.

'Don't be stupid,' she hissed as Aron climbed groggily to his feet.

'The most important piece of advice I give is: Kill or be

killed. You must be more aggressive than your opponent. Losing is not an option. You need to be able to flick on your aggression switch instantly. Bram and Dillon get up here.'

The class leant forward expectantly. Cora blanched, and Sade looked down at her feet, not wanting to watch.

Kill or be killed, Dillon repeated in his head, but it seemed ridiculous that he would ever have to kill. Bram climbed into the ring first. Keeping a wary eye on him, Dillon followed. Bram was already glowering at him and as he remembered their last conversation over Cora, he felt his own anger rising. This was more than sparring. This was personal.

Borzak handed Bram a dummy stake.

'Bram, I want you to attack Dillon. You're aiming the stake for his heart. Dillon, the second he charges, I want you to grab his arm, twist it behind him and, with a fast punch to the back of his hand, knock it out of his grip.' As he spoke, he demonstrated the moves against an imaginary opponent. 'Once you've dealt with the stake, you're going to knee him in the back and drop him to the ground. If that doesn't work, grab his stake arm with two hands and get close and knee him in the stomach three to four times until he drops it. It must be done super-fast with maximum aggression.' He turned to Bram. 'There are no rules, but leave out the mind games today.'

Dillon was still processing the moves in his head when Borzak roared, 'Start.'

Immediately, Bram lunged towards him, stake outstretched, hissing like an angry, black cobra. Dillon forgot what he was meant to do and stepped back so that the stake just missed his chest. Instantly, Bram launched at him again, stabbing the stake at his heart. Although it was fake, the force sent Dillon stumbling back, and he grunted in pain. Before he could get himself together, Bram dived at him again, throwing him backwards onto the floor and pinning him down with one knee. He jabbed the stake into his throat.

'Dead twice over, Dhampir,' he growled, dark eyes blazing with triumph.

'Excellent Bram,' Borzak growled. 'Dillon, what happened? This is exactly what I warned you about. You must be aggressive and fast in a fight situation.'

Bram removed the stake from Dillon's throat and released the pressure of his knee. With one hand, he swept his dark hair back off his high, pale forehead and turned to look outside the ring, his eyes searching for Cora. Without thinking, Dillon kneed him hard in the groin and as Bram fell back with a growl, he finally remembered to grab his arm with both hands and, darting in close, kneed him hard three times. Bram hissed with pain, doubled over and dropped the stake.

'Immobilise him, Dillon,' Borzak roared.

Dillon's slight hesitation allowed Bram to rear up again aiming his head for Dillon's chin. Dillon just managed to jerk out of the way but lost his balance. Instantly, Bram attacked and, grabbing Dillon's arm, he flipped him over his back, sending him crashing to the floor.

The fight had become a vicious battle for survival with Cora underpinning it all. Desperately, Dillon rolled to one side as Bram leapt on top of him. Neither of them was aware of anything but each other. They were so close, Dillon could see the fury sparking in Bram's irises, dark against his pale face, and smell the sweet, sour odour of his breath.

Anger flooded into Dillon and, as the taunts that Cora was just humouring him filled his brain, he felt the red mist descending. Roaring, turning Bram's anger against him, he shoved him away and, using both heels, kicked him hard in the stomach. This time, as Bram doubled over, he sprang up and smashed the side of his hand as hard as he could into the back of Bram's neck. Bram dropped to the floor and Dillon, snatching up the stake, pinned him down with the pointed end of the stake to his neck.

'Who's not good enough now?' he hissed under his breath, low to his ear.

Bram thrashed furiously as the channel of anger flowed back and forwards between them.

'Enough,' Borzak bellowed. 'Well done, both of you. An even match. Bram won the early part, Dillon the latter.'

Panting and not taking his eyes off Bram, Dillon straightened up, every nerve in his body still on high alert. Bram sprang up, incensed.

'I beat him – he attacked after I had won.'

'No,' Borzak corrected. 'You dropped your guard. I didn't say the fight was over. In real life you do not stop until you are completely sure your opponent has been immobilised.'

Bram slammed his fist into the pad at the side of the ring and, springing high into the air, backflipped out of the ring. Landing lightly on his toes, his haughty face marred by an irate scowl, he left the gym without a backward glance.

'I have to agree with Bram on this occasion, Borzak,' Mr Hunt, who had been watching avidly until this point, called out. 'Dillon would have been dead after the first part of the fight.'

Dillon directed a savage glare at him.

'Bram learnt an invaluable lesson today,' Borzak insisted. 'And so did the rest of the class. Opponents do not play fair in a kill or be killed situation.'

Mr Hunt's face darkened. 'A word please, Borzak.'

As they disappeared into Borzak's tiny office, Dillon climbed out of the ring. He looked for Cora, but she had disappeared after Bram. He felt his anger deflate into hurt. She had still chosen Bram.

In a daze, he barely noticed as Jeremiah pumped his hand and clapped him on the back. Ásta pushed past Sade, who was about to congratulate him, and, clearly turned on by the violence, pressed her excited body against his, filling his senses with her musky scent.

'That was impressive, Dillon,' she purred.

Dillon felt the heat flood into his cheeks and her shrewd green eyes darkened as she noticed, pressing even closer.

'Focus, Ásta,' Mr Hunt snapped, re-emerging from the office, a sullen Borzak following behind. 'You're up next with Celeste.'

Instantly, she jumped away from Dillon and, eyes narrowed, sauntered up to the ring. Celeste, her hair pulled into a long silver ponytail, somersaulted over the ropes and landed in a crouch. Despite the saunter, Dillon could tell that Ásta's whole body was alert. Her eyes never left Celeste's. Springing high into the air, she landed in a crouch two metres from Celeste and tucked her chin-length hair behind her ears.

Imperceptibly, the rest of the class inched closer to the ring, fascinated by their opposing characters. Ásta, as volatile as lava; Celeste, ice cold and implacable. Borzak joined them in the ring and, handing Celeste a fake gun, gave a little demonstration of what he wanted them to try out. Although both vampires nodded, neither took their eyes off the other for a second.

Borzak stood between them, arms outstretched to keep them apart. 'After the countdown,' he yelled, 'you start. Five . . . Four . . . Three . . .'

Ásta quivered with anticipation. Celeste was eerily still, her flared nostrils the only sign that she was pumped up. She had the focused intensity of a thoroughbred horse at the start of a race.

'Two . . . One . . . Go!'

As if they had been electrocuted, both vampires sprang at each other at such speed, Dillon almost missed it. Ásta was swifter and, grabbing Celeste's gun arm with both hands, she brought it down hard and kicked her sharp with full force. Celeste dropped the gun with a hiss of pain, and Ásta

274

threw her to the floor. As she grappled to pin her down with a complicated arm and leg wrap, she scrabbled for the fallen gun. This time, Celeste hissed with anger and writhed her long, athletic body like an electric eel underneath her. Their deadliness and highly charged emotions were sickeningly compelling. Dillon couldn't tear his eyes away.

Celeste freed an arm and, with an uncharacteristically wild, ferocious expression, like a trapped wolf, she lashed out at Ásta. Ásta was still too quick; slamming her hand into the floor, she snatched the gun up and placed it right at the centre of her forehead.

'Okay, okay, that's enough,' Borzak shouted.

Ásta refused to let go until Celeste, spitting with rage, finally admitted defeat.

'Perfect demonstration, Ásta,' Borzak enthused. 'You are a superb fighter. That is what I am talking about: super-fast, super-aggressive – don't give your opponent a second to think. Overwhelm them with the force of your attack so that they are on the back foot from the beginning. Celeste, you were excellent too, you just need to be faster.'

Ásta vaulted out of the ring, her face blazing with triumph, and sauntered up to Angelo. He made no attempt to hide how turned on he was by her display and pulled her close.

'Angelo, control yourself,' Mr Hunt snapped. 'I would like you all to continue to practise technique with Borzak on Tuesdays and your speed and strength on Thursdays, after lessons. Anyone who doesn't will lose the chance to compete in the Ice Challenge.'

'Really?' Bik said, as he swept out. 'I'm not missing Advanced IT on Thursdays.'

'Bik, you have Advanced IT every night – one night won't make any difference,' Jeremiah said, rolling his eyes teasingly at her.

As Dillon left the gym with them, Elias appeared from nowhere and pulled him aside. 'Madame Dupledge would like to see you in Professor Dukan's office,' he said quietly.

Dillon's heart thudded. Were they going to strip him of VE now?

'I'll catch you later,' he said, with a wave of his hand, to Jeremiah and Bik.

Professor Dukan's expression was sombre when Dillon opened his office door. The slight metallic scent of his office sparred with Madame Dupledge's sweet, intoxicating aroma. He had moved the Japanese screen away from the diamond-shaped window, and she was staring out at the moonlit lake.

'I trust you have adapted to life here at VAMPS now, Dillon?' she asked, turning to face him.

'It's been hard but I'm trying to, Madame.'

'Good, as I said, it is important that your behaviour is exemplary, especially now. As you know, both Professor Dukan and I have recently been away. Professor Dukan wanted to run further tests on your blood, and I had to meet the board of governing vampires. I'm afraid, despite increasing proof of the power of your blood, there is growing resistance to you being here Dillon.'

That was the understatement of the century, thought Dillon.

'A few of the governing vampires are –' she paused – 'traditional in their beliefs. Professor Dukan and I disagree. We need to strengthen our bloodlines and find ways to survive – "pure vampire" numbers are falling. Unfortunately, those who oppose us – including most of the Ancient pure blood families – have powerful connections.'

Bitterly, Dillon thought of his conversation with Bram.

'Luckily,' she continued, 'there are some enlightened and highly influential progressives we can rely on for support.'

Dillon wondered if she was referring to Countess Fassano.

'I don't want to alarm you, Dillon, but I would like you to be vigilant when you have to leave the academy walls. Until passions calm down a little, we can't be too careful. We think that the unknown vampire Chiro chased at the Flight Trial may have been attempting to kidnap you.'

Dillon felt a shiver of fear run down his spine. Thank God Chiro had been there.

'I have instructed Borzak and Chiro to increase their surveillance, so don't be surprised if you see them around.'

He had never heard her thoughts, and Madame Dupledge was playing it down, but the slight tightness along her jaw betrayed her tension. There was so much he still had to learn about the vampire world, but his election as VE had clearly set light to the touchpaper of resentment brewing between the modern and traditional vampire factions.

Professor Dukan, who had been grave and quiet so far, suddenly spoke up. 'It is not just your place here, Dillon. It is your blood. I have confirmation that you have a unique, highly precious vampire blood type. We still don't know what advantages it might give you, but many vampires would like to get their hands on it. We're trying our best to keep it under wraps, but there are already rumours circulating. I have a suspicion that one of the governors may have obtained a sample of your blood already.'

'How?' Dillon asked, a sudden sick feeling clenching his stomach. Sade was the only other person to have a sample, and she had been uncharacteristically cagey about it. She had said her sister could be trusted, but her family had sided with the traditionalists when parents had visited the school that night.

'The board came here early on and tried your blood. Madame Dupledge thought they would see reason once they tasted it, but there was an argument, and we think one of them may have used the diversion to take some of your blood away. It's the only explanation we have come up with. No one else has had access to your blood.'

Madame Dupledge was watching him closely and he tried not to think of Sade and what had happened to the secret blood sample.

She sensed his apprehension but, on this occasion, she misinterpreted its cause. 'Don't worry,' she reassured him, 'We will look after you.'

I doubt it, Dillon thought. He was much safer before he got here. No vampire had even heard about him, let alone his blood, for eighteen years when he lived with his father.

She stared at him more intently. 'I assure you that your father wouldn't have been able to keep you protected for much longer.'

This time, she had hit the nail on the head.

'How do you do that?' he blurted out.

She gave him a small smile. 'I can't always tell exactly what you're thinking. But I am a strong intuitive; it's like a highly developed sixth sense. I can feel a train of thought. Humans are even easier. Over the years, I have become highly practiced at tuning into it. When I was young, it would only happen at times of high emotion or conversely in a quiet moment where I let my senses roam free.'

The fragments of thoughts and feelings he'd picked up suddenly made sense.

'It's happened to me,' he admitted.

Her green eyes sparked with interest. 'It is not surprising,' she said, and then, as if regretting an indiscretion, her tone became matter-of-fact. 'There is usually one intuit in every year, some stronger than others. It is a wonderful talent, but it must be carefully developed. It can be dangerous if you become overwhelmed by another's thoughts and emotions. It's rare, but you may also develop "mirror touch synaesthesia".'

'What's that?' Dillon asked, frowning.

'It happens when you see someone else being touched and you physically feel it in your own body. You can literally experience another vampire's physical pain. If you discover that you have this – it is both a gift and a curse. By feeling what others feel, you understand what motivates them.' She paused. 'Sometimes you will be pleasantly surprised but, I'm afraid, often you will be disappointed by understanding some of the motivations of even your closest friends.'

As Dillon realised the significance of what she was saying, he felt almost crushed by its enormity.

Professor Dukan eyed him sympathetically. 'It's alright,' he said. 'If you have the full talent, Madame Dupledge will teach you how to protect yourself.'

Madame Dupledge nodded. 'I can help, Dillon, but let's see how it develops. We're starting mind power lessons this week– they'll cover the basics.' She thought for a minute. 'Be aware that as this talent develops, you may find you are extra sensitive after taking blood.'

'Okay,' Dillon nodded.

So far, the thoughts he had 'heard' had all been at moments of highly charged emotion: Cora's, when they were both in the sensory-deprivation room, Ásta's, when she tried to persuade him to drink Fred's illegal blood and Mr Hunt's, after the Flight Trial. His senses and energy were definitely heightened after Golden Blood so maybe his 'intuition' would also improve as he grew better at tapping into it.

'Just one more thing before you go, Dillon. I have discussed your position as VE with Mr Hunt and if you perform well in the Ice Challenge, it will no longer be under review. However, we will make a decision regarding your participation in the ski trip nearer the time. The risks are greater away from the academy.'

'Thank you,' he muttered, still stunned by the news of his possible mind skills.

Professor Dukan walked him out through his office.

'Try not to worry, Dillon,' he said. 'The mind thing will sort itself out. And as regards your blood, Chiro will keep an eye on you.'

16

Blood Bond

Dillon went straight to Sade's room and tapped on her door. He trusted her, but he needed to know why she was acting cagey about his blood sample. She opened it and beckoned him in. Bik was hunched over her laptop set up on the desk. Both vampires were brimming with excitement, even though Bik's eyes were hidden behind her dark VR glasses.

'Dillon, Bik and I got into Professor Dukan's computer and found out that you have this amazing blood no one has seen before,' Sade half-whispered as soon as he was inside.

She was so excited; he didn't have the heart to tell her that Professor Dukan had just told him the very same thing.

'Yeah, the problem is that because it's so unique, we can't match it to any of the blood recorded on the database. And we're still trying to find out who your mother is. What's odd is that when Bik tried to hack into your personal file, it came up with nothing. It's like it's been removed from the system.'

'Madame Dupledge has just told me a load of vampires are either determined to remove me from here, or they want my blood. Apparently, I'm a serious kidnapping target so she must be keeping my details under wraps.'

There was silence for a second as the two of them stared at him.

Finally, Sade spoke. 'Dillon, my parents are traditionalists, and against my wishes, they haven't supported you being here, but they would never condone that sort of thing.'

'I wasn't accusing them, but thanks, Sade.'

He remembered hearing her dad reason with Alexandru Danesti and he believed her.

'So there must be another hidden place in the system where they hide the ultra-classified stuff,' Bik said, 'I'm pretty sure I'll be able to access it eventually.'

'Won't they find out?'

Bik looked up from the laptop for a second. 'The CIA never did, Dillon. Nor the FBI, or MI6. I'm good at this stuff – that's why it's a waste of time for me to hang around the gym, despite what that meathead Borzak says.'

There was a soft knock on the door.

'Shit!' Bik swore and slammed the laptop shut.

Jeremiah, ducking slightly, stepped into the room and raised an eyebrow. 'How come I didn't get an invite to the party?'

'Because you're way too distracting,' Bik said, deadpan.

'Bik, you're up to something – I can tell. What have these two put you up to? Sade and Dillon, don't think I haven't clocked you skulking around.'

'Jeez,' Dillon exclaimed. 'Can't anyone do anything here without everyone knowing?'

Jeremiah chuckled. 'Of course not – unless you're extremely clever – like Bik and I.'

Bik smiled, and whatever she was seeing through her dark glasses flashed red and green across her glowing cheekbones. 'Very true. Jeremiah, I don't wish to have secrets from you so I will tell you.'

She glanced at Dillon, who nodded, despite Professor Dukan's warning – Jeremiah was different; he'd trust him with his life.

'Dillon has this crazy-rare blood no one's even seen before and we're trying to find out why the identity of his mother is a secret.'

Dillon curbed a smile. Bik fired out sentences like a machine gun.

Jeremiah whistled. 'Shit, Dillon, no wonder we all chose it.'

'Thanks,' Dillon muttered. He was starting to wish he had the most boring blood in the world.

'Really, Dillon. This is a big deal,' Sade said.

'Yeah, but it doesn't change anything, not really . . .' he stopped, realising that it had. Although Sade was excited, she was hovering on the other side of the room from him. Angelo struggled to control himself around him. Bram and his father were desperate to get rid of him. An unknown vampire had tried to kidnap him. He stared at the pictures of Sade's beautiful family, propped up on the desk.

'I don't want to be some pariah,' he finished dejectedly.

'I'm sorry, mate. You don't have a choice. Like Shakespeare said, sometimes greatness is thrust upon you. You just have to deal with it,' Jeremiah said.

'But that's just it, there's nothing great about me.'

'Sounds like a classic case of imposter syndrome to me,' Bik remarked.

'What's that?'

'You doubt yourself, don't believe in yourself, feel like fraud.'

Dillon was momentarily silenced. That was exactly how he felt. 'To be fair, Bik, I haven't exactly done much yet – I just have weird blood.'

'Start believing, Dillon,' Jeremiah interrupted. 'You were chosen as VE. You saved Angelo. You're a great flier. It means more than "weird blood". Start living up to it.'

Dillon stared at the three of them, each brilliant in their own way. He still found it hard to believe he could be as talented as them. 'It's just so much, so fast,' he said, finally.

'You'll get used to it.' Jeremiah clapped him on the back and, like the sun breaking through a cloudy sky, Sade smiled at him.

'We believe in you.'

His throat tightened with emotion; how could he have doubted her over the missing sample?

'Thanks,' he choked.

For an awkward second, none of them knew what to do with themselves, so in an overly hearty voice, Dillon changed the subject.

'As you two are so hot at finding stuff out, can you help me mug up on Countess Fassano before her visit? Bram and I have to greet her before the Ice Challenge, and I don't want to make a complete fool of myself.'

Sade waved at Jeremiah.

'Jeremiah's the vampire for that. He's always got his nose in a book. We're better at the science stuff.'

'Too true,' Bik agreed. 'You'll be in good hands with Jeremiah – he probably knows what shoe size she takes. He's a serious fan.'

'I'll admit I know a bit about her,' he said, bending over her and dropping a kiss on the crown of Bik's glossy blue-black hair.

Her cool façade melted a little as she batted him away and her voice softened. 'I'll see you later.'

'Where are we going?' Dillon asked, as Jeremiah strode off.

'The blood bar. I need fuel.'

Angelo, Fred and Aron were hovering outside the blood bar door as they arrived.

'Hey, Dillon. Just the vamp or dhamp I want to see,' Fred said, 'Aron overheard Chiro and Borzak talking about you. I've shortened your odds to 4-1 for the Ice Challenge but they're still good. You've *got* to place a bet now.'

Dillon tapped his pockets. 'Sorry, Fred. Nothing's changed and they're letting me take part for now but my position as VE is still under close scrutiny.'

'That's just bullshit, Dillon, of course they won't take VE away from you,' Fred protested.

Jeremiah extracted a platinum card from his back pocket. 'Put ten thousand on that, Fred.'

Frederick whistled. 'Jeez, Jeremiah. The gold-mining business must be booming.'

Dillon stared at Jeremiah. 'Are you mad?'

Like lightning, Fred had whipped out his phone, linked it to a slimline card machine and had taken Jeremiah's payment before he changed his mind.

'You won't get better odds than that,' he said and then lowered his voice. 'By the way, that fake stuff they serve in the blood bar tastes worse than animal blood. Angelo can't stand it. I've got some of the real stuff left if you want some?'

'We're good. Thanks, Fred,' Jeremiah said.

Dillon pulled Angelo aside.

'What are you doing? Don't get caught taking illegal blood. One more thing and you could be expelled.'

Without his nose plugs, Angelo shuddered slightly as he caught Dillon's scent. 'This is the last time, Dillon. I promise. My extra control lessons are helping.'

'Leave him alone, Dillon,' Fred protested. 'He's allowed a bit of fun . . . and he needs energy – Ásta's demanding.'

'Just be careful,' Dillon warned as they walked off.

'We've got Aron to protect us,' Fred called over his shoulder.

'I hope you're happy to lose that ten grand,' Dillon said apprehensively, as he pushed the blood bar door open.

'Call it an incentive to smash the hell out of Bram and win Cora's undying love.'

Dillon grinned. 'Well, to be honest I'd not be needing much of an incentive for that, but he's a lot more experienced than me.'

'So?' Jeremiah shrugged. 'You beat him in Combat, Hunt and Protect.'

The blood bar was empty and as cavernous as before. Jeremiah helped himself to a frothy shot and folded himself into one of the low-slung couches at the side of the bar. His legs were so long, his knees concertinaed up to his ears.

'That looks comfortable.' Dillon grinned and wrinkled his nose. He understood what Fred was going on about now; the blood smelt synthetic, fake – like decaffeinated coffee or saccharin compared to sugar.

Jeremiah didn't seem to care as he knocked it back. 'So, Bibiana Fassano. What do you want to know?' he asked.

'Just fill me in enough so that I don't come across as the village idiot when I meet her.'

Jeremiah chuckled. 'Fair enough. She comes from a powerful vampire family that ruled across Mexico and South America. Her father was destroyed for insubordination and she and her mother lived in exile for many years. Exile made her strong and she is ferociously clever. Controversially, she won a place here, although it was very different then, and her extraordinary talents made her a star vampire. She was voted Peak One and Peak Three VE – Madame Dupledge, her best mate, was Peak Two VE. The two of them became the stuff of legends.

'After leaving here, she spent years doing the equivalent of a PhD in the International Diplomacy Department and at the same time ran missions for the Vampire Secret Service. She overcame political infighting and several attempts to get rid of her but, eventually, she became the first female vampire leader of both departments. She is renowned for being ruthless, super-intelligent, spectacularly talented in all things to do with the mind and she has proved time and time again that she has giant *cojones*.'

Dillon paled. 'Jaysus, how the hell am I going to impress her?'

'Just waft some of your blood scent at her – that'll set her back on her heels.'

'Very funny. She sounds terrifying.'

'Yeah.' Jeremiah agreed. 'But, by all accounts, she is also incredibly beautiful, charming and –' he lowered his voice – 'so the rumours say, she has a magnetism that brings grown vampires to their knees.'

Dillon's mouth hung open. 'Holy shit.' He gulped. 'Does she have a partner?'

'Yes, he's from one of the Ancient Italian families. They

say it's not a "love" match, more of a powerful alliance – it's usual in our world.'

Dillon kept quiet about Sade's parents' desire for her and Bram to link up.

'Kids?'

'You mean vampire progeny. Not as far as I know. Many vampire couples are unable to have progeny though. It's why our numbers are falling.'

'What do you mean?'

'It's complicated – there's a strict hierarchy in the vampire world. At the top are the Ancients – pure-blooded vampires who are over a thousand years old. Pure-blooded means untainted with human blood.'

He grimaced apologetically at Dillon. 'The Ancients are the most powerful vampires. Nikolas Karayan, the head of the Vampire Council, is an Ancient. The next most powerful are the Nobles – pure-blooded vampires who are between three hundred and a thousand years old. Then there the Elders – pure-blooded vampires who are between twenty-five and three hundred years old. Most of our parents fit into this category although some families are more "powerful" than others. We are known as Fledglings – the offspring of pure-blooded vampires.

'It becomes a little more tricky after that as there are common vampires – the offspring of pure-blooded vampires and "changed" or ex-human vampires. Mahina is a common vampire, hence why there's so much fuss over her becoming the Peak Three VE. Dhampirs, as you know, are the offspring of vampires and humans. The lowest category is "changed" or ex-human vampires like Borzak.

'Over the years, pure bloodlines have grown weaker and, if dhampirs like you have powerful Noble or even Ancient blood on one side and an exceptionally talented human on the other, you can see how some believe you might re-invigorate the bloodline.'

'Ah.' Dillon nodded. 'I can understand that I might have –' he paused uncomfortably – 'Noble or even Ancient blood on one side, but my da seems pretty normal – even if I think he's amazing.'

'There was more to you than met the eye – maybe the same is true for your father?'

'Maybe,' Dillon agreed uncertainly and steered the subject back to more comfortable ground. 'What are Countess Fassano's greatest achievements?'

'She is credited with driving us towards modernisation and using our skills for bettering humanity rather than destroying it. She's brought us to all the most powerful tables in the world. You can look her up on Vampedia.'

'Vampedia? Are you messing with me now?'

'No! It's our online encyclopaedia. You can access it on an encrypted part of the internet that we use – ask Bik.'

'Okay, cheers Jeremiah. I appreciate it.'

'No sweat, I'll just have one more of these –' he raised his drink as if toasting – 'and then let's go.'

Dillon raised an eyebrow. 'Is everything okay?'

'Yeah, just fuelling up for my repeat blood homework.'

'Ah, sound – smart thinking.'

Dillon frowned as Jeremiah gulped back another shot, his hand shaking slightly on the cup.

'Are you sure Professor Dukan has got your requirements sorted?'

'Yeah, yeah, it's all good. I'm just making sure I don't fail again.'

On the way back to their room, Dillon remembered Fred's comment about Jeremiah's family mines doing well.

'Have your family always had an interest gold mining?'

'Yeah, my dad owns several gold and copper mines across the West Indies and Latin America.'

'I've never met anyone with their own gold mine.'

Jeremiah shrugged. 'My family have been around for a long time. It's easier to be in the right place at the right time when you outlive generations of humans.'

They had both stripped to get into their coffins when there was a tap at the door. Jeremiah wrapped a towel around his waist and opened it.

'Bloodlust homework,' Elias announced, handing Jeremiah another tray with a beaker of blood.

Jeremiah averted his nose and kept his lips firmly shut as he took it.

As the pungent smell hit Dillon's senses, he felt his fangs lower, pressing into his bottom lip, but it wasn't as bad as before. Everything paled in comparison to Golden Blood. Jeremiah grimaced and Dillon sensed his apprehension.

'Are you going to be okay?'

'Yeah, I'll be fine. I'll just hit my coffin and forget about it.'

'Okay, wake me up if you need me.'

He woke with the sense that something was wrong. As he lay in the dark of the coffin, he came over hot and sweaty and a faint spicy scent swirled around his mind.

I must not drink it. I must not drink it. I must not drink it. Shit. I can't do this.

Jeremiah's thoughts faded as fast as they had popped into his mind. It was like trying to keep hold of water in a sieve.

With a thud of fear, he sat up and crashed his head on his coffin lid. Cursing, he pressed it open. Through the darkened room, he saw instantly that Jeremiah's coffin lid was open, and his nose couldn't pick up the slightest hint of the blood.

'Jeremiah!' he hissed.

His open coffin remained still and silent. Dillon swore. Where the hell was he? The hot and sick feeling stayed with him as he pulled on some tracksuit bottoms. He sensed Jeremiah was alone somewhere cold and echoey. Maybe he'd gone to the pool. Sprinting along the corridor in a panic, he passed the shower-room door and skidded to a stop.

Opening the door, he followed the continuous sound of a soft, hoarse growling. Jeremiah was huddled against the tiles in the corner. His hazel eyes had turned scarily dark and bloodshot. The beaker of blood was three metres away in the other corner.

'I haven't had any,' he choked, not looking up.

Dillon sagged with relief. 'Thank Christ for that.'

Fighting the bloodlust had made Jeremiah weak. Propping him up with one arm and holding the beaker away from him in the other, he helped him back to his coffin. Jeremiah collapsed into it, shuddering.

'What about the blood?' he asked.

'Close the lid. I'll look after it,' Dillon insisted.

Still shaking but sighing with relief, Jeremiah sank back and disappeared under the coffin lid. Left alone with the blood, Dillon tentatively lifted the beaker closer to his nose. The initial hit was still pungent and his fangs shot out to their full extent but, hand shaking, he held on. Saliva spilled into his mouth and as his throat spasmed, he knew he was on the edge of his control. Swallowing hard, he willed himself to think of something else.

Instantly he thought of his father; if he wanted to see him again, he had to trust himself. With a sickening lurch in his heart, he remembered that Christmas was almost upon them. How could he have forgotten? He held the image of his father roasting chestnuts by the fire in his mind, remembering every detail of his face. As the memory warmed his heart, the fierce intensity of the bloodlust lessened, and he discovered that once the initial lust faded, he could detect a subtle bitter aroma that helped to reduce his craving for it — it was like he could tell the blood was bad for his system.

The next night, after Elias had arrived to collect the blood, Jeremiah thanked him profusely.

'I owe you big time, Dillon.'

'No problem, mate. You'd do the same for me.'

Jeremiah nodded and glanced at him curiously. 'How come you didn't have a problem with it this time?'

Dillon shrugged. 'I don't know – it doesn't smell so good after Golden Blood, I guess.'

'I s'pose not,' Jeremiah said and smashed his hand on his coffin in frustration. 'I'm disappointed in myself. I thought I could handle it.'

'Are you going to be okay for the ski trip?' Dillon asked.

Jeremiah's face darkened. 'I honestly don't know, but I've still got a bit of time to get a grip on it. First, we've got to get through the Ice Challenge.'

17

Blood Power

As December turned into January, the nights grew ever so slightly shorter. Dillon had settled into the twice-weekly blood-drinking, flying and combat-training routine. He was looking forward to the next stage of the Peak One syllabus – Enhancing Mind Power.

He and Jeremiah, cutting it fine as usual, joined the rest of the class for Madame Dupledge's first lesson.

Dillon sat next to Angelo, who immediately closed his eyes and slowly counted to ten.

'How are your lessons with Madame Dupledge going?' Dillon asked him.

Angelo opened his slightly bloodshot eyes and winced. 'They're going well, but sit further away, Dillon.'

He shifted his chair a couple more inches away as Madame Dupledge swept in and looked round the class.

'Mind power is one of the most sophisticated talents

296

vampires possess,' she said. 'It encompasses sensing emotions and thoughts, controlling emotions and thoughts and harnessing the brain's electromagnetic energy as a weapon. Some of you may have already started to experience a mind talent emerging. Countess Fassano has the most powerful mind reading talent in the vampire world. She can both receive and impart thoughts. I am a strong intuit; I can sense thoughts and feelings and, as you know, if a vampire takes blood from me, I receive a strong insight into their nature.'

Angelo and Fred squirmed in their chairs. Dillon sighed with relief that she didn't mention his possible mind skills, especially as he wasn't exactly sure what they were yet.

'Bram, I believe that you have started to exhibit skill at harnessing electromagnetic energy in the brain?'

Bram nodded.

'It is a wonderful skill. You must learn to use it with great care,' Madame Dupledge cautioned. 'You can inflict great damage, but it can be directed back at you, so over your three years here you will all be taught how to use mind blocks or shields.

'You may remember a recent outrage in the human world, where a few US and UK intelligence officers at a conference in Cuba developed debilitating symptoms of an "unknown" illness – humans have labelled it as a "Neurosensory Syndrome". Victims heard a constant high-pitched buzzing noise and reported experiencing pulses of pressure. Many suffered from headaches and brain fog. They were taken out of service until they recovered; some never recovered at all.

'Some believe the Ministry of State Security in China could be directing powerful microwave beams at them . . . others think it's the Russian FSB. But they can't find any conclusive evidence because . . . it's us.'

Dillon's mouth hung open in shock. 'Why would you do that?' he asked.

'For a variety of reasons, it may occur when an intelligence officer uncovers too much about our world or one of our vampires, or it may be that we want to direct world events in our favour. Sometimes we help the secret services or a president if they need a mole taken out or if we agree with their cause. We take extreme measures to retain our invisibility, only the people with the highest level of security clearance know about us.'

She glanced at him, sensing his disapproval. 'Remember, we take them out of active duty, we don't kill them.'

'How does it work?' Sade asked.

'A human brain can power a small lightbulb, ours are capable of creating much, much more electromagnetic energy. We're able to harness that energy and direct it in the form of high amplitude micropulses into another brain. The energy is absorbed by the soft tissues in both the brain and inner ear, heating them up, causing a pressure wave in the head that is interpreted as sound. In a worst-case scenario, the energy could fry the whites of the eyes like an egg, so it is to be used with great caution and only against legitimate enemies.'

Dillon winced, remembering how it had felt when Bram had experimented with him.

'What's the other type of mind talent?' Madame Dupledge asked.

'Compulsion,' Celeste said.

'Compulsion, the ability to coerce or brainwash another vampire or a human to do what you want. As you know, it is against the rules while you are at VAMPS to compel your peers or any of the staff. It is however a powerful skill and over the next three years you will be taught how to use it, how to recognise when a vampire attempts to compel you and how to block it.

'As protecting yourself is so important we will start with learning how to harness your mental energy to form shields. Some of you will be able to form mental shields better than others. Amongst the most powerful vampires, it is a game of cat and mouse between manipulating and directing mental energy and harnessing it to form mental shields.

'The ultimate mental shield will prevent the mind being entered or affected in any way. This means your mind cannot be controlled, damaged, read, influenced or communicated with. It is what you will aspire to by the end of Peak Three.'

She looked round the class. 'Is everyone ready? Bik please remove your glasses, they will affect your ability to connect with your inner energy.'

Scowling, Bik removed her glasses, and Madame Dupledge dimmed the lights further.

'Begin by closing your eyes,' she instructed. 'With your eyes closed, you will empty your mind of thoughts.'

Dillon shut his eyes and tried to empty his mind with difficulty. He could still hear the faint noises of the others in the room and Angelo's fingers fidgeting restlessly next to him. Madame Dupledge's voice washed over him.

'Relax and start to visualise the energy that flows within you as a magnetic force. Try to hold onto it and explore what it feels like.'

He sank a little deeper and tried to focus, searching for the energy deep within. Gradually, he lost sense of the classroom and felt himself going deeper. In his deepest centre, he found the spark of energy he needed for flying. He fought to hold onto it as Madame Dupledge's voice washed over him again.

'Once you have found it, see if you can manipulate it. Start to project it into a bigger shape so that it forms a shield of light around your mind.'

Finding it once more, he visualised it as a small spark, glowing white-hot. From deep within his mind now, he attempted to expand it but, like the top of a lighter snapping shut on a flame, he lost it abruptly and his eyes shot open.

Feeling spaced out and disorientated, he blinked a few times and glanced round the class. Angelo's eyes were already wide open as were Fred and Aron's. He smiled as he saw Sade clench her fists and grit her teeth as she attempted to hold onto her energy. The sight of Cora biting her lip, her long lashes fanning her cheeks, made his heart ache with longing. Celeste and Bram were scarily still, like marble statues, only the faint movement of their eyeballs under their eyelids showing that they were conscious.

Madame Dupledge had gone silent and her green eyes gleamed as she continued to stare at Bram. Suddenly, his eyes flicked open and he shook his head to bring himself back to the classroom.

'Well done, Bram, that's a great first attempt. You managed to partially block me,' she said.

Celeste looked like she was waking up from a coma. Her face was chalk-white and her eyes were dark and clouded.

'Rest for a minute, Celeste. Manipulating your mental energy can deplete you. It seems you were partially successful.'

'A little,' Celeste agreed, her eyes returning to their normal icy blue.

Dillon noticed that Jeremiah's eyes were still shut, only the slight tapping of his finger against his thigh showed that he was alert. Madame Dupledge watched him with interest and gestured to the class to remain silent. Finally, he opened his eyes.

'How did you do, Jeremiah?' she asked.

'Good,' he said, looking a little surprised. 'I am quite strong with mind blocks but today, I managed to hold it for longer.'

Dillon remembered how Jeremiah had stood up against Bram for him in the blood bar after he was elected as VE. It was typical that he hadn't boasted about his talent.

'Well done, Jeremiah.' Madame Dupledge smiled. 'You are strong indeed. Keep practising and Countess Fassano will want you at her side.'

Jeremiah sat up a little taller.

'Well done everyone, a very good first attempt. For the moment, until you are more confident, accessing mental shields should only be done in the classroom with me. As the Ice Challenge is coming up fast, I would like you to continue to practise your shields.'

After class was over, Sade approached him as they left the room.

'Can I speak to you?' she asked, standing a small distance away.

'Sure,' he said. 'Here?'

'No, let's go to my room.'

As they took the circular stairs down to the third floor, Dillon glanced at her. He missed the side of her that had made him feel like all was well with the world. He sensed she was upset.

'Are you feeling better now – about my blood?' he asked, quietly.

Her face fell. 'Your blood is particularly hard to resist but I have good willpower, Dillon. I just want things to go back to the way they were.'

He took her hand and turned to face her at the atrium on the fifth floor.

'So do I, but it's not your fault. You were just trying to help.'

She stepped away from him, an almost panicked look in her eyes, but not before Dillon felt an overwhelming sense of her shame and frustration.

'But I haven't helped. We found out about your blood, but Bik still hasn't cracked the code to the highly classified stuff.'

'It doesn't matter. What can I do to help?' he asked. He was desperate to contribute more than his blood to their efforts.

She shook her head. 'Nothing, it'll just take time.'

She looked so despondent so, on impulse, he stepped forward and put his arms around her. Instantly, she stiffened. Feeling she was about to bolt, Dillon tightened his arms.

'Give it a minute,' he whispered into her soft hair.

'I can't,' she whispered, trembling all over. 'We've tried before. Please let go, Dillon.'

Shocked by the extent of her reaction, he released her.

'Sorry, Dillon,' she gasped, surprising him as pink tears spilled out of her eyes and splashed onto her smooth cheeks. 'It's not your fault – it's mine. I'm a scientist. I should have known better.'

'Sade! Wait,' he called after her, as she dashed down the stairs away from him.

Wearily, he followed her down, cursing his blood. Why was it having such a strong effect on Sade?

He found Jeremiah topping up in Starbloods as usual.

'Tasty,' he said, raising his eyes at the enormous frothy blood drink he had just taken a sip from. 'You're missing out, Dillon,' he said, licking his lips. 'Any mind stuff makes me so thirsty.'

'I need to ask you something.'

'Okay,' he nodded. 'Fire away.'

'Suppose someone tasted my blood. Why would they have such a hard time controlling their lust for it?'

Jeremiah looked at him quizzically. 'What the hell have you been up to Dillon?'

'Nothing. Just answer the question,' he snapped and then seeing Jeremiah's slight start of surprise, he added, 'Sorry – I never grew up with any of this – it's all new to me.'

'Sometimes one vampire's blood is just particularly alluring to another vampire. Yours is especially tricky because it's a human-vampire mix and tastes incredible – better than Golden Blood, I should imagine.' He took another sip of his drink, leaving a line of red froth on his top lip and smirked at Dillon. 'It's even harder if you're attracted to them. Believe me, you can't get them out of your head.'

'Oh, right.' He was struck dumb for a second.

Jeremiah smirked again. 'Did that answer your question?'

'Yeah, thanks, Jeremiah. I'll catch you later.'

18

Blood Deal

As the Ice Challenge approached, spurred on by Jeremiah's bet, Dillon spent all his spare time practising. His mind-shield strength was improving, he was now able to hold the spark and grow it into a grapefruit-sized shield. The thing that kept him awake in his coffin was the thought of becoming trapped if they had to swim under the ice lake. Borzak had told them even their vampire strength wouldn't be enough to break the thick ice at the centre of the lake.

The rest of the year was feeling the pressure too and a tangible undercurrent of tension permeated the academy building. Ásta and Aron nearly came to blows during the combat training drills and even Fred was uncharacteristically snappy. Everyone had their own fears: Jeremiah was worried about taking on enough blood to maintain his energy, Sade was clearly still upset and avoiding him, and he'd barely seen

Cora alone since they had kissed on the roof – although he relived it time and time again in his dreams.

To escape it all, he borrowed Jeremiah's laptop and hid in one of the classrooms to do some last-minute research on Countess Fassano. The more he read about her, the more apprehensive he became about meeting her.

Jeremiah hadn't been joking when he said she was ruthless. Several vampires had met grisly ends on her watch. Reading between the lines, it seemed there were two things she couldn't abide: incompetence or disloyalty.

'Aren't you coming to watch the end of the Peak Two Challenge?'

He started and saw Cora watching him from the door.

'How long have you been there?' he asked.

'Not long.' She shrugged. 'Are you okay?'

Of course not, he wanted to snap. She'd hardly spoken to him for the past few weeks.

'Yeah, sure. Why?' he said.

'You look tense and, like I said, I wondered why you're missing the end of the Peak Two Challenge?'

'Shite!' He smacked his forehead. 'I forgot it's tonight.'

Cora grinned at him, and he felt the tightness in his chest loosen just a little.

'Come on then,' she said. 'Hunt's letting us catch a glimpse of it from the roof.'

'What do they do in the Peak Two Challenge?' he asked as they made their way up from the sixth floor to the top floor.

'You already know that our challenge tests our senses, stamina, agility, teamwork, flying and combat skills.'

He tried to ignore the pleasurable tingles up his arm whenever their hands brushed and concentrate on what she was saying.

'The main point of the Peak Two Challenge, along with other things, is to test transfiguration—'

'What's that?' Dillon interrupted.

'It's basically shapeshifting – like turning into a bat or a bird,' she said, energetically flapping her arms.

'Okay, I get it,' Dillon grinned, 'Carry on.'

'By the Peak Three Challenge we're expected to demonstrate our mastery of the highest mental skills like misting, mind reading, moving objects with the mind and manipulating the weather as well as superb flying, transfiguration and combat skills.'

Dillon raised his eyebrows. 'Misting?'

Cora gave him a playful nudge that sent little darts of electricity up his neck, suffusing his cheeks with warmth. 'Stop interrupting! Instead of flying or transfiguring, the most talented vampires can transform into a mist and appear or disappear at will.'

'Oh yeah.' He remembered Mahina mentioning that she was good at it. 'So what are the Peak Twos doing tonight?'

'I'm not sure exactly. Probably a lot of flying around as bats. Admittedly it's not the most exciting to watch – unless any of them are rubbish.' She grinned wickedly. 'Then it's funny, they might turn into the wrong thing or only half turn or change back at the wrong time.'

He stopped for a second and glanced at her, happy that the old Cora had resurfaced.

'What?' she demanded.

He shook his head. 'Nothing. It's just that it's like you've been avoiding me recently.'

Her face dropped. 'Every time we were together, it ended in a row or I hurt you. I didn't want to do that anymore. Besides, you were pretty pissed off and you asked me to leave you alone.'

They had arrived at the official entrance to the roof on the twelfth floor. Elias and a couple of burly assistants were acting as security.

'Go on up,' he said, waving them through.

The others were already up on the roof with most of the teachers. Jeremiah beckoned to him, but Cora dragged him over to stand next to Bram.

'It's about time you two stopped this stupid rivalry,' she said quietly, looking straight ahead.

Over the top of her head, his eyes met Bram's, and although Dillon didn't catch his thoughts, Bram couldn't have made them any clearer. They stood, one on each side of Cora, bristling with resentment.

'Here they come!' Cora exclaimed.

Dillon scanned the mountains in front of them. As the fast-moving shape from the east drew closer, he realised it was a triangle of bats. The cheer from the watching vampires abruptly changed into a gasp as, almost as Cora had predicted, one of the bats suddenly shuddered and dropped, transforming into a slight, pale-haired Peak Two vampire as he fell. Out of nowhere, another bat shot towards him like a speeding dart and transformed mid-air into Chiro, who grabbed the spinning vampire, preventing him from crashing into the mountainside.

'He must have used up his mental energy. Passed out most likely,' Bram commented.

Once again, the others cheered as the rest of the bats flitted over the roof and disappeared down the other side.

'Where's the other team?' Cora said, scanning the sky.

'Over there.' Bram pointed. 'Looks like they're having some trouble too.'

Again, Dillon saw what Cora had meant. Six stunning falcons swooped around a vampire girl who appeared to be changing from bird to vampire as she flew. Each time she flicked out of her bird state she seemed to lose more energy until on the last change she remained a bizarre half-falcon, half-vampire mix. It wasn't funny but Dillon caught Cora's eye and suppressed a smile.

One of the other falcons transformed back into the Peak Two VE, George Gyllenborg. Dillon saw instantly that he was a superb flyer and, in seconds, he was flying alongside her, holding her up, while she changed completely back to vampire. The watching vampires clapped and cheered as, flying as a team once more, two in vampire form, the rest as falcons, they too disappeared over the building.

'Great leadership from George,' Bram muttered, turning to Cora and ignoring Dillon. 'Let's go and cheer him up; he'll be devastated his team didn't win.'

As they left, Cora cast a backwards glance at Dillon.

Jeremiah came up. 'You okay?' he asked, watching Cora and Bram leave the roof.

Dillon nodded with a small, rueful smile. 'Yeah, all good – although that didn't exactly make me feel more confident about tomorrow.'

Jeremiah grimaced. 'I know what you mean. It's even worse for us – Countess Fassano will be watching.'

Early the next evening, the night of the Ice Challenge, a naked Celeste cornered a nervous Dillon in the showers.

'Is it true you get to meet Countess Fassano alone later?'

Dillon focused on a spot just beyond her left shoulder and shrugged. 'Not alone, but I'm greeting her when she arrives. Why?'

'I thought Bram might be winding me up.'

'Why would he do that?'

She shrugged. 'Because he's Bram. He likes to make out he's more important than he is.'

Dillon turned his head just enough to make eye contact with her. 'Why are you telling *me* this?'

'No reason. Although – it might help you to be less intimidated by him.'

'I'm not intimidated by him!'

She raised a sceptical eyebrow. 'Sure.'

'You haven't exactly been welcoming either.'

Celeste laughed lightly. 'Dillon. That's not my style. I'd like to meet the Countess – see if you can put a good word in for me.'

'I doubt I'll have that sort of influence. Like I said, we're only greeting her.'

Celeste ran her eyes down his body. 'Dillon, you're VE. I'm sure you can swing it.'

He held his ground but felt a slight tell-tale burn in his cheeks, as she ran her eyes slowly back up.

'Hey Dillon.' Ace strode in and dived straight under a shower. 'Hurry up, babe. She'll be here soon,' he called to Celeste.

Celeste leant forward until she was almost touching him and whispered in his ear, 'Don't forget, Dillon. I'll make it worth your while.'

Smirking back at him, she disappeared into the steam after Ace.

Jeremiah caught him on his way out of the shower room. 'What happened to you?' he asked.

Dillon shrugged. 'Nothing, just Celeste being Celeste.'

Jeremiah chuckled. 'Want to come up to the pool to check the conditions?'

As the soft orange sun began to sink behind the mountains, Dillon stared out of the floor-to-ceiling windows at the vast frozen lake and shuddered. Soon they would be battling it out underneath that solid, unforgiving ice.

'Shit, scary. Isn't it?' Jeremiah muttered.

Before Dillon could reply, three sleek helicopters appeared over the mountains on the far side of the lake and flew, silhouetted against the dusky orange-streaked sky, towards them.

The windows began to vibrate as they drew closer and he watched, fascinated, as the rotor blades whipped loose snow into circular flurries across the ice. The heat haze from the throbbing jet engines gave the horizon a shimmering movie-scene quality and, as the side doors slid open in unison, at least ten vampires swan dived out and swooped gracefully up the side of the building. Looking up, Dillon glimpsed them flying fast in formation across the roof before disappearing on the other side.

'Looks like Bibiana's here,' Jeremiah said.

'Does she always arrive like that?' Dillon asked, impressed.

'Yup, she never goes anywhere without at least three bodyguards – the others will be VSS operatives and maybe a couple of VIVs.'

'VIVs?'

'Very Important Vampires.'

'Shite.' Dillon's stomach clenched with nerves. 'I'd better go down.'

Once again, Aron loaned him the suit and shirt he'd worn for the Induction Ceremony. Dillon pulled the trousers on and, as he was all fingers and thumbs, Aron helped him do up the buttons on the shirt.

'Looking good, Dhamp,' he approved.

Normally Dillon was completely uninterested in his

appearance. His da didn't believe in vanity so he'd grown up with just a tiny mirror over the bathroom sink, but now, as he looked in the mirror on the inside of his cupboard door, he was fascinated. His blood-only diet had refined his looks: his face was alabaster smooth and more finely drawn, his eyes seemed to have darkened to a deep lapis-blue and the unruly dark hair falling over his forehead gleamed. All the fight training had honed his body so that his arm, shoulder and ab muscles now formed a perfect V, filling out the shirt like a Michelangelo sculpture.

Fred whistled when he turned up to inveigle a last-minute bet out of him. 'Woah, Dillon you're looking hench. Thank God, Aron is here to keep me on the straight and narrow. More importantly, the odds are still 4–1 for you to win the Ice Challenge.'

Dillon grinned and shook his head. 'Like I keep telling you, Fred, I don't have any money.'

'Borrow some, Dillon. Speculate to accumulate.'

'Okay, okay. Aron can you lend me ten Swiss francs or whatever currency Fred deals in?'

'Ten?' Fred looked at him in disbelief. 'The odds are 4–1, Dillon. That only makes forty. Put a hundred on and you make four hundred.'

'If I win.' Dillon reminded him. 'There's Bram, Ace and Aron to beat for a start.'

'Yeah, but their odds are 2–1.'

'Fred, I've got to go. Put me down for 10. But I'll have to owe you.'

'Okay,' Fred agreed sulkily. 'Hold out your hand.'

Before Dillon knew what he was doing, Fred grabbed his hand and ran his tongue across his palm. As his fangs shot out, Dillon struggled to pull away, but Fred held on with his surprising vampire strength and bit down into the skin just enough to make a crescent shaped mark. Dillon hissed with pain and Fred let go.

'There you go – vampire blood deal,' he grinned. 'Once marked with blood you must always uphold an agreement.'

'Fred, you idiot. I've got to meet the Countess now with a cracking great bite mark in my hand,' he roared.

Fred grinned, completely unconcerned. 'Keep your hair on. Look, it's starting to disappear already. You're a fast healer, Dillon.'

Bram and the other VEs were grouped in a tight huddle when Dillon hurried into Madame Dupledge's office, cursing Fred. Night had fallen, and a full moon gleamed through the diamond window. The others stopped talking as he approached, and Dillon guessed Bram had been discussing him. Mahina, the Peak Three VE, broke away from the circle, beckoning him over.

'Hi, Dillon. Bram seems to think he should do the talking tonight with Countess Fassano.'

Dillon scowled at Bram. 'It's true that I don't know as much about the vampire world, but I have read everything there is to read about her.'

'I'm honoured to hear it,' a soft voice remarked from behind him.

He swung round to see Madame Dupledge standing next to a striking vampire dressed in a tailored, midnight-blue trouser suit and high heels. She was taller than Madame Dupledge, with short, dark hair that was slicked back to display smooth olive skin, flashing brown eyes under arching black brows and strong, even features. She had one of the most animated faces Dillon had ever seen. He got the impression that she was interested in everything and missed nothing. As she examined him, he felt his throat go dry.

Sensing his awkwardness, Madame Dupledge introduced him. 'This is Dillon Halloran, our Peak One VE.'

'Ah, so you're Dillon. Congratulations, the first dhampir to join VAMPS. I've heard a lot about you.'

She continued to examine him with laser-like interest, and he had the sensation she was stripping away his outer layers like an onion.

Dillon swallowed. 'Thank you—' He broke off in embarrassment as he realised, too late, that he didn't know how he should address her.

A slight tilt of her head and an upward curve of her lips indicated that she wasn't mortally offended. 'I'm looking forward to seeing you in action later.'

His throat went dry again and his stomach clenched even tighter than before. 'Um, yes. There'll be action all right.'

Furiously, he kicked himself. What an inarticulate moron.

Bram stepped forward. 'Countess Fassano,' he greeted her in his beautiful, well-modulated voice, smiling with just enough sincerity to not seem sycophantic.

'*Domnule Danesti, ma bucar sa te revad,*' she greeted him, slipping into Romanian.

'*Multumesc* – you too. I trust your journey was pleasant.' Bram bowed and couldn't resist a little triumphant sideways glance at Dillon.

'Ah yes, the new Blackhawk copters are a treat.' She smiled. 'I hope you are enjoying your new role. You must be a great support to Dillon.'

Bram's eyes widened infinitesimally. 'Dillon only has to ask,' he replied smoothly.

Wow, thought Dillon, impressed, *he really is an operator.*

'I'm glad to hear it.' She smiled again. 'I'm sure I'll see your dedication to your role in action later.'

Bram's jaw tightened but he managed a smile. 'Of course.'

Turning to the rest of the group, she greeted Mahina and George, the Peak Two VE. 'Congratulations. I hear that you both excelled in your challenges,' she said. 'Mahina, we will talk later about your upcoming appointment.'

Bram's eyes glittered with envy as Mahina glowed with pleasure.

'Thank you, Countess.'

Madame Dupledge's mellifluous voice sounded even more musical after Bibiana's, low, soft-but-husky tones. 'I have much to discuss with Countess Fassano, but we will reconvene for the blood drinking at midnight, followed by the Ice Challenge for Peak One at two a.m. as planned. Mr Hunt is making the final preparations now. Bram, can you inform the rest of the Peak One students? Dillon, could you show

Countess Fassano to her coffin room on the fourth floor please?'

Dillon felt the pit of his stomach churn; what on Earth should he talk about?

Bibiana gave him a small smile. 'Ah, Dillon, perhaps you can enlighten me on what it's like to join VAMPS as a dhampir?'

She clearly needed no direction. As she loped out of the hall, Dillon hastened to catch up with her, and the four bodyguards covering the door and the lifts sprang to attention and split into pairs in front and behind them.

Jaysus, thought Dillon, looking at their huge biceps and fierce expressions, *a lot of vampires must want her dead*.

'Will we go via the stairs or the lift?' he muttered, nervously.

'Let's take the lift. I would like to visit the swimming pool floor first – the views from there are always incredible.'

One of the front bodyguards opened the lift doors and walked in first. Bibiana followed and the other bodyguard gestured to Dillon to enter. Self-consciously, he stood next to Bibiana as the second bodyguard joined them and she instructed him to press the button for the eleventh floor.

Bibiana's exotic, woody scent filled the close confines of the lift, making it hard for him to think straight. Awkwardly, he stared out of the glass sides of the lift and saw Bram, tight-lipped with anger, glare up at him as he left the hall.

Curbing a smirk, he groped for something to say to

Bibiana. 'Was it like this back in the day? When you were a student, I mean?' he asked.

She gave a low chuckle. 'No, I was here over a hundred years ago and it was very different, more of a cross between a fort and a castle.'

Dillon felt his eyes widen. Of course, what an idiot. He stole a sideways glance at her – like Professor Sandhu, she didn't look a day over twenty-five.

'When do vampires stop ageing?' he asked, without thinking.

She smiled slightly. 'In our early twenties. It's different for dhampirs, you age but incredibly slowly. Although it might be different for you if the reports on your blood are to be believed.'

'Oh, right.' He was silent for a second as he absorbed all the implications of that. Who hadn't been told about his blood?

The doors opened on the eleventh floor, but they remained in the lift as the other two bodyguards who had taken the stairs checked the space was safe. On their signal, the two bodyguards in the lift allowed Bibiana to leave. One guarded the door and the other, the secret exit to the roof. Cora was clearly not the only one who knew about it.

'Um, yeah. I still don't know what it means, to be honest,' he admitted.

She turned to him, and he found himself transfixed by the intensity in her mesmerising dark eyes. Wordlessly, she communicated with him, effortlessly slipping into his brain and sending him her thoughts: *It means you must be extremely careful. Madame Dupledge will protect you, but you must always be on your guard. It's imperative that you hone your skills quickly and then be prepared to make use of them. Your skills will be dangerous if they fall into the wrong hands.*

Unable to move or look away, he swallowed and nodded to let her know he understood, but in truth he felt fazed and couldn't quite believe what had just happened. Her eyes blinked, and the intensity of the moment melted away and she flicked her gaze back to the window. Immediately, he felt a strange feeling of loss. He found himself longing for her to look at him intently again but, turning abruptly, she headed for the lifts.

'Now, you need to prepare for the Challenge.'

'Countess . . . could I ask you something?' he asked, lengthening his stride to catch up with her.

As she turned her gaze on him again, once again he felt her incredible power as if a searchlight had found him in the dark. This time, she spoke. 'It depends on what it is.'

'Do you know anything about the vampire who was expelled from here last year and went missing?'

Her dark brows lifted in surprise. 'You must be referring to Zach de Courtenay?'

'Um, yes.'

As her eyes lasered into him, he felt defenceless, like she was staring into the very centre of his being. 'Ah,' she said after a couple of seconds. 'His sister, Cora de Courtenay. You are asking this for her?'

'Um, yes,' he said, marvelling at her power. There was no point in trying to hide the truth.

'And if I tell you, it will give you an advantage somehow?'

Unable to look away, he nodded, feeling his treacherous cheeks flush slightly. She thought for a second, making up her mind.

'I can tell you this,' she whispered softly, so the guards couldn't hear, 'he *is* an exceptional young vampire.'

Dillon, held his breath, waiting for more, but with the faintest of smiles, she headed straight for the lift, making it clear that the conversation was over. Instantly, the bodyguards jumped to attention.

As he re-entered the lift, Dillon felt crushed by the weight of his disappointment. Bibiana hadn't told him anything new that would help Cora. Now he would never win her from Bram.

Bibiana also seemed lost in thought, and they descended to the fourth floor in silence. Her bodyguards' eyes flicked restlessly, looking for hidden dangers. As Dillon left her outside her rooms, she thanked him.

'I'll see you at the blood drinking before the Ice Challenge,' she said, 'and remember what I told you.'

'I will. Thank you . . . Countess.'

19

Blood Ceremony

The others were hanging out in the coffin corridor when he returned. Avoiding Celeste, he joined Sade, Bik and Jeremiah.

'Woah, Dillon, you were alone with the most powerful female vampire in the world. How did it go?' Jeremiah teased.

'Shut up!' Dillon grinned.

'Bram and Celeste are beside themselves.'

'What's she like?' Sade asked, intrigued but keeping her distance.

'Intimidating,' Dillon said. 'It's like she can see straight through you. The four mountain-size bodyguards watching her every move don't help.'

'God, I wish she wasn't watching the Ice Challenge,' Sade groaned. 'It's way too much pressure.'

'Pressure is good, Sade,' Bik reminded her. 'It makes you raise your game.'

Sade shook her head. 'Depends on your personality.'

'You'll be too busy using that brain of yours to be nervous,' Bik insisted.

Jeremiah pulled Dillon aside. 'Is she really as compelling as they say?' he asked in an undertone.

'More.' Dillon grinned.

Jeremiah shook his head. 'Oh, Christ. Talk about upping the stakes.'

At midnight, Celeste sidled up as they made their way to the blood drinking. 'Don't forget to introduce me,' she whispered, floating off again before Dillon could reply.

The Ceremonial Hall had been transformed. The lights were turned down low and hundreds of tealight candles in brass holders lined long tables. The blood bags, hanging from their racks to the sides of the room, glowed red in the flickering light. Professor Dukan dashed about, double checking the arrangements. The tables had been arranged so that there was a long top table facing six perpendicular tables. Crystal flutes and damask napkins were laid at every seat.

Elias and his assistants scurried around directing everyone to their tables. The Peak Ones were on the left two tables, the Peak Threes in the centre and the Peak Twos on the tables to the right. Aron and Fred joined Dillon, Sade, Jeremiah and Bik. The Vampire Elects and Deputies sat in their assigned seats at the ends nearest the top table.

There was a hum of low, excited half-whispered conversation and the occasional instantly hushed chuckle. Once

everyone was seated, Mr Hunt, accompanied by several distinguished vampires, swept in. Dillon recognised Bram's father
from his haughty demeanour and dark, brooding expression.
They were followed by an entourage of burly, menacing-
looking vampires in black combat gear. The rest of the school
staff, swathed in floor-length cloaks, floated in after them.
Madame Dupledge and Bibiana were the last to arrive,
shadowed by her bodyguards and VIVs.

Madame Dupledge's luxuriant hair blazed red like the
blood bags against her creamy skin and Bibiana, panther-
sleek, prowled next to her, flickering eyes assessing the room.
Watching her, Dillon realised she was tense, and he wondered
why. Maybe, in her position, she was on permanent alert.
Everyone sat up and leaned forward, rigid with anticipation.

'Welcome to the Ice Challenge,' Madame Dupledge
announced, breaking the silence. 'This year we are especially
privileged that Countess Fassano has made time in her busy
schedule to visit us. She will be watching the challenge and
based upon what she sees, she might begin to make selections
for her trainee VSS.'

Aron's face turned the colour of pale ash; Ásta's eyes
burned with determination.

'As is traditional, we begin the Challenge with a blood
toast to wish the Peak One Challenge contestants good luck
and strength of mind and body.'

Elias's team began delivering individual blood bags to the
top table, and Dillon craned his neck to see what Bibiana
was drinking. He was too far away to see the label but then,

as the rest of the tables were served, he realised the blood type label had been removed and replaced with her name. Her favourite blood type was clearly a security risk and kept secret.

After the entire room had been given their blood except for Dillon, Professor Dukan went into the blood storage room and emerged a minute later, carrying a single bag with great reverence. The room hushed and every eye in the room watched as Professor Dukan passed the blood to him.

'Thank you,' he muttered, stiff with embarrassment.

'Be extremely careful when you pour it,' Professor Dukan instructed, 'and give the bag to me straight after.'

He nodded at Madame Dupledge.

'You may pour,' Madame Dupledge called out.

Angelo who had been twitching with the effort of restraining himself was the first to rip open his bag and fill his glass, Jeremiah was a close second. As the scent of blood filled the air, fangs shot out up and down the tables. Only the top table and some of the Peak Three vampires seemed able to control themselves.

As Professor Dukan hovered behind him, Dillon, hand trembling, poured the Golden Blood into his glass, following the lead of his classmates. Instantly, his own fangs shot out and, as the smell diffused into the air, Jeremiah and Sade, who were closest, swallowed convulsively, and their nostrils flared wide.

Madame Dupledge raised her glass. 'To a successful Ice

Challenge,' she intoned. 'May blood give you strength and honour.'

The room went silent, except for the sounds of gulps and sighs of pleasure. The top table, who had years of practice, sipped theirs with refined control and, as Dillon tipped his glass, he was aware that Bibiana was watching him closely. He attempted to drink slowly, but the minute the Golden Blood hit the back of his throat, a mad craving took over and he gulped the rest of it, relishing its exquisite taste. As golden fire scorched his throat and seconds later, his arteries, his vision blurred, and he swayed.

Hastily, Professor Dukan snatched the glass before he dropped it. 'Keep your head down for a minute, Dillon,' he whispered.

He could feel Bibiana's eyes boring into him and, with the super enhanced vision he developed after taking blood, he focused on the pattern in the napkin. As he traced one delicate stitch after the other, he heard Bibiana.

Quickly now, focus. You must gain complete control of your mind and body.

He jerked his head up and stared at her. She nodded infinitesimally, before she turned away and engaged the vampire next to her in conversation.

'Woah,' Dillon exhaled.

Jeremiah placed a steady hand on his shoulder. 'Are you okay?'

'Yeah.' He couldn't say that Bibiana had just spoken to him with her mind again.

Madame Dupledge stood again. 'Now, it is time to reveal the teams.' She paused, allowing the anticipation to build. 'Team Hawk: Dillon, Ásta, Cora, Jeremiah, Sade and Frederick—' Ásta hissed like an angry cat, and Madame Dupledge paused to glare at her. 'Team Eagle: Bram, Celeste, Aron, Angelo, Bik and Ace.'

'Yes!' Bram, Ace and Celeste pumped fists as the room erupted.

'Sorry vampires, I guess you drew the short straw,' Fred apologised.

'Don't be dumb, Fred,' Dillon reassured him, almost delirious with relief that he had Cora, Jeremiah and Sade on his side. 'We'll work together, and we'll win.'

'Congratulations teams.' Bibiana's soft, husky voice somehow managed to cut through the noise. Her powerful presence had everyone leaning in, straining to pick up her every word, bringing an instant hush to the room. 'I am delighted to be here and I'm looking forward to witnessing an impressive display of physical endurance and mental alacrity. The Ice Challenge is designed to take you to your limit and beyond. Its intention is to teach you valuable lessons about yourselves and how to conquer your fears.'

Dillon saw Sade bite her lip.

'My most important piece of advice is to do your best as an individual but always ensure your best efforts are for the good of your team. Good luck.'

There was a pause and then the room erupted into conversation. Dillon felt strangely bereft again. It was like her mesmerising voice had woven a comforting spell around him and now it had suddenly been ripped away.

'Thank you, Countess. Wise words indeed.' The room quietened once more as Madame Dupledge continued. 'Peaks Two and Three, you may wait here. We will meet on the landing stage on the side of the lake at two a.m. Peak Ones you may leave now. Mr Hunt will issue you with your final instructions and equipment.'

There was a scraping of chairs as everyone stood up. Several Peak Two and Threes clapped Bram on the back as he walked out, and he shared a brief, tense glance with his father.

As Dillon followed him, Mahina reached out and touched his arm. 'Good luck,' she murmured, 'and watch your back. It gets competitive out there.'

'Thanks,' he muttered, another attack of nerves punching him in the stomach. 'I'll try.'

Cora, who was standing next to him, scowled at her. 'You'd know all about that,' she hissed.

Dillon glanced at Cora in surprise and then remembered that Mahina had had something to do with hunting Cora's brother, Zach – the brother that he was no closer to finding out any more about.

20

Frozen Blood

Mr Hunt, flanked by Borzak and Chiro, met them in the gym. There was no sign of the burly VSS operatives. Dillon assumed they were setting up out on the lake.

'This is your equipment.' He pointed to twelve black backpacks laid out in a circle on the floor. 'It includes a waterproof suit, a GPS and vital statistics band, a small individual blood shot for emergency fuelling, sunglasses in case you get stuck after sunrise and a snow saw. You will decide if and when you need to use any of it. You can change into your challenge suits now. Lightweight boots are next to your backpacks.'

In silence, they stripped down to their underwear to change. As he pulled his suit on, he caught a glimpse of Cora and felt a rush of heat. God, she looked amazing. Quickly, he turned away and felt Ásta's mocking eyes on him.

'Nice chain, Dillon. How come I haven't noticed it before?' She smirked when he looked up.

Self-consciously, he tucked it into his suit and zipped it up to the neck.

'Where did you get it from?'

'My da gave it to me just before I came here – for good luck I suppose.'

'It looks vampiric.' She came closer and, lowering his zip, pulled the chain out, resting it on her upturned fingers. 'I'm pretty sure it's an Ancient vampire design. Look at the intricate metal work, and that stone is stunning. It must be worth a lot. Who is your mother again?'

Dillon noticed that Bram had heard and was watching surreptitiously.

'I don't know. I can't remember her.'

He slid it off her fingers and zipped it away again.

Dressed head to toe in black, they suddenly resembled the VSS; only the VAMPS crest on the front of the suit distinguished them. Dillon zipped the sunglasses and blood shot into the special pockets on his chest and hips. The last thing to go on was the GPS band, which he strapped tightly to his wrist, hoping it worked better than the one he'd had for the flying challenge.

'Listen up, everyone,' Mr Hunt continued, 'I won't repeat these instructions. There is an underwater drone operating under the ice in the lake. It has been placed there by a rogue vampire group who use them to smuggle cocaine and black-market blood. In this case, they are using it to hide a rare blood and stolen intelligence. Your task is to locate the drone, remove the blood and the data. Do not destroy the drone as it will provide useful intelligence. It may be booby trapped and it is likely that it will be guarded in some way. Remember, rogues will injure and immobilize you without compunction – a high-ranking vampire has already been staked to obtain the intelligence. Like the Flight Trial, do not take your phones as the signals can be tracked and could pose a security threat to the secret position of VAMPS.'

'Bullshit.' Fred coughed under his breath, hating to be parted from his phone for a second.

'The first team to return with the blood intact and all their team members will be the winners. Team Hawk will find further instructions on the western side of the lake and Team Eagle on the eastern side. I will give you the co-ordinates of their locations just before you leave. You will find all technical information about the drone and its position there. You will find your bases on foot, starting with a race down the mountain. You will NOT fly until you find your instructions. You need to conserve energy for the later stages of the challenge The only other rules are to avoid contact with humans and to stay within the thirty kilometre radius. Myself, Borzak and Chiro will be out there acting as referees in case there are any issues. Airborne drones will also be recording the events for the spectators but, essentially, you are now on your own. Compete as a team to win.'

Dillon swallowed and glanced round at the others; there were no whoops or high-fives now even amongst the most competitive vampires. He raised his hand. 'Are the rogues guarding the drone real?'

Mr Hunt scowled at him. 'They are top class VSS operatives who have been told to act exactly like real rogues. The only things they are not allowed to use are guns or stakes. You will be expected to attack them or defend yourself against them as you would in real combat.'

'Surely, we're not good enough yet to take on highly trained professionals,' Sade argued.

'That is the whole point, Sade,' Mr Hunt snapped. 'We're testing you.'

Sade opened her mouth as if she wanted to say something else and then shut it again as she thought better of it.

'Split into your groups,' Mr Hunt ordered. 'It is almost time to leave. Here are the co-ordinates for the information packs. Memorise them and destroy them.'

Dillon took the coordinates and joined Sade, Jeremiah, Cora, Ásta and Fred. Sade studied them carefully for a minute.

'Okay,' she said, pointing at a spot on the map. 'Got it.'

'Are you sure?' Ásta peered at the map. 'We don't want to mess it up before we've even got started.'

'If Sade says she's got it, she's got it,' Dillon snapped.

Ásta's eyebrows raised. 'Calm down, Dillon,. I'm just checking.'

'It's fine,' Sade interrupted. 'Ásta – I've got it.'

'Cool.' Ásta shrugged.

'Everyone ready?' Jeremiah asked.

They all nodded.

'Dillon and Bram are the default leaders,' Mr Hunt called out. 'But —' he smiled nastily — 'if the team feel they are not doing a good enough job, they may vote for an alternative challenge leader.'

Bram smirked, clearly confident that no one would want to oust him. Dillon blanched but Jeremiah punched his arm reassuringly.

'Let's do this thing,' Jeremiah said.

'You better be on this, Dillon,' Ásta warned.

'Thanks, Ásta.' Dillon scowled. 'You really know how to build someone up.'

She glared back. 'I want to win.'

'We all do, Ásta.' Sade reminded her.

'Yeah, just some of us more than others,' Ásta said, narrowing her eyes at Fred. 'He has to pay out big time if Dillon wins.'

'Ásta!' exclaimed Dillon. 'He wouldn't do that — would you, Fred?'

'Of course not!' Frederick blustered.

Dillon stared him right in the eyes. 'Frederick?'

'I won't.' Fred sulked. 'But don't blame me if I can't keep up with you guys when we're flying.'

'Listen carefully,' Ásta hissed. 'If you muck this up, I'll kill you.'

'There's no need for that, Ásta,' Cora exclaimed, putting an arm round Fred. 'You're going to do everything you can to help aren't you, Fred?'

As her beautiful eyes smiled into his, Dillon saw him melt.

If he had been torn between his bets and doing well, Cora, with one deep look, had converted him.

'Of course, I am.'

'You stick with me – I'll look out for you.'

Dillon recognised the slavish devotion in Fred's eyes. *Vampires would follow Cora to the end of the Earth*, he thought. There was something about her. Something bewitching.

'I've got your back too, Fred,' Jeremiah said. 'Just keep to your side of the bargain and do your best.'

'Time to go,' Mr Hunt called. 'We will leave from the emergency exit in the basement as it's on the front side of the mountain and you'll will have direct access to the lake.'

In silence, the two groups followed him through a door at the back of the gym that led to a concrete stone staircase Dillon had never seen before. Borzak and Chiro were waiting for them at the bottom and opened a heavy door with an impressive security system. Beyond that was a small roughly hewn cave tunnel with a smooth rock wall at the end. CCTV cameras and intruder lights lined the walls.

'Get ready,' Mr Hunt instructed. 'Remember, you have approximately four hours until sunrise to complete the challenge.'

The teams lined up. Dillon could feel the Golden Blood thudding round his body and as he looked across at his team – Ásta next to him, Sade carefully maintaining her distance, then Cora, Fred and Jeremiah – he felt the weight of responsibility almost crush him. He had to do this well, for them.

He could prove he was the leader they needed and cement his position as VE.

Borzak pressed a button and stood guard as the rock wall slid back with a gust of sharp mountain air. The inky star-splattered sky appeared behind it and Dillon leant forward onto the balls of his feet, his body as taut as a bow string.

'Go!' Mr Hunt roared.

After all the tension, it was a relief to start sprinting. They burst out of the entrance, and, pouring out like a waterfall over the edge, they raced down the mountain. After so many trials and tribulations, Dillon exalted at the sheer speed and surge of the vampiric power in his muscles as they bounded full pelt down the sheer, snow-covered mountain face.

At home, he'd been forced to slow down when winter snow had blanketed the landscape around the cottage and the path to the sea became treacherous. Now, his feet found purchase unfalteringly and in the silence all he could hear was the occasional gasp and grunt and the soft crunches as their feet landed lightly on the snow and bounded off again. Somewhere above them was the faint whine of a drone capturing the action for the bystanders. He glanced to both sides, checking everyone in the team was keeping pace, taking the time to give Fred a quick nod of encouragement. For a second, he relished the sense of teamwork and the simple pleasure in the strength and speed of his muscles. He wondered if this was how wolves felt when they ran with the pack.

Within minutes they were at the level of the lake, four

thousand metres below the academy, and the two teams fanned off to the left and right, sprinting with cheetah-like grace across the gleaming, snow-dusted ice.

'At this speed, it shouldn't take long to reach the place where the information is hidden. It looked like it was roughly halfway round the lake,' Jeremiah called softly.

'Okay, let's stick together and get there as fast as we can. Stay close to the edge in case we need cover,' Dillon called back.

They were really flying now, feet hardly touching the ice, and Dillon felt another surge of exhilaration. It was like he had springs attached to his legs and his body was as light as a feather. He had just run a ten-thousand-metre race and was not remotely out of breath.

'It should be coming up soon,' Sade called after they'd been running full pelt for ten or so minutes. 'I recognise the topography from the map. It was right on the side of the lake, just before that big outcrop.'

They skidded across the ice, coming to a standstill and scanning the towering ice surface.

'There's nothing here,' Ásta snarled.

Sade pulled out her map and examined the steep mountainside for a moment. 'I'm sure this is it,' she insisted. 'It must be higher up.'

'It looks like there might be something there,' Jeremiah said, pointing to a shadowy area halfway up.

'There's nothing down here so let's get up there fast,' Dillon agreed, peering up at the sky. 'We're vulnerable down here.'

'We could fly up there in seconds,' pointed out Fred.

'We could,' agreed Dillon. 'But Hunt said no flying until we reached the information point.' He paused, pointing up to the drone that hovered overhead. 'And we're being watched all the time. We'll have to climb. Everybody agree?'

The group nodded their approval. Ásta and Cora, the best climbers in the group, took the lead, scaling the steep snow-covered rock with ease. Frederick stayed at the back. Dillon heard him swear as he slipped a few times, but he kept up. Ásta whooped softly as she reached a small ledge.

'This must be it!'

A small, black gap fringed with icicles was just visible.

'Keep quiet until we're inside,' Dillon warned and crawled under. 'Woah, would you look at the size of it!'

Even in the dark as he straightened up, he could see it was huge. Once they were all in, they switched on their torches and the deep glittering blue walls lit up like a moving sea, frozen in time.

'It's stunning,' agreed Sade, turning round and round. 'Like an ice cathedral.'

'Come on, this is not a sightseeing trip,' Ásta snapped, indicating a black flight box at the side. 'The instructions must be in there.'

She snapped open the locks and pulled out a waterproof file. Inside were intelligence style notes and the estimated position of the hidden contraband.

'Get over here, Sade,' she beckoned, and Dillon smiled to

himself. Sade had clearly proven herself. She scanned the map in seconds.

'It's on the far side of the lake, furthest from the school. The only way to get to it undetected is under the ice,' she announced.

'Shite. That lake is at least twenty kilometres long,' Dillon swore. 'Can we seriously do that?'

'Dillon, we swim fast. It's fine,' Cora said. 'We're already halfway along it.'

'True, but we are not completely invincible to the cold,' Sade warned. 'We're fast, but it will start to slow us down.'

And I will have to breathe at some point, thought Dillon.

'We should test that we can break through from underneath,' he suggested. 'We don't want the whole team lost under the ice.'

'Oh, come on. Don't be such a pussy, Dillon,' Ásta growled. 'The other team will have swum half the lake while we're still pissing around making emergency exit holes.'

'I think it's worth it,' Dillon insisted.

Ásta stared at him, hands on hips. 'We don't have to come up to breathe Dillon – it's a waste of time for all of us except you.'

Dillon felt his stomach contract. 'Okay,' he agreed, finally. 'We swim as close to the surface of the ice as we can. Then we can break through if something goes wrong.'

'Cool.' Ásta jumped up.

'Everyone else agreed?' Dillon asked. 'Just one more thing,

GPS doesn't work under water, how will we know where we're going?'

'We're vampires. We have an inbuilt sense of direction,' Ásta snapped impatiently.

Sade scanned the map again. 'It lines up exactly with the tallest peak on the south side. It's the one we flew over on our first flight here. Look –' she pointed to the map – 'it is quite distinctive. It looks a bit like a crown, one large peak flanked by two smaller peaks. We have to swim due south. The contraband is between one and two kilometres from the south shore. We just have to hope it is emitting a sonar ping and we'll be able to pick it up. If not, it's going to be a bit like searching for a needle in a haystack.'

Dillon's stomach clenched again. 'Would it make more sense to swim round the edge then, even if it's longer?' he queried.

'It's twenty kilometres in length but approximately fifty if we go round the shoreline,' Sade calculated.

'Come on, Dillon,' Ásta snapped. 'Stop messing around. Let's take the fastest route and get the hell there before the others.'

'I'm just making sure there isn't a cleverer way,' Dillon snapped back.

'What's the plan if we find the contraband first?' Frederick asked.

'Fly out of there like bats out of hell,' Cora said, grinning at him.

'Enough planning!' Ásta screeched. 'We'll deal with it

when it happens. Flying is faster. Swimming is less detectable. We'll make a decision.'

'Alright, remember, if we get split up or something goes wrong before sunrise, meet back here,' Dillon reminded them.

He bent close to Sade as she tucked the information in her suit and whispered in her ear. 'How long do you reckon I've got under ice?'

She jerked her head away. 'A good half hour, maybe more. Your vampiric system may take over completely,' she muttered, shielding her nose with her hand.

'Okay, thanks.' He too turned away, saddened that she still couldn't handle being near him.

One by one they ducked out of the ice cave and took off, swooping like swallows down to the ice.

Frederick whooped 'Yeah, baby!' as he wobbled into land.

'Shush, you idiot!' Ásta hissed.

Working so fast his arm blurred, Jeremiah plunged a stake into the ice and sawed a triangle around it. Then he grabbed the stake and pulled hard, biceps bulging. With a sucking, popping noise the ice triangle flew out and he staggered backwards.

'Well done,' Ásta approved.

Dillon shuddered; the hole revealed a sinister triangle of inky black water.

'Ásta, you lead, then Cora, then Fred, then Jeremiah, then Sade and I'll bring up the rear. Keep together—' He broke off as Ásta sat on the edge of the ice hole and plunged into the ice feet first. A second later, she dived like a dolphin, feet breaking the surface with an arch of waterdrops and disappeared.

Dillon felt his heart go cold. For a second, he glimpsed her eerie, shadowy figure under the surface of the ice before she disappeared again. Cora followed, dropping into the water and emerging like a seal, hair plastered back, eyes wide with exhilaration.

'It's stunning under here,' she gasped before diving back under.

One by one they followed her until only Dillon was left. Despite his fear of being trapped, he had no choice but to plunge into the black depths after them. He couldn't abandon his team.

The cold water hit him, and his chest tightened like a vice. He was used to swimming in the Atlantic, but this was something different altogether. Instantly, he panicked and clawed to the surface, gasping. *I can't do this*, he thought. *I'm going to fail in front of everyone.* The faint whirring of the drone above brought him to his senses. Taking a deep breath, he submerged himself once again and this time he was ready for it. He dived and kicked hard after Sade. Glancing back, he fought a wave of claustrophobia, the hole was already just a tiny glimmer of light.

'You can do this,' he snarled through gritted teeth, kicking further into the water.

Sade was just about visible in front, and he stretched out, once again, amazed at the power of his limbs. He felt no need to breathe as he surged through the water. The ice filtered the moonlight shining on the surface, lending an opaque mystical colour to the water. He swam right up to the underside of the ice, marvelling at the patterns of trapped bubbles and spectral ice sculptures projecting downwards. It was a different world – beautiful, desolate and peaceful. All he could hear were the strange cracking noises of the ice and the swooshing of his limbs carving smooth arcs through the water.

Sade's feet were just in front of him now, and he could see the ghostly figures of the others strung out in front of her. He sensed they were heading due south as planned. The ice above him was shooting past, and he realised they must be swimming at an incredible pace. For a while, he lost track of time, lulled into a deep relaxation by the incredible submerged peace.

Slowly the realisation that he was starting to feel the cold crept up on him, and a painful cramping sensation started to pulse in his legs. When the edges of his vision started to blur, he finally had to acknowledge that he was running out of oxygen. Golden Blood obviously only took him so far.

He kicked hard and stretched out to grab Sade's boot. The whites of her eyes gleamed in the eerie, moonlit water as she looked back. Dillon pointed up at the ice and ran a finger across his throat. She kicked forward and tapped Jeremiah's boot and slowly everyone came to a stop, treading water. Ásta scowled and gestured forward.

Jeremiah stabbed at the ice above with his saw. It barely dented it. He ran his hands along the ice until he came to a large, trapped bubble and tried again. The ice was weaker and the saw stabbed through enough for him to force it in but, despite his huge strength, it was hard work from underneath. Dillon began to panic. As his chest convulsed, he clawed at the ice.

Snaking shark-like through the water, Cora swam up to him. Her eyes held his, steadying him as she unzipped the pocket on his chest and removed the blood shot. For a second, Dillon froze, as she inserted it into her mouth and bit down to break the seal.

'What the hell are you doing?!' A stream of bubbles blew out of his mouth as he swore.

For a second, her eyes widened as she realised Dillon's shot contained Golden Blood, and he saw her shudder as she struggled to stop herself swallowing. She pressed her lips against his and shot the blood from her mouth into his. The instant electricity as their lips touched sent the blood shot surging through his blood stream, pumping the precious Golden Blood and its gift of oxygen, refuelling the parts of his body that had started to shut down.

For a few blissful seconds, he forgot about the others and even the importance of the challenge. He didn't want to let her go, but she pulled away, leaving him feeling lost and dazed. *Okay?* Her eyes asked and he nodded.

Ásta swam up and gestured impatiently for them to hurry up. As they began shooting through the water again, Sade turned away and overtook Fred to join Ásta at the front. A faint shout echoing through the water told him that the other team were ahead of them and he cursed himself for holding them up. In the distance, they could just see the other team, all six swimming fast in a horizontal line. They had obviously decided remaining undetected under the ice was the safest option too.

Dillon caught Ásta up and pointed down. It would be colder further from the surface, but they would be less visible and could swim below the others. Silently, they dived and, swimming together now, they flowed smoothly through the water. Dillon felt a sudden burst of Golden-Blood-induced confidence – they were going to win this thing.

The other team were about one hundred metres away, swimming close to the ice and weaving through the downward ice projections. With no obstructions, hidden in the murky depths, Dillon's team were catching up. Sade tapped her ear indicating that they should start to listen for the drone.

It was womb-like in the deeper dark water and with the repetitive flowing strokes through the water, he deliberately allowed himself to float into a trance-like state. His mind drifted and suddenly, without warning, he picked up Bram's fierce thoughts, obsessed about beating him. It seemed that the recent Golden Blood had made him more receptive, just as Madame Dupledge had predicted. He just hadn't noticed before. He winced as a strange crackling noise travelled through the water and he realised Bram was projecting his energy to try and locate the drone. Dillon grinned to himself as he felt his frustration that it wasn't working.

Among the cacophony, faint electronic beeping noises flickered into his brain. He signalled to the others to stop by cupping his ear, motioning them to stop and listen. Together, they formed a circle, floating face down as Dillon trained his mind on the beeps. Confident he had a fix on them, he closed his eyes and began swimming again. He sensed Cora and Sade on either side of him as he changed direction, heading southwest.

The freezing cold was starting to affect their vampire systems now and Fred struggled to keep up the pace. Aware that the other team were still above them but hadn't yet picked up the sonar ping, they silently dived deeper into the murk. As the visibility decreased, they kept close, feeling their way through the water like they had in the sensory challenge all those weeks ago.

Closing his eyes and concentrating hard on the increasingly loud sonar pings, Dillon stopped. He could just make out something that looked like a mini spaceship nestling on the tattered weeds at the bottom of the lake. Four legs supporting small, spinning rotor blades protruded from a glass-domed cylindrical centre. There were no wires, only what appeared to be sensors and a flashing light. Under the glass dome, they could see a tightly wrapped package.

Frederick, suddenly revived, made a circle of his finger and thumb and nodded before diving closer and gently running a light finger over the surface of the dome. A piercing noise strangely distorted by the water went off and the drone shot off towards the surface. Jeremiah flung out a long arm and grabbed hold of it, but the cold had weakened his phenomenal strength and it dragged him sideways through the water. Dillon and the others, their limbs like lead, vampire hearts bursting, struggled to catch up as the drone sped towards the surface, its rotors creating streams of bubbles.

Alerted by the noise, and not so weakened by the temperature of the deep water, Bram's team torpedoed towards them and Aron smashed the heel of his hand into Jeremiah's chin. Jeremiah's head shot back but he managed to keep hold of the drone as Aron circled to attack again.

Scowling with fury, Ásta found the strength to attack Aron from behind, sending him tumbling through the water. They were close to the surface now, and Dillon saw that the drone was aiming for a glimmering circular hole in the ice about half a metre wide. Whatever was awaiting them above, at least they wouldn't be trapped beneath the ice.

Ace dived forward as the drone hit the surface and broke Jeremiah's grip. Both teams watched as it flipped over, and the mini rotors lifted it from the surface of the water like a helicopter. If the situation hadn't been so tense, Frederick's awed expression would have been comical. Bram reacted fastest and hurtled after it. Dillon followed a second behind and, as he neared the hole in the ice, he shut his eyes to find the spark of energy he needed to fly. Bram burst through first with a shower of water droplets and soared into the star-strewn sky. Dillon broke the surface of the water straight after and gasped as the bitter cold air shocked the energy out of his body. He plunged back through the hole and crashed into Ace and Ásta, sending them tumbling back down into the water.

Cora realised what had happened and shot after Bram. From below the surface of the water, Dillon saw her burst through the hole and disappear as she switched straight to flight. Ásta grabbed him as she followed and together they exploded out of the water. This time Dillon was ready, and he rocketed up as his body, suddenly free of the dense water, shot upwards so fast that Ásta was forced to let go.

Blinking water out of his eyes, he shook his head to orientate himself. The drone was still rising; Bram was right on its tail, with Cora close behind. He saw Bram lunge forward and grab one of the drone's legs. A huge bolt of blue light lit the night sky and radiated up Bram's arm. At the same time, a VSS vampire swooped out of nowhere and rammed into him, sending him somersaulting towards the lake.

Dillon lurched and stalled mid-air as an agonising pain streaked through him and he understood that, somehow, he was still tuned into Bram. Cora faltered too, unsure whether to go after Bram or the drone that had begun to lurch from side to side. The VSS vampire circled and accelerated towards her, and Dillon felt a volcano erupt in his veins as now, her fear flooded his unshielded brain.

He saw Ásta's pale, startled face as he flew past her like a bullet shooting from a gun. White-hot heat ripped round his body as he threw himself headlong into the VSS vampire. He went flying backwards, and Dillon saw Cora close in on the drone.

'Careful, Cora!' he howled as she reached out for it.

Ásta engaged the vampire in a vicious dog fight as Cora touched the drone, and Dillon almost fainted with relief as she pulled it towards her. Below him, Bram crashed into the ice with such force that he broke through it and disappeared below the surface. Cora screamed. Another agonising burst of Bram's pain racked Dillon's body and he threw himself into a steep nosedive.

'Help Cora!' he screeched to Sade and Jeremiah as he shot past them and the rest of Bram's horrified team.

He plunged deep into the black water and spotted Bram sinking, his face strangely serene without the habitual sneer. He grabbed hold of his suit, kicked hard for the surface and hauled him onto the ice. A vicious shard of ice protruded from the side of Bram's chest.

'Shite, Bram. Bram, can you hear me?' Dillon gasped, retching as another wave of Bram's pain bent him double.

Bram's beautiful, fined-boned face looked as if it had been carved from the ice he lay on.

'Help! Someone help!' Dillon screamed but eight more VSS had joined the battle and the others were all engaged in the desperate fight for survival in the sky above.

He had no idea what to do. No one had talked about emergency first aid for vampires. Bram's wound was held open by the vicious shard, preventing him from healing. Pulling the shard out, on the other hand, would surely allow precious blood to flow out of his body even faster. That was what happened to humans, and he couldn't risk it not being the same for vampires. He couldn't get this wrong.

Dillon had no choice; Bram was almost translucent now. Blood, the vampire life force, was the only answer he had. Wincing, he bit hard into his wrist. Immediately, blood welled up and dripped onto the ice. For a second, he paused, then he took one more look at Bram and wrenched the ice stake out. If Bram could heal himself again, this was the best way Dillon could think of to help him. Bram convulsed and then shuddered as Dillon placed his wrist over his mouth and let his blood seep into his mouth. With a deep groan, Bram gulped and latched on, sucking with deep, powerful swallows.

Dillon could almost feel his blood travelling into Bram's arteries, its powerful heat warming him back to life. Bram's dark eyes fluttered open, and Dillon saw confusion flit across them. Abruptly, he felt the mind connection between them shut down.

'The drone. It gave you a massive electric shock. You crashed through the ice. An ice shard stabbed you in the chest,' he said.

As realisation dawned, Bram struggled to control himself and, with enormous effort, he knocked Dillon's wrist away. 'What the fuck!'

Dillon licked his own wrist to stop the bleeding and once again felt the surge of power in his blood. 'I had no choice.'

'It's against the rules,' Bram hissed and cried out as he tried to sit.

Dillon almost threw up when he saw how misshapen Bram's shoulder was.

'Feck the rules, Bram! Did you want to die?'

Bram looked up, searching for the camera drone and his team. He sighed with relief when he saw it above the others, recording the action. The dog fight above them was becoming more desperate.

'It'll be fine – I can feel it healing. I need to lead my team,' he snapped.

He sprang to his feet and paled again as he clutched his shoulder.

'How long will it take?' Dillon asked.

Bram gasped with pain. 'It's started already.'

'Can you fly?'

'Yes, I'll be fine.'

Agitated, Bram looked up again. Four more VSS vampires flitting like bats across the sky had joined the battle. Outnumbered now, Ace, Bik, Ásta and Jeremiah fought them, using every trick Borzak had taught them. Sade and Frederick were struggling to keep Celeste and Bik away from Cora and the drone.

'Shite,' Dillon swore, as a VSS vampire flung Ásta across the sky. 'I've got to go.'

They both took off at the same time, but Bram lurched downwards as his injured shoulder threw him off balance. Dillon had done all he could to help him. Bram was healing. It was safe to leave him behind.

His focus was on Cora as he flew up so didn't notice the

VSS vampire streaking towards him. Like a pillar of iron, the vampire crashed into him at full speed, knocking the air out of him and sending him tumbling through the sky.

Dillon fought to regain his flight line and, as he turned, wild-eyed to face the vampire, he membered Borzak's words: *Kill or be killed*. Even so, the cold hatred in the vampire's burgundy eyes and the speed of the attack took him by surprise and, once again, he found himself flipping through the air. The vampire swooped and slammed into him again and Dillon momentarily blacked out. When he came to, he felt a thud of fear, sensing that the vampire's aggression was excessive for a training exercise. Desperately, he tried to gather himself for the next attack as the vampire snaked in, lips pulled back over his extended fangs. In a split-second move that surprised Dillon, he struck once again, holding him in a vicious choke-hold. Immediately, an agonising vice-like pain enveloped Dillon's brain, and he realised the vampire was projecting exceptionally strong mind power. He tried to ignite his inner mind-shield but the pain was already turning him limp.

'Fight, Dillon!' screamed Cora as the vampire began to fly fast towards the mountains, away from VAMPS.

Hearing her voice, Bram, who was still flying falteringly below, looked up and saw them. Dillon glimpsed the conflict in his face as his hatred battled with the knowledge that Dillon had just saved his life. Then, like lightning, he whipped out his ice saw and hurled it with his good arm. For a horrible second, his vision blurred by pain, Dillon thought Bram had aimed it at him but, as the vampire let out an agonised hiss, he saw it embed deep in the back of his head. Dillon's stomach heaved, and he swallowed compulsively as they began dropping through the sky like stones. Half-frozen with horror and entangled in the vampire's still-tight grip, Dillon fell with him for several metres.

'Fucking fly, Dillon!' screeched Cora again.

Shuddering, he came back to his senses and pushed himself away from the plunging vampire. Below him, he saw the vampire crash into the ice and lie there inert. Chiro flashed past him, followed by Borzak, his face grim with anger.

Something must have been going seriously wrong for their teachers to be intervening. There was no time to find out what was going on; Bram had already turned and was flying unsteadily back towards his team.

'Go Cora, Celeste's behind you,' Dillon yelled.

Cora flew straight at Celeste and banked at the last minute, tricking Celeste into shooting past her. As she set off across the ice, Dillon rocketed after her. Bram screeched a warning at Ace, who backflipped and swooped upside down, twisting in mid-air as he righted himself and set off in pursuit. Dillon heard Bram behind him howling in pain as he forced his arm forward into the full flight position.

Tears from the force of the wind streamed out of Dillon's eyes as he moved up to Cora's shoulder and they streaked across the ice. The weight of the drone was affecting Cora's aerodynamic shape and Ace was gaining on them.

'Shit, Ace is good,' he hissed. 'I'm not sure how long I can keep this speed up.'

He could feel his energy reserves were lower after giving Bram some of his precious blood.

'Hold my hand,' Cora shouted back, holding onto the drone with one hand and reaching out with her other.

He reached out and, as they clasped hands, the bolt of energy catapulted him forward. Cora underestimated the sudden burst of speed and let go of the drone. They both watched in horror as it spun in crazy circles and smashed into pieces on the ice below them. The central glass canister containing the precious blood and intelligence data rolled along the ice.

Instantly, Ace went after it, and Dillon, already stretched to the limit, pitched forward into a vertical dive. Every muscle in his body strained as he fought for control. He felt his eyeballs press into the back of his skull, and he almost blacked out as he flattened out just above the surface and skimmed along the ice. Ace was right behind him, and Dillon had to focus on holding his line as one mistake would mean it would all be over. Keeping the rest of his body straight as an arrow, he scooped up the canister and banked upwards hard. Ace shot past as Dillon soared straight back up towards the stars.

Two VSS vampires flying at full pelt swept in from the side. Dillon swerved, flying sideways now just as Cora caught up with him. Fighting for control, they swooped back round and saw the others spread out across the sky.

'We have to help them,' he roared at Cora as the vampires swept in, ready to attack again.

'Stay with me,' she shouted back. 'They're after the cannister. The others will sort themselves out.'

'You're a strong flyer, Cora. I'll distract them and give you a head start.'

'Dillon, I don't th—'

'Stay low,' Dillon shouted, chucking the cannister at her before swooping back up. It was a split-second decision that he instantly regretted as he saw Sade smash her boot into a vampire's face and Frederick, roaring like an enraged bull, finish him off with a diving head butt. Jeremiah and Ásta swooped in to protect them on the outer sides.

'Fly,' he roared at them.

'Go Ace!' Bram howled at the same time.

With jaw-dropping athleticism, Ace executed a perfect top-speed flying display as he outmanoeuvred the vampires on his tail and shot after Cora.

Cursing, Dillon gave chase, but Aron flew straight across him, deliberately disturbing the airstream. Dillon lost control, spinning through the sky towards the lake. Desperately, he tried to pull up, but he was too low. The ice flew up to meet him and, just as he braced himself for impact, he ricocheted back into the air as a strong hand grabbed the back of his suit.

'Woah!' whistled Jeremiah, inches above his body. 'That was close.'

'Very,' he just had time to gasp as he re-established his flight line.

'Go get them,' Jeremiah roared as he let go.

Cora was weaving all over the ice trying to hold Ace off. Not caring that his energy reserves were waning and his emergency blood supply was gone, Dillon yelled at his team to keep close and threw himself into a final burst of speed. He sensed the energy draining out of him as the air pressed against his limbs.

He caught up with Bram, who was now flying fast but unbalanced with Angelo. Ace and Cora were still engaged in the deadly airborne dance ahead of him, with Celeste chasing behind. Somehow, every time Ace drew close, she managed to slip out of his grasp, and Dillon heard him curse with frustration.

Aron tried to upset his airstream by flying across him again, but Dillon, now wise to his tactics, flipped to his side and, despite his core muscles burning with the strain, he managed to grin as Aron, flying too low, lost control himself and crashed into the ice below, rolling over and over.

He was at full stretch now and, shooting past Celeste, pushing his entire body to the limit, he reached out and, as he had practised for years on the rugby pitch, tapped Ace's heel. Instantly, Ace lost his flight line and flipped high before plummeting headfirst into the ice. Dillon couldn't resist a smile to himself as he swept over, delighted that one of his human skills had finally come in useful.

The school was in sight now; he could hear the roars of the watching vampires as he edged next to Cora. Flying at the edge of his limits, he couldn't look round to check that the others were with them.

'Slow down a bit, Cora,' he screeched.

'Are you mad?' she howled back.

'I don't know where the others are.'

'Don't make the same fucking mistake twice, Dillon. You've got to trust in the team. Let's just get there.'

He was almost flying on empty. His legs were turning numb like he was dragging them along.

'I'm not going to be able to keep this up for much longer,' he yelled, gritting his teeth now with the effort of keeping up with her.

'Just keep going, Dillon,' she screamed. 'You can do it.'

The viewing platform, lit up by the first fiery streaks of dawn, was fast approaching now, and Dillon's body began to spasm in agony. Together, they shot over the crowd of watching vampires, and he glimpsed Madame Dupledge and Bibiana look up at them.

Circling back, Dillon's heart nearly burst with pride as he saw Ásta, Jeremiah and Sade flying in tight formation like the red arrows, cajoling Frederick who, by sheer force of will, was keeping up. He still wasn't the strongest flier, but he was doing it. Bram's battered team trailed behind, weaving from side to side.

Dillon summoned the very last vestiges of his energy and, with one almighty push, joined his team as, completely spent, they all dropped out of the sky in unison to land in front of Madame Dupledge and Bibiana Fassano. Cora handed the cannister to Madame Dupledge with a small, exhausted bow.

His legs trembling with the effort of remaining standing,

Dillon turned to his team. 'You're incredible, every single one of you,' he said, his voice shaking with emotion.

The bat-like VSS vampires swooped in, followed by Bram's team, who landed clumsily. Dr Meyer rushed towards them, but Madame Dupledge stopped her.

'Well done Team Hawk,' she said. 'We have witnessed inspired acts of bravery and some truly impressive physical feats tonight. Both teams should be proud of themselves.'

Countess Fassano stepped forward. 'Team Eagle, of course, you are devastated but I want to commend you for your immense spirit and talent. Bram Danesti, you proved tonight that you are exceptionally brave and a worthy leader. Keep displaying those sorts of skills and I would be proud to have you in the VSS.'

Despite her kind words of consolation, Bram's face was still ravaged with pain and anguish at losing the challenge and he fought hard to hide his emotion.

'When Chiro and Mr Hunt return, Madame Dupledge and I will review tonight's events to confirm the winners and colours will be awarded accordingly.'

21

Blood Colours

Dr Meyer whisked Bram, Ace and Aron straight to the Sanatorium. Dillon thought longingly of his coffin, but Ásta dragged him along with the rest of the team to the pool to celebrate.

'We did it!' she crowed.

Dillon stared at Sade. 'I can't believe you kept the VSS vampires off Cora.'

'Yeah,' she joked. 'I kicked some ass tonight!'

Fred raked his hands through his hair. 'Damn, Dillon, I'm pleased for you and everything, but I really didn't expect you to win. I'm kicking myself for not lowering your odds. At least I've made a packet on Aron and Bram.'

Dillon tried to affect sorrow, but he couldn't resist a wry smile. 'Sorry about that, Fred. How much is it that you owe me? Forty isn't it? Remember your fangs in my palm?

'Yeah,' Jeremiah added. 'I'm expecting my full payment too – forty grand isn't it, Fred?'

Fred paled. 'Thank Christ, no one else believed in you, Dillon.'

'Um, thanks Fred.' Dillon grinned.

Ásta moved closer and, looking up at him through her spiky black lashes, ran her hands over his chest. 'You were impressive tonight, Dillon.'

'We all did it,' Dillon protested, transfixed by the movement of her fingers with their short, blood-red painted fingernails.

Ásta ignored him. 'All that brooding, untapped passion. We could be explosive together.'

Her heady, musky scent drowned his senses as she slid her hand down lower.

'Don't you want to check on Aron?' Dillon gasped, shifting away.

'Dillon, he's a vampire.' She grinned. 'He'll be fine. Dr Meyer will give him some extra blood to help him heal faster.'

'I could do with some of that,' Jeremiah groaned. 'That ice swimming totally depleted me.'

'I've got my blood shot,' Ásta offered, fishing it out of her pocket.

'You should still see Professor Dukan. You burn up a lot,' Dillon cautioned.

'Cheers, Dillon. Yeah, I'll go and see him,' Jeremiah promised.

Spotting Angelo arrive with the rest of Bram's team, Ásta sauntered off and Jeremiah leant forward.

'What happened to you out there?' He asked underneath his breath.

'I don't know, one of the VSS vampires lost it. Bram got him off me.'

'Shit.' Jeremiah whistled. 'I never thought I'd see the day that Bram would do anything for you.'

'Me neither.' He didn't mention giving Bram his blood.

'I'd better go and cheer up Bik,' he said. 'She'll be furious she didn't work out how to pick up the sonar ping first.'

Dillon searched for Cora and saw her staring out the windows at the slowly brightening sky.

'Hey,' he said joining her.

'Hey,' she said.

They were silent for a minute.

'I saw you save Bram's life,' she said, quietly.

'He saved mine too so we're quits.'

'You gave him blood.'

'I had to.'

'No, you didn't, but I'm glad you did.'

'Cora,' he turned her towards him. 'I asked Bibiana about your brother but she didn't tell me anything, only that he is an exceptional vampire. I'm sorry, I guess you already know that.'

'Dillon,' she said, her eyes glowing huge in the soft dawn light. 'Don't you get it? She said he *is*. That means he's alive. Now I've just got to find him.'

Reaching up, she kissed him softly and tenderly on the cheek.

'Thank you,' she whispered.

'I may be able to talk to her again,' Dillon said, leaning towards her, longing to connect with her again, but she was agitated and distracted.

'I better check on Bram,' she said, pulling away and he fought hard to hide his disappointment.

'I can't ignore him; he's hurting,' she said, softly. 'Try to understand. His pride is wounded and he's struggling knowing that you – the dhampir he's supposed to hate – saved his life.'

The problem was that he could understand, he had felt Bram's pain and agony and, deep down, he had to admit that he too was struggling to acknowledge Bram's incredible bravery and leadership. As he watched Cora make her way round the pool to the door, he felt a dark, exhausted gloom descend and, slipping out after her, he went straight to his coffin.

His mood was still dark when Madame Dupledge called him and Bram into her office the following night. Her expression was serious.

'I have spoken to Chiro and Borzak, and Mr Hunt has analysed your wristband data. It seems that two serious incidents occurred last night. Dillon, perhaps you might like to explain what happened to Bram?'

Dillon glanced at Bram, noticing that he looked even

paler than usual, and his eyes were deeply shadowed. His face was hauntingly beautiful. To his surprise, Bram shot him a quick conspiratorial look rather than his usual angry glare.

He began hesitantly. 'Bram tried to capture the drone, but it appeared to give him a massive electric shock – perhaps because he had been using his electromagnetic abilities. He crashed through the ice and, when I dragged him out, I saw he had been pierced through the chest with an ice shard. I pulled it out and stayed with him until he revived.'

Madame Dupledge raised her eyebrow and he battled to keep his mind blank. 'Is that all?'

'Yes,' he nodded, forcing himself to hold her gaze.

'How did you know Bram had been injured? Did you see him fall?'

'I saw the electric bolt but then –' Dillon glanced at Bram again – 'I felt his pain.'

Madame Dupledge nodded slightly. 'Did you help him revive?'

He felt a surge of unease and he could feel Bram willing him to stay silent about the blood. Madame Dupledge had made it quite clear on the first night that it was one of four rules that could not be broken. She was watching him intently and he knew he had to block Bram's feelings.

'I held my hand over the wound until it healed,' he said, praying that the camera drone hadn't captured what had really happened and felt a wave of relief from Bram sweep over him.

She switched her attention to Bram. 'Bram, is that how you remember it?'

'Yes,' Bram said, staring her straight in the eyes.

She inclined her head. 'And the second incident?'

'One of the VSS vampires had lost control,' he said. 'He wouldn't release Dillon, so I threw my ice saw at him, and Dillon was able to free himself.'

'You had no prior knowledge of this attack?'

If Bram did, he showed no sign of it, and he shook his head. 'Of course not.'

'Very well, I will see you later at the award ceremony, Bram. Dillon, Countess Fassano would like to speak to you.'

Dillon's heart thudded; he knew he wasn't strong enough to block Bibiana from reading his mind, and Bram flicked a warning glance at him as he walked out the room. Dillon heard Bibiana greet him at the door and then, the exotic, spicy scent that usually preceded her hit him. Instantly, her powerful presence filled the room. Professor Dukan was with her, and he closed the door, leaving her bodyguards in the atrium. She joined Madame Dupledge next to the desk.

'I hope you have recovered from your endeavours yesterday, Dillon?' she enquired.

'Yes, thank you, Countess.'

'We are concerned that there was another attempt to kill or kidnap you,' she growled, straight to the point. 'If so, it is a serious breach of security, and I have launched an immediate investigation. The vampire in question is currently under guard while he heals. After Bram's quick thinking disabled him, Chiro and Borzak were able to subdue him and bring him in for questioning.

'As we know, your blood is incredibly strong, Dillon, and Professor Dukan believes it is growing stronger. You could be an incredible asset to us, and my department will hunt down anyone who attempts to take control of you. Chiro and Borzak will continue to guard you whenever you leave VAMPS. Do you understand the gravity of your situation now?'

'I guess.' He shrugged, his dark mood making him long for his life in Ireland when he didn't have to deal with any of this. Would he ever get to go back home?

'Very well, you may go.'

'Just one more thing –' as he opened the door to leave her voice dropped to its slowest, lowest and softest octave – 'did Bram Danesti force you to give him your blood in the Ice Challenge?'

Her searchlight gaze bored into him, and his heart thudded. Of course, they already knew all about it. They knew he and Bram had lied. Standing tall, he stared straight back at her, and his voice rang out clear and direct. 'No, he didn't. Bram was out of it. I thought he was dying. I did it to save his life.'

There was silence for a second. *Now the shit's really going to hit the fan*, he thought.

'Thank you for your honesty, Dillon,' she said, finally. 'You may go . . . and less of the swearing please.'

Once again, he was surprised at just how effortlessly she could read his thoughts.

★

Bram slammed the wall in fury.

'Why the fuck did you tell them?'

Dillon had found him in his room, staring at the torn VAMPS crest on his battered challenge suit.

'They knew already.' Dillon tried to control his temper to reason with him. 'I told them it wasn't your decision.'

'If I lose colours over this,' Bram hissed, 'I'll kill you. Stay away from me. Just stay away. Your blood is messing with my head.'

Dillon raised his hands and backed away. 'Fine, suits me,' he snapped.

Clearly Bram's moment of soul searching was over. He was back to being as combative as ever. Bleakly, he wondered if they would strip him of VE for certain now.

The Peak Two and Three vampires had already begun to congregate in the ceremonial hall so there was no time to find Jeremiah and Sade. Muted conversations trickled down through the building:

' . . . Dillon Halloran will get his . . .'

' . . . Bram Danesti's blown it. . .'

' . . . No way, you heard what Countess Fassano said to him . . .'

' . . . What do you reckon Mahina will get . . .?'

As Dillon ran lightly up the stairs, the building lights dimmed and moonlight filtered through the glass roof, lending a soft luminescence to the ceremonial hall. Flickering candles lit a temporary stage and a reclining chair with tattoo needles was set up next to it. A vampire with an intimidating black flame tattoo covering the whole of his neck and creeping up in tendrils over his jaw waited next to it. For the first time, Dillon felt his stomach flutter with nerves.

The rest of his year were already grouped together with the Peak Two and Three vampires in front of the stage. Ásta and Aron's faces were stony with nervous anticipation. Dillon noticed that Bram hadn't arrived yet.

Jeremiah gave him a thumbs up and raised his eyebrow. 'Okay?' he asked.

Dillon shrugged. 'I'll tell you later.'

Bram silently slipped in next to Cora just before Madame Dupledge swept in with Mr Hunt and took their places at the head of the stage. Bibiana followed, flanked by two of her bodyguards.

'Welcome to the 181st Ice Challenge Awards Ceremony,' Madame Dupledge called out. 'These awards recognise great bravery, commitment and skill. Once again, we are extremely honoured to have Countess Fassano here to award the colours.'

Bram's jaw stiffened with tension, and Dillon's heart twisted as he saw Cora gently touch his hand. Bibiana stepped forward.

'There are four categories of colour award at VAMPS. Quarter Colours, Half Colours, Full Colours and, for exceptional vampires, the Peak Performance Ring.

'Half Colours are a tattoo of the outline of the VAMPS crest and its motto. Full colours contain a drop of blood from our three founders and complete the tattoo. The Peak Performance Ring is made from a mix of antique silver and the ashes of our most famous Ancient vampire forebear, Dargan Afanas. At its centre, the black onyx represents courage and strength.

'I would like to award the Peak Performance Ring to a vampire who has become exceptionally talented and wields her immense powers with dignity and restraint. She excelled in the Peak Three Challenge, and she embodies the modern, progressive vampire that VAMPS aspires to. Mahina Ikaika, come and collect your award.'

Dillon felt a lump in his throat as Mahina glided up to the stage, struggling to hold back her emotion, and Countess Fassano slipped the glimmering ring over the index finger of her left hand.

'Well done,' she said. 'Wear it with pride.'

The hall burst into applause and her friends hugged her as she rejoined them.

Next, Countess Fassano awarded Celeste, Sade, Angelo and Jeremiah with Quarter Colour pins. She presented Fred with a pin for teamwork and perseverance. Grinning happily, he high-fived Aron and discreetly stuck a middle finger up at Celeste.

The hall went silent as Countess Fassano paused and a heavy tension filled the room.

'First to receive the honour of Half Colours for immense bravery, dedication and leadership is . . .' Dillon's heart thudded ' . . . Bram Danesti. Well done, Bram.'

The hall burst into applause again, and Dillon expected to see blazing triumph on his face, but Bram looked down, visibly struggling to contain his emotion. Only when Cora embraced him, triggering a chorus of whistles did he manage a small smile. Looking dazed, he made his way to the stage and bowed to Bibiana who shook his hand and said something in his ear.

The tattooist attached his needles and gestured to Bram to lay down. Removing his shirt, he revealed smooth, lean chest muscles and beautifully sculpted abs disappearing into the waistband of his trousers. Several vampires in the other years eyed him hungrily as he lay on the chair. He closed his eyes as the tattooist, casting a shadow over him, began to tattoo the outline of the ancient VAMPS crest with the motto *'In Tenebris Refulgemus'* – *In Darkness We Shine* – along his inner arm.

Afterwards, he rejoined Cora, chest bare and Dillon felt another agonising stab in his own chest as she kissed the tattoo to cheers and more whistles.

'Next to be awarded Half Colours . . .' Once again, Bibiana's husky voice silenced the room ' . . . for combat skills, physical strength, mental strength and team motivation: Ásta Einarsdottir.'

Ásta punched the air and Angelo, closely followed by Aron, hugged her, lifting her feet off the floor. There were a few glances from the other vampires in Dillon's direction and he felt his stomach churn. He wasn't going to get colours because he'd given blood to Bram. He'd be lucky not to get kicked out. He barely noticed as Ásta stripped her top off without any embarrassment and lay down on the chair to receive the crest below her collarbone.

Aron received Half Colours across his muscle-hewn back and, even as he beamed with pride, a single pink tear leaked down Fred's cheek. The final two Half Colour awards went to Cora and Ace. As Dillon watched the tattooist ink the motto in a crescent at the base of Cora's slender, white neck, just above her shoulder blades, he felt conflicted emotions, pride, longing and anxiety that he would never be good enough for her. Dillon's already tortured heart constricted in agony and he turned away.

Most of the Peak Threes were awarded Full Colours. George Gyllenborg, the Peak Two VE, was awarded Full Colours for outstanding leadership and skill in the Peak Two Challenge. Dillon felt shame begin to prickle down his back as Sade and Cora glanced at him sympathetically.

Jeremiah shook his head furiously and hissed, 'This is total shit.'

Bibiana raised her hand for silence.

'And finally, for immense courage, teamwork, compassion and . . . for saving the life of another . . . ' she paused as the vampires stirred,' . . . I award Full Colours to Dillon Halloran. As you all know, it is a great honour for a Peak One student to receive Full Colours.'

The hall erupted and a buzzing filled Dillon's ears as Jeremiah, clapping him on the back, pushed him towards the stage.

'Well done,' Bibiana said softly. 'May the strength of our ancestors guide you always.'

Lifting a small ampoule filled with crimson liquid high so that it glinted under the moonlit roof, she handed it to the tattooist.

'Where would you like it?' he barked, the tattooed fire tendrils moving disconcertingly across his jaw as he spoke.

Dillon's mind went blank for a second, and then he thought of his father. 'On my chest, above my heart,' he said.

The tattooist nodded and, in a daze, Dillon stripped off his shirt, subtly removing the attention-grabbing chain and pendant with it. Ásta wolf-whistled loudly, and he glimpsed Mahina smiling as he lay on his back on the chair and stared up at the glass roof. The strong, metallic smell of blood made his nostrils flare as the ampoule was opened but he was in such a state of euphoria that he didn't even feel the fine needles pierce his skin. He knew that there was no turning back now. He might be half human but he was now forever marked as a vampire.

22

Blood Warning

The tattoo healed almost instantly, and every time Dillon looked at his bare chest, he traced the rich and vibrant black crest with its dark-red words: *'In Tenebris Refulgemus'* – In Darkness We Shine.

'Dhamp, you're going to wear that thing off,' Jeremiah teased the following evening.

He couldn't explain how it made him feel; like his election as VE wasn't a sham, like he was meant to have a place at VAMPS. For the first time, even though he was different to the others, he didn't feel like an outsider.

The others were already in Madame Dupledge's classroom when he and Jeremiah walked in. There was an air of excited anticipation as they waited for Countess Fassano to deliver her lesson on International Relations and Vampire Diplomacy. Ásta, wearing a low top, kept twisting round to show off her newly tattooed colours, much to Celeste's irritation.

Dillon's heart twisted when he saw Cora and Bram sitting close together; after congratulating him on his colours, she had disappeared with Bram for the rest of the night. He didn't understand her; he had found out about her brother for her and yet she was still choosing Bram over him. Had Bram's bravery and moving display of emotion finally won her over for good? He remembered Bram saying that she was drawn to underdogs. Is that all he had ever been to her? Now he had proved himself, she was no longer interested?

He barely heard Angelo as he sat down.

'Show me your colours again,' Angelo repeated.

Forcing his mind off Cora, Dillon lifted his T-shirt.

'It looks so good,' he sighed enviously.

'I'm sure you'll get yours next year,' Dillon mumbled, covering up again.

'Yeah.' Angelo's face darkened. 'As long as I survive the ski trip.'

'You will,' Dillon said, and he meant it.

Angelo had been working hard at his extra lessons with Madame Dupledge, and he trusted him now, but he still found it disturbing when Angelo hovered close to his neck and counted slowly to ten. Thankfully, it was happening less than it used to.

With a gust of her bittersweet scent, Madame Dupledge swept in. 'Unfortunately, Countess Fassano was called away in the middle of the day to deal with a diplomatic emergency,' she announced.

The air of expectation deflated like a balloon.

'Damn,' Celeste hissed under her breath, and Bram struggled to hide his disappointment.

'I know you were looking forward to her lesson, but she has promised to return as soon as the emergency has been dealt with. In the meantime, this is a good opportunity to make sure that you are fully prepared for the ski trip.

'Your performances in the Ice Challenge have proven that you all have the courage for the next stage of your development into modern vampires. However, over the next few weeks, I would like you to practise your control techniques and inform me if you feel you need any help. Jeremiah, Professor Dukan has studied your vital statistics during the Ice Challenge and has adjusted your blood rations, if you would like to see him after the class.'

Dillon saw the relief on Jeremiah's face, and he wondered why he had refused to acknowledge that he needed Professor Dukan's help for so long.

'Professor Sandhu will be here in a minute to go over some of the final preparations for the trip. Ah, here she is . . .'

'Hello everyone!' Professor Sandhu greeted the class cheerily as she glided through the door dressed in a colourful kaftan, her long hair trailing down her back.

Madame Dupledge turned back to the class. 'I will leave you now. A reminder. You will not be able to progress to Peak Two at VAMPS unless you pass the ski trip test, so make sure that you are fully prepared.'

Next to Dillon, Angelo twitched nervously.

'Thank you, Madame Dupledge.' Professor Sandhu, smiled round the class. 'Well done, everyone. The Ice Challenge was extremely entertaining to watch, and you all did so well.'

She pulled a box out of her bag.

'Your mouthguards are ready so please check that they fit,' she said, handing them out as she walked through the class.

Dillon slotted his in. It was tight but he felt that was a good thing. The next minute, Professor Sandhu opened her blood vial and wafted blood around the room.

'Smile, please.'

As they all bared their fangs at her, only Fred's mouthguard slipped slightly out of position, allowing his fangs to shoot halfway out.

'Just my luck,' he moaned.

'It's okay, Frederick. It's better to have found out now,' she reassured him. 'Come to me for a refitting after the class. I also need you all to take your clothes sizes so I can order suitable après-ski wear for you.'

Celeste and Ásta scowled.

'I'd like to choose mine myself,' Ásta said.

Professor Sandhu raised an eyebrow at Ásta's extremely low top.

'I'm not sure that's such a good idea, Ásta. Don't worry, I know what you young vampires like.'

Dillon saw Ásta eye Professor Sandhu's lurid kaftan sceptically but even she dared not hurt her feelings. Straight after the class, even though it was late in the evening, Dillon went to the blood room to call his father. As he had hoped, it was empty and to his surprise, his father answered on the second ring.

'Da, I got my colours,' he said, proudly.

His father chuckled. 'Well done, Dill. Of course you did. I suppose you have a great tattoo across your chest?'

'How did you know?' Dillon asked.

'Your m— Madame Dupledge told me.'

'Oh,' said Dillon momentarily silenced. Obviously, Madame Dupledge had a hotline to his father that he didn't. 'Well,' he continued, 'I just wanted to tell you – and that we've got one more test before we graduate from Peak One.'

His father's warm voice became grave. 'Be careful, Dillon. Just watch your back.'

'What do you mean?' Dillon asked.

'It seems you've ruffled a few feathers. Don't trust all vampires equally and don't let your guard down for a second.'

'Now you're worrying me, Da. What do you mean?' Dillon said, feeling an inexplicable fear chill his spine.

'I'm sorry. I just want you to look out for yourself.'

Dillon started as a small group of hench Peak Threes entered the blood room and made it clear they wanted the space for themselves.

'Da, I've got to go. I'll call you in a couple of weeks, after the trip.'

Uncharacteristically, his da seemed reluctant to let him go.

'Dillon . . . I love you, son. I've loved you from the moment I set eyes on you, and I'll always love you, no matter what.'

A lump rose in Dillon's throat and a terrible sense of foreboding gripped his heart.

'What's wrong? Are you okay? You're scaring me, da.'

'Don't worry about me. Just look after yourself – you hear me?' he commanded with a vehemence Dillon had rarely heard from his dad before.

'Trust me – I'll try, da. But it's hard . . .' Shaking, Dillon broke off the call before emotion got the better of him.

The Peak Threes stared at him, and he hurried out. He was ashamed he was feeling so fearful, tearful even. Inexplicably, he also felt a pang of jealousy, paranoia even, that Madame Dupledge had become his father's confidante. They seemed as thick as thieves. Before it had just been him and his da. Everyone seemed determined that he should find out about things last, and now his da was in on it too.

23

Blood Hurts

Dillon kept a low profile for the next few weeks; he was tortured by the sight of a loved-up Cora and Bram and uneasy after the conversation with his father. He would have loved to talk to Sade about it, but she too was avoiding him. It was a relief when the night of the ski trip, the last hurdle, finally arrived at the beginning of March.

After Professor Dukan supervised their blood ration, Professor Sandhu instructed the whole year to gather at the entrance atrium so that she could inspect their appearances and issue last-minute instructions. Despite Ásta and Celeste's reservations, the ski clothes she had ordered were chic and expensive-looking. Dillon had never known such well-fitting luxury.

Professor Sandhu tutted when she saw Ásta's skin-tight outfit. 'Did you give me the right size, Ásta?' she asked.

'Yes, of course Professor. Ski gear must come up small,' Ásta said, breezily.

Professor Sandhu looked sceptical, but she said no more, calling out to the group instead. 'Make sure you have your glasses and your fang and nose guards on you.'

Dillon tapped the slim box in his ski jacket pocket to make sure he had them and noticed Angelo do the same.

'Now remember, stay under the radar,' she warned. 'You will attract attention, so don't let it go to your head. Don't make fast movements, don't get too close to humans and be on your guard the whole time. You want to be in control at all times. Good luck and, even though this is an important test –' her mischievous blue eyes sparkled – 'have fun.'

Standing next to her, Madame Dupledge frowned slightly. 'Just not too much fun. I will give you further instructions when we reach Zermatt – the helicopters have arrived.'

Dillon felt a thrill of excitement as they left the academy building and flew down to the three sleek helicopters waiting on the ice. Even knowing that Chiro was watching over him didn't dampen his spirits.

Bending low, he, Jeremiah and Bik jumped into one of the helicopters, along with Sade, Ásta and Angelo. Chiro scrambled in next to the vampire pilot and Sade sat in the furthest seat from him. Dillon tried to smile at her but she avoided making eye contact. Sighing, he stared out of the window as the helicopter's engines roared and they lifted into the air.

Ásta whooped, 'Freedom!'

He watched the fang-shaped academy building disappear and dismissed a slight feeling of foreboding at the thought of appearing as a dhampir amongst humans for the first time.

Flying fast and low, they reached Zermatt heliport in less than two hours. As the helicopter circled the mighty Matterhorn Mountain, Dillon marvelled at the picturesque ski village below. Out of the corner of his eye, he saw Angelo discretely slip his fang guard into his mouth.

The cheery lights from chalet windows and glowing outdoor lamps lit the way from the heliport to the cable car terminal. Humans in colourful ski jackets and warm hats were everywhere: crowded into après ski bars, spilling out of cosy restaurants and strolling along the pretty cobbled streets.

'How can they bear to walk so slowly?' Celeste asked.

Even Dillon, having spent almost five months amongst vampires, found the pace pedestrian. He was taken aback at how rosy and dishevelled the humans looked compared to the cool, porcelain perfection of the vampires.

Angelo soaked up the smorgasbord of humans before him. '*Dios mio*, Dillon,' he moaned under his breath. 'There's so many and they smell so good.'

'Shush, Angelo,' Dillon hissed, looking round, 'You can do this.'

Angelo winced as a human girl brushed past him. 'You're right. I can do this,' he said, caramel-brown eyes earnest. 'I have been practising so hard.'

'Practising what?' Ásta asked, pushing between them.

'Abstinence,' Angelo said.

'Oh God, how boring,' Ásta said and stalked off to talk to Celeste.

The cable car terminal was quieter than the streets, only a few people were heading up the mountain at this time of the night. Madame Dupledge, dressed in a faux-fur gilet with tight black trousers and boots, stopped to give them their last-minute instructions.

'We have split you into two groups for the first part of the evening as all of you descending on a bar at the same time will create too much of a disturbance. Ásta, Angelo, Jeremiah, Cora, Celeste and Frederick, you will join Dillon. Sade, Ace, Aron and Bik will join Bram. Bram's group is slightly smaller because of the size of the bar.'

Ásta smirked at him, and Dillon felt the same flutter of foreboding.

'Dillon's group will spend an hour and a half at the exclusive Benjy's Ice Bar up on the slopes. Bram's group will go to the equally exclusive Z bar on the river. Both groups will meet afterwards at the Nightjar club in the centre of the village. We have chosen the venues because the clientele is young and glamorous. Borzak will be in town and Chiro will be on the mountain, but both will keep a low profile unless there is an emergency. You will meet them at two a.m. on the dot outside the Nightjar. Do not drop your guard for a second. You are expected to mingle but be very careful not to become too close to the humans. Remember all the work we have done in our desires lessons and if you feel you are losing control, employ all the techniques we have practised. Mr Hunt and I will wait at the VAMPS chalet on the edge of the village for the duration of our trip. We will head back there after the Nightjar. Remember how important this trip is in terms of your development as modern, responsible vampires.' She smiled. 'Be on your guard but I have trust in you, and I believe in you. This year, Dillon's group have a slight advantage in that Dillon will be able to guide you. Good luck all of you.'

Madame Dupledge and Mr Hunt disappeared towards the village. Sade glanced at him nervously as she joined the rest of Bram's group, and he smiled at her; he had no doubts that she would be okay. She had brilliant control, except when it came to his blood. He turned away as Bram kissed Cora goodbye.

'Be careful. Stay out of trouble,' he heard him say.

Dillon and his group headed into the terminal and attempted to keep a low profile as they waited for the next cable car to trundle in. A few humans got off, skis slung casually over their shoulders and stared curiously at the vampires as they stepped in from the other side.

'It smells so human,' Angelo moaned, licking his lips as the doors shut and they lurched off up the mountain.

Dillon had never been skiing. As the cable car swung upwards, the slope beneath them glistened like royal icing under the floodlights and he watched a few snowboarders carving graceful S-shaped curves down the mountain.

Celeste stared moodily out of the cable car window. 'God, I just want to get this over with. Humans are so intellectually and physically inferior to us. They're only good for one thing.'

'Nice, Celeste,' Dillon said, 'I am half human. Could you explain that so my "inferior" human side can understand?'

'Yeah, well, Dillon, at least you act more vampire than human nowadays.'

'Yeah, Dillon, you've changed so much,' Angelo said. 'Even though I have better control – I actually don't want to suck your blood out all the time now.'

'My heart's broken,' Dillon said with a grin.

'And you've got really handsome,' Celeste said, with a sly glance at him. 'The human girls are going to find it hard to resist you.'

'Ah, get away with you. I'm nothing to write home about,' he said, avoiding Cora's grin and staring out the window to hide his awkwardness. 'Get ready,' he added, noticing that they were almost at the top, 'time to join the human race.'

Only the cable car attendant was around when they disembarked, and Dillon, glancing back, saw him staring after them in amazement. It was already so different from his last experience in the world of humans. The path to the ice bar was marked out with warm festoon lights and a rustic wooden sign. The sound of loud pumping music and laughter floated across the crisp mountain air, titillating them with the prospect of pleasures to come.

Angelo's pace quickened. 'Woah,' he grinned, licking his

lips as they turned the corner and saw it for the first time.

Benjy's Ice Bar turned out to be more like an ice village; several large domed igloo-style buildings had been built into the mountain side, and a long crescent-shaped outdoor bar had been carved from ice in the centre. Thick faux-fur blankets were laid on outdoor bar stools and people were crowded around two ice luges at one end of the bar. Skis and snowboards were propped up against wooden racks and up lights made the clear ice of the bar glow like a neon-blue surfboard. The views over the floodlit ski slopes and the twinkling village below were incredible. Outdoor heaters suspended from tall poles kept the chill off and young people dressed in designer ski gear clutched steaming drinks while they jigged around to the music.

'Right, this is it – keep your heads down. Don't draw attention to yourselves and think human,' Dillon reminded them.

'I could never be that dumb,' drawled Celeste.

Even though the crowd was glamorous and young as Madame Dupledge had said, he noticed that they were still creating a stir as they walked towards the bar. People stopped, drinks halfway to their mouths, and stared. Close to the bar, he realised with a shock that the ice luges were nubile male and female torsos. A group of trendy snowboarders was chanting each other on as they poured shots into the top of the shapely female ice luge and drank them as they trickled out, ice cold, at the bottom. Girls screamed with laughter as they limbo danced under the male torso and attempted to catch vodka in their mouths before it splashed onto the snow. Dillon stared and Ásta grinned.

'I had no idea humans could be fun,' she said, 'Let's have a go. What do I order?'

'Vodka, I think,' he said, 'Just one, remember.'

She sauntered up to the bar and smiled at the barman. 'Six vodka shots, please,' she said, staring straight into his eyes.

The poor boy flushed bright red, and he blinked rapidly. 'No problem,' he stammered, fumbling with the shot glasses. 'Any particular flavour?'

Ásta leaned forward over the bar. 'What would you recommend?'

Sweat beaded on his forehead, and he pulled at the trendy camouflage snood around his neck. 'Raspberry is nice.'

'My favourite colour.' Ásta delivered another devastating smile, and he almost dropped the vodka bottle he had picked up.

The cute, blonde-haired bargirl working with him had noticed Angelo and Jeremiah standing behind Ásta and was staring at them in open-mouthed admiration. Angelo smirked back at her until he saw Ásta's frown and whipped out a pair of dark glasses which, rather than diminishing his appeal, made him look even more rock-star gorgeous. The bargirl turned pink and smiled at him, starry-eyed.

'For God's sake,' Ásta exploded, under her breath. 'How pathetic.'

'What?' Angelo shrugged. 'She can't help it.'

'Just remember, Angelo, whatever you can do, I can do better,' she said as she handed out the shots. 'Come on,' she beckoned, sauntering over to the ice luges. The snowboarders were so absorbed, they didn't notice her at first. 'My turn now,' she said huskily to a shaggy-haired boy who was about to go next.

'In a minute,' he said, not noticing that his friends had gone silent.

As he twisted down to drink, he glimpsed Ásta and the rest of the vampires grouped behind her and his jaw dropped. The vodka shot splashed across his face as, spluttering, he stood up and stared.

Ásta, in her skin-tight jacket and boots sashayed up to the female torso. 'Dillon, pour the vodka in for me,' she called over her shoulder.

'I'm not your slave,' he muttered, following her, nevertheless. 'Ready?'

'Of course,' she winked at the shaggy-haired boy who was still transfixed by her, vodka dripping off his face.

He poured the raspberry vodka in at the top of the female torso, and Ásta watched it trickle through and then, slowly and sensually, she extended her tongue and lasciviously licked the blood-red liquid up as it trickled out.

'Surprisingly nice,' she said, running her tongue over her lips.

Dillon saw the snowboarders' eyes glaze over. *Shite*, he thought, as other people in the bar realised something was going on and started drifting over. This wasn't a good start.

'Another shot, Dillon,' she commanded, feline eyes dark with excitement.

'Come on, now. I'm sure someone else is waiting for a turn,' Dillon said.

'Don't be such a spoilsport,' she snapped.

'We're not supposed to be drawing attention to ourselves. The whole bar is transfixed by you,' he hissed back.

'God, Dillon. Sometimes you are so boring.'

'I'm VE,' he hissed. 'I'm supposed to be helping you to blend in.'

'Just pour,' she snapped.

'One more and that's it,' he said and tipped another shot in.

As Ásta lapped and sucked at the liquid again, a small red trickle dribbled over her chin and, straightening up, she wiped her mouth and slowly licked each finger. The boy next to her looked ready to combust, but no one dared approach. Her eyes had turned even more feline and, as Professor Sandhu had said, it was as if they could sense something dangerous sparking off her.

Angelo had no such reservations and, eyes blazing, he gulped his shot straight from the glass and kissed her passionately. The crowd sighed, unable to take their eyes away from them, and Dillon remembered how he had felt when he'd first seen the vampires. Their glamour was magnetic and irresistible.

'Ásta, I'm not sure that's what you call blending in,' Cora said.

Ásta, still locked onto to Angelo's mouth, flicked her middle finger in Cora's direction.

Professor Sandhu had said alcohol had less effect on the vampires, but Dillon noticed it made their eyes glitter slightly.

'This stuff is okay,' Fred said, approvingly. 'Not as good as my bottled blood, but not bad.'

'I'd like a go,' Celeste said huskily, and Dillon glanced at her in surprise. He hadn't noticed her watching with the others. Her ice-blue eyes were huge and dark, and she had an air of suppressed excitement.

'Maybe later,' Dillon said, worried that Ásta's display or the vodka shot had kindled some sort of dark passion in her. 'The crowd is getting restless.'

Furiously, she scowled at him.

'Let's check out those intriguing igloo things,' Cora said to distract her.

Aware that the eyes of the entire crowd were following them, Dillon ducked under the arched entrance to one of the igloos. Inside, through a short corridor was an incredible indoor bar with jungle animals carved into the ice walls and a vaulting ice ceiling. More faux-fur blankets covered the seats, and lanterns placed in tiny ice alcoves lit the gleaming walls. Strings of LED lights draped the bar.

A chilled, hypnotic beat and conversation filled the room, and people lolled at low tables, knocking back vodka cocktails.

'You get a table. I'll get more vodka,' Fred offered, eyes gleaming.

Dillon grimaced. 'Fred, I think we've had enough.'

Fred's face fell. 'Ah! Come on, Dillon. We need to blend in. One more isn't going to hurt.'

'Okay, but this is the last,' Dillon warned. 'I'll order it.'

He ordered a jug of the winter vodka cocktail. 'Can you make it weak, please,' he said to the girl behind the bar.

She stared at him admiringly. 'Are you models?' she asked, flicking her long brown hair over her shoulder, revealing a pretty ear studded with earrings and lowering her sooty lashes.

'What? No, we're, um, we're students.'

'Really? Acting students?'

'No, just ordinary students,' Dillon shrugged, wishing he'd put more thought into a cover story. 'Student students, you know. Studying . . . stuff.'

'Really? You don't look like students. Would any of you like to come to the Nightjar afterwards? A group of us are heading down there after work. Why don't you give me your number? I'm Lola, by the way.'

Dillon thought for a minute. 'Sorry, I don't have my phone. Maybe we'll see you there—'

He broke off as she suddenly leant forward and kissed him. All he was aware of was her warm lips and the hot smell of the blood under her skin. He felt his head spin and, as his fangs started to pop out, he shot back in alarm, clamping his mouth shut.

'I'm sorry,' she said, misreading him. 'I don't know what came over me. I don't normally do that.'

'It's not you. I just find you very attractive,' Dillon muttered with his mouth shut.

Fred, standing next to him, grinned. 'He'll be there later,' he said, winking at her and picking up the jug of vodka cocktail.

'Brilliant, Dillon,' Celeste exclaimed as he placed the glasses on the table. 'Leading by example, I see.'

'It wasn't my fault,' he turned to Fred. 'Was it?'

'*Ja*, the poor girl was devastated by your irresistible allure.'

'I just ordered the drinks,' he protested.

'Yeah, and you smouldered those stunning blue eyes at her, I bet,' Ásta teased.

Dillon blinked, no one had ever told him he had stunning eyes before.

'Sit down, Dillon,' Ásta said. 'Stop looking so confused. Golden Blood has made you very attractive. You're quite the stud nowadays.'

Dillon felt a very faint heat warm his cheeks.

'Look, you don't even turn bright red like you used to. Although, I rather miss that. It's extremely titillating for us vampires.'

'I don't,' Angelo said. 'The human blushing thing drives me crazy.'

Dillon noticed that the humans at the other tables were staring. 'Keep your voice down, Angelo,' he hissed, pouring himself a drink. 'And stop calling the other *people* in the bar "humans". They can hear, you know. Now – *slainte!*' he said, raising his glass.

'Slantcha?' asked Fred.

'It's Irish for "cheers",' he explained.

'Ah, like "sante",' Fred said, raising his glass in return.

'*Slainte!*' chorused the rest of the group, downing their drinks in one.

Dillon noticed that the alcohol gave a pleasurable burn – nowhere near as heady as blood but nice enough. The bar was filling up as people, intrigued by the group of beautiful vampires, piled in. The vampires were equally fascinated by the situation.

'It's amazing how much they drink,' marvelled Fred. 'They are losing control of their senses. We could clean up.'

'Fred!' exclaimed Dillon.

He shrugged. 'Just saying.'

Dillon looked around. Fred was right; people were losing their inhibitions. Several were swaying drunkenly to the music in the centre of the bar. A couple of girls with butter-scotch tans and slight goggle marks braved approaching their table.

'Want to dance?' the prettiest one said, slurring slightly and quite unable to take her eyes off Jeremiah.

'Thank you, maybe later.' Jeremiah smiled and both girls flushed red under their tans.

'It's like lambs to the slaughter,' Ásta hissed, watching the giggling girls stumble back to join their friends, casting longing backward glances at Jeremiah.

Fred grinned. 'I'm going to act human and get some more drinks. Everyone in?'

'No more, Fred,' Dillon said.

'It's fine, Dillon. It's not affecting us,' Fred insisted.

He dragged Jeremiah up to help him and the entire room paused. The pretty barmaid's eyes glazed over when Jeremiah smiled at her.

Fred returned to the table grinning. 'Jeremiah is like a tiger amongst pigeons. He's set this place on fire.'

He was right, Dillon sensed that the room was becoming more and more highly charged. The intense allure of the vampires was adding an extra frisson to the usual hard partying après-ski atmosphere.

Ásta's eyes were beginning to glitter dangerously and so were Cora's. Fred and Jeremiah slotted their mouth guards in. Dillon could feel the alcohol mixing with the Golden Blood in an extremely pleasurable way. Back home, he'd enjoyed a pint with his father in their local pub, Mulligans, but this was something else.

'Come on, guys. Let's dance,' Ásta said, peeling her jacket off to reveal her minute black crop top. Fully aware that it showed off her toned curves, she slowly swayed to the centre of the room, throwing the jacket to Angelo.

Dillon winced. 'Angelo, you better get up there.'

Angelo stripped off his own jacket and they began to gyrate slowly and sensually together. More and more people piled into the centre and formed an admiring circle around them. Celeste pulled a reluctant Jeremiah up and, tossing her long silver blonde mane, she began dancing provocatively with him. The atmosphere was becoming more and more feral.

Left alone at the table, Cora's eyes met his. 'Will you dance with me, Dillon?' she asked, her sea-green eyes glittering.

He drank in her beautiful face, but she had barely spoken to him since the Ice Challenge. 'I'm not sure that's a good idea in here,' he muttered. 'It's getting out of hand.'

'It's fine,' she said ignoring him and reached for his hand, sending little electric shots shooting up and down his arm.

On the edge of the crowd, she started swaying, her vampire senses keeping perfect time with the music, and moved closer.

Dillon stepped back slightly as his head reeled. 'What are you doing?' he whispered as he felt the inevitable heat start to scorch round his body.

'Just having fun,' she whispered, nuzzling his neck and tickling his ear with her lips, driving him crazy.

'Don't,' he whispered. 'You've made it clear you'd rather be with Bram.'

'Shush,' she said, pressing closer. 'Bram's not here. Let's just have some fun.'

Dillon's head reeled. He'd been longing for this since the Sanatorium on his first day at VAMPS. From somewhere inside, he found the will to hesitate. 'Why now?'

'We won't have another chance to get out.'

Dillon glanced at the other vampires. Fred was behind the bar, learning to make cocktails. The crowd was still mesmerised by Jeremiah, Celeste, Ásta and Angelo and drawing in closer to them.

Things were definitely getting out of control, but he couldn't think straight, Cora's intoxicating scent clouded his brain and he felt almost hypnotised by the insistent beat of the music. The combination of the Golden Blood he'd drunk before they left and the vodka were making him feel dizzy.

A surreal feeling like he was dreaming took over and he didn't stop her when she led him to an arch covered with a fur curtain and slipped behind it. There was an ice corridor and another two doorways draped with heavy faux-fur coverings. Inside the first one was a cosy, circular igloo room with more furs piled on a raised platform in the centre. Long, white, tapered candles flickered around the edges of the room.

'I heard a couple of girls say that people pay for the experience of sleeping here overnight,' Cora whispered.

Inside, it was cosy and womb-like. Dillon felt like he was in some long-imagined dream as Cora pulled him against her and raised her lips to his. Once again, he held back.

'I still don't understand?' he whispered, looking into her eyes.

'You found out my brother was alive,' she whispered. 'And I want to.'

The heat that had been building between them all term unleashed and suddenly he couldn't get enough of her. Cora pulled back slightly and peeled his jacket off. Fingers trembling, he unzipped hers and as he traced her perfect curves with his hands, she shuddered, pulling him closer. Her hands crept underneath his T-shirt and caressed his chest, slowly moving down to his waistband. She teased the area just below his hip bone, slipping her fingers in the gap between his skin and belt. Involuntarily, his abs tensed, and he gasped with pleasure. A moan escaped his lips and, unable to resist any longer, he pulled her onto the furs, frantically ripping off the rest of their clothes.

For a second, he paused. In the soft light, her body glowed pale and smooth, her long limbs entwined with his. Thirstily, he lowered his mouth to her neck and traced the scent of her blood that had driven him crazy for months. Gently, with feather-light licks, he followed the path of her carotid artery from her neck to her breasts. Gently, he bit on her nipples and felt them harden under his tongue. Growling, she arched her back in pleasure and his head reeled at the taste of her skin. Growling again, this time with more urgency, she arched towards him again.

'Harder,' she whispered.

He responded, sucking deeply, her little growls of pleasure driving him crazy. Gently pushing him away, her eyes glittered huge with desire and never left his as she changed position and slowly lowered herself onto him. Dillon's head shot back – the sensation was exquisite. As they began to move together, he could feel the heat building and building, and he lost sense of anything other than the sensation of her body on his. Suddenly, she stopped, leaving him quivering on the brink of pleasure and bent her head. He felt her teeth graze his neck and sink into his skin. He cried out as his blood turned into molten fire. His fangs shot out reflexively and, without knowing what he was doing, he reciprocated, sinking them into her slender neck. They both cried out as an exquisite double eruption shuddered through their bodies. Cora collapsed on top of him and for a minute or two, they lay in each other's arms, trembling with the aftershocks of pleasure.

'Fuck me, Dillon!' Cora whispered.

Dillon couldn't resist a smile. 'What, again?'

Cora pressed her mouth against his chest to stifle a giggle. Gradually, he became aware of the noises of the bar beyond the fur curtain and feeling returned to his limbs.

He took her face in his hands. 'Sorry, did I hurt you?' he whispered, gently licking the crescent-shaped mark on her neck to make it heal faster.

'You could never hurt me,' she said.

The sound of cheering broke out in the bar.

'We better get back,' he said, scrambling for his clothes. 'They'll notice we're missing.'

With vampire speed, they dressed. Just before she reached for the curtain, he pulled her back. 'Cora—'

She put her finger on his lips. 'Don't spoil it . . .'

She disappeared back into the bar. He wasn't ready to face the others yet. In a daze, he followed the ice corridor past the other igloo room to another arch that led him outside. Hugging himself, he stared up the inky night sky and the hundreds of stars splashed across it. His body still tingled all over, and he felt more alive than he ever had in his life – it was way more intense even than Golden Blood. He took in a few controlled, big, deep breaths and willed his heart to slow down. He missed her already and feared it was an event that could never be repeated. She was with Bram. He could never find out.

The sound of shouts from the bar brought him back to reality. As he pushed his way through the heavy furs, the smell of hot humans brought him to a standstill, and he felt saliva run down the channels in his tongue.

The situation had deteriorated. Jeremiah, his eyes bloodshot and jaw quilted with the effort of maintaining his control, held a shaggy snowboarder and Angelo at arm's length. Ásta had her arms around Angelo, trying to calm him. His eyes were black and wild, and he was making a low, growling noise. Celeste's eyes glittered red with excitement as she poured petrol on the confrontation and taunted the snowboarder. Dillon felt the passion in his veins turn to rage as he approached her.

'What the fuck are you doing?' he hissed.

'Nothing,' she hissed back.

He turned his back on her and appealed to Angelo. 'Calm down, Angelo. It's not worth it. You've worked so hard.'

Somehow Angelo heard him, and Dillon saw his eyes, huge and predator-like, reduce in size and begin to look slightly more normal.

'We've got to get out of here, now,' he said to Jeremiah.

'We needed to do that ten minutes ago,' said Jeremiah,

lisping as his fangs strained against the mouthguard. 'Where the hell were you?'

'I went to explore,' he said, adjusting the collar of his jacket self-consciously,

Cora's bite mark had healed but it still felt like flames were licking up his neck.

Jeremiah glanced at him for a second and raised his eyebrows, knowingly.

'Let's get out of here,' Dillon said, ignoring him.

He nodded and let go of the snowboarder who lunged forward but was held back by his mates.

'She was the one who danced with me! She sucked my neck!' He shouted as Jeremiah dragged Angelo out. 'You're all fucking weird.'

Celeste blew him a kiss and, sauntered imperiously out after them. Dillon ground his teeth; she irritated the hell out of him. Ásta backed out behind her, not dropping her guard for a second. The rest of the crowd watched them leave in awed silence.

Cora was still trying to persuade Fred away from the cocktails.

'We've got to get out of here quick,' Dillon hissed.

Cora glanced at him, and he felt his neck ripple into flame again. She grabbed Fred, scooped up their jackets and joined him. Little aftershocks of electricity shot round his body as she brushed against his arm. The sharp mountain air brought them to their senses. The party in the outdoor bar was still in full flow.

'Celeste, you put us all at risk of losing control in there,' Dillon said, looking behind to see if anyone had followed them. 'You can't court attention like that and then turn on them.'

'What century are you living in, Dillon? I should be able to behave exactly as I like without some moron mauling me,' she said, indignation creasing her brow.

'In our world, yes. Not in the human world where they're irresistibly drawn to you. We're not supposed to attract attention to ourselves on this trip.'

'How dare you reprimand me, Dhampir,' she hissed, eyes sparking. 'If you were so worried about it, where were you, VE?'

Her eyes flicked towards Cora, and he felt another strange flutter of foreboding.

A loud, terrified scream sent sudden chills down his spine. A girl ran round the side of the igloo bar.

'Call the emergency services,' she screamed, 'there's blood everywhere!'

Angelo and Fred perked up.

'Stay here,' Dillon snapped – he didn't want those two anywhere near fresh blood.

'I'm coming with you,' Celeste insisted.

Dillon hesitated. 'Okay,' he said finally.

She wasn't his favourite vampire, but she had exemplary control. As fast and as hard as they dared, Dillon and Celeste pushed their way through the crowd. The cute outdoor barmaid lay unmoving at the side of the igloo bar next to the bins and empty drinks boxes. Her face was a horrible blue-grey colour. Her once blonde hair and the snow around her head were stained red. His fangs broke the surface of his gums and pressed into his guard once again and, disgusted with himself, he had to place his hand over his nose to block the smell.

A medical student rushed up and bent low to check if she was breathing. With a grim expression, he unzipped her ski jacket and began to administer CPR. Dillon turned to Celeste in horror, the girl's neck was ravaged.

Chiro suddenly appeared at his side. 'Get out of here now,' he growled. 'The others are already on the way to the cable car.'

Chiro guided them to the edge of the crowd and, with a furtive glance to check no one was watching, he pushed them into vampire speed. They reached the cable car terminal in seconds.

'We can't fly,' he hissed, 'the floodlights are too bright.'

'What happened?' Cora whispered.

'A girl was attacked. It looked like her throat had been ripped out.'

Cora's eyes opened wide. 'How could that have happened?' she asked, glancing at Dillon.

A paramedic skidoo roared up the mountain, sirens blaring followed by police and mountain rescue vehicles. As they climbed into the cable car, they heard the chug of a police helicopter overhead.

'What happened?' Angelo asked.

'Don't talk,' Chiro growled, pacing round the cable car and peering out the windows.

Madame Dupledge and Mr Hunt were waiting for them at the bottom. Borzak sped towards them as fast as he dared with Bram and the others. Once they were all together, Madame Dupledge addressed them.

'There has been a serious incident. It seems a human girl has been killed. Chiro has reported that it looks like a vampire attack. Our plans to stay the night have been cancelled and the helicopters are waiting to take us straight back to VAMPS. We will start a full enquiry immediately. Mr Hunt and I will stay here to begin damage limitation.'

As the helicopters lifted off and swooped over the floodlit mountain, Dillon stared down at the flashing lights and the cordons. A skidoo dragging a sledge with the girl's body covered with a blanket sped down the mountain to an ambulance waiting at the bottom, leaving a pink trail of smeared blood on the pristine mountain slope.

24

Blood Betrayal

Aside from the thrum of the engines, there was absolute silence inside the helicopter. Shocked and sick to his stomach, Dillon looked around at Cora, Celeste, Angelo, Fred, Ásta and Jeremiah; their faces, still as marble, revealed none of the inner turmoil he was feeling. Except for Celeste, he'd seen them all struggle with control – Angelo in particular. Had he underestimated their powerful instinct to drink fresh blood? Could one of them have ripped that girl's throat out? Even though he didn't want to, he had to ask.

'Did anyone see anything?' he asked.

'You and Cora were the only ones who disappeared,' Celeste said, looking between them. 'I presume you can account for each other.'

Without knowing why, the flutter of foreboding burst into a flood of fear, and his eyes flicked towards Cora. 'We went outside for some fresh air,' he said.

'Cora came back on her own,' Celeste continued. 'I suppose you needed more "fresh" air.'

'The vodka went to his head,' Cora said. 'He was feeling overwhelmed.'

'Strange that you left him on his own then,' Celeste said, raising an eyebrow. Her ice-blue eyes were hard.

'What do you mean?' Dillon said.

'It was your first time amongst humans as a half vampire.' Celeste shrugged. 'Maybe you lost control?'

Incredulously, he stared at her. 'I've lived amongst humans all my life. I could never kill a girl like that. Surely you don't really believe that?'

Celeste shrugged. 'Bloodlust does strange things to vampires.'

'I'm a dhampir,' he snapped.

'How convenient. You called yourself a vampire earlier,' she said, flicking her hair dismissively.

'Leave it you two. Madame Dupledge will find out what happened,' Jeremiah said. 'I'm sure it has nothing to do with us. Maybe there was a rogue around, or she was attacked by a wild animal.'

'I don't know why they couldn't sort it out and let us carry on,' Fred said, oblivious to the tense undercurrents fizzing around the helicopter. 'I wanted to check out the Nightjar.'

Ásta stared moodily out the window. 'Yeah, the one night we were supposed to have some fun,' she said.

Next to Dillon, Angelo's dark eyes glowed with relief. 'Dillon, it wasn't me,' he confided, under his breath.

Dillon tried to swallow the fear that was still rising in his throat. 'I know. You did great, Angelo,' he said and turned to look out of the window.

His mind was spinning. How was he going to explain his absence without dropping Cora in it?

The frozen lake flashed under them as they approached VAMPS. Only a relatively short time ago, he had been the hero of the Ice Challenge, the toast of VAMPS. He had an impending feeling of doom. He had betrayed Bram, and now he was going to pay for it.

Professor Dukan and Dr Meyer met them at the entrance.

'Terrible business,' Professor Dukan said, pacing up and down. 'Madame Dupledge has sent a message that you should go straight to your rooms. Do not talk to anyone except your roommate. She will speak to you individually as soon as she gets back.'

The minute they were in the lifts, Bram came up to Dillon. 'What the hell happened?' he hissed under his breath.

'Not sure.'

'Were you together the whole time?'

'Pretty much.'

Bram's eyebrows drew together, and he opened his mouth to speak.

'No discussion please, Mr Danesti,' Professor Dukan cut in. 'This is a serious matter.'

Silently, they walked down the corridor to their rooms. When Sade reached her door, she glanced at Dillon. Her eyes were huge with concern. He gave her a small smile but inside, he felt sick, like he'd betrayed her too.

As soon as he shut the door to their room, Jeremiah turned to him. 'Do you want to tell me?' he asked.

'You know. Cora and I went out for some fresh air.'

'Come on, mate, this is me you're talking to. The tension has been building between you two since you first set eyes on each other and then suddenly you disappear together and come back all starry-eyed. Fresh air alone doesn't do that.'

'I didn't come back starry-eyed,' Dillon protested. 'I came straight over to help you sort Angelo out.'

'It's okay, mate. I'm not going to tell anyone,' Jeremiah said. 'And for what it's worth, I trust you. You are the only one unaccounted for, but I can't see you ripping out a pretty girl's throat – even if bloodlust did take hold.'

'Um, thanks mate. Like I said, all I did was get some fresh air to clear my head.'

'Like I said, I believe you. Thousands wouldn't.'

'You're sure no one else left the bar?'

'Only you and Cora.'

'I know I didn't do it, so it must have been someone who wanted to make it look like it was one of us. Someone with a grudge against VAMPS.'

Jeremiah was watching him closely. 'What's up?'

He shook his head. 'You don't think Bram and Cora could have set me up?'

'What? No! Cora's not like that.'

He sighed with relief. 'Yeah, you're right. I'm just being paranoid.'

'It's going to be a long evening. I'm going to chill before it all kicks off,' Jeremiah said, opening his coffin.

Dillon sat on the floor with his back against the wall and put his head in his hands. It was a relief when Chiro came for him at dawn. Madame Dupledge paced up and down her office, alone. She stopped when she saw him.

'Shut the door behind you please, Dillon.'

Dillon thought he glimpsed a stricken expression cross her face before she turned to him and stared at him, deathly serious.

'Dillon, I want you to be honest. Did you attack that girl?'

Dillon started and stared back at her. 'No, of course not!'

'Celeste told us that you were the only one missing from the bar last night. During our damage limitation, we found evidence of your unique blood mixed with the girl's blood.'

His heart, which had slowed right down, suddenly started beating hard and fast again. 'What? I swear, I saw her at the bar but not again until the alarm was raised.'

'How do you account for your time alone then?'

He couldn't tell her that he had needed some space to savour the incredible aftershocks of being with Cora.

'We had a few vodkas. It combined with the Golden Blood. I felt dizzy. We went to get some fresh air. Cora wanted to get back; I needed some more time.'

'Even though you are VE and were supposed to be keeping

an eye on the others – especially considering you had some of the more volatile vampires in your group?'

He was silent, then he said, 'I guess it wasn't my finest decision, but I got things under control as soon as I came back in.'

'Having satisfied your own bloodlust?'

'No, I told you, I had nothing to do with that. I feel the attraction of human blood, but –' he paused – 'I believe I can control it.'

He was struggling to come to terms with her sudden hostility towards him.

'Your blood DNA at the scene is damning, Dillon.'

'I can't explain that, except that everyone knows I have unique blood. It would be easy for someone who wanted to get rid of me to frame me.'

'A little far-fetched that someone would go to all that trouble, don't you think?'

'No more far-fetched than accusing me of something I didn't do.'

She studied him for a second and despite the rising dark panic threatening to overwhelm him, he sensed her conflicted emotions.

Finally, when she spoke, her voice was strained. 'I am sorry, Dillon, but I really have no choice. Unless information comes to light that proves your innocence, I have to put you in isolation, and you will face a full vampire trial. If you are found guilty, in accordance with VAMPS rules, you will be put to death.'

Shocked rigid, Dillon stared at her, unable to comprehend what was happening to him. 'Death?' he gasped. 'You'd have me killed?'

She glanced at the door and spoke fast in a low voice. 'You must act very carefully now, Dillon. There are several powerful vampires who want you removed from this school. You must try to remember anything you saw or anything that might help your case. In the face of the evidence against you, I am in an extremely difficult position. I championed for you to come to VAMPS and I can't be seen to support you without the risk of being ousted myself.'

'So, you don't believe I did it and yet you're prepared to throw me under the bus?'

Her emerald eyes glittered. 'Losing my position wouldn't help either of us,' she said coldly.

'How am I meant to defend myself? I want to speak to my father. Don't I get a lawyer or something?'

'It doesn't work like that in our world. The trial will uncover the truth. It is best like this.'

Dillon stared at her incredulously. 'This is medieval. I want to speak to my father.'

'Your father knows that this is the way it's done.'

'There is no way my father would stand by and allow this to happen to me,' he said fiercely. 'I want you to contact him, and I want to see him. I am half human; it's a basic human right.'

'In a vampire court, your vampire side takes precedence.

There is not much your father can do. He knew the risks when you came here.'

'He could not have known that I would be somehow set up or framed for something I didn't do.' He was begging her now. 'Promise me, you will contact him.'

'I will try, but as I said, there are powerful forces against you.'

He was clutching at straws now. 'In that case, what about my mother? If she's from a powerful vampire family, my father must be able to ask her to help.'

'Dillon, I will do what I can, you will just have to trust that. Remember that I am under scrutiny too. There is not much time. Chiro will take you to the holding cell now. You will remain in isolation until the trial.'

It was like a nightmare he couldn't escape. He turned and stumbled towards the door. Suddenly, he turned back. 'Your intuition would tell you that I'm telling the truth. Why can't you use it?'

'Dillon, I am a strong intuit, but I am not immune to vampires who can block me, and you have been growing stronger at evading me.'

Dillon blinked, surprised. He hadn't known that and yet, now he thought about it, he had blocked her on a couple of occasions – especially with Bram after the Ice Challenge.

'My evidence would not be accepted in a trial where there is concrete evidence of your blood at the scene. Countess Fassano's mind-reading abilities are so strong, she is the only vampire they might accept. I have already made a request to the Vampire Council but there is no guarantee they will allow it.'

A wave of rage rolled over him, pushing out the panic; he hadn't wanted to come to a vampire academy. All along he had felt like a pawn in some greater plan with no control over what happened to him.

'You and my mysterious *mother* engineered my place here,' he spoke through gritted teeth. 'I never wanted to come. I didn't ask to be Vampire Elect. I didn't ask to drink blood, or swim for miles under solid feckin' ice to fight rogue feckin' vampires! I didn't ask for any of this! None of it. And every step of the way you –' he pointed angrily to Madame Dupledge – 'You tasted my blood. You said it was special. That I was special. It doesn't make sense. *Why* would I do something like this?'

He steadied himself, closing his eyes and focusing on soothing memories: Cora steadying him beneath the ice; Cora kissing him to take flight; Cora in the ice room at the ski resort, looking deep into his eyes. And as he did, he felt an echo of the strength she brought him. He opened his eyes, looked at Madame Dupledge, and continued.

'It's your responsibility to get me out of this but all of you only really care about yourselves, don't you? So fair enough – go ahead, Madame Dupledge. Save yourself. It's what every vampire does. Isn't it?'

★

He was pleased to see her wince as he turned and left, but it gave him no satisfaction. Cora had been right when she had warned him that Madame Dupledge wasn't as powerful as she seemed. It had happened to her brother and now it was happening to him. Chiro led him to the bowels of the building. At the very bottom, deep inside the mountain, was a small cell with reinforced steel doors. At the door, Chiro paused.

'I don't believe you did it, Dillon. I saw you outside and then go in,' he growled under his breath. 'Whoever did it, was clever enough to evade me.'

Dillon turned to him gratefully. For some reason, Chiro had always had his back.

'Thanks, I appreciate that, Chiro. Did you tell Madame Dupledge?'

'Yes, but there are some strong forces at play. They are hung up on the blood thing. I will do what I can to find out more. The cameras are watching – you have to go in now.'

As Chiro began to swing the door shut, Dillon turned to him and spoke urgently under his breath. 'Sade might be able to help you. She is extremely clever and has contacts in high places. Her sister works in some top blood testing lab.'

'I'll try, but it won't be easy.' Chiro grimaced and clanged the door shut.

Dillon heard his soft footsteps scurry away and felt the anger drain away allowing despair to wash over him. The cell had been carved out of the mountain and was a complete contrast to the rest of the building. The walls and floor were bare rock, and it had a damp, earthy smell. A single coffin rested on the floor and the only light came from the small green light on top of a surveillance camera. It made a faint whirring noise as it followed him around the room.

He was still struggling to come to terms with the abrupt change in his fortunes. For hours he paced the cell; the brief miraculous time he had spent with Cora seemed like it had happened in another life. His mind travelled back and forth through a never-ending loop, plunging from the ecstasy with Cora to the horror of the dead girl, searching for any clue to explain who was trying to frame him.

At some point tiredness overtook him and he lay, exhausted, in the coffin. It was hard and cold, completely unlike the luxury version he had become used to. Still, sleep eluded him as his mind continued to churn over every detail of the ski trip; desperately, he tried to remember if he had seen anyone or anything that would make sense of what had happened.

Finally, he must have fallen into a fitful sleep, full of hazy dreams. In one, Cora's lust-glazed face morphed into the pretty barmaid's as he bit her neck in ecstasy. She writhed in equal rapture, and he found he couldn't stop drinking her blood. The sensation of it spilling down his throat, so warm and fresh, was exquisite until her eyes, half Cora's, half the barmaid's, grew wide and frightened. She thrashed against him, but he still couldn't stop.

He woke sweating, heart pounding, and felt his mouth for evidence of blood. Terrified, he threw open the coffin lid and lay there, too frightened to move. The feeling of drinking the girl's blood had been so visceral, so realistic, that for a minute, he wondered if a fit of bloodlust could have overtaken him without him even realising it.

'Dillon.'

He started as Chiro silently appeared and bent over the coffin. He spoke fast and under his breath. 'Things are moving fast. Like I said you have some powerful enemies, but you also have a powerful ally.'

'Who?' he whispered, shaking his head to try to clear the vision of the dead girl.

'I'm not sure. There's a lot of secretive stuff going on. Your friend Sade is helping.'

His heart swelled as he thought of Sade. He longed to see her.

'Jeremiah, he is your friend, no?' Chiro asked, eyes gleaming red in the dark.

'Yes, why?'

'He says you confessed that it was you when you were in the room together.'

Dillon's whole body went icy cold.

'Jeremiah?' he asked stupidly.

'Yes, Jeremiah,' Chiro growled.

He felt like he was losing grip of reality, that he was plunging downwards off the side of a cliff. He sat up and retched over the side of the coffin. Chiro waited until he had finished.

'Did you?'

He struggled to lift his head. 'Jaysus, no, of course not. I don't understand; he's always stood up for me.'

'Like I said, it seems like you've got powerful enemies.'

'He wouldn't do that,' he repeated.

'He's done it. The trial is set to go ahead in two days.'

He couldn't rid himself of the sensation that he was falling, that there was no hope. He clutched Chiro's arm to steady himself. 'Can you remind Madame Dupledge, I must see my father.'

'She's under a lot of pressure. Alexandru Danesti and Eric Torstensson are after her scalp.'

'Alexandru Danesti must be behind this,' Dillon said bitterly. 'He's been trying to get rid of me since the beginning.' He laughed mirthlessly. 'I wish he'd succeeded earlier. I'd take expulsion over death any day.'

'Stay strong,' Chiro growled. 'I've got to go now. I've been in here too long already. Professor Dukan will deliver some blood before the trial.'

Dillon's mouth watered at the thought of blood, but sick with himself after the recent nightmare, he immediately forced it out of his mind. The small cell was beginning to drive him crazy. It was impossible to know how long he'd been there already. As he climbed out of the coffin and paced up and down, he was tormented by his father not wanting to see him, Jeremiah's betrayal and paranoia that Bram and Cora had set him up. His eyes were gritty from lack of sleep and his skin felt dry and shrivelled from lack of blood.

He had no idea how much time had passed when he heard a faint tap on the other side of the metal door.

'Dillon?'

He recognised Sade's voice instantly but mindful of the camera, he turned his back to the door and leant against it and put his head in his hands as if in despair.

'Sade?' he whispered. 'How did you find me? You know there are cameras?'

'Chiro told me – I've dealt with the cameras, but I only have a minute. Are you okay?'

'No, how can I prove I'm innocent stuck in here?'

'We're on the case. Hold tight.'

'How could Jeremiah betray me?'

'I don't know yet, but don't worry Dillon – we'll find out. I've got to go.'

'Sade—'

'Bye, Dillon.'

He heard her footsteps sprinting lightly away.

'Thanks,' he whispered, and he slid down the door, landing in a heap on the floor.

He had heard that you found out who your friends were in a time of crisis, and he hugged his stomach as the pain of Jeremiah's betrayal gripped him again. He thought of his difficulties with the bloodlust tests. Maybe he wasn't the vampire he seemed to be.

At some point, he pulled himself together. If Sade was putting her neck on the line, he had to try to keep strong for her. He racked his brains for any tiny detail he might have missed but, once again, he came up with nothing. He had been completely absorbed by Ásta's display with the ice luge and he found it hard to remember anything in the ice bar except for his mad desire for Cora.

The more he thought about it, the paranoia that Cora had set him up, increased. Why else would she have suddenly changed her mind? Every time they had got close before, she had made it clear that she had to be with Bram.

Eventually, aware that he was driving himself crazy, he attempted to relax his mind in the hope that he would pick up Cora's or Jeremiah's thoughts. When he struggled to pick up a single thing, he realised it was pointless; the cell was probably fitted with mind-blocking technology.

Sleep, when it came again was fitful and full of nightmares. Each time, he woke screaming 'No, da!' as his father insisted that he must face his death like a true vampire. Shaking, sweat dripping, he had to battle to remind himself that his father would never do that. He grew weaker and more deranged. He had completely lost track of time by the time the metal door opened again and Chiro walked in, followed by Professor Dukan.

Professor Dukan looked almost as bad as he felt; his hair was dishevelled, his tie was askew, and his eyes were slightly wild and bloodshot. 'They have decided you can't have Golden Blood anymore,' he said. 'Are you strong enough for the trial? I have brought another type, but it may make you worse.'

As he leant forward to show him the bag, he whispered,

'Dillon, I am investigating the DNA of the blood at the scene. Sade was sent a sample from an unknown source, but we are short of time. Delay where you can.'

Dillon's nostrils flared at the sight of the blood and his fangs shot out, piercing his cracked bottom lip. 'It's fine. I refuse to take blood anyway,' he said. 'In protest against my treatment. If I survive this, I'm going home to Ireland, going back to the way things were – just me and my da, no more of this vampire shite.'

Professor Dukan gasped. 'You can't,' he said, twisting his long fingers in agitation. 'Your potential is too great.'

'So one minute I have "great potential" and the next they're talking about putting me to death? Where's the feckin' potential in that?'

Professor Dukan winced. 'You must stand up for what is right. You can't change something that is wrong by giving up.'

'Think of Sade,' Chiro growled.

Sade's soulful, earnest eyes flickered into his mind, and he put his head in his hands. Wordlessly, he reached for the blood and drank, even though every gulp felt like a betrayal. It tasted bitter and he felt it burn his throat.

Glancing up at the camera, Professor Dukan continued in a louder tone. 'The trial starts at midnight tonight. As is traditional, it will be held at the peak of the East Mountain and will be attended by Madame Dupledge, the governors of the school and the entire Vampire Council. The judge is the head of the Vampire Council, Nikolas Karayan. He will call witnesses to the stand to testify against you. You represent yourself and have the right to call on any witnesses in your defence.'

Dillon's head reeled. 'Can witnesses testify anonymously?' He was thinking of Cora. If she had set him up, then Bram would already know, but if she hadn't, then he didn't want to betray her – unless he had to.

'Possibly, it is at the discretion of Nikolas Karayan. Chiro will be back to fly you to the East peak before midnight.'

His formal tone indicated he was talking for the benefit of the surveillance camera. As he turned to the door, he whispered, 'Keep calm. Anger will play into their hands. Think who you would like to speak for you.'

Chiro nodded. 'Stay strong,' he said, as he closed the heavy door.

The blood hit Dillon's system hard. Rather than oiling it like Golden Blood, he felt his body cramping and, for a minute, he thought he might throw up. He was already weak, and he felt worse as it chugged, sluggishly through his system.

Desperately trying to marshal his thoughts, he ran his hands through his hair, noting that it felt lank and brittle. No one, except Chiro had seen him outside the bar but Chiro had no actual proof that it wasn't him who had killed the girl at another time. He didn't know if he could trust Cora anymore and Jeremiah, his protector, his rock, had betrayed him. Madame Dupledge's hands appeared to be tied, and she couldn't use her intuition against the blood DNA evidence. Only Countess Fassano offered some hope, but there were no guarantees that she would agree to read his mind or that they would allow her to. He was entirely reliant on Professor Dukan and Sade coming up with something in time.

By the time Borzak and Chiro returned just before midnight to collect him, he was weaker still and cramps still racked his body. He could barely stand as Borzak pulled his arms behind his back and snapped silver restraints around his wrists.

'Why are you doing that?' he asked. 'It's obvious I'm too weak to escape.'

Borzak shrugged his huge shoulders. 'It's the way things are done.'

Flanking him on either side, they held him up as they walked him up through the building to the fifth floor. There was no sign of the others, but just as they reached the door, Angelo appeared on the stairs and called out.

'We're not allowed to talk to you, but I know you didn't do it, Dillon. I don't care what anyone says.'

Dillon turned and stared at him. 'Thanks, Angelo,' he managed, overcome with emotion.

Borzak and Chiro led him over the tiled school crest through the inner door to the concrete tunnel beyond.

'Ready?' Chiro asked.

He nodded and, with Borzak holding one arm and Chiro the other, they flew through the outer door and up the side of the academy building. As they flashed over the stunning glass roof, he wondered if he'd see it again.

25

Blood Trial

Out of nowhere, two VSS operatives, dressed in their usual black, joined them, one flying just above and in front, the other behind. Chiro used his considerable flying skills to make it a flight to remember, and Dillon tried to forget his weakness and the fact that it could be his last, as they swept down steep mountainsides and sliced through stunning, narrow gullies. The landscape grew wilder, and they flew into an eerie, pale mist that swirled around the foothills and filled the dark valleys. Dillon, unable to see anything more than Chiro's red gleaming eyes next to him, lost any sense of where he was, becoming so disorientated he no longer knew where the sky and the earth were. Chiro gripped him tighter, and he sensed they were beginning to climb. Suddenly, almost at the peak of the mountain, they shot out of the cloud and Dillon gasped. Green lights swirled overhead, illuminating the sky with ethereal green radiance.

As they flew higher towards the light spectacle, the mountain peak levelled out into a spectacular plateau ringed with fire torches. In the centre was a large luminous rock, roughly hewn into the shape of a rectangle. Madame Dupledge and a surprisingly frail, ancient-looking vampire dressed in a long ermine cape waited for them next to it. Their pale faces reflected the shifting lights above and gave them an otherworldly appearance.

They were surrounded by a circle of formidable vampires dressed in red, hooded robes. Ice gripped Dillon's heart as the flaming iron torches revealed their exposed fangs. An outer circle of vampires dressed in long black robes included Alexandru Danesti. His hard black eyes looked even more disturbing under the shadow of his hood and with his gleaming fangs exposed. Sade's parents and Eric Torstensson – Celeste's father, wearing an ice-cold expression just like his daughter's – stood next to him.

Chiro brought them in to land and to Dillon it felt like he was floating on a platform, high above the clouds. The VSS, silent as shadows, circled above them like eagles above an eyrie. There was no doubt that he was alone at the top of the world and at the mercy of an ancient vampiric system he barely understood.

As Borzak removed the silver restraints around his wrists, Madame Dupledge spoke.

'Dillon, this is Nikolas Karayan.' Her musical voice sounded strangely sombre, and he almost stepped back in shock. Her exposed fangs gave her a savage, menacing beauty that he had never seen before. 'He is the head of the Vampire Council and will oversee your trial.'

Nikolas's intense, pale eyes scrutinised him with interest. 'At last, I meet the dhampir who has been causing so much unrest.'

As Dillon stared back into his eyes, he felt fear grip him. Despite Nikolas's almost brittle appearance, he was without a doubt the most intimidating vampire he had ever seen. His tongue froze and his anger deserted him.

'Sorry,' he stuttered stupidly. 'I never meant to.'

Nikolas smiled, exposing razor sharp fangs. 'Ah, so endearingly human,' he said, turning to the circle of vampires around them. 'Never apologise, Dillon, until you know what you are apologising for. Is it your fault that you were sent to the world's most exclusive finishing academy for vampires? Or is it the fault of those who believed a dhampir might change our world for the better?'

He dared not look at her, but Dillon sensed Madame Dupledge flinch infinitesimally.

'And now you find yourself in this terrible position, accused of killing an innocent human girl in a fit of blood-lust. An act that is expressly forbidden while you are a student at VAMPS as it risks upsetting the delicate alliance between the human and our vampire worlds. As is customary, we will hear the evidence against you and then you will have the chance to defend yourself.

'The aurora borealis only appears above this mountain once every two years; it is remarkable that it should appear for your trial tonight, don't you think? Maybe it is a coincidence but maybe it is fortuitous. Does the vision of the borealis signify that you are special, Dillon?'

Dillon swayed and Chiro gripped his arm to hold him up.

'I haven't a clue.'

'Let go of him, Chiro. Stand back,' Nikolas snapped.

As soon as Chiro let go, Dillon half-slumped to the ground.

'Get up,' Nikolas insisted.

Trembling with the effort, Dillon managed to stand. Behind the circle of vampires, he noticed the rest of his year arrive and take their places beyond the outer circle. Immediately, he searched for Jeremiah, and he felt the pain like a punch to the stomach when he saw the animosity radiating out of him, extinguishing the small spark of hope that his betrayal was a mistake. Bram stood next to Cora, staring at him with a strange half-triumphant, half-bitter expression on his face. Desperately, he searched Cora's beautiful face for signs of guilt. She was pale and drawn and, as her vivid eyes locked on to his, he saw the regret. His knees buckled slightly. What had she done to him?

'Can the first witness for the prosecution come forward please?' Nikolas called out.

A wave of sickness washed over Dillon as the vampire circle parted to let Celeste through.

'What is your name?'

Celeste faced him; her silver blonde hair gleaming iridescent in the lights. She looked both stunning and assured.

'Celesté Torstensson,' she said, and despite her cool voice, Dillon sensed her suppressed excitement.

Nikolas nodded approvingly. 'Can you tell us what happened on the night of the trip to Zermatt?'

'Right from the beginning, Dillon let the evening get out of hand. He allowed some of the more reckless vampires to drink human alcohol and make exhibitions of themselves. When we went inside, the situation deteriorated and even though the atmosphere was becoming dangerous, he disappeared with Cora. When Cora came back, he wasn't with her. In that time, things became even more volatile. As VE, he should have been there. When he did eventually turn up, his eyes were glazed, and he looked dazed although I didn't understand why at the time. Jeremiah got us out safely and Dillon accused me of inflaming the situation to detract the others from his own guilt. Then we heard the screams and I saw that a human girl had been killed. It wasn't just for blood; her throat had been ripped out. It was clearly an out-of-control bloodlust killing. Dillon –' she turned and pointed at him – 'was the only one who left the room alone. It couldn't have been anyone else.'

There was a faint stirring amongst the circle of vampires. Dillon's legs shook with the effort to stand up. Her evidence sounded damning.

'Thank you, Celeste.' Nikolas's lips pulled back in a smile that only succeeded in making him look more sinister. 'Alastair Hunt, come forward, please.'

Mr Hunt glided forward and his cold raven eyes swept

over Dillon. Ever since the night of the Flight Trial, Dillon had known he couldn't trust him, and he understood that Mr Hunt would do everything in his power to get rid of him. Under his beak-like nose, his lips twitched with the effort of containing his jubilation.

'Madame Dupledge and I were alerted by Chiro. As soon as the year one vampires had been flown out, we began to assess the situation. The girl had been brought down the mountain. I compelled the mountain rescue team and was able to examine her. As Celeste said, it was quite clearly a vampire attack. Madame Dupledge contacted Countess Fassano and she pulled the strings at the hospital. One of our VSS operatives on the ground completed her examination and took the necessary blood samples. They made the wound look more like an animal attack and circulated the information that the girl had been attacked by a wild wolf.

'The samples were flown straight to our secret labs in Zurich and DNA of a unique blood type known to be Dillon's was found. We believe he must have been trying to heal the girl with his own blood when his bloodlust was satisfied, and he realised what he had done.'

Dillon gasped. 'I didn't. I don't know how my blood got there. There must have been a mistake. This is wrong.'

'There is no mistake.' Mr Hunt delved inside his black cloak and handed Nikolas an envelope. 'These are the lab reports, matching the blood type at the scene with Dillon's.'

Nikolas paused dramatically before opening the envelope, and the vampires in the outer circles craned forward slightly as he scanned the contents. 'Thank you, Alastair. I can confirm to all those present that the report shows a direct match.'

Dillon's heart, once vampire slow, began to beat faster. As one, the watching vampires leaned forward as they heard it. Mr Hunt bowed and, with one more cold glance at Dillon, returned to the outer circle of vampires.

'Will the third witness come forward please?' Nikolas called out, his expression theatrically grave.

As Jeremiah made his way to the centre of the circle, Dillon's knees gave way again. As he looked up at his room-mate, he felt crushed by the weight of the contempt blazing out of his eyes.

'I was with Dillon on the night of the ski trip. I saw him leave the bar with Cora and return after she did. I have got to know him well as we share a room and I noticed imme-diately that he looked different. He seemed excited and, as Celeste said, his eyes were glazed. When the screams started, he didn't want any of us to go with him, he only allowed Celeste because she insisted. In the helicopter afterwards, he denied that he had anything to do with it but when we got back to our room, he confessed that the vodka combined with his attraction to Cora had unleashed a terrible blood-lust. When he saw one of the bar girls taking empty bottles around the back of the building, he lost control. He said he must have blacked out but when he came to, he was horri-fied when he discovered what he had done and so he bit his wrist and fed her his own blood. When he realised it was too late, he panicked and left her there.'

Dillon stared up at him. 'Jeremiah, come on. Why are you doing this? I never said any of that. Never.'

He searched Jeremiah's face but there was no sign of compassion, just cold contempt.

'Quiet!' Nikolas's powerful voice, at odds with his frame, reverberated around the circle. 'You will have your chance to speak. Thank you, Jeremiah. You may return. Dillon, call your first witness.'

There was silence. Dillon slumped and his mind went blank for a minute.

'Chiro,' he blurted out.

Chiro shuffled to the centre of the circle, looking even more awkward and unimposing on the ground than usual. When he began speaking, his voice was unusually hesitant.

'I was patrolling the skies above the ice village. I transfigured into a bat because of the risk of being seen in the floodlights. There was a mass of people around the outside bar but I was flying quite big loops of the whole area, so it wasn't always in my direct sightline when I was checking the forest on the other side of the pistes. I was just completing a loop when I saw Dillon outside the ice bar, but he was just standing there staring at the mountain and the sky. When the alarm was raised, I got them all out of there.'

'Thank you, Chiro. Just so we are all completely clear, can you confirm a couple of small points for me,' Nikolas asked.

Chiro nodded uneasily.

'You said you weren't in direct sight of the location at all times?'

Chiro nodded again. 'As I said, I was flying big loops and as a bat, I am less noticeable, but I am slower because of my size.'

'I see, and you didn't see Dillon come outside?

'No, he was already outside when I flew over.'

'So, he could have killed the girl in a fit of bloodlust before you saw him,' Nikolas asked.

Chiro looked at Dillon. 'I suppose he could have, but he wouldn't have had much time.'

'Thank you, Chiro. Who is your next witness, Dillon?'

As Chiro shuffled off, Dillon was in turmoil, the evidence against him was overwhelming, but he would still rather die than betray Cora. He almost blacked out when he heard her clear voice ring out.

'I would like to give evidence.'

He was too weak and befuddled to argue.

Shaking off Bram's restraining hand, Cora pushed her way through the circle of vampires and stood by the glimmering rock. In the firelight, her eyes were the same colour as the sky above her. She had never looked so boldly beautiful or nervous as she held his gaze.

'The reason Dillon left the ice bar was because of me,' she said, in her cut-glass English. 'The atmosphere in the bar was carnal. It unleashed an explosive desire in us.'

Dillon felt his body heat up with the memory, and he found the energy to meet her eyes.

'I suggested that we leave the bar. Dillon was reluctant at first, but I persuaded him. As soon as we were alone –' Cora paused, searching for the right words – 'our need for each other escalated and we were physically intimate. It was incredibly intense because the spark between us had been building for months. Both of us were left shaken, but for Dillon, I think I'm right in saying, it was particularly overwhelming as it was the first time he had been with a vampire.'

Despite the truth of her words, Dillon winced.

'Afterwards, I went straight back to the bar in the hope that the others wouldn't realise that we'd gone. Dillon was still feeling overwhelmed by the intensity of what had just happened, and he said he needed some fresh air. He wasn't gone for long and when he returned, he had the same expression he'd had when I left him. It wasn't bloodlust.

'The minute he got back, he took control of the situation. Celeste had enflamed the room by dancing incredibly provocatively and taunting a human boy. When he reacted and Angelo felt compelled to protect her, Jeremiah stepped in and then Dillon got everyone out.'

Except for the howl of the wind around the mountain top, there was absolute silence when she finished speaking. She tore her gaze away from Dillon and found Bram.

'I'm sorry, Bram,' she said, her bottom lip trembling with emotion. 'I never intended to hurt you.'

As they stared at each other, Bram was unable to disguise the naked pain and anger etched onto his stony face, and Dillon bowed his head in shame.

'Ahem,' Nikolas broke the spell.

Dillon sank further onto his knees. The rollercoaster of emotions had further depleted his limited energy.

'Your passionate defence of Dillon is admirable, Cora, but even so, you cannot say where Dillon was in the period he was outside without you. You cannot prove that your –' he paused – 'liaison did not set off a bloodlust in Dillon. Tell me, did he take blood from you?'

Cora hesitated a fraction and then she lifted her chin and stared him straight in the eyes. 'Yes,' she said finally.

There was a slight hissing sound from some of the vampires and Nikolas raised his eyebrows.

'Did you take blood from Dillon, despite knowing it was against academy rules?'

Cora bit her lip. 'Yes, but I wasn't really aware of my actions at the time.'

'Very well, Madame Dupledge will discuss the implications of your transgression with you later.'

As she returned to stand next to Bram, who stared straight ahead, his jaw rictus tight, Dillon was hit with a sudden flood of revelations. Maybe Bram hadn't set him up. They had become rivals over Cora and because of his election as VE. His high-powered family had taught him to be arrogant and to manipulate the system for his own gain, but ultimately, Bram was an honourable vampire and a genuinely good leader. That was why Cora had been won over by him. Now here he was staring death in the face, and he wondered, not for the first time, if the Blood Tasting had got it right.

'You have one more witness, Dillon,' Nikolas reminded him.

There was no one else left to act as a witness for him; there was no sign of Sade or Professor Dukan. At least she had been spared Cora's testimony.

'I'll speak for myself,' he said, hanging on to the strange luminous rock to hold himself upright. 'I didn't kill that girl. It's true that I have many faults, but I don't believe out-of-control bloodlust is one of them.' He forced himself not to think of the terrible dream in the cell. 'Cora's testimony is true. I went outside because I was completely overwhelmed by what had just happened.'

Out of the corner of his eye, he noticed Bram shudder.

'I needed some time before I returned. I know that as VE, I shouldn't have left the bar and I managed the situation badly. I know that Bram would never have done that. What Chiro says is true, I was seeing the world through new eyes, even the sky and the view across the mountains looked different. I can't have been out for more than five minutes. There wouldn't have been time for me to get round the building and attack that girl before Chiro saw me. I never confessed to Jeremiah because there was nothing to admit to. I am willing to have my mind read to prove that I am telling the truth.'

Nikolas affected sorrow. 'Ah, I am sorry, Dillon. Countess Fassano is the only vampire qualified enough to read minds in a trial situation and I'm afraid she declined our request.'

Dillon's grip on the rock faltered; no one else could save him now.

'Dillon, the council and governors will now transport to confer and decide your fate.'

The two inner circles of vampires instantly disappeared, leaving the outer circle alone with Chiro and Borzak. Dillon slid down the rock utterly drained. For a second, no one said a thing.

Cora turned to Bram again, her voice shaking slightly. 'Bram, what can I say? I'm so ashamed. Dillon and I . . . we've always had a spark . . . things got out of hand that night. Please believe that I didn't intend to hurt you.'

Bram's fists were clenched with suppressed emotion. His eyes were dark with pain and when he spoke, his jaw was tight with tension.

'I believe you Cora, but I'm not sure I can ever forgive you,' he said in a low voice.

Cora swayed as if his words had hit her physically, her face drained and as shadowed with pain as his. Dillon's own pain gripped his stomach and he doubled over as he remembered Bram's words that he was no good for Cora and he'd hold her back.

Ásta snorted. 'Come on guys, since when were we vampires exclusive? You're acting like a pair of lovesick humans. Unless a miracle happens, Dillon is not going to be an issue for much longer.'

'Ásta!' Angelo exclaimed, glancing at Dillon.

Ásta adopted an aggressive pose, and Dillon realised with surprise that she was upset.

'He's been well and truly stitched up by someone.' She spun and with her fists lifted, confronted Jeremiah. 'What's in this for you, you fucking traitor?'

Jeremiah crouched forward in a defensive stance and hissed. 'I just told the truth.'

'Yeah,' Ásta taunted. 'Celeste got to you, did she?'

Celeste snarled and Jeremiah sprang at Ásta, but she was ready for him and somersaulted high into the air, landing next to Dillon. Aron, Fred and Angelo immediately sprang into the air and landed lightly next to her. The two groups faced one another, fangs out and growling, low in their throats.

There was a disturbance in the swirling green kaleidoscopic skies above them as the Vampire Council returned and surrounded the small group next to Dillon.

Nikolas turned his cold eyes on them. 'Interesting. It seems that Dillon evokes strong passions amongst you. Return to your positions immediately. We have reached a verdict.'

Defiantly, they helped Dillon stand.

Nikolas's light, mocking tone changed instantly. 'Leave him,' he snarled.

Trembling, Dillon faced him as the circle parted to let through the vampires who had turned out to be his loyal friends.

Nikolas surveyed him. 'Dillon, as you know, your presence as a dhampir at our most exclusive finishing academy has wrought division and rancour – even amongst your peers. Some of us thought you held the key to our future; it seems they were misguided. We have conferred and the majority agree that you have been found guilty and should be put to death.'

Madame Dupledge, standing next to him, bowed her head.

'No!' Cora cried out. 'He didn't want any of this.'

Dillon felt strangely numb as if the words washing over him had no meaning.

Nikolas continued. 'In the traditional manner, the council shall each feed upon your blood until you are dead. As Countess Fassano is missing, we will collect a vial for her.'

Dillon gasped. Of course, he should have known that only vampires could come up with something so macabre.

Nikolas beckoned him forward. 'Dillon, you became a vampire. Now face your death like one. Remove your shirt.'

Fingers shaking, Dillon undid the buttons of his shirt. As he pulled it off, his tattoo, '*In Darkness We Shine*', seemed like a sick joke. The stone in the chain around his neck burned hot in the light of the flickering torches and Nikolas's eyes narrowed as if he recognised it. Pausing, he stepped forward to examine it more closely.

'Where did you get this?' he asked.

Dillon shrugged. 'I don't know. My father said it was a gift from my mother.'

Nikolas looked momentarily disconcerted and he glanced at Madame Dupledge, who stared at him, her face stricken.

He closed his eyes and appeared to be wrestling with something. Dillon sensed his mind whirring.

Finally, he seemed to reach a decision and opened his eyes again.

'It may prove to be unfortunate, but rules are rules,' he said. 'Borzak, help Dillon onto the stone.'

Borzak lifted him and placed him face up in the centre of the stone. It was smooth and cold against his bare back. Dillon traced his tattoo with his fingers and turned, searching for Madame Dupledge.

'Tell my father I love him,' he choked. 'Tell him I did nothing wrong.'

Madame Dupledge swallowed and fought hard to hide the emotion on her face. He heard a low growling noise from his friends as the inner circle drew closer towards him.

Flamboyantly, Nikolas lifted an ornate pewter box and sprinkled a light, musk-scented ash on Dillon's throat. Chanting unfamiliar, ancient words, he traced strange symbols on his skin. Finally, he bent towards him, and Dillon saw his thin, pale lips had stretched back to reveal the full extent of his long ivory-coloured fangs. Instinctively, his limbs thrashed as he tried to get away, and Borzak slipped the restraints on once again, weakening him further.

Closing his strange pale eyes once more, Nikolas lowered his mouth to Dillon's throat. Close up, he smelt old and musty, like a long-abandoned sarcophagus, and Dillon shuddered, instinctively turning his head away from the smell. Nikolas on the other hand paused, clearly relishing the intoxicating, unique scent of his blood. Pausing to inhale more deeply, Dillon sensed his barely controlled craving for it. Dillon closed his eyes. His whole body tensed as he waited for the piercing of fangs into his skin that would end his life. In his mind's eye he focused on his father's face. He wanted it to be the last thing he saw.

The incision, when it came, was fast and efficient and Dillon jerked as Nikolas's dusty, dry lips pressed hard against his throat.

'Wait!'

Dillon recognised Professor Dukan's voice and felt a gust of air whisper across his bare chest.

'We have found evidence of Dillon's innocence.'

His eyes snapped open.

'It is too late,' Nikolas snarled, reluctantly retracting his fangs and raising his head an inch but still crouched over Dillon, his eyes red with bloodlust.

'You cannot make the decision to put vampires from the school to death without the consent of the entire council. Countess Fassano was not present.'

'She was informed. I repeat – it is too late, Professor Dukan,' Nikolas mumbled, spitting out the copious amounts of saliva that had begun to stream over his lips.

'I have evidence that it was Celeste Torstensson who killed the girl on the night of the ski trip. The unique blood found at the scene was stolen from a sample at the school. It is Dillon's but the sample is old; his blood profile has changed since he started taking Golden Blood, and his vampire side has continued to develop. It is important that we learn from him, not destroy him.'

Dillon heard a wave of hissing and as he stared into the magical green sky, swirling above him, he wondered if he was dreaming. Had Nikolas drunk his blood already?

'I found the empty vial that had Dillon's blood sample in it in the pocket of the jacket Celeste was wearing that night. I know it was Dillon's because I took the sample.'

There was another hiss of surprise, but the sound of Sade's low, gruff voice convinced him he was awake. As he turned, he stared wonderingly at her exquisite, glowing face. She was an angel sent to save him from the jaws of death.

'Nikolas, it is only fair that we hear Professor Dukan. Dillon did not have the full three witnesses,' Madame Dupledge said, her sombre voice barely concealing her tension.

Slowly, Nikolas straightened up. When he faced the circle, he had gained control of his bloodlust and his bloodshot eyes betrayed just a hint of how much he had wanted Dillon's blood. Ignoring Madame Dupledge, he addressed the council and governors, his voice still husky.

'You have already heard what Professor Dukan and Sade have said. They know the consequences if what they say is untrue. Are you prepared to accept their testimonies here and now?'

Eric Torstensson, Celeste's father, pushed his way to the inner circle and swept his hood back. 'This is an outrage,' he shouted, his face twitching with agitation. 'A complete fabrication of the truth. We all agreed that the dhampir should be put to death.'

A low hissing swept around the circle again as the vampires conferred and, ignoring Eric Torstensson, nodded at Nikolas.

'Celeste, come forward.' His voice was low and menacing.

Celeste held her head high and joined her father. Only a faint twitching muscle in her cheek betrayed her fear. Nikolas faced her.

'An extremely serious charge has been made against you. Professor Dukan has accused you of stealing a sample of Dillon's blood, killing a human girl and planting his blood at the scene. If the council accept his charge, you are also guilty of lying to us. What is your response?'

Celeste paused to glance at her father, and Dillon saw her eyes cloud with pain. As they stared at each other, Dillon had the strange sense that dark storm clouds of fear, doubt, confusion and deep sadness were swirling and building inside her mind, trapped behind the perfect façade she had maintained for so long.

Sade's gruff voice broke the silence once again. 'There is one more thing. A tiny diamond was found in one of the samples.'

She turned to Celeste, her own eyes dark with sorrow. 'I'm sorry, Celeste,' she said, 'but I can't stand by and let injustice occur. I think it is the diamond from your left fang.'

Finally, the storm broke in Celeste and, as she tore her eyes from her father's, the agonising words spilled out. 'It's true,' she said, facing Nikolas, wounded and beaten, but still proud.

There were gasps and rumbles of shock.

'No, Celeste,' Eric snarled. 'He's guilty. There's no proof the diamond is yours.'

'It's over, father,' Celeste said quietly, her voice raw with pain.

Nikolas looked at them and frowned.

'Show me your fangs, Celeste,' he requested.

Celeste allowed her fangs to descend and approached the sacred rock. Nikolas peeled back her top lip and leant forward to peer at them closely.

'I can confirm that there is no diamond on her left fang,' he announced after a second.

'That doesn't mean anything!' shouted Ace and tried to push through the circle but was held back by Aron.

Nikolas ignored him. 'Tell me one thing. Why?' he asked Celeste.

She spoke slowly and haltingly. 'I hate him. He doesn't belong at VAMPS. He's a dhampir. Bram, myself or Ace were far more suited for the role of VE; we have been bred for it. All along, Madame Dupledge gave him special treatment and privileges he didn't deserve.'

Dillon stared at her in surprise. Her words had a ring of truth, but they didn't match the turmoil in her mind. He couldn't believe she hated him enough to want him dead. As if she knew what he was thinking, Celeste's eyes met his. Perhaps it was the release of emotion, Dillon having come so close to death, or perhaps it was Celeste's agony, but, like a dam bursting, her thoughts flooded into his mind.

He clutched his head as they crashed over him, feeling a history of troubled thoughts and painful emotions as if they were his own. Ever since her mother's death, she had tried to please her powerful father and had been at the mercy of his terrible rages. Her ice-cold composure was a sham, a carefully constructed facade to protect herself.

Although he was still weak, he sat up, clinging to the rock for support. 'Wait, she doesn't deserve to be put to death – she has been manipulated by her father.'

His voice resonated around the circle of vampires, surprising him with some newly found strength. Several of the older vampires hissed between their fangs. Eric Torstensson glared at him, his eyes like daggers. Nikolas raised an eyebrow.

'Interesting that you should defend the architect of your brush with death. Nevertheless, Celeste has broken two VAMPS rules, the consequences of which are made very clear to you at the Induction Ceremony. She also lied to the council in front of the sacred rock.'

'I understand,' Dillon spoke again. 'But she has been at the mercy of her father for years and he has taken advantage of her guilt over her mother's death to manipulate her.'

'An impassioned defence, Dillon, but may I ask how you have suddenly come to understand Celeste's actions?'

Dillon hesitated. He glanced at Madame Dupledge.

'Sometimes I am able to receive thoughts. Madame Dupledge believes I may be an intuitive.'

Nikolas's eyes flicked to the chain around his neck.

'If it is so, explain to us how and why Eric Torstensson, a powerful and respected member of the governor's circle, would manipulate his daughter, risking her entire future and his own, in order to bring down a dhampir.'

Dillon closed his eyes. The gateway into Celeste's mind was still open. 'Eric Torstensson was one of the governors who tasted my blood early on. He felt its strength and he became obsessed with it. He wanted Celeste to steal more from the samples kept at VAMPS, so that he could investigate further. Finding the sample that Sade took was a gift for Celeste and when she sent it to him, he used the world-leading testing facilities at his pharmaceutical corporation and discovered that eventually, my blood will become —' Dillon paused — 'my blood will become self-regenerating, meaning that I will not be dependent on ingesting blood like most vampires.'

There were several gasps and hisses of surprise.

'For years, Eric has been working on a secret process, similar to a vaccine, that could be injected into vampires to change their DNA and eliminate bloodlust. He flew into a terrible rage, knowing that my blood could undo everything he has worked for, let alone the potential billions he would make. He concocted the plan for the ski trip. Celeste knew that if she didn't follow his wishes, it would ruin his life's work. It took her no more than a few minutes to kill the barmaid while the rest of us were distracted around an ice luge. My disappearance with Cora was a gift, giving her story credibility.

'All her life, Celeste has had to learn to hide and control

her emotions from her father. Her mind talents have become strong, and she learnt from him early on how to compel others. She was able to convince Jeremiah into believing that I had confessed to him.' He swallowed. The sudden knowledge that Jeremiah hadn't betrayed him after all was almost overwhelming.

There was silence. Dillon stopped speaking and the wind howled round the plateau as the vampires looked to Nikolas.

'Absolute fantasy,' spat Eric, his eyes dark slits of rage.

Nikolas ignored him and turned to Celeste. 'Dillon claims he is an intuitive and explained via his access to your mind that your father controlled your actions. We cannot accept the testimony of an intuitive alone. Do you accept the truth of his words?'

Without looking at her father, Celeste nodded, her eyes dark with agony.

'Very well. I have made my decision. I shall spare your death, but you are expelled from VAMPS with immediate effect. Eric Torstensson, your father, will be imprisoned and tried separately. If found guilty, no mercy will be shown to you Eric.'

Eric screeched, directing his fury at Celeste. 'You've ruined everything,' he snarled. 'The word of a so-called "intuitive" dhampir would never have held up against yours.'

She stood motionless and as he suddenly disappeared into thin air, leaving her alone, she revealed no emotion, as if she was expecting to be abandoned.

Nikolas sighed and signalled to the VSS operatives hovering above. 'Find him,' he snapped.

Celeste shut her eyes and Dillon sank back again as he felt her agony and conflicted emotions blast into him once again. She detested what her father had put her through, but she blamed Dillon for his demise with a cold, implacable fury. At the same time, even though she reviled his access to her mind, she knew that she owed her life to him.

She let him hear one more thought before Madame Dupledge led her away. *You should have let me die.*

Another blast of her agony and shame washed over him before Ace pushed through the circle and stopped her. Taking her into his arms, he whispered, 'I'll come after you.'

She kissed him slowly and lingeringly on the lips. 'Don't. You deserve better. Just let me go.'

With a bored expression, Nikolas turned to Dillon. 'So, Dillon, you survive; the aurora borealis was fortuitous after all.' Once again, his eyes flicked over the chain. 'Your unique blood and the *passions* you inspire will require further investigation. We will need to ensure you will benefit our vampire community and, if your blood has the properties Professor Dukan and Eric Torstensson profess, how we might *protect* such a resource.'

As he listened, Dillon knew that Nikolas craved his blood, especially having had a taste of it, and he suppressed a shiver. Turning abruptly, Nikolas clicked his fingers, and the Vampire Council instantly disappeared, leaving just Alexandru Danesti and Sade's parents.

Dillon shuffled over to Sade, who was still standing next to Professor Dukan, her huge brown eyes still wide with shock.

'Excuse me, Professor,' he said.

Silently, Dillon and Sade stared at each other.

'I'd be dead if it wasn't for you,' he said in a low, unsteady voice.

Ignoring her parents, who were glaring at her, she stepped closer and tentatively absorbed his scent. Closing her eyes for a minute, she stepped back.

'Dillon, I'm really sorry I've been acting so weird with you, but I'm almost over the bloodlust. I was so worried it was me who had drunk your blood sample when Celeste stole it that I convinced myself I couldn't be around you.'

'You would never hurt me,' he said, feeling his voice well with emotion. 'I've missed you.'

26

Blood Forever

Fred, Angelo, Aron and Ásta rushed up to Dillon.

'*Dios*, Dillon, I thought you were a goner,' Angelo said, drawing a line across his throat to emphasise his words.

'Why didn't I take bets?' Frederick moaned. 'I'd have made a fortune. No one expected you to survive.'

Dillon smiled weakly. 'Thanks guys and Ásta, seriously, I really appreciate you standing up for me.'

'You've turned out to be okay for a dhampir,' Ásta said gruffly.

As Sade went over to her parents, who were talking to Mr Hunt with sober unhappy expressions, Dillon noticed Bram having an intense argument with Alexandru.

'It's over, father,' he heard him say as he shrugged his father's hand off his arm. 'Dillon's VE.'

'What has happened to you?' Alexandru hissed. 'A dhampir never deserves such an honour.'

Bram sighed, the pain of Cora's confession still visible on his face.

'I don't care about VE anymore. He's earnt it. He can have it.'

'Is this all about her?' Alexandru asked, glaring over at Cora, who was standing, shell-shocked and miserable, alone.

Bram didn't answer, and Alexandru hissed again. 'Stay away from her, Bram. She's like her brother. She's no good for you. She humiliated you.'

Ignoring him, Bram stalked off.

Furiously, Alexandru clicked his fingers, and instantly, two bodyguards dropped out of the sky, landing on their feet either side of him. As they took off, he shot Dillon a look of pure loathing before circling dramatically over Bram.

'I'll speak to you when you've calmed down,' he growled down at him and disappeared.

As the wind chilled his still-bare chest, Dillon watched as Bram stopped opposite Cora, and he saw the raw pain in their eyes as they both stared at each other.

He desperately needed to speak to her; she had put everything on the line for him, including losing the possible link to her brother. Did that mean it was over with Bram?

But, as she tentatively reached out for Bram's hand, he saw that it wasn't over between them, and he had to turn away to protect himself from the pain that he knew would come later.

Mr Hunt, stonyfaced that the trial hadn't despatched Dillon, began calling out instructions. 'Everyone head straight back to VAMPS with me and Professor Dukan. Borzak and Chiro, remove Dillon's restraints and fly with him.'

Sade's parents, looking angry and tight-lipped, were clearly warning her to stay away from Dillon, refusing to even look in his direction.

'Sorry,' she said, rejoining him after they had gone. 'You know their feelings. They are ambitious for me. What happened with Cora and Bram by the way? They look devastated.'

He realised she had arrived after Cora's confession. He reached out for her hand. 'It's complicated. I'll tell you later. Will you fly with me?' he asked.

She smiled and slid her hand into his. Chiro supported him on the other side and as they took off, Dillon took one last look down at the now empty plateau. It felt like another lifetime since he'd first seen it, half-crazed with fear.

As streaks of dawn appeared, they swooped up the side of the school. Dillon realised for the first time, it felt like he was coming home.

There was just one more vampire to face. Jeremiah was waiting for him in their room, his handsome face a mask of shame.

'Dillon, I'm so sorry. I'm ashamed and shocked that someone could compel me so easily without me suspecting a thing. Trust me, I'd never do that to you intentionally. My head's completely fucked . . . I feel like such a bloody idiot. I'm sorry. What can I do to make it up to you?'

It was too much for Dillon's emotionally frazzled brain to deal with. The blazing contempt in Jeremiah's eyes at the trial and the sense of utter betrayal followed by the overwhelming relief that it was Celeste had left him drained.

Urgently, Jeremiah spoke again. 'I should have been strong enough to block her.'

Dillon's eyes were heavy now – all he could think about was his coffin. 'She hid her strengths, Jeremiah. It's a lesson for us all,' he slurred. 'Look, I'm not trying to make you feel worse, but I'm going to need a bit of time . . . ' He paused as he saw the flash of pain across Jeremiah's eyes.

Jeremiah nodded, taking it on the chin. 'I understand. I'll sleep somewhere else tonight.'

Dillon looked away, unable to witness Jeremiah's hurt any longer. 'Thanks,' he said quietly.

He heard Jeremiah gather a few things together and leave the room, closing the door softly behind him. Dillon slumped against his coffin absolutely drained. He felt numb. After nights of intense turmoil and coming within a fang's length of death, his mind was finally closing down.

There was a tap on the door. Dillon struggled to raise his eyelids as it opened, and Chiro peered round.

'Madame Dupledge wants me to guard you whilst you sleep today – just as a precaution after the events of last night.'

'Thanks for your help last night, Chiro,' Dillon managed to slur as he lifted the coffin lid. 'I'm sorry. I've got to sleep now – it was all a bit much.'

Chiro's red eyes gleamed. 'It's not surprising,' he growled. 'You've been through a lot. Don't worry now. I'll be here.'

'Than . . .' As Dillon half fell into his coffin, his voice petered out.

He knew he still had to apologise to Bram, but it would have to wait. As the lid closed with a gentle click and darkness enveloped him, he passed out into a dead sleep.

He woke suddenly with the sense that something was wrong, the coffin felt like it was swaying from side to side. In a panic, he opened the lid.

He squinted as the light from a dusky sky, tinged with red and gold, filled the coffin, and he sprang out, landing in a crouch on the wooden deck of a boat. Two figures silhouetted against the falling sun turned to him.

'At last,' his father said, smiling. 'Dillon, even though she wasn't around, you need to know that your ma never stopped loving you. She had to make the —' he swallowed as his voice cracked — 'the unbearable decision to leave you to protect you. Now, at long last, it is time for you to meet.'

He turned to the striking vampire standing next to him. 'Dillon, this is your ma.'

Bibiana faced him, somehow looking softer and less powerful than he remembered her. The fiery stone at the centre of the triangular pendant around her neck flickered like flames, exactly the same as his own.

'I have waited a very long time for this day . . .' she said, smiling tentatively, her husky voice raw with emotion.

Dillon stared at her, lost for words. Never in his wildest dreams had he imagined that Bibiana Fassano was his ma.

'I'm sorry to have removed you before you completed the year at Peak One,' she continued. 'Emotions are riding high after your acquittal and until things calm down, having you *disappear* for a while seemed like the safest option.'

She beckoned at someone behind him and his jaw fell open as Chiro emerged at the side of the coffin.

'Chiro is the best bodyguard in the vampire world. He and I have been together for a very long time. I trust him implicitly – please believe that neither he nor I would have let Nikolas Karayan take your life.'

Dillon's eyes widened in disbelief as he found his voice. 'You let him get feckin' close.'

'Dill,' Gabriel remonstrated and Dillon winced as Bibiana placed a gentle hand on his da's arm.

'It's okay, Gabriel. He's been through a lot.'

She turned back to him, and he felt the intense power of her scrutiny.

'I empathise with your anger, Dillon,' she said, her eyes examining every detail of his face. 'Please try to understand that it was complicated. There were things I had to put in place before the vampire world found out about you. I had to keep you and your father safe.'

'It took eighteen years?' Dillon snapped.

He hardened his heart as she allowed him to feel the agony it had caused her. Bleakly, he wondered if he would ever be able to return to VAMPS, to the vampires who had become his close friends and to Cora.

'Yes, you will,' she said. 'Only, this time, you will return as the son of Countess Fassano.'

Acknowledgements

Massive thanks to Jo McGrath who came up with the idea for *VAMPS* and gave me the chance to fulfil a dream. It's been a joy to collaborate with you and Walter Iuzzolino at The Writers' Room; your narrative suggestions were always spot on. I'm also grateful for your steadfast encouragement – particularly when the going got tough in the middle section and I was struck down with Covid. Writing *VAMPS* was hard but it was also great fun. I hope I have done it justice.

Thanks also, to Ronnie Trouton for making Dillon and Gabriel sound more Irish and for the other helpful suggestions. It was great to have a male perspective on some of Dillon's thoughts and feelings. I have a yearning now to visit to the west coast of Ireland for wheaten bread and to swim in the Atlantic on a misty morning.

Another huge thank you to Simon & Schuster for commissioning *VAMPS* after my first three chapters. I'm particularly grateful to Judith Long for her excellent, extremely helpful editorial observations and her unerring ability to spot where I hadn't quite thought something through and to Clare Hey for her vision and enthusiasm in championing the project in the first place.

Many thanks to John O'Connell for reading the manuscript and for offering his impeccable grammatical advice.

Authors often mention that writing fiction can be all-consuming. I didn't realise just how much until *VAMPS*. I'm incredibly grateful to my friends, my Pilates friends/clients and my family, who understood and were generous enough to cut me some slack.

Special heartfelt thanks are for my mum and dad – you're my 'rock in a storm'. Thank you so much for your help and support.

Zac, Benj and Lola, I'm so proud of you – you're the best bits of my favourite characters. You're also my world. Much love and thanks for making me laugh.

Finally, my love and most grateful thanks go to my husband, Rob. I couldn't have done it without you.